Cicely's Sovereign Secret

Cicely's Sovereign Secret

A Story of King Henry VII's Private Matter

Sandra Heath Wilson

buried
river
press

ISBN 978-1-910208-37-3

Buried River Press
Clerkenwell House
Clerkenwell Green
London EC1R 0HT

www.halebooks.com

Buried River Press is an imprint of Robert Hale Ltd

2 4 6 8 10 9 7 5 3 1

Printed and bound in Great Britain by
CPI Antony Rowe, Chippenham and Eastbourne

Preface

IN THE SPRING of 1483, the children of the late Yorkist King Edward IV were declared illegitimate by their own uncle, the new King Richard III. His second niece, the perceptive and loyal Cicely Plantagenet, hardly knew him, but from the outset was fiercely drawn to this charismatic man, with whom she shared tremendous affinity and, rarest of all, his trust.

With Richard, Cicely discovered her intensely passionate nature, and how honourable and sensitive he was. They were uncle and niece—forbidden to succumb to desire—but they shared complete, unconditional but secret love before Richard had to defend his realm, his cause and his life against the invading force of the Lancastrian pretender, Henry Tudor.

Richard was slain at the Battle of Bosworth Field on 22 August 1485, and his death left Cicely grief-stricken, alone, and carrying his child. He was to be branded a wicked tyrant, but she knew the true man, and defended his memory, even to Henry Tudor's face. Her love for Richard would never be shaken, no matter how strenuously and cleverly his conqueror sought to ruin his good name.

Clinging to her lost love, and anxious for her unborn

child, Cicely found herself ensconced in the court of the Lancastrian usurper, whom she did not regard as fit to aspire to Richard's throne. Henry was ruthless, cold, dangerous and enigmatic, and Cicely's bitter elder sister, Bess, had become his unwanted, hate-filled queen.

About to be shamed and ruined by bearing an illegitimate child, Cicely was saved by Henry's half-uncle, Jon Welles, who offered marriage and acknowledged Richard's child as his own. It commenced as a contract, but became much more, although what she felt for Jon could not compare with the powerful emotion aroused by Richard.

Henry was not as cold as he seemed, but harboured a suppressed passion for Cicely, the sister he could not have. He was determined to possess her, and forced her into his bed with threats to harm those she loved. Cicely loathed Henry for Richard's death, but his serpentine charm, vulnerability and surprising skills as a lover often made hating him impossible.

Throughout, she knew he was a mortal threat to her secret son, to Jon, and to all Yorkists, especially her adored cousin, Jack (John) de la Pole, Earl of Lincoln, who was accepted to have been Richard's heir. While she and Jon were estranged, she and Jack became lovers, and she gave him her heart. He became the second great passion of her life.

To Cicely, Jack was the rightful King of England, but then in the summer of 1487 he became embroiled in a plot to put a pretender called Lambert Simnel on the throne of England. Through Jack she was lured into dangerous plots and secrets of which Henry would dearly have liked to learn. Her anxiety for her charming, irresistible cousin grew daily, because the affinity she shared with him was an echo of that shared with Richard.

The Simnel rebellion wrought havoc in the realm, with Henry emerging the victor. Jack was believed to have been killed in battle, but Cicely rescued him. Henry suspected that the body he buried on the battlefield with a willow stave through its heart was not that of the Earl of Lincoln.

The last Cicely saw of her cousin and lover was on the river stairs at Westminster Palace, with his inscrutable accomplice, the older Welshman known to her only as Tal. It was a cold winter night, with fluttering torches and falling snow, and Jack's farewell smile had been so beloved in the streaming flames and leaping shadows.

She did not know if she would ever see him again, but she *did* know that Henry still ruled her life and that he was closing in upon her little boy. Would she ever be free of him?

Chapter One

IT WAS CHRISTMAS, and the night air cracked with cold as two well-muffled horsemen rode the final snowy mile towards Knole, the Kent palace of the Archbishops of Canterbury.

One rider was the Lancastrian king, Henry VII, perhaps the most calculating and devious monarch to ever rule England; and one of the luckiest and least deserving. A month short of his thirty-first birthday, tonight he was pursuing a very delicate and dangerous private matter. His companion was the only man in whom he had confided, and that only partially. If the whole truth came out, there would be renewed and widespread rebellion, even within his own ranks, and the hitherto defeated House of York would surely reunite and overthrow him. It was vital to him that this private matter remained just that—private.

Knole was in darkness, in the hands of a few of Henry's most trusted servants. Not even Archbishop Morton himself was there, knowing better than to question the dangerous usurper he himself had conspired to put on the throne.

Two of Henry's Yorkist foes were also waiting covertly. One was the Plantagenet prince he had cause to fear the most, the other he would have been dismayed to identify.

Purely by chance, they had wind of the sensitivity of the meeting, and hoped to learn all they could. To them the thirty years of war between York and Lancaster were far from over, and it was their goal to remove Henry from the throne he had usurped through the betrayal and death of the Yorkist king, Richard III.

A bribed servant had left a ground-floor casement unfastened, and now the intruders waited at a small-paned upper window overlooking the quadrangle. They wore black, and their faces were smeared with soot, making them impossible to see in the unlit passage, where the tapestries and Christmas greenery were shadowy. Several torches flickered below, and a lantern shone beneath the gatehouse to their left. To their right was the roofed, columned gallery that sheltered two entrances to the great hall, where Henry's secret would surely be revealed. The Yorkists certainly prayed so.

The more important of the two was 25-year-old Jack de la Pole, Earl of Lincoln, Richard III's trusted nephew and intended heir, who was believed to have died in battle against Henry during the summer. But Henry knew of his secret survival, and hunted him doggedly. Everything about Jack told of strength, courage and purpose, coupled with an appeal that won men to his banners. With tumbling, almost black curls and dark, shining eyes, he was more handsome and alluring than was good for the well-being of the fair sex, with whom he had seldom failed.

His older companion, identified only as Tal, was in his early fifties, a fit and rugged man, fair-haired and of noble birth. The scent of cinnamon lingered around him, suggesting far warmer lands than the Welsh borders from which he hailed. Strangely, the large, orange-gold topaz ring he always wore seemed to suggest the same thing. Perhaps because it brought the sands and heat of the desert to mind.

Both were nervous, but Tal truly doubted the wisdom of

tonight's venture, even though Knole was virtually empty. '*Diawl*, Jack, this is bloody madness.'

'All I need is for you to identify the boy. If he comes.'

'I only *glimpsed* him on a windy night on a French quay! That is *all*.'

Jack was irritated. 'You are our chance of making this identification. If the boy we expect tonight is the same one watching when Henry left to invade England two years ago, then surely our suspicions are confirmed.'

'I still cannot provide *proof*, Jack. The fellow who sent word to us in the first place is dead at the hands of Henry's toads, and although I paid that priest well, half then, the other half depending on result, he clearly played me for a fool. I have sent a trusted man back into Brittany, but it will take time. I have no idea yet who the woman was, except perhaps the boy's mother.'

There were sounds from the gatehouse end of the passage, a door opening and men's voices. They must have been outside, because they stamped their boots and cursed the cold. Jack and Tal also heard whining and the slither of large paws on a wooden floor.

'Shit! One of the mastiffs!' Jack glanced at a nearby door. 'In there! Quick!'

Tal needed no urging, and they slipped swiftly out of sight, but before closing the door, Jack took a phial from his purse, and smeared some of the contents down the jamb.

Then, the door closed, he and Tal pressed back against the wall, daggers drawn. They hardly dared to breathe as the men and the hound approached, still complaining and stamping their feet occasionally.

Jack crossed his fingers superstitiously as the hound began to whine within inches of the door.

One of the men noticed. 'What is it, Nero?'

The hound suddenly sneezed and the men laughed. 'Come on, you useless cur!' one said, and to the intruders' relief, Nero left willingly enough as the men moved on.

Jack straightened from the wall. 'That was too fucking close.'

'What did you put on the door?'

'Orange oil. Many dogs do not like it. We struck lucky with Nero, blessings be upon him! He may have picked us up, but the oil spoiled his sense of smell.'

Tal opened the door cautiously, and peered out. Everything was as it had been, and he emerged slowly, sheathing his dagger. 'If we had any sense, we would leave *now*, while we know we can.'

'We *must* learn Tudor's secret.' Jack put his dagger away as well. 'Tell me again what you remember about the boy.'

'Well, I would say he is an arrogant, sulky brat. He seemed about twelve, so will be at least fourteen now. The woman kept him close. She was pale, and looked unwell to me, but beautiful and probably older than Henry.'

'With whom she had no fond leave-taking?' Jack pressed.

'Not a sign of it. Our only facts are that she and the boy were there, and Henry was of intense interest to them.'

'Yet, we expect the boy to come here tonight. There is much more to this than appears on the surface, but God alone knows what. Royal by-blows are common enough.' Jack had been puzzled from the outset.

'Henry's purpose tonight might be some other Tudor nonsense.'

'Henry does not deal in nonsense,' Jack replied quietly.

Tal grunted. 'He is unbalanced, like a door on one hinge.'

'Only sometimes. As to the boy … we only have to observe and then leave as secretly as we came.'

A rafter creaked, and both men stiffened, but then there was silence again. Tal breathed out slowly. 'Sweet God, we perceive danger in everything.'

'The day we do not, will be the day we are snuffed.'

'Then I trust you hear its soft steps when you dally with the queen's sister.'

Jack smiled too. 'Ah, my sweet, sweet Cicely. No wonder Henry thinks he married the wrong sister. His queen mishandles him quite amazingly.'

'Whereas Viscountess Welles handles him most deftly, from all accounts.' Tal grinned. 'And if it were known she also has *you* to handle deftly as well, she would be envied by English womanhood.'

Jack chuckled. 'Henry despises me because of her, almost more than my Yorkist blood. He will never win her.'

Tal studied him. Jack de la Pole seemed to be just a likeable rogue, but was discreet, perceptive, clever and unshakably loyal to his House. There was no doubt that had he succeeded Richard III, he would have been a worthy king, and far more popular than Henry Tudor could ever be. Tal felt more than loyalty to Jack, he felt paternal love, too.

He was taller than Jack, and muscular, without the extra weight that so often accompanied age. His shrewd eyes were green, and his long fair hair liberally streaked with grey, a true blend of salt and pepper. Bowing to the vagaries of fashion had never been his way, and he made a point of always being in need of a good shave. He was inscrutable, with hidden depths and unshakeable resolve. As well as an air of being revenge personified.

Not sensing the scrutiny, Jack pulled a philosophical face. 'I have Cicely, but must share her with her husband and her snake of a brother-in-law. Her husband I can endure, not least because I like and respect him. Jon Welles may be Henry's half-uncle, but he would have brought his 10,000 men over to me at Stoke in the summer. I would not have lost the battle then. But Henry Tudor I detest. More than I ever imagined possible.'

Tal glanced at him, about to say something but then

thinking better of it.

Jack read him well. 'The Seventh Commandment? Well, we cannot all be as saintly as you, Tal. Censure me, by all means, and Tudor, but think ill of my lady at your peril, for I will not allow it, even from you. She is Tudor's lover because he blackmails her by threatening those she loves, to wit, her husband and me. Tudor is obsessed with her, do you not see it? She may only be eighteen, but she is a rare creature, so warm, excitingly carnal and pleasing that men adore her. Her husband certainly does, and so do I. She has a great heart, and has always loved truly, beginning with—' He stopped. 'Well, it matters not with whom it began. There is a magic about her, and saint or not, even you must have imagined being in her bed.'

'Do not misunderstand me, Jack. I hold Lady Welles in great esteem. My unspoken comment was to wish you could both be free to marry.'

Jack always found him perplexing. 'Where is *your* wife now? Kingston l'Isle or Calais?' He called it Callis, as did most Englishmen.

'Neither. I have sent her to my sister at Kenninghall, where she is now more holy than the Virgin herself, and even dresses as if in Holy Orders.'

'Good God.'

'We all, men and women alike, take a chance with marriage. Sometimes we are fortunate, but other times we have the Devil to thank. *I* have Woden to thank.'

Jack stared. '*Woden*?'

'Oh, pay no heed. It is all nonsense. Jack, I am sorry if you thought I disapproved of you and Lady Cicely. Broken marriage vows are a particularly sensitive subject for me. And not because of my own marriage, as I think you know well.'

Jack's expression changed, and he clapped a reassuring hand on the older man's shoulder. 'Yes, I know. And understand.'

'My feelings run too high sometimes.' Tal was rueful.

'As when you drink your sorrows to drive them away, only to make them worse? Too much wine does you no good, Tal.'

'You know it seldom happens. I usually drink sparingly.'

Jack clapped his shoulder again, and then they looked down into the quadrangle in silence, before Tal asked, 'When will Tudor arrive, I wonder?'

'Any time now,' Jack replied. 'The secretary in the great hall began to pace an hour ago.'

'Who do you think he will bring?'

'There are few he dares to trust.'

The clatter of hooves echoed suddenly into the court-yard, and Jack smiled grimly. 'He must have heard us, God rot his innards. And only *one* companion?'

'They are both so muffled I cannot make anything out, even which is which.'

'Henry is on the roan. I would know the dragon of Cadwallader a mile away at night, hooded, in black on a black mount.' He watched closely as the riders reined in and grooms ran to tend the sweating horses.

Henry swung a leg over his pommel to jump down to the snow. He was tall, slender and graceful, and did not remove his hood, but the face of the second man was suddenly revealed in the dancing torchlight.

Jack was startled. 'Sweet Jesu! Jon Welles!'

Dismayed, he gazed down at Cicely's husband. Jon, Viscount Welles was in his late thirties, an impressive man with long legs and a firm frame. He was clean-shaven, with carved features, and his wiry brown hair was greying at the temples. His eyes, Jack knew, were a particularly vivid, penetrating blue.

Jack did not know what to think. Henry was suspicious of his half-uncle's failure to arrive in time at Stoke Field, so

15

why in God's own name trust him with a matter that was self-evidently dangerous and sensitive?

Tal watched the two men exchange words. 'I thought Welles was one of *us* now.'

'So did I. His force would have been decisive.'

'If he ever intended to fight. Maybe he prefers to wait and see.'

Jack shook his head. 'No, he was honestly delayed.'

'Well, he appears to be Henry's man again now.'

The two men disappeared beneath the gallery towards the great hall, and Tal nudged Jack. 'Come, to our purpose then, and God protect us.'

'Amen to that.'

They moved stealthily towards the stairs that led down to the ground-floor lobby. From there an egress opened straight in front of them to the quadrangle gallery, and to their left was a door into an identical passage beneath the one they had just quit. It was in a room at the far end of this second passage that the casement through which they had gained entry was to be found.

To the right of the lobby was a short, narrow way to the wedged-open door of the firelit great hall. The two men crept silently towards it, alert for any sign of guards or mastiffs. They halted by the doorway, which was next to the dais that elevated the archbishop and his guests above others. The long, white-clothed trestle table concealed the interlopers from those by the fireplace halfway down the hall. Henry and Jon talked in low voices as they stood before flames and crackling logs. A small table and a chair had been placed in readiness.

The diminutive secretary—white-haired, bearded and clad in dark robes—hovered uneasily by the table, where several documents were in readiness for Henry's signature and seal. Sticks of sealing wax were there too, one of them bright yellow. Jack and Tal had been told that the unidentified woman on the quay at Honfleur always used yellow sealing wax, and had sent Henry an enigmatically forged letter. It contained nothing more than the briefest of appeals for help, but his shocked reaction had been witnessed by Cicely and Jon Welles.

Jack indicated the wax to Tal. '*That* cannot possibly be coincidence! This meeting *has* to be about the boy,' he whispered, and then the scent of Christmas pine and yew enveloped him as he slipped behind the dais to the other side of the hall. Tal followed, and they settled to observe.

Henry seated himself in the chair, and stretched his long legs towards the fire. His cloak, sleeveless coat, gauntlets and soft velvet hat had been tossed carelessly on the floor. He wore a grey doublet slashed with purple, and clinging hose that disappeared into thigh boots. It could not be said he was handsome, but he was certainly memorable, with long, reddish hair, high cheekbones, a long, prominent nose, narrow chin and pale complexion. His mouth was straight and wide, and his eyebrows arched above strangely hooded eyes, the left one of which had a cast that made his gaze unnerving.

His elbows rested on the arms of the chair as he gazed into the fire, his hands together as if in prayer, his fingertips tapping idly to his lips. He seemed relaxed, but the air he exuded was of icy unapproachability. Henry Tudor's emotions were always hidden. Stifled even.

His blood right to the throne was paltry, and came through an illegitimate royal line, the Beauforts. He also claimed dubious descent from Cadwallader, the last king of Britain. His emphasis on his Welshness had brought him support and a clear passage through Wales to confront Richard at Bosworth. Much good it had done his homeland, for he had done nothing to improve its lot.

Jon Welles paced nervously. He too had removed his outer clothes, revealing a sleeveless wine-red coat over a brown doublet and hose. The spurs on his thigh boots jingled now and then, and as he ran a hand through his hair, Jack noticed the turquoise ring Cicely had given to him. It had belonged to her father, King Edward IV.

The secretary cleared his throat. 'Your Majesty, I crave your leave to speak.' At Henry's nod, he continued. 'Your Majesty, you indicated as urgent the writ for the apprehension of certain murderers and robbers. It has now been prepared, and I have taken the liberty of bringing it for your signature and seal.'

Henry's uneven eyes swung to him for a moment, and then he nodded. Everything was placed before him, and he read the writ with the help of a magnifying glass produced in readiness. His eyesight was not that of a young man, probably due to too many nights spent in candlelight, perusing complicated accounts into the small hours. He was known for his parsimonious diligence.

'Damn all villains,' he muttered. His voice was soft, his accent tinged with Welsh, and occasionally with French or Breton. Accepting the proffered quill, he wrote his signature with great care—as he did everything—and then the secretary held a stick of wax to a candle. Finally the royal seal was appended.

Jon Welles observed Henry. 'You need spectacles,' he said bluntly.

'I am not an old man yet.'

'Then permit me leave of absence the next time you hunt.'

'*Er mwyn y Tad*!' Henry responded, annoyed.

Tal translated for Jack. '"For God's own sake!"'

The spurt of anger caught at Henry's chest, and he coughed hollowly. Consumptively. Gripping the chair, he strove to overcome a threatened paroxysm. At last he succeeded, and waved the secretary from the hall. 'Go, and do not return unless sent for. And be sure to close the door.'

The relieved secretary obeyed, and Henry nodded at Jon. 'Close the other door as well, we need privacy.'

Jon did as instructed, and returned to the fireplace. 'Why this elaborate theatre, Henry?'

'Partly to tweak Morton's self-important nose, partly to intimidate my guests, who will be confronted by a huge empty palace, firelight and me at my grimmest. Such drama, do you not think?'

'Drama? We have sneaked away from court like naughty children.'

'It pleases me to keep them guessing. My advisors think they are in command. It does them good to find they are not.'

'That is all very well, Henry, but this is not wise. Morton's palace? An isolated cottage would surely have been more sensible?'

'I cannot impress in a *cottage*, and the thought of Morton having to relinquish his palace is pleasing. Besides, if there are interlopers, the mastiffs will sniff them out.'

'You play with fire.' Jon came to stand across the table from him, his tall figure outlined against the flames. 'I think you are making a grave mistake. You should have left it all well alone.'

'I have responsibilities.'

'Maybe, but in this instance they are *not* here in England.'

Henry leaned back in his chair. 'You think I am foolish?'
'Yes.'

'Maybe, but the decision is made.'

Jon leaned his hands on the table. 'You *do* know that this whole business is high treason?'

Jack and Tal looked at each other. *Treason*?

'Against whom, Uncle? Well? Who is the king? Me, and I can hardly commit treason against myself.'

'You can commit high treason against England,' Jon

replied levelly. '*That* is what you are expecting me to condone.'

Henry's strange gaze was upon his uncle. 'Are you about to be difficult? Because if so, let me remind you that you have a delightful wife.'

Jon froze. 'You threaten Cicely?'

'Of course not, Uncle. I treasure her even more than you do.' Henry smiled, but it did not reach his wintry eyes.

'So, *that* is why I am suddenly in favour again? Because you can use Cicely to ensure my discretion and obedience?'

'Take it as you please.'

Jon returned to the fire to kick a partially burned log.

Henry watched. 'Oh, dear, I think you are out of sorts with me.'

'I dislike you when you behave like this.' The log received another kick.

'Have a care, uncle mine, for although I may occasionally permit Cicely to be rude to me, *you* do not merit such latitude, even if you *are* my mother's beloved half-sibling.'

There was silence, during which the fire crackled and despatched sparks up the vast chimney.

'Where is Lincoln?' Henry asked suddenly.

'Lincoln? The *earl*?'

'Well, strangely, I am fully cognisant of the whereabouts of the city and county,' was the sarcastic response.

'I have no idea where he is. You and Cicely tell me he survived Stoke Field, and I must believe you both, but I certainly have not seen him since he fled the country in February.' This was a very great lie indeed, as the two eavesdroppers knew well.

'Cicely has not confided more?' Henry was disbelieving.

Jon looked at him. 'Cicely does not *know* any more, save that he survived Stoke, but badly wounded. Then he was abducted, although why or by whom is still unknown. You are aware of all this, so why question me more?'

20

'Because I want to know just how close she was to Lincoln,' Henry said quietly. 'She *does* rather love her close relatives, mm? She certainly loved Richard far more than a niece should her uncle. As my dearest wife did too, of course. But in Cicely's case, Richard reciprocated, did he not? I firmly believe that her short-lived child was his, not yours.'

Jon was not cowed. 'Henry, I can tell you here and now, upon mine own honour, that Cicely and Richard were *not* lovers.'

Tal's face had become quite a picture. This was the first he had heard of Cicely and Richard. Or of a possible child.

Jack knew that Richard had been Cicely's lover, and that the union resulted in a son, Leo, of whom Richard had never known. Jon Welles had protected her through marriage, but then fate intervened and it became expedient to pretend the boy had died within hours of his birth. Now almost two, he was known as plain Master Leo Kymbe, and was being brought up by the family of that name in the countryside of Lincolnshire. Being Richard's son, he was now the only person for whom Jack de la Pole would be prepared to give up his own claim to the throne.

Tal whispered. 'Is this true, Jack? About the Lady Cicely and Richard? And a child?'

'No.' Jack would never divulge Cicely's secret. Not yet, anyway.

Henry was still fixed upon the thought of Cicely and Richard. 'It was incest,' he breathed, sitting forward, his body suddenly as taut as whipcord. 'Damn his soul, he bewitched her, seduced her, satisfied her and taught her everything she knows of making love. And she knows so *very* much, does she not? She adores to be adored and to adore in turn. And it is because of him. *He* brought her to life, and made her the marvellous creature she is now. I *know* he did! He haunts me, and sometimes I feel him watching me, laughing. He is still with me, Uncle. *Still!*'

Chapter Two

JON GAZED UNEASILY at his royal nephew. 'Sweet Jesu, Henry, you make him sound like a wizard.'

'He was!' Henry struggled for composure, and became level again. 'Jealousy is the ravening wolf within, is it not?'

Jon did not answer.

Henry closed his eyes. 'I make love to her, but know she does not love me. Physically maybe, but not in her heart. You have more of her than I ever will, yet even you do not have as much as others, mm? Richard will *always* have the lion's share, and then, perhaps, that tomcat Lincoln. No, do not deny it to me again, for it is the truth. Have you *seen* her when she defends Richard's memory? She shimmers with love, and for him she would challenge Beelzebub to mortal combat. *I* want that love from her, but know I never will. Even a king cannot have everything he wants.'

'What do you expect when you have forced her into your bed? Yes, she loved Richard, and will always be loyal to him, but that is not the same as the love *you* suspect existed between them.' Jon was the soul of reason. 'I promise you her child was mine, conceived in Nottingham, in June 1485, and born a month too early in 1486. St Valentine's Day, no less. Richard was not wizard enough to divine what was happening under his nose.'

'Richard initiated her,' Henry insisted, 'then you had her, and then Lincoln, who is risen from the dead to haunt me!'

'You lash yourself, but do not actually *know* anything. No matter how many times you make love to her, no matter how skilled your caresses, she will *always* be York.'

'Oh, do I not know it.'

'Either accept it, or leave her alone. But please do *not* whinge about it, least of all to me. She is my wife and I intend to keep her. And while you harp on about incest, it does not seem to prevent you from flouting the Bible yourself in order to commit adultery with her. She is your wife's sister and your half-uncle's wife, yet I believe you even went so far as to want to set her up as your official mistress, in spite of the uproar that would cause.'

'Was that why you did not support me at Stoke Field?' Henry's left eye wandered a little until it gazed as steadily as its fellow.

Jon did not flinch. 'It was not possible to wade 10,000 men through that flood at Huntingdon. Otherwise I *would* have been there.'

'On which side, I wonder?' Henry murmured, and moved on before Jon could challenge the remark. 'Why have you not confronted me over her?'

'You think I would defend *my* honour at the expense of hers?' Jon replied. 'She wishes me to say and do nothing, and I am sure enough of her love to do as she requests.'

'How craftily you insert that last. Small revenge.'

'But revenge for all that,' was Jon's response.

Henry gave the ghost of a smile. 'True. Oh, I know my madness over her. She is my full moon, and I bay. How I wish *she* was the daughter of York I vowed to marry, not her sow of a sister. God fuck Edward IV and his bigamy! And to make her legitimate, I was forced to make her missing brothers trueborn too. I actually *returned* to them their better blood claim to the throne than my own!' How it curdled his blood to even think of it. 'Just what in the name of Hell itself happened to those boys after Richard sent them away, mm? Where? I can *claim* that he had them murdered in the Tower to secure his stolen throne, but I know he did not. Does Richard's sister have them in Burgundy, waiting to spring an invasion upon me?'

'I cannot answer that, Henry. And without their bodies, you cannot point a convincing finger.' Jon could almost sympathize with his half-nephew's quandary, but the fact still remained that the children were all illegitimate, and Richard had become the rightful King of England. The repealing of Richard's title to the throne did not really make any difference in the eyes of many, including Henry himself, although he would never admit it.

Henry unfolded from the chair as fluidly as a cat, but then turned as perhaps a dozen horses entered the quadrangle. He glanced urgently at Jon. 'What happens now is of vital personal importance to me, and I know how much I ask of you.' Then he smiled, and this time it reached his eyes, changing him completely.

Watching from the dais, Jack observed that suddenly irresistible charm, for it coaxed forgiveness from the unforgiving. This other side of Henry Tudor sometimes tore Cicely's heart.

Voices were heard at the far door from the quadrangle, and Henry spoke again. 'We will use Breton, it is less likely to be understood by unwelcome ears.'

'As you wish, but my Breton is poor. I was not there as long as you.'

Behind the dais, Tal breathed out heavily. 'Shit. I only have a smattering of Breton.'

'I have none at all,' Jack replied.

Henry had spent the first half of his life in Wales, and

24

the second half exiled in Brittany and France. He was fluent in all three languages, and in Latin.

Footsteps approached, and then a burly, middle-aged man in a fur-lined leather cloak entered the hall, his arm around the shoulders of a boy of fourteen or so. The man's square face was ruddy, and the scarf of his swathed grey hat was wrapped several times around his throat.

The boy was tall and strong for his age, with a haughty demeanour. He had fair hair that hung low around his neck in a continuous under-curl, and his royal-blue cloak was embroidered with gold. But everything about him was somehow displeasing, including the sullen set of his mouth.

The man made low obeisance to Henry. 'Your Majesty, I am Guillaume de Boulvriag, tutor, your obedient servant. I bring you the boy—'

'Speak Breton!' Henry ordered sharply.

The man flinched, but then bowed again, and reintroduced himself in his native tongue, which, while not being the customary language of the Breton nobility—French being preferred—was still much used in the west of Brittany, where Henry had been kept under house arrest.

The tutor ushered the boy forward, bowing frequently as he introduced him as Roland, with a surname that sounded like 'du Coskerr', but Roland himself did not bow or speak at all. Instead, he treated Henry as an equal.

Henry's face was a mask as he addressed the boy, but the only answer was a hoisted chin. The king proceeded to prowl slowly around the pair, like a patient predator. He surveyed Roland from head to toe all the time, before halting in front of him and speaking in a reasonable tone that would have been a grave warning to those who knew Henry Tudor's ways.

De Boulvriag hastened to speak in Roland's defence, but Henry held up a hand, still awaiting a polite response from the boy. When there was none, he suddenly cuffed Roland's ear, hard, causing him to stagger back and clamp a protective hand to the side of his head. Sinking belatedly to his knees, he bowed his head.

Henry spoke sharply in Breton.

Jack thought it was akin to '*I am the king, and you will show me complete respect*!' Although, perhaps not as politely put, because Henry's language was often colourful.

'Well, Tal? Is it the same boy?'

'Yes. The boy's surname is probably du Coskäer, a noble Breton family. They also call themselves de Cosquer or de Vielleville in French, all of which I believe will more or less translate as "old town".'

Henry and de Boulvriag conversed, but too quietly for their words to carry. Their manner gave nothing away. Roland continued to kneel, his head hung obediently, although there was still a touch of arrogance about the set of his shoulders.

All was suddenly forgotten as an inner door burst open and Nero dragged his unfortunate handlers into the hall. The great mastiff was fawn in colour, speckled with dark grey, and slavered as it pulled towards the group by the fireplace, but then it halted, its black-masked face alert, its flopped ears suddenly pricked as it looked towards the dais. An ominous growl throbbed deep in its throat.

Jack's spirits plunged, and he put a wary hand on Tal's arm.

Jon's attention flew towards the corner as well, and he approached the dais, drawing the dagger on his belt. The mastiff began to give voice—loud, savage baying that resounded between the hammer beams overhead. Henry was taut with alarm, while Roland scrambled fearfully into de Boulvriag's protective arms.

As one, Jack and Tal bolted for freedom, black-shrouded figures dashing towards the door Jon had closed. As they struggled to pull it open again, Jon hurled his dagger instinctively, not knowing at whom he aimed. It pierced Jack's left shoulder and managed to embed itself, forcing him to grunt in pain. The door opened, and Jack ran on in agony, to the staircase lobby and then into the passage opposite. Tal paused only to shove the wedge back into place, to delay pursuit. He did the same with the passage door, which he locked and bolted for good measure. After kicking the wedge to jam it, he heard Jon, the mastiff and its handlers bursting out of the hall.

Tal ran to Jack, who had halted only yards away, leaning his right shoulder weakly against the panelled wall. 'Come, Jack, I will help you.' He put a supporting arm around Jack's waist, and hauled him along as quickly as he could.

Shadows loomed and shrank in the torchlight from the quadrangle, and shouts and Nero's racket filled the air. Jon shouted furiously behind them, 'Fuck the archbishop! Just beat the bloody door down!'

Nero became even more frantic, and the door jolted as men tried to force it open with their shoulders.

Tal tried to half-carry, half-drag his wounded companion, determined to get him out of the casement somehow, but the injury was too painful. Jack had to stop again, wincing at the searing pain.

'I cannot, Tal, I will hold you back. You will be caught trying to haul me through that window.'

'I am buggered if I am leaving you here!'

'You must! Do you want us *both* to fall into Tudor's clutches?' Jack glanced back at the door, as some of the Breton men from the quadrangle lent assistance. The battering redoubled, and it was clear the lock and wedge could not hold for long. He closed his eyes as pain engulfed him.

'Sweet God above,' he breathed, and then looked urgently at Tal, who was about to pull the dagger from him. 'No, leave it. I will bleed like a stuck pig and leave a trail in the snow, even supposing we get that far.'

'I *can* get you out!'

'No. For fuck's sake, Tal, be sensible. I am *not* going to be able to escape. It is too damned far to the horses. One of us has to get away with the knowledge we have gained tonight. It has to be you. Listen closely, Cicely's son lives and *is* Richard's. The boy may yet be York's future, do you understand? His name is Leo Kymbe. Tell her you know. If I am eliminated, as I know I will be, Henry will remove my brothers as well. Leo could well become *vital* for York. Give me your word, Tal.'

'But—'

'Your *word*!'

Tal nodded reluctantly. 'You have it, my friend.'

'And tell her I love her. Now, get out of here while you still can.'

The commotion at the door was tumultuous and the mastiff seemed almost demented. There were tears in Tal's eyes as he ran.

Jack watched the final flick of his cloak disappear into the room at the end of the passage, and then edged his own way into the first room he came to, leaving a smear of blood on the jamb. He managed to rub more orange oil over it, and then closed the door behind him. The room was illuminated by the cold sheen of the moon and snow outside. He staggered to the window, wondering if he could get out somehow, but it was sealed, and he was in too much pain to struggle one-handed. So he turned back his heavy cloak as much as he could to ease the weight on his left shoulder, and leaned against a table, facing the door, his dagger beside him.

At last the lobby door surrendered, and the chase streamed into the passage, led by Jon, who carried a torch. He was accompanied by the Bretons, and the baying mastiff with its handlers. The frantic hound avoided the orange oil and pounded on along the passage after Tal. Jack smiled.

'I am back here, you stupid cur.'

The clamour dwindled through the doorway at the other end of the passage, and then the great hound's baying changed into apparent confusion. Had Tal's scent been lost? Jack prayed his friend had made good his escape. He heard the chase move on, out of the passage and along towards the gatehouse. Then, a minute or so later, Nero's baying carried from outside.

Jack tried to gauge whether or not Tal might have eluded capture, but then it all seemed to die away, and into the silence there fell the soft tread of a single man. The steps faltered. Perhaps the bloodstain on the stonework had been noticed. Candlelight shimmered beneath the door, and an almost animal instinct told Jack who was coming. The door opened slowly, cautiously. The man appeared, tall, slender and graceful, clad in grey, with russet hair to his shoulders. Henry. He came into the room, the candlelight swaying over his face as he gazed at Jack.

'I *knew* it was you, de la Pole. Soot cannot disguise you, or save your life now.'

'So it would seem.' Jack's brown eyes were dull with pain, but he picked up his dagger, so Henry knew he was armed. 'What do you do now, eh, Tudor? Save me in the hope of extracting information? Or do away with me once and for all while you have the chance ... and then pray Cicely never learns you took the life of her most beloved cousin? What a dilemma.'

'No dilemma, my friend, for I do not intend to risk you being nursed back to health *again*.' Henry placed the candlestick on the small mantelshelf. 'I want to be rid of you, once and for all. England has only one sovereign, and that is me. York will never return. *Never*! My uncle's dagger is about to make a much worse wound, so much worse that

29

it will kill you. From loss of blood, if nothing else. *He* can take the blame, and I will reward him well for saving me. How he then deals with his wife is his business.'

'You really have no soul, you Welsh tick. Well, get on with your unholy work, enjoy the sensation of driving into *my* flesh for a change.' Jack tried to laugh.

Henry's face was stony, but his movements, hitherto slow and commanding, were suddenly swift and vicious. He seized a chair and hurled it at Jack who, caught off guard, moved aside too late. The dagger was jolted from his grip, and Henry was upon him in a second, grabbing him by the hair and jerking him forward to fall prostrate on the floor. Spots of blood scattered on decorative tiles, and Jack was in too much pain to fight back. Henry stood over him, a foot on either side, and reached for the dagger's hilt, meaning to twist the blade cruelly before driving it further in. But then he paused, and decided to inflict even more pain first.

Jerking Jack's cloak aside and moving Jon's dagger in the wound, he reached for his victim's left arm and twisted it back cold-bloodedly, until it must surely dislocate. Or shatter. So excruciating was the pain that Jack screamed. Henry wrenched the arm again, and as the joint began to dislocate, Jack fell helplessly into a blinding light. Oblivion claimed him.

Henry relished inflicting physical torture on the man he *knew* Cicely loved. White-hot jealousy like this had pushed him to consign Richard's illegitimate son, John of Gloucester, into madness. Now Lincoln would suffer the same. Henry exposed Jack's other arm. He would take his time, and do more damage.

His back was to the door, and he did not hear Tal's soft step. He knew nothing until he was clouted with the candlestick he himself had brought to the room. He felt a sickening pain, saw a blur of lights, and lost consciousness.

Tal closed the door softly, and bent to Jack. He knew

Jon's dagger had to be removed, but not before due preparation. Seeing the partly dislocated left shoulder, he froze. The only wound Jack had sustained originally had been caused by the hurled dagger. Now he was in this pitiful state. Henry had been reaching for the *other* arm, having clearly already done great damage to the first shoulder. The intention had been to hurt Jack as much as possible before despatching him!

Tal was tempted to put an end to the hated king there and then, but the time was not right. Instead he cut several strips from Henry's fine silk shirt, and then contented himself by aiming a particularly vicious kick into the apex of the royal legs.

Returning to Jack, he manipulated the left shoulder back into place, and as Jack stirred, clamped a hand over his mouth. 'No squawking, my friend!' he hissed.

Jack had no time to think as the dagger was pulled swiftly out of his shoulder, and the pad of silk pressed down to staunch the flowing blood. Tal worked swiftly, tying the pad in place as strongly as he could, and finally making a sling.

Jack sat up and saw Henry's motionless figure. 'Good God!'

Tal was surprised by the reaction. 'How much do you remember?' he asked, pausing alertly as they both heard shouts outside, and the more distant baying of two mastiffs, but the sounds soon faded again. The house itself was as silent as the grave.

'I recall being in the great hall. That's all.'

Using as few words as possible, Tal explained how he left the house. 'I had to come back for you, my friend. So I left a trail in the opposite direction from our horses, until I came to a stream, then I waded back towards the house. I re-entered as I had left, and found Henry standing over you, about to maim your right shoulder, as he already had your left. I hit him as hard as I could with a candlestick. The bastard was having fun torturing you, and then I believe he meant to murder you. To rid himself of Cicely's cousin and lover.'

Jack was dumbfounded. 'Have *you* killed *him*?'

'No. That would let him off too lightly. I want slow revenge.' Tal tested the window. 'Damn it!'

'We have to use the other window, as before,' Jack said.

'Can you manage?'

'There's only one way to find out.'

'I will support you, but if you give a single mew, so help me I will knock you unconscious again and bloody well carry you. Do you understand?'

'Perfectly.'

Helped from the floor, Jack swayed, requiring a strong arm around his waist, but he managed to walk to the door. Tal peered out into the passage, and then became motionless, his arm tightening warningly around Jack. He could *feel* that there was someone hiding nearby. But he could not see anything. The torches still flared in the quadrangle, the shadows loomed and then shrank again, but no one else seemed to be present. The feeling hung unpleasantly, and so did his heart, but then he decided to risk it and hurried Jack along the passage towards the end room. No one raised the alarm, and when he glanced back, no one appeared. Whoever it was clearly had as good a reason as theirs for staying out of sight.

Getting Jack into the other room and closing the door behind took only moments, and once inside, Jack leaned against a wall.

'Are you all right?' Tal asked anxiously.

'Could not be better.'

'You will do, my friend. Now, we are going to go through that window, and you will have to find the strength to help. I will climb out first. Then I want you to lean out and then down as far as you dare. You will begin to slip forward, but I will stop your fall and ease you down gently. I will see you safely away from here, I vow it. Thank God Almighty that Henry's desire for secrecy means so few men on guard, eh?'

Jack smiled weakly. 'Just stop talking, and get the fuck outside.'

Tal climbed easily onto the windowsill and pushed the casement to look out. The sounds of the search could be heard from two directions, too distant to be of immediate concern. Torches bobbed to the south, and there were lanterns to the west, but to the northwest, where their horses were hidden, all seemed quiet. Tal dropped down six feet or so into the snow, and then looked up, his breath silvery in the cold.

'Now!'

It seemed an age before Jack leaned over the ledge and did all he could to ease himself further and further out. Then, slowly and painfully, he lowered his head and shoulders until Tal could reach up to grasp him as he began to fall. It required all Tal's strength to pull him down and support him without causing him too much pain.

Jack took a few moments to recover, but then nodded. 'I am ready.'

Tal caught him around the waist again, and they started for a clump of bushes as fast as Jack could manage. If anyone came that way, the footprints to and from the broken window would be suspicious, but at least there was no blood from the wound, to identify the owners of the prints. Yet, at least.

They reached the bushes, and Tal pulled Jack into cover, glancing around warily. The torches to the south were nearer now, and coming their way!

'*Diawl!*' he breathed. 'We cannot linger like sweethearts.'

'No stolen kisses?' Jack grinned.

33

'Not even one.' Tal supported him again and then made a swift break for the edge of a small wood to the northwest, where their mounts waited.

By the time they reached the sheltering trees, Jack was getting weaker. There was blood oozing from around the dressing now, and then, to Tal's utmost dismay, approaching lanterns glimmered ahead. The wood was being swept from the far side! And there were more mastiffs, at least two! He redoubled his efforts, convinced they had time to get away. The horses waited patiently, with blankets over them to keep them as warm as possible. Tal brought the chestnut.

'Can you manage if I shove you up?' he asked quietly, urgently.

Jack nodded, and Tal lifted him easily, but saw how he swayed in the saddle.

'Hold on for dear life, damn it! I have not got you this far, only for you to fall off like some old woman!' He turned the horse to face east, and the roundabout way they had chosen to get to and from London.

But as he went to mount the second horse, a mastiff caught wind of them and began to give voice.

'Fucking Nero!' Jack breathed in dismay.

'Get going! *Now!* You know the way!' Tal slapped Jack's mount on the rump, and it leapt away.

The mastiff became more excited, and then its voice changed as it broke free of its handlers to give chase.

'Sweet God above!' Tal breathed, glancing after Jack, whose strength was doubtful for a hard, prolonged gallop.

There was only one thing for it, the mastiff had to be confronted. Dagger drawn, Tal urged his frightened horse directly towards the sound of the great hound. He saw the creature bound out of the snowy darkness and prepare to leap at him. The horse was terrified, but Tal was a strong rider, and as the hound hurtled at him, he bent to not only meet it, but stab it in the neck as hard as he could. The animal yelped and fell away.

Tal spurred his mount on again, in the opposite direction from Jack. He had to draw pursuit away from his wounded friend. The horse was not only relieved to escape, but also fresh and rested, and carried him through the trees swiftly. He heard shouts and knew the searchers had seen him. Some of them were riders, but Tal knew they would not catch him now.

He prayed no one would see Jack, and after riding across some open parkland, where there were too many prints for his to be picked out, he reined by another small wood. To his utter devastation, he saw Jack's riderless horse galloping past the front of the house. He recognized it by the long white stocking on its near foreleg.

Rigid with dismay, he watched the lanterns bob through the other woodland and then the searchers emerge, some on foot, some riders, with the single remaining mastiff. One man was leading a horse, over which something had been slung. It was some distance away, a formless silhouette, but it looked like a body. As he watched, the horse stumbled and the body slipped sideways before falling into the snow, where it lay absolutely still. Jack? What else could he think? Salt stung Tal's eyes.

The body was gathered and tossed over the horse again, without respect.

'That is the royal Earl of Lincoln, you ignorant clods!' Tal breathed, painfully aware of the comparison with Richard's fate after Bosworth, when he too had been thrown ignominiously over a horse.

Choking back a sob for the Yorkist prince he loved as a son, Tal turned his mount to begin the lonely ride back to London.

Chapter Three

AT TWO IN the morning three nights later, when Christmas Day had passed, London was peaceful beneath the stars. It was bitterly cold, with hard-packed snow still lying in the ancient streets. Smoke ascended vertically from the countless chimneys cloaking Ludgate Hill, and church towers and steeples rose like spines. St Paul's cathedral pointed skyward like a huge finger, while far below, the Thames at low tide was a narrow silver ribbon.

There was little movement on the river, the close-to-freezing water having retreated from most of the quays and wharves. Even London Bridge was quiet, its tenements pressing together as if for warmth. Henry VII's capital was a scene of night-time tranquillity, and all seemed well.

Somewhere between the river and the cathedral, in the maze of streets and alleys of Cordwainer Ward, was St Sithe's Lane, where stood Pasmer's Place, residence of Viscount Welles and his lady. It was not the largest property on the lane, by any means, but it was certainly one of the most pleasing, set around a courtyard behind a protective wall, with a small enclosed garden behind. Named for its owner, John Pasmer, a prosperous merchant, member of the Skinners' livery company and of the influential

Staple in Calais, it was very comfortable and luxuriously appointed. Pasmer now chose to live elsewhere in the capital, and was often in Calais, so he derived a useful income by renting the mansion to the king's uncle. He owned a number of properties in London and around the country, and had tenants in most of them, some very well-to-do. There was no doubt he would die a very wealthy man.

Viscountess Welles lay alone in the bed she should be sharing with her husband, but he was still absent with Henry. She was small, with fair skin, dark grey-brown eyes and defiant, dark-chestnut hair that could so often become a tangle. Her rounded figure was narrow-waisted, with full breasts, and she was not what people expected of a Plantagenet. Her sister Bess *was*, being tall, lissom and beautiful, with straight red-gold hair to her waist.

Cicely smiled in the firelight that shone through the bed drapes. Richard had been slight like her, with the same hair, but no one mistook *him* for anything other than a Plantagenet. She thought of the uncle for whom she would always feel such forbidden yearning and love. Neither of them had sought it … or been able to deny it. So much had been shared with him, and the sharing had been divine. She entered eagerly into every carnal delight, and it was at quiet times like this that she remembered him most, longed for him most, and could almost touch him again. This, in spite of Jon and Jack, both of whom she loved so much in the present. Especially Jack.

Jon she cherished, steadily and truly. He had become her husband to save her from the ruin of bearing a child out of wedlock. Richard's child, as Jon was well aware. For that she would *always* hold him dear, and be glad of him in her bed. But the desire she felt for him was not the almost ferocious passion first stirred by Richard. She had never expected to know such intensity again, but had found

37

something very close to it with Jack, who had always been in her heart to one degree or another, since he rescued her from drowning in childhood. With him there was an echo of Richard, and a link to all the joy that had gone forever.

She felt a sliver of guilt, for it was wrong to think of other loves while in Jon's bed. Where was he? He and Henry had left Greenwich Palace for Kent six days ago, but no one at court seemed to have any idea of their purpose. Bess knew nothing, nor did Henry's omnipresent mother, Margaret Beaufort, Countess of Derby. Which suggested that Henry was up to something very devious, into which he had dragged his reluctant half-uncle.

It was very unusual for Jon not to tell her where he would be, and he had promised to be home for Christmas Day, but she had celebrated alone. Henry, on the other hand, was wont to disappear from time to time, but not even Sir Reginald Bray knew where this time. Nor did the ambitious Dudley, while Morton looked as if he had been forced to eat a mess of feathers. These men defended their powerful positions jealously, but Henry was not a king who could be controlled, and they were forced to work very hard to stay in favour.

Cicely wanted Jon home again. Henry could stay away forever as far as she was concerned, because his return would mean a summons to his bed, which she did not want. Conscience made her pause. She was unfair to him. Yes, he had made her go to his bed, and yes, he had taken Richard from her and thus destroyed her happiness, but when she was with him there could be such tenderness and pleasure that she despised herself for it. She was prey to her own senses, and to his. Henry Tudor was a thoughtful lover, sensual, skilled and subtle. How she wished it were not so, but she revelled in fleshly joys. Even with him.

A lone horse entered the courtyard from the lane. Jon? She slipped from the bed and went to fold the shutters back and breathed on the frosted lattice. Yes, it was him! After brushing her hair, she dabbed rosewater on her skin and then donned a warm robe to wait for him by the fireplace. But he did not come. Puzzled, she lit a candle and went down to the deserted great hall, where she soon saw him by the fireplace.

His one hand was on the mantel, and in the other he had a cup of wine. He was gazing down into the blaze he had clearly just revived. His cloak and hood lay over a bench, and he was unaware of her. There was an air of complete dejection about him, as if his spirit had been crushed.

What was wrong? 'Jon?' she said, and the hall picked up her voice.

He turned in dismay. Without the direct firelight his face was pale and distracted, and she saw his cheeks were wet.

Appalled, she discarded the candle and ran to him, but he shook his head and held up a hand. 'Leave me, sweetheart. Please.'

'Not when you are like this, Jon.'

'Now is not the time, Cicely. I must compose myself.'

'Tell me what is wrong.' She went closer to put a gentle hand on his sleeve.

He pulled away. 'I will tell you in due course, but *please*, leave me for now.'

'Is it Henry? What has he done?'

'*He* did not do anything. I did.' Jon tossed his untouched wine into the fire, where it hissed and frothed violently.

Then, to Cicely's astonishment, he hurled the cup as well. She saw how his shoulders shook as he wept silently. It was terrible to see such a strong man so shaken by ... grief. Yes, it was grief. Moving behind him, she embraced his waist and rested her head against his back.

'Please tell me, let me comfort you.'

His hands gripped hers, and she could feel his struggle

to regain composure. It was a minute or more before he turned. 'I would *never* have harmed him, you know that. I would not do such a thing to him. Or to you.'

'Who are you talking about, Jon? Has something happened to Henry? Is that it?'

Jon gave a mirthless laugh. 'Jesu, if only it were, unless you count a good kick in the crotch and being knocked out for a while by a blow to the head, neither of which affected him much, except in his temper and pride. No, sweetheart, it is not Henry.' He gazed steadily and eloquently into her eyes.

Awful realization began to slide coldly over her. 'Jack?' she whispered.

'Forgive me, Cicely. Forgive me ...'

'He is hurt? I must go to him!'

'You cannot, sweetheart.' He closed his eyes. 'Jack really is dead this time, and I killed him.'

She stepped back involuntarily. All sound seemed to stop, as did the air itself. It was Sheriff Hutton again, and the moment she had learned of Richard's death. The same disbelief and pain, the same vacuum and inability to think or accept; the same conviction that it was a nightmare from which she *must* awaken at any moment.

'No. I ... do not believe it.' Her voice seemed to echo from within.

'Do you think I would lie about such a thing? To you, of all people? I know what Jack meant—means—to you, but he is dead, because of *my* dagger. I *swear* I did not know it was him. I thought it was an attempt to assassinate Henry. There were two of them, both in black hoods and cloaks, their faces blackened, but I believe now—by his height and build—that the second man was that meddlesome bastard ... Tal.'

He hesitated over the name in a way she noticed, even in her state of distress. Jack had introduced Tal to her as

Taleisin ap Gruffydd, which she did not believe was a real name at all. Did Jon *know* it was false? The only occasion at which she knew Jon had seen Tal was briefly, by torchlight on the river stairs of Westminster Palace, when he had asked her who Tal was.

'Why did you think it was Tal? You only saw him that once, and—'

'It was him, Cicely.' Jon's tone was level.

She breathed in deeply, to make herself concentrate, but Jack was smiling at her again; she could hear his laughter, feel his touch, share his kisses and know the joy of being one with him. He was still here. He *had* to be! But the awfulness tightened within. She would never see him again, and the heartbreak was almost insupportable.

Jon reached out. 'If I could take back those seconds, I would. I know he was your lover, and that you felt towards him almost what you felt for Richard.' His next words distracted her. 'Sweetheart, I may have thrown the weapon, but I would have sworn the blade did not penetrate enough to kill him. To slow his escape, yes, but not to take his life. With care and attention he would have survived, yet he was found dead. And no, I do not think it was Tal's work,' he added, 'unless he feared Jack might be "persuaded" to talk to Henry.'

'Tal would *never* do that.' She closed her eyes, her hands clenching into tight balls as she willed Jack to walk into the hall and prove it all to be untrue. But he did not.

Jon was answering her. 'Maybe he would wish to *save* Jack from Henry's merciless attentions?'

She shook her head. 'No, I will not believe it. Who found him?'

'The searchers roused to comb the grounds retrieved his body, but Henry found him before then.'

Her thoughts paused. 'Henry?' she repeated slowly, suspiciously.

Jon hesitated, and then drew her to a chair by the fire and sat down to pull her onto his lap. He put his arms around her, and she leaned against him. Intimacy was established. At first he could not find words. Jack's death had shaken him to the marrow, and so had his own guilt.

She spoke first. 'I know you would not have hurt Jack deliberately, but you must tell me everything. I owe it to him. Where did it happen? Why were you there?'

'I cannot tell you everything, sweetheart, because I am sworn to secrecy by Henry, and believe me, it is something so dangerous that you should not be exposed to it. But I *will* say that it happened in Kent, a meeting about something of infinite delicacy that Henry only partly confided in me, and I wish he had not. But somehow an inkling of it must have been discovered by Jack and Tal.' He described everything again, speaking of Roland only in passing, as simply 'a Breton boy'. He ended at the moment he wounded Jack and the two intruders had made their escape. 'Both of them got away, it seemed, but later it turned out that Jack had not.'

'And Henry was the one who found him?'

'Yes, sweetheart, and I know that is suspect in itself, but he was not to blame, for he suffered an assault that could *not* have been self-inflicted. He said he was searching within the house, while the main chase was outside in the grounds, and he entered a room to find Jack already dead. But then he was hit on the back of the head with a candlestick and knows nothing more. He awakened to find half his shirt cut away. Jack's body had gone, but there was blood where he had lain. His accomplice—Tal—must have come back for him. There is no other explanation.'

'I am loath to take Henry's word for anything.'

'Subsequent events convince me he was telling the truth. There was a thorough search of the grounds, although there were not many men to do it, and a single horseman was seen escaping. He disappeared into a wood and was not seen again. I believe it must have been Tal. He managed to kill a mastiff, and shortly afterwards, Jack's riderless horse was found by the house. I know it was his because there was blood on the reins, and ... this was caught on the pommel.' He took out a small pouch, in which were some strands of long, curly, almost-black hair.

Jack's hair. Salt pricked Cicely's eyes, but the tears did not fall.

Jon replaced the hair in the pouch, and pressed it into her hand. She pushed it into her purse, along with all the other precious mementos of her loves. She only dared to carry them in the house now.

'Where did they find him?'

'In the woods somewhere. I do not know exactly where. At first I only knew about the horse, but then saw a body being brought back to the house, flung over the back of another horse, but I did not go to inspect it. I could not. I preferred to remember Jack de la Pole alive.'

A sob choked in Cicely's throat, and she slipped her arms around Jon's neck to hide her face in the crook of his neck.

'Anyway, Henry was in no condition to leave for London as originally planned, nor was he to be for several days, so we tried to sleep for what was left of the night. I could not, and paced the passages. That was when I saw ...'

'Yes?'

'A body, wrapped in a shroud, being carried across the quadrangle and out beneath the gatehouse. I went to another window and saw it being taken to a hollow, where a grave had been painstakingly dug. Not easy, the ground was frozen. The body was placed in it and covered. Then, well, there was a willow overhanging the hollow. Need I say more?'

'A stave through the heart?' she whispered, remembering Jack's supposed makeshift burial on the battlefield

43

at Stoke. Someone else's body, mistaken for his, had been placed in an unmarked grave and pierced with a willow stem. Now, that same dishonourable burial had been re-enacted, but truly this time. How like Henry to condone it. No, worse, he would have *ordered* it!

'So, my love,' Jon continued quietly, 'Jack really is dead this time, and as I was the one whose act brought it about, I have to take the blame.'

She hugged him tightly. 'Where did it all happen? I need to know where he lies.'

'So that you can go there and weep over him? If you do that, Henry will know that I have said things to you that he has expressly forbidden. It is best you do not know.' Jon took her hand to be sure she paid full attention. 'Cicely, this secret of Henry's is one thing for which he will put himself first. *First*. Do you understand?'

Cicely sat up on his lap as her thoughts raced back into the summer just past. 'This boy of whom you are being so careful to say nothing … Henry once almost blurted to me that he had two children, not only Prince Arthur. You told me then *never* to mention it. Your warning was that he would not hesitate to forfeit me to save himself. I must now put two and two together, and—'

Jon interrupted her urgently. 'Do not make that connection, sweetheart! Please. It's dangerous.' He paused. 'Did Jack or Tal ever mention this secret meeting to you?'

'No.'

'You would not deceive me?'

'No! I never spoke to Jack again after that night at Westminster, when you and I saw him with Tal on the river stairs. When *you* affected not to know Tal, although now I suspect you did.'

He ignored the last sentence. 'I would dearly like to know how they learned enough to be there that night, sweetheart. Henry was meticulous about keeping it covert.'

44

Jon touched his fingers to her cheek. 'I repeat, you are not to mention to *anyone* that Prince Arthur is not Henry's only child.'

'Why does Henry not simply acknowledge this boy? There is no shame in siring a child before marriage, least of all for royalty and the nobility.'

Jon met her eyes squarely. 'That is up to him, and remember, we do not know who the mother might have been. There are any number of reasons why such a child might remain unacknowledged. You are to heed my warning, because when Tal approaches you—'

'Why would he?'

'Do not be artful, my love. You know he will want to tell you about Jack, if only to incriminate me to the full.'

'Why would he want to do that?'

He evaded the question. 'And if, by any chance, you have been dabbling in more than you should, then Tal is even more likely to be in contact. *Is* there a set plan to topple Henry?' he asked then.

'A goal, maybe, which all true Yorkists share, but I do not know of any firm, organized plan.' She spoke almost absently. Her thoughts were wandering again. Remembering. Seeking a reunion that was impossible …

'My sweet Cicely, I fear to lose you now.' Jon's blue eyes were anxious.

She put her arms around his neck again. '*Never* think it, Jon Welles. My regard for you burns as steadily as ever.'

But my heart breaks for Jack.

Chapter Four

CICELY HEARD FROM Tal the next day. Snow was falling heavily, and she was in the parlour with her maid, Mary Kymbe, disentangling embroidery threads, a task that did not require concentration. Christmas had lost all meaning and joy, and the garlanded leaves and other decorations seemed almost spitefully incongruous. Cicely dared not display mourning, and wore bluebell velvet trimmed with white fur, a gown Jack had admired.

The emptiness within was so like that other emptiness, when she had lost Richard, and she remembered a poem he had written as a very young man. He had realized his wife, Anne, loved her dead first husband more than him, but now the words meant so very much to his niece.

To be without you is to fade a little within.
To not hear your voice is to lose the sweetness of music.
To forfeit your smile is to be plunged into darkness.
To never feel your touch is to lose all sense of being.
To know you have gone forever is to steal away all joy.

She fumbled with the colourful silks, and Mary glanced at her sympathetically. The maid was one of the Kymbes of

Friskney manor in Lincolnshire, who cared for Leo, under the guise of him being the son of Mary's brother, Tom. Elderly Mistress Kymbe, Mary's aunt—who had been deaf for many years now, but could read lips—was the midwife and wisewoman who delivered Leo, and now played the role of grandmother to him.

The maid was pretty, with soft brown eyes and brown curls, and was of an age with Cicely. She was gentle and kind, and her loyalty to Cicely was unshakeable. There was no sweetheart in her life, not from lack of offers, but because Mistress Kymbe, who had 'the sight', predicted that a true and lasting love would come to her, and his name would be the periwinkle flower. Mary believed the cryptic statement.

There was much more to Mary than appeared, for she was the old lady's pupil, and very receptive and accomplished indeed. She knew all the medicinal herbs and beneficial flowers in her aunt's garden at Friskney, where there were also plants of a more arcane degree. Charms, cures, salves, potions and many other strange things were to be found in the old lady's casket, and now Mary had a similar casket that was filling slowly as she acquired new skills. Apart from 'the sight', Mistress Kymbe had another great gift, 'the cunning', and she perceived both to be slumbering in her niece. She foretold that one day Mary would possess greater knowledge, power and skill than her own.

Cicely was glad of the maid's quietly comforting presence, because Jack's death had sucked her vitality away. She was desolate, and wished Jon did not have duties today. When he was with her it was easier to bear, but Henry had come upstream to Westminster from Greenwich that morning. He came alone, and summoned Jon. Did it concern the same secret from Kent? Henry Tudor's reluctant lover did not care if he had a thousand secrets to try to hide, or if they brought about his downfall.

A page came in with a sealed note. 'An urgent message for you, my lady.'

Urgent? Cicely read quickly. It was brief. *Now. As before. T.*

Earlier in the year, Tal had waited in the lane to take her to Jack at the Sign of the Red Lion in nearby Budge Row. It had been the eve of Jack's flight from Henry's closing net, and they had made love for the last time in a dingy upstairs room at the rear of the premises. She rose quickly to look from the window, but the snow was so heavy that everything beyond the courtyard wall was obscured. Tal was waiting out there again now, but this time it could not be to take her to see Jack.... Her lips pressed together as she fought back the ever-close tears. She told Mary she would go alone. Whatever Tal had to say was for Lady Welles alone to hear.

His imposing figure appeared out of the swirling snow as she emerged from the courtyard, a lonely figure in hooded cloak and pattens.

'My lady?'

'If you think to take me to the Red Lion again, I—'

He interrupted quietly. 'The landlord asks no questions, my lady. I fear it must be the same room, too, because it is all he had. Forgive me, but we must talk privately, preferably in some comfort. A fire will have been lit, and there is a chair.'

And a bed, she thought, but no Jack to warm it. She signified consent. What else could she do?

'My lady, last time we pretended to—'

'Be sweethearts? Yes. I agree to that as well.' No one glanced twice at cloaked lovers.

He slipped an arm around her shoulder, and she rested her head against him. It was oddly reassuring, but as they walked towards Budge Row, it seemed that Jack's shade walked with them. She even glanced down at the snow, but there were only two sets of footprints. Soon they neared the court of shops, where stood the wooden, red-painted lion from which the small inn, really little more than a tavern, took its name. The hostelry was thronged inside, but no attention was drawn as they threaded their way to the staircase at the far end of the taproom. The innkeeper, having already been paid, did not even glance up.

Cicely entered the remembered first-floor room reluctantly. She felt Jack's presence so keenly.

'Tal, I would rather have simply walked around in the snow than come here.'

'A king's daughter cannot be expected to trudge the snowy streets.' He began to help her with her cloak and hood.

She wasted no time on pleasantries. 'Tell me what happened.'

'Your husband has not told you?'

'I would like to hear it from you as well.'

'Please be seated, my lady, that I may sit too. I am old enough to be your father, maybe even your grandfather, so take pity, I pray.' He indicated the only chair, which was by the smoking fire.

'I prefer to stand.'

'As you wish.' He removed his outer clothes and placed them on a table, being careful to take what she took for a small book of hours from the pocket inside the cloak. It was bound with red silk, and embroidered in silver with a droop-eared hound that seemed familiar.

'Is the hound your cognizance, Tal?' she asked.

'No.' He placed his gauntlets over the book, to deter further questions.

She felt embarrassed, until he indicated the chair again. '*Please* sit, my lady, for I feel awkward talking like this.'

She sat on the edge of the bed instead, and on almost reaching foolishly for Jack's hand, made herself concentrate on Tal instead. This was the first time she had been able to observe him properly. The snow reflected from rooftops outside, giving him a cool sheen, and she had a feeling he was connected with military matters. He wore a very plain leather brown tunic, belted low on his hips, and the gold chain and its religious pendants. She could imagine him at the gates of Jerusalem, holding Christ's banner aloft and brandishing a sword.

From their first meeting, she had felt he subjected her to judgement, and so, rather childishly, asked him about the book again, because she knew he did not want to discuss it. 'Your book of hours is very beautiful.'

'It is a book of poetry.'

The answer took her aback. Now he was a Crusader poet?

He countered question with question. 'Did you know that your husband considers the matter that led to Jack's death to be treasonous?'

She was thunderstruck. 'I—I know he considers it to be dangerous and does not want me to become involved in any way, but … *treasonous*?'

'I agree with him. Events at Knole were—'

'Knole? I only knew it was Kent. Jon would not say where, or why, but he *did* describe what happened.' That explained Morton's mess of feathers, she thought.

'My lady, does Jon Welles believe *he* killed Jack?' The question was blunt.

'He does, but at the same time he questions it.'

'Does he think *I* did?'

'No. Neither of us does, unless it was to spare Jack from terrible torture.'

Tal's eyes were bright. 'I loved Jack de la Pole as if he were my son, and would have lain my life down for him. Instead, he laid his life down while I escaped. Can you imagine how wretched that makes me feel?'

She nodded. 'I believe so.'

He recovered a little. 'Your husband is right to doubt his sole responsibility for what happened.'

'Jon told me that someone assaulted Henry and cut up his clothes. I imagine it was you.'

'Why should I deny it?'

'You did not kill him when you had the chance?'

'And have the Tudor and Lancastrian wolves close in to devour England during Arthur's minority? Filled with hatred I may be, but I still have my faculties. I want Tudor and his offspring hurled aside, so ridiculed and deserted, they can *never* take the throne again.'

She nodded. 'I understand. So, you then took Jack's body...?'

'Body? Oh, he was not dead then.'

Her lips parted. 'But Henry said—'

'I would not believe a word that Welsh turd said, even with his hand on the Bible. Perhaps least of all with his hand on the Bible. All I know is that I went back to that room and saw the King of England standing over Jack, who was most certainly alive. By then he was not only wounded by your husband's dagger, but his left shoulder had been almost wrenched from its socket, to cause him as much agony as possible. And Henry was reaching for the other shoulder. He was torturing the man he hated.'

'Surely not even Henry would—' she began, a little foolishly.

'Do not be naïve, lady! Have you forgotten what he did to John of Gloucester?'

Cicely looked away. 'So, if you had not returned when you did...?'

'Henry would have murdered Jack.'

She fought against believing it, not of the Henry who could be so warm and gentle. But she knew he had another side, a deeply unpleasant side that he could not always control. And that he sometimes *chose* not to control. He could be like a dry plant pod, suddenly shattering so that its seeds catapulted in all directions. That was the uncertain temper of Henry Tudor. All could be quiet, until that sudden snap …

Tal continued. 'Jack only remembered being in the great hall, but I know what happened after that. I managed to get him out of the house.' He described the flight to the horses. 'I thought he had got away. I do not know what happened after he left me, except that I saw his riderless mount and then the searchers leading a horse with his body flung over it like panniers.'

Cicely told him what Jon had told her. Tal turned away, his voice tight. 'So, Jack de la Pole has had an even more humiliating burial than Richard?'

'Yes.' She swallowed. There was silence, until she asked, 'What was so very important about that meeting? And how did you and Jack know?'

Tal drew a long breath. 'We learned from an agent, since murdered. Henry has a bastard son, whose name has since been confirmed to me as Roland du Coskäer.'

'If you think to surprise me about this boy, you do not. I know Henry has a by-blow, although that is *all* I know. The name means nothing to me. And I only know because Henry let it slip himself.'

As she spoke, a snatch of conversation with Henry returned to her, when she had asked about the woman he had once loved.

'*Who was she, Henry?*'

'*No one I wish to speak of.*'

'*Did she hurt you so much?*'

'*She did not hurt me, Cicely, I hurt her. By leaving her.*'

Tal spoke again. 'Roland's mother is a woman called Tiphaine du Coskäer, born de Rieux. Both families are Breton and noble. Her brother is now Chief Minister of

Brittany, so she is not a serving girl.' He described what he had observed at Honfleur, when Henry left to invade England, and then added pointedly, 'She was consumptive, I am sure, so if Tiphaine passed it to Tudor, then he may very well pass it to you. You do understand that?'

'Yes.' She knew the danger.

'We wander from the point. Suffice it that I identified the same boy at Knole.'

'But the reason Henry has not acknowledged him may simply be that he is *not* his son,' she pointed out.

'Oh, he is Henry's. Do you not see the connection between his name and Prince Arthur's? They are called after ancient heroes, demonstrating Tudor's dynastic ambition, to show he does, after all, have an ancient blood right to the crown. Even his choice of personal saint, Armel, is another reference to Arthur. Both are Welsh, and both mean "bear". Tudor is steeped in it. Oh, he is clever, for who does not know the stories of Arthur and Roland? I imagine that if he has another son, the name Oliver might slip into the scheme of things.'

'Perhaps it is simply that the boy was born on 16 June, which is Roland's Day, I understand. And it is the date of Stoke Field,' Cicely added.

'My lady, if there is treason around this boy, you are probably in the best position to find out more.'

She became cool. 'You wish me to make love with Henry and then make subtle enquiries in the fond aftermath?'

'I would not put it quite like that.'

'Perhaps, but it is what you mean. You think it easy for me, but then you are of a puritan turn of mind, are you not? Displaying your religion like a trophy. Perhaps you are really a Templar. However, as it happens, Henry is not a man who *can* be questioned. If I learn anything between the covers with him, it will be because he wishes me to know.'

'With all due respect, Lady Cicely, I am *not* puritan, and know well that you could draw blood from Tudor's stony heart if you wished.'

'You flatter me.'

Tal shook his head. 'Even this miserably pious pilgrim can see your spell, as did Jack.'

'Is that a subtle reminder?' she asked.

'Of what?' He looked at her.

'The night I first met you, when Jack took his horse Héraut to be stabled secretly at the tavern in Gough's Alley. He drew me aside and said there might come a day when my closeness to Henry would be needed.'

'Did he? I did not know.'

She wanted to disbelieve him, but knew he spoke the truth. In the silence that followed, she thought the faint scent of thyme drifted in the air. The scent of … Jack.

Tal saw the expressions cross her face. 'Lady Cicely?'

'The scent of thyme, when none is there, is said to indicate the presence of a ghost. Did you know that?' Jack was all around her again.

Tal went to the fireplace and took a poker to the smoking coals. She could see that he was struggling about what to say next. 'I must say something to you, because Jack told me to.' He turned to face her, his hands clasped behind his back.

'What is it?'

'I know you have a son by King Richard, a boy now named Leo Kymbe.'

Chapter Five

Shock engulfed Cicely. Jack had told this man her greatest secret? How could he? How *could* he? She rose from the bed and went to the window to compose herself. The white rooftops and smoking chimneys were only partly visible through the falling snow.

'How you must *really* condemn me now, Sir Saint,' she said at last. 'First I betray my marriage vows with Henry Tudor and then with Jack, and now you discover that my first lover was my own uncle. Incest and adultery aplenty, resulting in a child. And here I am, alone in an inn bedchamber with *you*. Maybe I am intent upon more unholy seduction, *far* beyond redemption in your pious eyes.'

'Mock as you will, my lady, I can assure you that your honour is not in danger from me.'

'And yours is even safer from me.'

A glimmer of a smile played upon his lips. 'Yes, I am sure it is.'

It was not easy to convince herself that if Jack had trusted him, then she could as well, because there was something about Tal that continued to disconcert, not least that he was keeping something else from her, apart from his real name. And—always—there was that sense of being judged and found wanting.

'Lady Cicely, it is none of my business whose bed you share, but Jack made *Leo* my business.'

'Apparently, my cousin's fingers were crossed behind his back when he promised not to even consider the Yorkist implications until Leo reaches his majority.'

'He only told me because the circumstances were so extenuating. Jack *was* a man of his word. A man of *immense* honour.' Tal spoke a little sharply, and then tried to soften the moment. 'You are determined to dislike me, are you not?'

'Because you are the way you are.'

'Which is…?'

'Sanctimonious.'

His lips parted in astonishment, and then he laughed. 'Indeed? Oh, if only you knew how wrong you are. But think what you will, it is of no consequence, but I *can* be trusted.'

'Then I expect of you what I expected of Jack.' She drew a fingertip down the partly misted window, wishing Richard could return to guide her. 'You want me to divulge what I learn from *Henry*, a man who trusts no one, and whom no one should trust. When I am away from him I see him truly, it is only when I am *with* him that he affects me in ways I wish he did not. I can want him so very much. Do you understand? There, now you will need to pray for me tonight, to save my wicked soul.'

'Your soul is not wicked, my lady.'

'Then it must only be my wicked body.' She resumed her seat on the bed. 'If I *do* happen to learn anything from Henry, how may I contact you?'

'I lodge at Flemyng Court in St Andrew's parish, near the King's Wardrobe. The house has bay windows through three storeys, and faces the entrance to the court. It cannot be mistaken. Failing that, I will be found in Calais. To reach me there you must approach the skinner, John Pasmer.'

'The man who owns Pasmer's Place?'

Tal nodded. 'He has tentacles everywhere, and is a very useful agent.'

'So he *does* support York. I always felt he did.' She recalled the fat merchant, with his mustard-hued clothes and too-tight leather bonnet with the badge of the Calais Staple. His beaming smile and affable nature made him seem unlikely to be involved in danger.

'Pasmer joined the Staple when Richard was king, and acted for him on many an occasion. Then he aided Jack as much as he could, and will continue to support York. He has no time for Tudor or Lancaster and is a good friend. You may have faith in him.'

'What if you *and* Master Pasmer are in Calais?' she asked sensibly, wondering why Tal would be there at all.

'The priests at St Andrew-by-the-Wardrobe are loyal. It is not only near Flemyng Court, but is where my mother and other members of my family are commemorated or interred, so I have connections there. But please, to safeguard yourself and everyone else involved, be very circumspect in your approach.'

She looked at him. 'I know how to be discreet, sir.'

'Yes, I rather suppose you do. However, if you need to see me in person, I will do my utmost to come to you. Please be assured of that.'

'Why would you do that for me?'

'You were dearly loved and trusted by Richard and Jack, and so my duty is clear. I will help and protect you.'

Yet when she met his eyes, she was still unsure of him. *Why?* 'Are you a genuine Yorkist?' she asked then.

He was offended. 'Yes! I wish to overthrow Tudor and destroy his line's chances of *ever* ruling again, and then I want York returned to the throne.'

'And—?' There was more, she could tell.

'And my underlying cause, my reason for *everything*, is the restoration of a beloved sibling's honour. Your father stole it, Richard gave it back, and now Henry has stolen it again. Of three kings, I serve and respect only Richard. And his line,' he added.

That line being Leo, she thought, her heart tightening. 'Richard would have put Jack on the throne, so your allegiance now should be to his brother, Edmund de la Pole,' she said. 'He must be fifteen now, and will therefore reach his majority soon enough. Is he not at Oxford at the moment?'

'As I understand it, he is in London for the Christmas season. Have you met him?'

'No.' Edmund was her first cousin, as was Jack, but she had never even seen him.

'Then let me enlighten you. He is very smooth-tongued and charming, but at times startlingly headstrong, coarse and oafish. His hair consists of very long, auburn curls that surround his head in a great mane, and he could be considered a beautiful youth, maybe even a devotee of folly bells, but is apparently only interested in women.'

She knew that folly bells were said to be the trinkets of fashionable men who preferred their own sex.

'Jousting and other manly sports are his delight,' Tal continued, 'so he cleaves to others of the same inclination. He is very good at them all, but arrogantly so, and likes nothing more than to prance around on his new white stallion, showing off its paces and his own, and also proclaiming his ability to afford some of the costliest red leather and gold trappings in England. Perhaps his arrogance is what makes him so efficient and skilful, but there is a sordid and tawdry side to him that is alarming in one who would call himself the White Rose.'

'You describe *Jack's* brother?' She found it hard to believe. 'Even so, Edmund has the bloodline, and with guidance might be moulded.'

'Edmund is for himself alone, and I cannot bring myself to support his claim. No matter that he is Jack's brother and Richard's nephew, he will be bad for England.'

'As bad as Henry?' she asked coolly.

'The point would be debatable, believe me. Richard chose Jack for more than just his blood. He would *never* have chosen Edmund, but would rather have raised his illegitimate son, John of Gloucester, to be his heir. Lady Cicely, I know you fear my ambitions regarding Leo, but neither you, nor Leo himself, has the right to decide about his future.'

'That is not for you to decide, either.'

'When you lay with Richard, you gave life to a boy of great importance, whether or not he is baseborn of incest. There are precious few royal scions of the House of York still living, and Henry will scythe his way through them until they are eliminated. Edmund de la Pole *and* his younger brother, Richard, will be high on his list, you may count upon that. Leo, too, should the facts about him reach royal ears. You have to confront the unpalatable truth, Lady Cicely. Leo will *always* be in jeopardy, but he may also become York's last hope.'

'Who are you to speak to me of this? And do *not* insist that you are Taleisin ap Gruffydd!'

'It is my name, my lady.'

'You think me gullible?' She glanced at the book of poetry, but the silver hound was hidden beneath his gauntlets. She had seen that hound badge somewhere before. Maybe Jon would know.

Tal looked at her. 'I have one last message from Jack,' he said quietly.

'Yes?'

'I am to tell you he loves—loved—you very much.'

It was too poignant. Sorrow tolled through her like a funeral bell, and the pain was too great. She bowed her head and gave in to silent weeping.

Tal felt at a loss. 'He asked me to tell you, Lady Cicely.'

She struggled. 'Please take me home. Jon will return soon, I hope. I need to be with him.'

'Of course.'

It was late evening before Jon returned to Pasmer's Place. Cicely waited in the parlour, where settled coals and logs glowed in the hearth, and candlelight picked out the tapestries and panelling.

He was angry to learn where she had been, and with whom. 'The *Red Lion*? Have you taken leave of your senses, Cicely?' he cried, slamming his goblet of wine down on the table.

'You were not here to ask, Jon, and I *had* to hear what he would say.'

'Which was?'

'That Jack was not dead when Henry found him.'

Startled, Jon gazed at her. 'What, exactly, have you been told?'

'Nothing that would incriminate you, as you seemed so sure Tal would do. Quite the opposite, in fact.' She then repeated the story of how Tal had managed to get Jack on to a horse, and what he had seen afterwards.

Jon listened very carefully, and then took a deep breath. 'And that is all?'

Her eyes widened. '*All*? How much more do you wish? Jack was alive, and Henry knew it! Henry dislocated Jack's shoulder, and—'

'Can you prove it? No. And Jack is certainly dead now, the last person with him being Tal!' He removed his doublet and almost threw it aside, a sign of there being far more to his reaction than appeared on the surface.

'I can tell you that Tal did *not* end Jack's life, but tried to save it,' she said. 'Oh, Jon, surely you do not believe Henry's version of events?'

'I always doubt him, and if what Tal says is true, it means Henry is *deliberately* saddling me with the sole responsibility for Jack's demise.'

'Yes. Even I do not wish to think he would do that.' She paused. 'There are other things I know from Tal that *you* certainly did not tell me.'

'Other things?' A guarded look entered Jon's eyes.

'That it happened at Knole, for instance, and that you and Henry met with a Breton man and a boy named Roland.'

Jon relaxed; clearly what she said was not what he anticipated. Feared, maybe. 'I wish to God Tal had held his tongue. If you should let slip your knowledge, Henry will believe *I* told you.'

'You already know the lengths to which I will go to protect you, Jon, and that will never change. I would cut out my tongue rather than endanger you. Or Leo, of whom Tal also knows.'

'Oh, my cup runneth over,' Jon groaned. 'You *do* realize that we dangle by threads if all this gets to Henry's little rosebud ears?'

'Yes.'

Jon paced, and then returned to her. 'So, pretty-maid Edmund de la Pole—God spare us!—fails to be appealing. No Jack he. But then, Henry will already have death warrants for every Yorkist male he can think of in an idle moment while passing a stool.'

'Jon, why is Henry's secret treasonous?'

'Jesu, lady, that sly insert was worthy of Henry himself.'

He was right, she thought, a little ashamedly, for she had done it to catch him off guard. It was Henry's favourite ploy.

'I plucked the word for effect,' Jon said then. 'I do not actually know what lies behind it all.'

'That, sir, is a falsehood.'

'Maybe, but it is all I intend to say, are you clear?'

She nodded. 'But at least answer this. Tal's badge appears to be a flop-eared silver hound. Do you know it?'

'No.'

Yet another falsehood, she thought.

'Cicely, Tal will bring perdition upon us. I do not care if he was close enough to Jack to share the same pair of hose, you are *not* to communicate with him again. Never! *Jamais. Nicht. Nunquam.*'

She lowered her eyes, signalling consent but hiding her true intent. She would see Tal again if necessary, and do all she could for the protection and furtherance of York. Richard's House. Leo's House. As the last crept into her mind, she began to accept that she could not obstruct her son's destiny. Whether or not she, or even Leo himself, might wish otherwise, his lineage was already his fate. But she did not accept it yet. Not yet.

Now it was Jon who changed the subject. 'Henry, who is still in a foul mood, is to go to the palace at Esher in a week or so.'

'Which is of interest because...?'

'Because I am to be there too.'

'Why?'

He spread his hands. 'I think maybe Roland, but am only guessing. I have a feeling your presence will also be required, and *not* for the obvious lascivious reason. He ordered me to hold my tongue about the boy, which means you must too. You know *nothing* of Roland, do you understand?'

'Yes,' she replied. But her chin came up in that mulish way he knew so well, and he smiled.

'Oh, Cicely, am I going to have trouble with you?'

The smile was one of those that endeared him to her so much, and she forgot her displeasure. 'I do love your smiles, Jon Welles, even when you are being aggravating and deceitful.'

'Deceitful?'

'I know you have been less than honest with me tonight. Several times.'

He had the grace to look a little guilty. 'But otherwise, I am still your dear husband?'

'Perhaps.' She took his hand. 'In fact, definitely. I need you now, Jon Welles.'

'I trust it is a disgracefully, shockingly, shamefully *carnal* need?'

'Libidinous to the ultimate degree.' The desire had come from nowhere.

They had spoken of such momentous matters, but now, without warning, he had stirred the wantonness within her.

He was amused. 'My lady, has it never occurred to you that I know exactly which smile to employ in order to get what I want from you?'

'You would not be so calculating.' She moved closer.

'Ah, you forget that I share blood with Henry, so can be just as sly and manipulative.'

'Well, I *could* say that I know that you think you know, but that you do not know what I know. I do know, however, and intend to act on my superior knowledge.'

'I *think* I understood that.'

She smiled and began to unfasten his shirt.

'Here, in the parlour?' He pretended to be shocked.

'Well, we can go down into the great hall and summon the servants if you desire an audience. Or I could wait, and catch you by surprise when we break our fast in front of everyone in the morning.'

He grinned. 'If only I had the courage to call you out on *that!*'

'So, you will settle for here, now?' She slipped her fingers inside his open shirt and let them wander through the dark hairs on his chest. The warmth of rosemary was blended with his fresh masculinity, and her senses stirred still more. She was so glad to be his wife, and so glad that he loved her. Their practical contract had become so much more than just an arrangement.

They undressed and lay together before the fire, purposely omitting the locking of the parlour door. They felt daring and foolish, choosing the risk of discovery over the secrecy of a curtained marriage bed. It was almost a forbidden passion.

She leaned over him as he lay on his back. The firelight was mirrored in her eyes, and flushed her breasts to deep rose. Her alert nipples cast little shadows as she brushed them to and fro against his chest. He had such a good body. Small wonder two beautiful witches had fought so hard to keep him, she thought.

She leaned down to kiss the pulse at his throat, running the tip of her tongue over it while her hand explored the damp hollow beneath his arms. The perspiration was clean and fresh, and the hairs fine, dense and clinging. Her lips moved from his throat and down to his nipple. He gasped and arched a little, for it was so sensitive, but she did not spare him. Her lips and teeth played sweet havoc with him, even as her hand moved from his armpit down to that other forest of hair, out of which there now sprang an arousal that heralded a dazzling union to come. Yes, dazzling, because she needed him so much right now, and knew that he needed her. She would not think of Knole, nor would he; instead, they would join together in an act of love that would banish everything for a while, and give them back to each other. But then there was shouting in the snowy courtyard.

Jon was furious. 'What in God's sweet name—?' Then he became still as they both heard the king's messenger seeking to deliver a message to Lady Welles.

Cicely's heart sank, and the pleasure of lovemaking was banished in an instant. Henry was summoning her!

Chapter Six

HENRY'S APARTMENTS AT Westminster were decked for the season, but in a manner as restrained as the man himself. They had once been Richard's rooms, and Cicely remembered so much as she knelt before his usurper.

Henry's gold velvet robe was tied loosely at the waist, revealing the reddish hair on his chest. His hair was damp, because he had bathed, and the warm air drew out the scent of cloves on his skin. There was no sign of him having been attacked, he seemed as perfect as ever, except for his wayward eye, and he was still as fascinating as a beautiful but deadly plant.

She wore a particularly revealing plum brocade gown—the one he liked most—and was sure to bend forward a little, to display her shoulders and the soft, curving shadow that disappeared between her breasts. On entering his presence, she had deftly removed the pins in her hair, so that her chestnut tresses tumbled free. Her only jewel was the emerald ring he had given to her. The purse at her waist contained no mementos, only the things any woman would be expected to carry with her.

Tonight, she had done all she could to make herself desirable to him, because she had to retain his favour if she was to protect herself, Jon and Leo. And at the same time she had to pretend not to know anything of events in Kent, except the bare fact of Jack's death. Certainly she could not mention Knole itself. Nor could she think of Jack being tortured, because preoccupation with *that* horror would prevent her from even smiling at this icy king who could also burn with such fire too.

'It is good to see you again, Cicely.' Henry raised her, cupped her chin in his slender fingers, and made as if to kiss her, but released her again and moved away.

'You honour me, Henry.' The kiss that was not a kiss disturbed her. He had never done such a thing before. Why now?

'How are you, *cariad*?'

'As you see, I am well.' The Welsh word for sweetheart always sounded good on his lips.

He looked at her again. 'More than a week without you is a long time.'

'And so I only get a pretence of a kiss?'

'Ah. Well, perhaps I fear the response will be a pretence too.'

'You do not fear any such thing, Henry Tudor, not after all this time.'

His eyes seemed more hooded than before. 'You still make me very aware that you are York and I am the enemy.'

She summoned a smile. 'And so you are. Henry, I am ashamed to enjoy you so much.'

'There's honesty for you.'

'I *do* enjoy you, Henry. How can you possibly not know *that* by now? My treacherous little muscles, remember? They give me away every time.'

His strange eyes were like the North Sea in November, and there was no sign of the cast in the left one. He was *trying* to unsettle her. Was it to rattle her into revealing if she knew anything she should not? She decided to forestall him.

'Jon has told me what happened to Jack.'

'I thought perhaps he would. His part in it, at least.'

'He blames himself.'

'Yes, I imagine he must. It was … unfortunate, but his aim was perfect. Now I will never interrogate your cousin.'

She had to look away. 'Jon also told me you were attacked. Are you all right?'

'Enough to have a grim temper, yes. Candlesticks and my scalp were not meant to come into contact.'

He did not mention his other, more embarrassing injury, so she pretended not to know of it. 'Where did you have Jack buried?'

'That need not be of concern to you, Cicely.'

'He was my cousin.'

'And more.'

'No.'

He gave a cool little laugh. 'Deny it if you wish. His whereabouts are nothing to do with you. As far as England is concerned, he lies beneath a willow at Stoke Field, with a living sapling growing through his treacherous Yorkist heart.'

She knew it would be wise to turn the conversation. 'I … I believe I have yet to thank you properly for the emerald.' She spoke brightly and raised her hand to show him that she wore it.

'The giving of which was perhaps a little clumsily handled.'

She looked at him. 'I know you, Henry Tudor, you enjoyed yourself because of the embarrassment it caused. Including to me.'

'You? Cicely, it was a mark of my high regard.' He seemed genuinely surprised.

'You did it immediately after Jon and I had exchanged

those totally unnecessary second vows of marriage, which *you* insisted upon, and you did it in front of Bess and all the courtiers present. Bess did not deserve to be humiliated. Nor did Jon. Nor did I.'

'How very remiss I seem to have been.' He went to a window overlooking the Thames, where lanterns marked the whereabouts of the few vessels plying the low night tide. His movements were sinuous, and his manner unhurried. 'I laid claim to you with that ring, Cicely. It was a defiant gesture. No more and no less. If it humiliated others, they must put up with it, but never think I intended to belittle or mortify *you*. If I did, I regret it very much. I would never wish to hurt you.'

'You would if it suited you.'

He glanced back with the hint of a smile. 'Being apart has not softened your tongue or dampened your spirit.'

'I sincerely trust not. Being rude to you is one of my greatest pleasures.'

'Another being to fuck me.'

'I wish it were not so,' she replied honestly.

'I know that too.'

'We are adulterous sinners, Henry.'

'On my death bed I will implore the Almighty for clemency, pay to have masses said for me in perpetuity, bestow lavish gifts upon Holy Church, forgive everyone I can think of, and thus ensure my time in Purgatory is brief and my entry into Heaven prompt and irreversible. Oh, and just before I go, I will whisper in Arthur's ear that he is to forget my so-called mercy and behead *everyone* I protected by so foolishly giving my word. *And* he will be told to punish those covered by some damned treaty or another.'

'How very unchristian.'

'As are my thoughts at this moment, because I so want your lips to play sweet merry Hades with me.'

'Then they will.'

He came around her to caress her shoulders gently before kissing them. 'You are an exquisite jewel, Lady Welles,' he whispered.

Her eyes closed with pleasure. She could not help it, he was irresistible.

Next he coiled her hair over her left shoulder to unfasten the gown, as he had so many times before. He eased the rich plum brocade gently down until it slipped around her ankles. She wore nothing else, and closed her eyes as his lips moved enticingly into the crook of her neck.

'I need you so much, *cariad*,' he whispered.

His touch was so unerring that her secret struggle increased.

He turned her to face him. 'I pray that tonight you will not threaten me with the codfish.'

It was their little silly joke, that when he displeased her she would lie beneath him like a codfish on a slab. Then he smiled at her, and it was in his eyes as well as merely on his lips. A man's smile could do so very much. A few hours ago it had been Jon Welles, and now Henry. She was confronted by the mostly hidden Henry, loving, warm, amusing and engaging.

'Oh, Henry …' She could hardly speak, her emotion was so great. Was this what it was to have one's heart truly torn? 'What are you called in Welsh?' she asked then, for this other Henry needed a name.

Surprise lit his eyes. 'Apart from *twll tin*?' He smiled again.

'What does that mean?'

'Arsehole.'

She smiled. 'No doubt your fellow countrymen do call you that, for you have not done much for them, but it is not what I mean.'

'My Welsh name is Harri Tudur. Why?'

'Because that is who you are right now. I see you, Harri,

looking out from the cold shell of Henry Tudor. The true man is with me now.'

'Harri Tudur died a long time ago,' he said abruptly. 'In April 1471, when my life changed forever.'

'The Battle of Tewkesbury? When you were a boy? No, Harri Tudur is here now, with me. I know which man I have been lying with, which man I laugh and smile with. Admit it, please.'

He put his hands to her waist, caressing her skin with his thumbs, and then leaned to whisper in her ear. 'As you wish. I am Harri Tudur.'

She closed her eyes, for the gentle attention played havoc with her senses. Shame warmed her skin, because she wanted him. She always wanted him, for the way he satisfied her every need, and then did it again.

He wrapped a lock of her hair around his finger. 'My waking moments are spent in imagined sin with you,' he whispered.

She smiled a little wickedly. 'I will not remind you that you have a wife with whom you can sin whenever you wish.'

'Do with *Bess* the things I do with you? Jesu, she would believe that Old Nick himself had possessed me, and she would rush to take the veil if I actually attempted to explore her body with my tongue.'

He was right, she thought. Bess was as warm and responsive as a stone. 'Am I to be on my knees before you, or beneath you on a bed?' she asked flirtatiously.

'Here. Now.'

In a trice she was back at Pasmer's Place, saying something so very similar to Jon. '*So, you will settle for here, now?*'

She went to her knees and parted his robe, to find his excitement already evident. He smiled. 'My anticipation is unbearable.'

'Then let me help,' she breathed, the muscles in the apex

of her legs trembling with an excitement of their own as her hands enclosed the base of his erection and eased the tip towards her lips. Her eyes closed as she kissed him, tasted and cherished him.

His beautiful fingers moved richly in her hair, stroking and loving, and she heard him whisper her name.

Desire plundered her, and she was lost amid so many pleasures that time almost seemed to halt. She exulted in possessing Henry Tudor, because he was at her mercy now, his relief dependent upon her command. And she was relentless, prolonging his ardour until she thought he would no longer be able to bear it. Oh, the joy of this particular man, whom she both hated and desired.

She heard his breath catch as he reached a point from which there was no return. He was the prisoner of his own desire, and as he finally surrendered, his entire body flexed with pure physical reward. She accepted all, exulting in the moment, and weak with the fulfilment he gave. Her arms moved around his thighs, as she continued to glean ripples of joy from him.

His fingers coiled lovingly in her hair as he let her take all she wished of his body. 'Jesu, *cariad*, I think I have died in ecstasy,' he said softly.

She wondered how close this was to love. Now, when he was so warm and gentle, when they had shared such euphoria, and he trusted her so much, there was communion. She did not *want* to believe anything ill of him. Anything at all.

He pulled her up into his arms, then took her hands to stretch them down as far as he could without forcing their grip apart again. The action brought them together, body pressed to body. He hid his face against her hair and swayed almost imperceptibly. It was so subtly and undeniably erotic that she could not have broken free, even had she wished to.

It was some time before he released her again. 'The comfort of the bed, I think, mm?' He took her hand to lead her through the small lobby to the king's bedchamber. Richard's bedchamber, but everything was different now. Even the bed. Richard's had been hung with murrey and blue, Henry's was green and white, embroidered with bright-red dragons. It was grand and four-posted, carved and gilded, with intricate drapes that were almost closed upon the inviting hiding place within.

She slipped through the gap between the curtains, and lay on her back, a hand stretched out to him. 'Come, Your Majesty, I will permit you to lie in your own bed.'

'Why, thank you, gracious lady.' He tossed his robe aside and climbed in with her, leaning over her for a moment as if to say something important.

The firelight caught his face, his eyes, and she saw something written there. 'Henry?'

But he lay beside her. 'My dream is still to one day have you all to myself. No inconvenient uncles, cousins, husbands, only my good self to satisfy your sweet desires.'

That was not what he had been about to say, she thought, trying to fathom the expression glimpsed in his eyes. What had it been? Something that caused him pain, she decided. Mental pain, not physical.

He gave a quick laugh. 'And instead of you, I have your sister, with whom I am as brief as humanly possible.'

'Five strokes, I believe you once said.'

He smiled again. 'It depends upon how much thinking about you has preceded it. If I get myself to fever pitch, I can do it in three. Once there were only two. I do not think she knew I had been there at all.'

'Poor Bess.' But she smiled.

'Poor *Bess*? Have you any idea how demeaning it is to have to bed a woman whom I loathe and who loathes me? It is my bounden duty to make her fruitful and hope for heirs, but there is no pleasure, love, tenderness, no joy or those sparks that can make my life so very worthwhile. Only you can grant me those things, *cariad*.'

Without warning, he hauled himself up restlessly, and sat back against the carved headboard. 'Do the people believe I am only king because I married your sister and put Edward IV's blood back on the throne?'

His voice had changed, and the abrupt question took her by surprise. 'No! You are king by conquest, Henry, and have united York and Lancaster *since* then, through marriage. I should imagine everyone knows that.'

'Do they?' There was subtle warning in everything about him now. 'I will *not* be known as *her* consort!'

Alarmed, but endeavouring not to let him see it, she reached up to touch his cheek soothingly. 'You are not known as that, Henry. You were the king before you married her, not *because* you married her.'

His capacity for violence loomed over her again, that dark suspicion that often eclipsed his mood. Suddenly, he was the king who had tortured John of Gloucester and then paraded what was left of him in front of the entire court. The king who could well have taken pleasure in dislocating Jack's shoulders as a prelude to murdering him. When *this* Henry was to the fore, there was no saying what he might do.

As if to prove the point, he snatched her hair at the nape of her neck, and twisted it cruelly. 'You fear me now, *cariad*?' His eyes glittered in the candlelight.

'Is this what you want of me? My fear?' She was frightened, but her spirit rebelled. She would *not* bow to this! Her struggles were useless, because his grip only tightened, and she had to hold her hair to stop the pain. 'I thought you wished me to love you, Henry Tudor. Instead, I am nothing more than your toy, to be treated with scorn whenever you choose! Especially *after* you have been lightened of your load!'

'I can survive on your fear.'

She stopped resisting. 'You always swear that when you change like this, no matter what you say or do, beneath it all you still love me. Is it no longer true?'

He gazed at her as if he did not understand.

The hesitation gave her heart. 'Please, Henry, you are really hurting me.' Her eyes had never been larger or more brimming with tears. Richard had told her how devastating her charm could be if she really wished, and right now, she certainly wished, but she had no idea if it could possibly rescue her from further violence.

'You cause me distress, every minute of every day, madam,' he snapped.

'And inflicting it on me instead will change that?'

Again he looked as if he had not understood, but his grip relaxed.

She tried to find her way to Harri Tudur, who was surely somewhere not far within. 'Oh, Henry, if you distress me, you will find that when you want me again in a short while, I will indeed be that cold, limp codfish.' She made herself give him a tiny conciliatory smile.

She saw bewilderment flit through his eyes, before he released her, slowly, uncertainly. His confusion was touched with fear. Of himself? Did he even know what had just happened?

But then it had all passed, as swiftly as it came. He leaned his head back again and closed his eyes. 'Saints above, lady, you can always tame me.' There was a long pause. 'You play me on a line, I think.'

'I do not play you, Henry,' she replied untruthfully. 'I only want you to be happy.' *You have no idea how much I wish it. When* you *are happy,* I *am not at risk!*

He looked at her again, his face still caught in the shaft of firelight. 'Did I hurt you, *cariad*? Please, tell me.'

'Do you know what happened, Henry?' she asked gently, for his pain now was quite pitiable.

'No. At least ... but I can see by your face ...' He pulled her up into his arms, and kissed her with a different violence. The violence of a man who sought to put things right with the woman he loved. 'Hold me, *cariad*. Show your forgiveness.'

She slipped her arms around him in genuine reassurance, for how could any woman withstand such wretchedness? His distress was as much a chain around her as everything else about him.

He sank his fingers through her hair again, but gently now, so lovingly. She knew it was not pretence. 'I do love you, Cicely. How many times must I say it?'

'As many times as you need to, Henry,' she answered gently.

'The darkness is upon me so swiftly ...'

'I know.' She stretched up to kiss his mouth again, and a floodgate of emotion was opened as he returned it. Everything he was, every part of his being poured into that kiss. She could feel his strength and his weakness, his love and all that he tried so very hard to suppress.

'I can only speak of this to you, my love,' he whispered then. 'You are the only person I trust with my private dreads. What might I do one day? I fear it so. If I ever truly hurt you, I would die of the wretchedness and guilt.'

She moved her cheek against his. 'I know your unhappiness, Henry, I understand it.'

He drew away ruefully. 'Except at Huntingdon.'

'Your black self was in command that day.'

They had kept an assignation at a Huntingdon inn, and he had suddenly believed her to be part of a conspiracy to kill him. In his fear and rage, he had struck her to the floor and said such terrible things, before leaving. Yes, he had terrified her that day, but she could have stopped him from leaving. One gentle word, as just now, about the codfish, and he would have been in her arms again, craving the same forgiveness he craved now. He was crucified by himself. None other. And the time had yet to come when she could turn her back on him forever. Maybe it would never come.

'*Cariad*, I believed I had lost you that day, and knew I had brought it upon myself. I have never felt so bleak.'

'I am still here, Henry.' She touched his face again. 'Come, lie down with me again and hold me close.'

Deep under the coverlets again, he gathered her into his arms. 'I am so sorry you have finally lost de la Pole.'

Her eyes had been closed, but now flew open again.

He said no more, and she felt him settling and relaxing against her. Soon his breathing became regular. She lay there, gazing up at the elaborate folds of the bed canopy, caught in the moving shaft of firelight that pierced the crack in the curtains. It was a long time before she drifted into a dreamless sleep.

Chapter Seven

CICELY AND HENRY were startled from sleep the following morning when someone knocked discreetly at the bedchamber door. Three, and then three again. A signal.

Henry sucked in his breath. '*Fuck* Fryon!'

Étienne Fryon was Henry's secretary in the French language, and had also served Richard and Cicely's father. She knew him by sight, but had never spoken to him. His presence this morning was evidence that at least some of the forthcoming royal business would be conducted in French.

Flinging the bedclothes aside, Henry leapt out of bed, and then immediately doubled up, clutching his crotch. 'Sweet Jesu, Mary and all the angels!' he gasped.

Cicely hastened to him in alarm. 'Henry? What is it?'

He recovered enough to look at her. 'It would seem I have to admit that I suffered a more demeaning injury than the blow to the head. A damned hard kick up the arse. Well, not quite the arse, just halfway between it and my dick! It hurts first thing, but eases off when I have been moving around for a while. I tell you, if I ever catch that bastard, his cock and nuts will be sliced off and thrown to the dogs!'

She hid her mouth with her hands, wanting to laugh but, unsure whether he said it with humour or not.

'One laugh now, lady, and yours is the pretty arse that will be kicked.' There *was* humour, albeit reluctantly, because he knew how he appeared, bent over, holding on to himself.

She moved closer, and pushed his hands gently aside, to replace them with her own. 'There, I am sure that is a balm, Your Majesty.'

He met her eyes. 'You think I cannot pierce you this morning because of an embarrassing little bruise?'

'So now it is a *little* bruise?'

'Kings brush pain aside.'

'Do they indeed?' She smiled and worked gentle fingers into him. 'Hmm, I see that everything still functions as it should.'

'It cannot help but do so when you are near.' He relaxed a little, bent his head to kiss her, and moved himself sensuously in her hands. 'Oh, I would dearly like to return to that bed, but I really cannot. It will take long enough to robe me, as it is.'

She slipped a soft fingertip inside his foreskin. 'Even when I do this? Are you sure?'

He smiled. 'No, although a good fuck would set me up for the day, but I have to act the king now, and need your help with my garbing. Then, when you are dressed too, you must leave by the door behind that blue tapestry.' He nodded towards it and then went to rinse his face from a bowl.

Her father's many lady-loves had used that door, but Cicely knew that no such thing had happened here in Richard's time. At Nottingham, however, there was another such door that *she* had used to go to him. If only she had realized sooner that she loved him so very, very much. How many more times might she have used that door?

Henry had picked up a towel, but paused as he observed her thoughtfulness. 'Your expression tells a story, Cicely. What is it? Did you come to Richard here through the same door?'

'I did not go to and from my uncle at all in the way you suggest. Please do not spoil this, Henry.'

'You have secrets that it drives me to lunacy to think of.'

'Secrets that do not exist,' she answered, appearing angelic. 'The story behind my expression a moment since is simply that I was reminded that this and a similar door at Nottingham were indeed used by my father's many doxies. And it was not *my* uncle who told me about it, but *yours*.' She would have to be sure to warn Jon she had said such a thing to Henry.

'My uncle? Jon Welles, I presume?'

'Well, certainly not Jolly Jasper, who does not speak to me at all, let alone about such a subject.' Jasper Tudor was Henry's full-blood uncle, and had taken him into exile after Tewkesbury. Now Jasper was Duke of Bedford, and disapproved entirely of Cicely Plantagenet's place in Henry's life. 'Jon was in my father's household,' she went on. It was true enough. Jon had even been one of the many present at her father's deathbed, although she had only recently learned of it.

Henry nodded. 'Your father was excessively profligate, I grant you.'

'Hardly a secret, and hardly an appropriate criticism when *you* are suggesting I follow in the same footsteps, creeping out secretly after gracing your bed. You, Henry, are the Tudor pot that accuses the Plantagenet kettle of being burnt, and are in no position to condemn my father, when you have gone even further and endeavoured to make his daughter your official mistress. Shame on you.'

'Ah, you have a point, of course.' He smiled again, and then glanced towards a window. Snow was falling, large, heavy flakes that descended almost vertically, because there was no wind.

She took great care with his clothes, because a king had to be perfect in every detail. She had once dressed Richard, not in royal robes, for it had been at the hunting tower near Sheriff Hutton, when they had been together for the last time. But the emotion she had felt then had been almost intolerable. There was emotion now, but it was not the same.

Henry smiled as she combed his hair with great care, trying not to touch the bruise left by the candlestick. 'Have you no urge to scratch me with all the force you can muster?'

'Not at all, although I will oblige if you so desire?'

He put up his hand to rest it gently against her cheek. 'I desire much from you, my love, but not that.'

Next she brought his heavily jewelled, silver collar of pearls and rubies. It had a new pendant she had not seen before, in the shape of a solid silver dragon that coiled upon itself, biting its own back. It was both beautiful and cruel, and had diamond eyes that glittered wonderfully, as if the precious stones had somehow been miraculously cut to catch the light.

Henry watched her studying it. 'A perfect allegory of me, do you not think?'

'Yes.'

'You are not supposed to agree.'

'Then do not ask such questions.'

He laughed a little. 'I am put in my place again, I believe.'

'Take care of yourself today, Henry.'

'I do every day. There is no one more skilled at caring for his precious hide than me, I assure you.' He gazed at her. 'Oh, it grieves me to have to *dress* you, for to be sure you are a heavenly vision in all your God-given loveliness. Rich garments are not needed to make a joy of you, my Plantagenet princess.' He proceeded to dress her in the plum brocade gown and then placed her hooded, fur-lined cloak around her shoulders.

The signal knocks sounded again, probably with great reluctance, because delivering Henry Tudor a second reminder was not an enviable task. More voices were now audible in the outer room.

'I must go,' he said regretfully. 'I will send for you when I go to Esher on 10 January. No doubt you already know.'

'This is the first I have heard of Esher,' she replied with saintly untruthfulness.

'I thought maybe—' He broke off. 'Well, no matter. I will want you there.'

'And I will come, you know that.'

'Because you still wish to protect my uncle?'

She lowered her eyes. 'I rely upon you to honour your word, Henry. You have me, and so will not harm Jon. Do you still promise me that?'

'Yes. He will not come to any hurt at my hands.' He went towards the door.

'Nor the hands of any of your creatures,' she added quickly.

'How mistrustful you are.' He turned, rubbing an eyebrow. 'You have my word, Cicely. I will not be the cause, directly or indirectly, of anything ill befalling my half-uncle. There, is that specific enough? I would not wish you to suspect me of being snake-tongued. Now, I must begin my duties or I will still be doing them at midnight tonight.'

'No, by then you will be poring over your accounts, which is a self-inflicted task.'

'So I will and so it is.'

'And your eyesight will continue to suffer for it. You really should let others do it for you.'

'Never. Accounts and expenses I trust only to myself.'

She smiled. 'So, you are still as mean as they say.'

'*They* had better not say it in my hearing, which is as sharp as ever it was.' He caught her hand and raised it to his lips. 'Do not return to Pasmer's Place alone. I know you chose, foolishly, to come here unescorted, but I will not have it that you return in the same way. Which reminds me ...' He went to the table where he attended to documents, and hastily scrawled 'safe pass' and his initials on a piece of paper, sanded it, shook the sand away and then handed it to her. 'Show this at the palace doors, and guards will see you safely home. And leave *now*, or you may be seen by the waiting crowds when I open this joining door.'

As she moved towards the tapestry, he spoke again. '*Cariad* ... do not grieve for Lincoln. The fellow was not worth your tears. You are better off without him.'

She halted. With those few words, however intended, he had resurrected Knole again, and thus the question of his innocence.

He smiled apologetically. 'Forgive me, I merely sought to ... comfort you.'

She did not answer, but drew the tapestry aside and slipped through the door behind it. But then she halted without closing it behind her, and listened as he went out to the main apartments. All conversation ceased in the outer room as a trumpeter announced him. Maybe if he had not made her think of Jack again, she would not have done anything more, but he had. And she did.

There was no time to think. She peered around the tapestry. The door had swung to, but not completely, and she knew that if she could get behind it, she would not only hear what was said, but see much as well. Surely no one would come into Henry's bedchamber, except Henry himself, and she would have time to escape again. Would she not? She hesitated, but then gathered her skirts, holding them close for fear a fluttering hem might be seen, and emerged from hiding.

Pressing back behind the hinged side of the other door, she found the voices were indeed louder, but there were so many that it was impossible to understand anything. She peeped through the gap, and the first faces she saw belonged to Henry's favoured advisors, Sir Reginald Bray and Edmund Dudley, who resembled a barn owl and popinjay respectively. The way they glanced around reminded Cicely of Henry's 'imp', a little man who was like Mistress Kymbe, and could read lips and report everything that was being said, even if the conversation was taking place some distance away. Henry had no doubt learned a number of secrets that way, some of them dangerous to those who had thought themselves able to speak in confidence. Heaven protect all Yorkists if Bray and Dudley ever mastered that art.

The Frenchman Étienne Fryon stood with several other secretaries. He was dark, slight, expressionless and purse-lipped, with eyes like bright coals. His black robe had a collar of starched white pleats, and his flat-crowned hat was tied beneath his chin. But it was the tall man beside him whose presence made her heart lurch. Tal!

She was so startled that she jerked back, as if he might somehow see her. For a moment or two she struggled to control her shock. Had Tal been playing Judas all along? No, it could not be! He had been helping Jack to *escape* … had he not? Taking a huge breath to calm herself, she looked through the gap again.

He wore a slate-blue tunic, with a *Lancastrian* collar to which was attached an equally Lancastrian red rose pendant, and there was a hound brooch pinned to his black hat. That same hound she had seen on his blue silk book. Was he Henry's agent after all? A cold finger now ran down her spine. No wonder he was so secretive! Was she in the utmost danger for having begun to trust him?

She had to know more, so she remained where she was,

83

looking into the other room, which gradually emptied. She could hear the voices more clearly, but not Tal's. Perhaps he had left without her seeing? She looked through again, moving from side to side as much as she could in order to see as much as possible. Then she glimpsed him, talking to a huge man whom she knew to be Sir John Cheney, and who had suffered the ignominy of being unhorsed at Bosworth by Richard, a much smaller man with— by then—a broken lance. Immensely tall and muscular, Cheney was about forty years old and *very* strong, with untidy, dark-blond hair that hung down to his shoulder blades, and a long face with cheeks that seemed to fold towards his nose. His silver bull's horns badge depended from the front and back of his Lancastrian collar. She did not like him, for not only had he fought against Richard, but against Jack at Stoke.

Both men moved out of her sight completely, but she heard Cheney's great guffaw of a laugh, and Tal's quieter amusement. The room became quieter after that, and just as she decided Henry was on his own and might come back at any moment, he spoke amiably to someone.

'Ah, Sir Humphrey, my Silver Hound, we are private at last. I trust Calais is in good order?' The tone was amiable.

'Calais thrives, Your Majesty.'

It was Tal's voice at last. Sir *Humphrey...*?

'And how is your wife now?'

'Well enough.'

The brevity of the response was not lost upon Henry. 'It is known that you have difficulties,' he said, not unkindly. 'Cheney tells me she is no longer at your residence in Kingston l'Isle.'

'No doubt he wonders if I have done away with her, Your Majesty. He is wont to make mischief. The truth is that she is now with my sister in Norfolk.'

'I have learned to my own cost that rumour and

84

innuendo are unavoidable crosses to bear.'

'But at least you—' Tal broke off.

'At least I...?'

'I would not wish to be misconstrued or deemed insolent.'

There was a pause. 'Indeed not, but I am curious.'

'I was going to say that at least you had pleasure before being talked of. I did not.'

'Ah, yes, so I did, but the entire host of Winchester angels would fall from grace because of the lady in question.'

Cicely's lips parted. They were referring to *her*! The court had been at Winchester for Prince Arthur's christening, where she had carried the baby, and Henry had forced a passionate kiss upon her. To be fair to him, he believed they were completely private ... but they had been discovered by Jon, Henry's mother *and* Jasper Tudor! Jon had left her for some time after that, because she had lied to him about the nature of her closeness to Henry.

Now Henry spoke in Welsh. *'Mae cariad yn holl-bwysig.'* Then he had an afterthought. 'Coming from whence you do, sir, I wonder if you have Welsh?'

'No, Your Majesty,' Tal replied dishonestly.

'Perhaps it is as well.' Henry turned briskly to documents before him. 'You are Marshal of Calais, sir, do you believe there is anything there that is in need of my particular attention? My intervention even?'

So, Tal *was* a military man, Cicely thought, and an important one at that.

'Calais is loyal, Your Majesty, and will always serve the king.'

'As it served Richard and Edward?' Henry asked quietly.

'It honours the institution of the monarchy, whoever actually sits upon the throne.'

'Well, as I am now your third king, I suppose I have to believe you. So, I trust you sufficiently to advise that my policy at the moment is to mediate between Brittany and France. My ambassadors are doing all they can to divert the prospect of armed interferences. I prefer peace at all costs, having had a surfeit of strife since Bosworth.'

'Yes, Your Majesty.'

'If you have to wonder what my stance is on a certain matter, I wish you to bear this desire for peace in mind. I want you to attend to this list, wherever it is....' There was a slight rustle as Henry sought among the papers on his desk. Then he coughed. 'Too much dust, I think,' he said to Tal. 'Ah, here it is.' Papers rustled again.

Tal was sympathetic. 'Heaven spare us all from the monstrous mountain of documents that looms on all sides, Your Majesty. Administration is self-perpetuating.'

'Indeed. Now, I wish you to leave for Calais immediately. And as you have my undivided attention, is there anything else you wish to discuss?'

'There is one thing, Your Majesty. A personal matter.'

'Speak.'

'I am considering another pilgrimage, and wish to approach you in due course regarding the granting of another licence. You were gracious enough to bestow one in April last year.'

'Ah yes, piety.' Henry exhaled. 'You did not go to Rome after all, as I recall.'

'No, Your Majesty. My duties prevented it.'

'Is it Rome again?'

'Mount Sinai. St Catherine's Monastery.'

Cicely thought of the crucifix and St Catherine's wheel.

Henry spoke again. 'I see no present reason why not. Just take care to have your duties fully covered this time. It would be a shame to have to abandon your second pilgrimage.'

'Thank you, Your Majesty.'

'You may go, then.'

Cicely hurried back to the tapestry and through the hidden door, which she closed as quietly as she could. She then fled along a secret passage, through a succession of short, confined ways, to another doorway at the bottom of a flight of narrow steps. There she stopped, for there was a trilling of female giggling on the other side. The ladies' mirth was at the expense of an unfortunate young minstrel whose split hose had revealed an undergarment trapped between his buttocks. Finally, a more authoritative lady collected herself.

'Come, ladies, to our duties. Lady Margaret will punish us if we are not there in time.'

There was a lot of throat-clearing, more smothered giggles, and then silence as they hastened away towards the nearby concourse. Cicely waited a minute or so, to be sure there was no one to see her creeping out, and then she opened the door. She was at the closed end of a brief side passage that adjoined the main concourse towards the river stairs.

But as she hurried along it, she saw Tal again. He was going the same way, carrying his cloak. Her dismay increased as he was accosted by Sir John Cheney, in a manner that revealed the two to be not merely acquainted, but good friends.

She considered turning back to use the entrance to the great courtyard, but as Cheney went swiftly on his way, Tal observed her. His dismay clearly matched hers, but he approached. She stood her ground stiffly, and as he straightened from a respectful bow, made sure he saw her glance lingering pointedly on his Lancastrian collar.

'I have to leave for Calais on the next tide, my lady, but think we need to talk first.'

She said nothing as she permitted him to usher her into a deserted chamber. He was careful to leave the door wide open, for there was not to be any hint of anything untoward between the Marshal of Calais and Lady Welles, and there were too many people passing to and fro for them to be overheard.

To him it was just a convenient room, but Cicely had been there before. A minute or so, no more. With Jack. Stolen, hazardous minutes, because Henry was hunting him. Yet here he had been. Oh, her brazen, beautiful Jack. In this room they had exchanged their last words. Their last kiss.

But Tal did not know, and she did not intend to tell him. Confrontation was already inevitable, because of this man's clearly Lancastrian connections, of which Jack could surely not have known. Could he? Suspicion and doubt ruled her now.

'Who *are* you?' she demanded. 'I already know you are the Marshal of Calais, because I eavesdropped upon you with him this morning, and that you are Sir Humphrey … but what is your surname?'

'You eavesdropped? From the bedchamber, no doubt?'

'Where else?' She held his gaze almost fiercely.

'I am Sir Humphrey Talbot, my lady.'

'Talbot? So *that* is why you are called Tal? Taliesin does not enter into it?'

'Correct. The silver talbot hound—some call it a running dog—*is* my badge, and is why Henry is wont to call me his Silver Hound.'

'He trusts you.'

Tal raised an eyebrow. 'He also trusts you, does he not? I think you now understand why I wish my true identity to be concealed.'

'Did Jack know?'

'Yes.'

'About … this?' She indicated the red rose pendant on his collar.

'Yes. I kept nothing from Jack, nor he from me. We were

close and trusted each other. But I *am* always known as Tal to my friends.'

'Among whom I now number?'

'If you so wish it, my lady.'

'I do not know that I wish it at all, sir, because you are also clearly friendly with Sir John Cheney, who is Henry's man to the marrow.'

'Cheney is my immediate neighbour in Berkshire. He usually resides in Kent, but also possesses, among others in the county, the manors of Compton Beauchamp and Bishopstone, only a few miles from Kingston l'Isle, where I reside. So he is right on my doorstep. I do whatever is necessary *not* to draw attention to my real allegiances, Lady Cicely, so I am all charm and reason to him.'

'He also opposed Richard and Jack,' she said then. 'I suppose you can be all charm and reason about *that* as well?'

'I have to be. What sense is there in being Henry's *secret* enemy if I openly pick fights with those who support him? You are Henry's lover, so perhaps I should quarrel openly with you as well. His good mood this morning was clearly because he spent the night with you. He all but glowed. You are *very* good for him. What would Richard and Jack think of *that*?'

Cicely conquered the desire to walk out.

'My lady, if an opportunity presented to do away with Cheney and not even be suspected, I would do it.'

She saw how he fingered the crucifix around his neck. 'So, you *are* after all a Crusader knight of sorts, are you not, Sir Saint? *Another* pilgrimage? One wonders for what dreadful sin you wish to be absolved this time.'

'I hope it will be two sins, Lady Cicely. One long since committed, the other yet to be achieved. I will have much to atone for at the Day of Reckoning, believe me, but I will *not* wish either sin had never been.'

'You speak so lightly of sin that I wonder if you are, after all, Jack's murderer.'

'You *know* I am not, my lady.'

She did not respond.

He glanced out at the concourse, but they were still not attracting particular attention. Those who looked saw only a conversation between acquaintances. 'I can understand your anxiety, my lady, but wish to allay your fears. Perhaps we should talk in true privacy. May I conduct you home? We can talk on the river.'

'Is it wise for us to be seen together?'

'We have already been seen, my lady, but as it happens, there is no reason why I should not approach you like this today, because your husband and I are old acquaintances. We were in your father's household together. So I merely offer you the use of a particularly elegant barge in which to return to the city. It is the least I can do on such a cold day. I am sure even Henry Tudor would understand that.'

'Old acquaintances? But—' Why pretend? She already accepted that Jon was hiding truths.

Tal smiled. 'Oh, he recognized me. I should imagine he was merely interested to know by what name I had been introduced to you. You see, he has a secret too, Lady Cicely, one he and I share, but I doubt he will *ever* speak of to you.'

Chapter Eight

TAL'S REVELATION SHOCKED Cicely. She thought back. Yes, maybe Jon *had* been seeking the name, she simply had not realized it at the time. But what was this new secret? Viscount Welles was going to be questioned!

'And please do not call me Humphrey,' Tal requested. 'I cannot abide the name. It sounds like an escaping fart.' He presented his arm, but no sooner had they emerged into the passage again than they came face to face with Henry's formidable mother, who was accompanied by a flurry of ladies-in-waiting, whose giggling and whispering told Cicely they were the ones she had heard earlier.

The former Lady Margaret Beaufort had borne Henry when she was very young indeed—only thirteen, some said—and was still only in her forty-fifth year. Diminutive and decidedly rodent-like in appearance, with a thin face and pointed nose, she had sharp little eyes that were as hooded as her son's. Her nose was as large and her eyebrows similarly arched. She even had the same small chin. No one could ever doubt that she was his mother, for they even shared many odd little mannerisms, such as rubbing an eyebrow, or putting fingertips together and tapping lips. For all her small size, she was a daunting woman, second in importance to Henry himself. Certainly he put her before his wife in all things. But did he put her before his lover as well? Cicely could not help but wonder.

Margaret always wore black robes and a white wimple, and was invariably found with a prayer book in her thin, quick hands. She presented an utterly pious face to the world, but there was *nothing* she would not do for Henry, upon whom she doted to the point of obsession. Piety had no place in the way she had calculatedly schemed and plotted to see him on the throne, and it was mostly at her instigation—and Archbishop Morton and the treacherous Stanleys—that Richard met his death at Bosworth.

Thomas, Lord Stanley, was her fourth husband, now elevated to Earl of Derby. He had kept his forces from fighting at all that terrible day. Never had a fence been more surely balanced upon until the very last second. Henry's life had been endangered, because Richard almost reached him, and Cicely wondered just how much of a grudge Henry might bear on account of it. And against Thomas's brother, Sir William, who deserted Richard at the pivotal moment, and threw his considerable force on Henry's side. But in Henry's eyes they had both waited until the final seconds. It was said that the strange and wonderful beast called the elephant would never forget anything. Henry Tudor was just such a creature.

Cicely, too, could be an elephant, and would be avenged, no matter how long it took. If she *ever* learned anything to Morton's or the Stanleys' disadvantage, she would see that Henry was told.

Margaret halted, her clever eyes flitting swiftly from one to the other. 'Sir Humphrey. Lady Welles.'

'Lady Margaret,' Tal murmured respectfully, bowing low.

Cicely curtsied. 'My lady.'

'I did not know you were acquainted.'

Tal smiled disarmingly. 'I am escorting Lady Cicely safely home on such a very cold morning. She is, after all, the lady of my old friend, Lord Welles.'

Margaret's face changed at the mention of her much loved half-brother. 'You and my brother are friends?'

'We served together in the household of Lady Cicely's father.'

'Ah, yes. That is not a time I wish to remember,' Margaret answered, and then smiled pleasantly enough. 'I bid you both good day,' she declared, before walking on, her ladies hastening after her.

'There, you see?' Tal murmured. 'Henry will soon learn of it, but will accept as she does. After all, I am too old a fellow to be a threat in the lists of love, mm? And I *do* know your husband.'

They left the palace to go out into the white winter day. The sky was still yellow-grey, but for the moment the snow had stopped. It lay in a deep carpet of white, flawless and beautiful. Cicely paused before reaching the river stairs, because this was where she had seen Jack go out of her life forever. After being with her in that same room she had just left, she had watched him board a private barge with Tal, and then sail away into the driving snow of a winter's night.

'I … still cannot really believe Jack is dead,' she said.

Tal turned to her. 'But he is, and we *both* have to accept it.'

'Maybe we have to, but I do not *want* to. I still love him so much.'

'At least you have the consolation of knowing he loved you too, my lady.' He hesitated, unsure of the moment, but then ushered her gently on towards the crowded steps.

It was low water, so all larger vessels were out on the river, with only small skiffs at the steps. Passengers for the barges and other more substantial vessels had to be ferried out to them. There was still a great bustle, but her attention was drawn out across the gleaming mud to a gilded barge of particular grandeur. The badge it flew – a white lion on a red background – was that of the Mowbray Dukes of Norfolk and Earls Marshal of England. That badge had been absent when last she saw the vessel. There had been no identification at all.

She said nothing as Tal assisted her into a skiff. She knew they were going out to the barge, which rocked gently on the current, but as the skiff was rowed towards it, she looked at him. 'You are connected to the Mowbrays?'

'My younger sister, Elizabeth, is the Duchess of Norfolk. Surely you remember that? There being such a close connection with your family, albeit briefly.'

Cicely was ashamed to have forgotten. Lady Elizabeth Talbot had married the last Mowbray duke, and they had only one child, a daughter, Lady Anne Mowbray, who had died when she was only eight. She had been married to the younger of Cicely's two brothers, whose disappearance from the Tower when Richard came to the throne was still such a mystery.

Steps had been lowered to the water and Tal assisted her aboard with great courtesy and care, before issuing instructions to the crew master to go downstream to Three Cranes wharf. She was ushered to the cabin superstructure. It was richly accoutred inside, a main cabin and what appeared to be a side cabin with mattresses for sleeping. The barge was capable of long river journeys.

When they were seated and provided with wine, the page who had served them was waved away, and Cicely was alone with the man who professed to be Henry's enemy, but was apparently not only his trusted Marshal of Calais, but also Jon's unacknowledged friend.

The gilded barge rocked as it came about on the swirling Thames, and Tal regarded her steadily. 'What is it you wish to know?'

'What is it you mean to tell?' she countered.

He raised an eyebrow. 'I imagine you heard everything that passed between the king and me?'

'Yes, and I noticed you denied knowing Welsh.'

'A prudent precaution.'

'Is that also why you profess to me that you support Richard, yet I know Sir Humphrey Talbot did not fight for him at Bosworth?'

'Because Richard bade me stay in Calais, and that is what I did, although I wished to be at his side.'

'You are a man of influence in Calais, snug in Henry's favour and enjoying many privileges, so why do you risk it all with Yorkist plots?'

He smiled. 'I have no intention of explaining *that* to you just yet, my lady, until I am as sure of your trustworthiness as you need to be of mine. After all, if I merely *converse* with Henry Tudor, you do far more and with much greater intimacy. I can be trusted, my lady, if only because of the immense regard I have for Richard and Jack.'

The air always prickled when she was with him, and she did not like it. 'How can I ever feel *comfortable* when you wear your disapproval like a mask?'

He got up irritably, twisting his topaz ring around several times. '*You* are the disapproving one, Lady Cicely, naming me pilgrim, Crusader, Templar and saint. You mock my piety and suggest that I could be Jack's murderer, so do not accuse *me* of unfair conclusions!' He turned away. 'My lady, *you* are a danger to *me* if Tudor's fond caresses have finally secured you to him.'

For a few moments, she was too angry to respond, but with the hesitation came common sense. Jack had trusted him completely, so who was she to express doubt?

'Perhaps we should begin again?' she ventured slowly.

His lips twitched into what may have been a smile. 'I forgive you if you forgive me?'

'Too childish for you, perhaps?'

'No, not at all, my lady. I am content to begin again, for I think we need to be on good terms.'

'Then let us start with something innocuous. Why do you wear cinnamon?'

'Because in hotter lands it serves to keep insects away, flying *and* crawling. Then I found that I liked it as well, and so have used it ever since. Does it offend you?'

'No. It makes me think of the Holy Land. Please, do not take that as another snipe.'

He smiled.

'I … feel a little uncomfortable calling you Tal, when you are so formal towards me. I would prefer to be plain Cicely.'

'I cannot be so familiar with a king's daughter.'

'Yes, you can. It is my wish.'

He studied her for a long moment, and then went to replenish their cups. As he resumed his seat, the barge swayed gently on the swirl of the uncertain low tide, which would surely soon turn. He leaned his head back, gazing at nothing in particular.

'I find it difficult to confide my secret at all, so please do not think it is a personal slight to you. I need to be absolutely certain of my facts, and have proof of them, before I can act, so I will not tell you all. But some of the history is already known to you.'

'What do you mean?'

'Before marrying your mother, your father was pre-contracted to someone else.'

'Yes, to Lady Eleanor Tal … bot.' She faltered over the word as her memory was jolted for the second time. Her father had been secretly wed to Eleanor *before* he 'married' her, Cicely's, mother, Elizabeth Woodville. Eleanor lived on for four years, and was his rightful queen. Edward's children by Elizabeth were all illegitimate.

Tal nodded. 'Your father died intending the treason of

putting his baseborn son on the throne of England, when he *knew* that by then his only true heir, legitimate and not attainted, was his brother Richard. That is why I have always held your father in contempt.'

'I am so very sorry, Tal.'

'So am I. Eleanor was the woman who put Richard on the throne of England.'

'And my father, as much as Henry, was the man who killed him,' she said quietly.

Tal tasted his wine. 'And here I am, the brother of a Queen of England, but merely *Sir* Humphrey. The title of my father, the 1st Earl of Shrewsbury, descends through the children of his first marriage. The barony of de l'Isle descends through my mother's first marriage, which leaves poor little Humphrey of the second marriage with nothing at all.'

She was sympathetic.

But he smiled. 'It is galling to have lofty connections, without any of the benefits. I am actually a cousin of several degrees to you, and therefore to Jack, and to the present Earl of Warwick, who slaves in Henry's kitchens as Lambert Simnel.'

Warwick was the son of the Duke of Clarence, the middle brother between Edward and Richard. Before being executed and attainted for treason in 1478, Clarence had sent his two-year-old son and heir to safety in Burgundy. A changeling was substituted in England, and no one knew, except the Duchess of Burgundy, to whom Clarence had written, describing a scar that would identify his true son. There had been no such scar on the 'Warwick' captured at Bosworth by Henry, but there *had been* on the boy known as Lambert Simnel, for whom Jack had fought at Stoke, and whom Cicely herself had met on the eve of the battle. The unfortunate changeling had been imprisoned in the Tower ever since Bosworth, along with John of Gloucester, while the real Warwick, who had been crowned King Edward VI in Dublin Cathedral, could have escaped at any time from the royal kitchens.

Tal sighed. 'Warwick wants nothing more to do with the House of York, and it is understandable, but, like Jack, I believe a man should follow his destiny.'

There was a brief silence, before Cicely said, 'Warwick is not a man.'

'But he *will* be, as Leo will one day too. They are both of royal York blood, and Leo is a king's son.'

Cicely spoke of Richard's old friend, Francis Lovell, instead. 'Do you know what happened to Francis? His body was not found at Stoke, and he was seen crossing the Trent to escape, but—'

'Lord Lovell is well, and keeping his corn-coloured, bewigged head low in Burgundy. He is unrecognizable, but made himself known to me one day at Calais. He and a number of other Yorkist fugitives are sheltering under the duchess's auspices. They await something, but I do not know what, nor would Francis confide when I last saw him. There are whispers that do not amount to rumours, if you understand what I mean. An atmosphere.'

'My brothers?'

'Anything is possible when nothing is known.' Tal drew a long breath. 'Richard sent for me before he laid claim to the crown. He sent for my sister Elizabeth as well to tell us that he had learned of Eleanor, and that he believed *her*, not your mother, to have been truly his sister-in-law. He apologized for his brother's actions. He actually *apologized* on your father's behalf. I respected him so much for that. Jesu, if ever there was a man who could have been a great king, it was Richard. I was proud to be his adherent, because I liked him for himself, and because he restored Eleanor's honour.'

He paused, and Cicely could see that he was almost overcome, but then he recovered and continued.

'Now ... *now* there is Henry, who to suit his own purposes has declared your parents' marriage to be true after all, and thus he has dishonoured Eleanor all over again. I love her memory too much to stand by again and do nothing. I stood back at the time because she begged me to. I even received my knighthood from your father, and he advanced me to the position of Marshal of Calais! My mother was granted rewards. We were bought, Cicely. To my eternal shame.'

'Do you *really* think you could have done anything? My father was the king, and for all his charm and brilliance, he could be pitiless. He would have disposed of you quickly enough. I imagine Eleanor knew this. Tal, I know what it is like to fear for loved ones and want to protect them. The circumstances may not be the same as Eleanor's, but the principle is. She was your sister and could only protect you from your rash loyalty by holding you to a promise. Why else do you imagine men like Jack and my husband apparently failed to protect me from Henry? I *chained* them with promises. I understand how Eleanor felt, Tal, and I admire her for it. I also admire you for standing by your word.'

'You think I should continue to stand by it?' He asked it quietly, with meaning.

She began to realize. 'Henry? Is *he* the sin that is not yet committed?' She felt such a mixture of emotions in that second that she trembled.

'I want him off the throne, with no hope whatsoever of ever regaining it. Or of his line regaining it. I want him damned to perdition, do you understand? That is why I did not kill him when I had the chance. It would have let him off too lightly.'

Cicely gazed at him, trying not to shiver. This was a side of Tal that cast him in an entirely different light.

'I have long had secret plans in place to bring the Calais garrison over to York. The men are loyal to me. I held

Calais for Richard, and if Jack had won at Stoke Field, I was to have brought men over to secure London and the Thames. Now, once I have tangible proof of his private matter, and *know* I will be able to rid England of him and his blood, there needs to be a new Yorkist leader in readiness, so those same plans will be implemented.'

She stiffened. 'But what of the "atmosphere" in Burgundy?'

'What good is something that is nothing more than smoke in the wind? Warwick wants no more of it, Edmund de la Pole is unthinkable and John of Gloucester is witless. Would you wish to resort to other, more distant royal cousins … or to an undeniable heir?'

'Leo is baseborn, Tal, no amount of wishing on your part can put that right. Richard and I were uncle and niece and were *never* married.'

'Do not be naïve, Cicely. If there was a pre-contract with my sister, there can be another between you and Richard.'

She gasped. 'You would *forge* such a thing?'

'Did you become lovers while his queen still lived?'

'No!'

'And he never once mentioned marriage?'

She hesitated, because Richard *had* mentioned marriage, even though he knew it would be virtually impossible. And at the very least inadvisable, even supposing the Pope would have granted dispensation. They both knew they broke the laws of Holy Church and that they should not have loved at all.

Tal watched her. 'So, he did mention it.'

She did not want to answer, but knew she had to. 'Yes, Richard mentioned marriage, but it was a romantic desire, not a practical suggestion, and we both knew it. Certainly it was not the same as my father with your sister. I lay with my uncle before any mention of marriage, and I lay willingly with him again after the brief thought of matrimony had been discarded. Our love was everything. You have no idea … at least, maybe you do.'

'You surely do not imagine I have reached this ripe age without ever experiencing love? I may give the impression of being constipated by religion, but I am not.' He glanced away. 'Love has visited me in a way it should not, and *please* do not leap to the conclusion that it concerned another of my own sex! Nor has it concerned my sisters or any other woman forbidden by blood. My sin is to love another man's wife, and to know that if I had been offered the chance, I would have consummated that love, even though her husband was a man towards whom I felt the utmost honour and respect. I would not have even *thought* of the Bible or Holy Church.'

He stopped, and then added, 'I could say this of Jack's feelings for you, even though he really liked Jon Welles. But I was not Jack, because my lady did not glance twice at me. Nor did I try to seek her attention. I knew she was indifferent to me.' The wryest of smiles was directed at her. 'Nor am I speaking of you, should you dread an imminent confession of undying passion.'

She coloured. 'I did not think it for a moment.'

Getting up, he glanced out of the door to see how far they were from Three Cranes wharf, from where he would escort her safely up through the narrow London streets to St Sithe's Lane. The wharf was visible now, and the barge had already commenced to manoeuvre. Bitter cold swept into the cabin, and he closed the door quickly.

'Soon we will no longer be guaranteed privacy, Cicely. So what are we to be from now on? Allies in a common cause?'

As the gilded barge approached Three Cranes, she thought of Jack, whom she had encountered one day on the steps there. It had been her belief that he was importuning a pretty, yellow-hooded whore, but it had been the other way around. *He* had been accosted, and the woman had not been just a whore, but one of Henry's spies, intent upon finding out all she could about the gallant nephew whom Richard III had intended as his heir. Then she thought of Bess, Prince Arthur and Henry, before returning to Richard, Jack, Leo and Jon. Loyalty to the latter left her no choice.

'We are allies, Tal,' she said quietly.

But he knew she did not find it easy to work against Henry. 'Cicely, if your feelings for Henry are stronger than you wish to admit—'

'Of course they are!' she cried. 'Of *course* I feel for him! Do you think I could lie with him, laugh and smile with him, and make sweet love with him and *not* feel? He has an effect upon me that goes further than any coercion there may once have been. Do you understand? Sometimes … sometimes I can almost love him. But I love my House too, and I loved Richard and Jack infinitely more than Henry Tudor. Yet that does not make it any easier to set myself—however secretly—against the private man. Harri Tudur. *He* it is who loves me, who battles so constantly with—' She broke off sharply, for Henry's innermost secrets were not Sir Humphrey Talbot's business. They had been entrusted to her, and she would honour that trust.

Tal studied her. 'But you have made your decision, have you not? You are for York, and you will stand by it?'

Would she be a viper in Henry's breast? *Could* she? 'Tal, what was it he said to you in Welsh? Just after he mentioned Winchester?'

'*Mae cariad yn holl-bwysig*? It means "Love is all important". You have the King of England at your feet, Cicely.'

She closed her eyes and bowed her head. 'All I can tell you of his plans is that he intends to go to Esher soon, but I do not know why. He has instructed Jon to be there, and wishes me to attend as well. Jon guesses—only that, no more—it may be to do with Roland du Coskäer. I do not think I am to be there simply to warm the royal bed.'

He nodded. 'I believe we have said everything we should. As I have already said, I will be leaving for Calais the moment the tide turns. My vessel, the *Elizabeth* is here at Three Cranes, ready to sail with a cargo of wine. I will be aboard. Do you remember everything I said about how to reach me?'

'Yes.'

He smiled. 'I wish you well, Cicely.'

Cicely rested on returning to Pasmer's Place ... until suddenly Mary was shaking her urgently.

'My lady! My lady!'

Cicely sat up in alarm. 'What is it?'

'An urgent message!'

'From whom?'

Mary's eyes were huge, and she held up a fragment of paper, upon which someone had drawn three leopards' heads.

Jack's badge!

Chapter Nine

CICELY'S HEART SEEMED to shake within her, and the crackling of the fire in the hearth was so sharp that it echoed. 'Mary, it cannot be. Lord Lincoln is dead,' she said quietly.

'The messenger, named Edgar, begs you to accompany him to a house in Flemyng Court, near St Andrew-by-the-Wardrobe, my lady. And I am to go with you, and be sure to take my casket.'

Flemyng Court? Would Tal have left for Calais, still pretending that Jack was dead, if he was not? Cicely did not know what to think, except that her distrust of Sir Humphrey Talbot was returning. But she had to be sensible, and was it *sensible* to think Jack might be alive after all? Jon had seen the riderless horse and the burial in the willow hollow.

'Does Edgar say anything else, Mary?'

'That there is a cousin in need of you, and of my knowledge as a wisewoman, my lady.'

Cousin? Now Cicely's heart leapt. Might it really be Jack who sent for her? Or could it be a trap? But set by whom? She had to go, though. If it could be Jack, she would *never* fail him.

'Bring the pale-blue velvet, Mary,' she said quietly, then

thought again. 'No, wait.' If it *was* Jack, she should not go openly as Viscountess Welles. 'We must be in as much disguise as we can. I will wear that brown gown of yours, and you stay in the grey.'

The maid was horrified. 'My lady?'

'Just bring your gown, Mary. I am ordering you. And … is there anyone in the stables you deem trustworthy enough to have him prepare two unremarkable horses for us?'

'Yes, my lady. I will attend to it.' The maid hurried away.

Flemyng Court lay in the west of the city, and from Pasmer's Place, Edgar conducted the two women along the busy mile of snowy Thames Street, one of the most crowded and prosperous thoroughfares in the capital. The messenger was a short, wiry man of forty, with sharp grey eyes and an air of being well able to take care of himself.

The fresh snow had already been cleared into piles at the side of the street, and the sky was clear and blue now. London sparkled in the cold sunlight.

Thames Street extended from Tower Hill in the east, to Blackfriars, where it met Puddle Dock Hill, just before reaching the city's western wall. The hill led up from the river, where the towers and battlements of Bayard's Castle rose from the waterside, alongside the stretch of quays and wharves called Puddle Dock. The castle had once been the main London residence of the House of York, and was where her father had been proclaimed king … and where Richard had reluctantly accepted the crown pressed upon him by the Three Estates. His regret had been evident to all, but there was no choice. He *was* the king. And so had begun the inexorable path to Bosworth.

Along the way towards Blackfriars, there were merchants' premises of almost every description, from spicemongers and apothecaries, to shoemakers and silk merchants. Street vendors shouted their wares, carts bumped along with eggs, cheese and milk, and winter vegetables from the many country farms just beyond the city walls. Gentlefolk brushed with the most common of souls, weaving to and fro along the cobbled way, while whores leaned from upper windows, their bosoms on full view.

Cicely hardly noticed anything. She felt as if she had been holding her breath since the moment Mary had brought the leopard's head note.

Mary was more alert to everything, and was soon conscious of someone following. She turned in the saddle, and saw a youth of about sixteen, very elegant and well mounted, with an exceeding fine head of auburn curls. He was intent upon them. The maid reined in. 'My lady?'

Cicely turned, and so did Edgar.

The maid manoeuvred her mount closer. 'Please, do not look behind me obviously, but someone is following us.' She described him to them. 'I do not know him at all, but no common man would be able to wear such garments, and that white stallion will have set him back a fat purse. As will the red leather trappings. He is of noble birth, *very* conscious of it, and not afraid to be seen, except by us.'

Edgar leaned forward, as if to adjust Cicely's bridle, but cast a sharp look behind.

'Do *you* know him?' Cicely asked nervously. The description Mary had given brought Tal's description of Edmund de la Pole to mind. But ... why would Edmund be following them? Unless ... It must have something to do with Jack.

Edgar was nodding. 'Yes, I know him. It is Lord Edmund de la Pole. In fact, I am probably the one he has recognized.'

Cicely's heart sank. Jack did not like his younger brother, so this could surely not be benevolent interest. 'So it *is* Lord Lincoln to whom you take us now.' She would *never* forgive

Tal for withholding this from her!

'Yes, my Lady. His life is in great danger, and he has a wound that should be tended to properly. Secretly. It is not far now to the end of Thames Street, and I can cause a diversion before then. There is a small herd of cattle approaching from Blackfriars. I will stampede them, and they will disrupt everything behind us. Lord Edmund will have his work cut to keep his fancy horse under control, let alone pursue us. Lady Cicely, I will then set my horse for our destination, and I wish you and your maid to follow with as much speed as you can. We can reach Flemyng Court without the fellow knowing anything.'

'Or lead him straight there,' Cicely replied.

The messenger shook his head. 'I will know if he is still following, and will lead him a merry Christmas carol. He is a little too conspicuous to blend into any convenient background. That is where arrogance gets him. If he is up to something he should not, then riding out like a peacock on a unicorn is not the way to do it. Come, we will continue slowly, and the moment I set the cattle agallop, we are to kick on at speed.'

They rode on, and as the docile cattle came alongside, Edgar suddenly began to whoop, whistle and yell, and much to the fury of the drover, brought a small whip down upon the rumps of several cows. There was instant uproar as the panic-stricken beasts surged forward in confusion. Edgar spurred his horse on along the street, and the two women followed. Thames Street was left in chaos behind them. Mary glanced swiftly back, and saw that Edmund had been unseated, and was struggling to keep hold of his frightened horse's reins.

The three riders galloped past Baynard's Castle, alarming a cartload of chickens in cages, and then up Puddle Dock Hill, which would eventually pass the Royal Wardrobe, where all the robes and other clothes were stored. But before then it ran alongside the church of St Andrew-by-the-Wardrobe, close to which was a warren of overhung streets and alleys. But there were also fine residences, including those of Flemyng Court.

St Andrew's Church loomed above the rooftops as the riders gained the narrow way into the shelter of the court. Tal's house was exactly as he had described, with bay windows through three storeys, facing them as they entered. It was a handsome house, befitting the Marshal of Calais, and as Cicely reined in breathlessly, she scanned the windows. She was only yards from Jack!

Edgar jumped down and helped Cicely and Mary to alight. 'We have lost him, my lady! But go straight inside, while I take the horses out of sight, to be sure. You are expected. Please, hurry!'

They caught up their skirts, Mary struggling with the heavy casket, and in a moment they were in the house. They heard the clatter of the horses, and then silence outside.

A steward hurried to greet them. 'Lady Cicely?'

Cicely flung her hood back and nodded.

He immediately sank to his knees.

'Please rise, sir, my rank is hardly of consequence under the circumstances,' she said, waving her hand for him to rise again. 'Is Sir Humphrey here?'

'His lordship arrived after Sir Humphrey had left to present himself to the king first thing this morning, and then sent word that he was leaving for Calais aboard the *Elizabeth*. By the time the man I sent reached Three Cranes, the vessel had departed.'

So, Tal was not guilty after all.

The steward bowed respectfully. 'Please, if you will follow me, my lady, I will take you to his lordship.'

The house *felt* as if it was Tal's residence, she thought as she ascended. His character was imprinted in everything, almost to the point of leaving behind a trace of cinnamon.

Yet there was nothing that she could have pointed to and been certain it belonged to him, except, perhaps, the tapestry of Calais facing the stairs on the first landing. Yes, that was his.

The boards creaked on the second-floor landing, and it was much cooler as she was led to the door of one of the principal bedchambers at the front of the house. It had to be the room with the topmost of the bay windows, she thought. The steward knocked upon the door, opened it, and then stood aside for her to enter. Mary remained discreetly outside.

Cicely moved slowly, her hem rustling and her steps muffled on rush matting. *Please God, let Jack be waiting for me....*

His voice warmed her frightened heart. Just one word. 'Sweetheart?'

Her eyes fled to the curve of the window, and the black outline of a man against the cold sunlight. He moved, and she could see him at last. Jack! Her lips said his name, but not a sound came out. He smiled, his dark eyes shone and his almost-black curls were as unruly as ever. He wore clothes she recognized at Tal's, and he was a little pale and drawn, but it was *him*. The living man, not an illusion conjured by the terrible grief within her.

His left arm was in a sling, so it was his right hand he extended. She ran to him with a glad cry, and his lips found hers again in a kiss that was ablaze with love. Once again she knew the joy of thyme on his breath and in his hair, and the sheer wanton gratification of his body against hers. Death had not claimed Jack de la Pole after all, he had come back to her! Her prayers had been answered, and this time it was not imagination, which was all she had now of Richard.

He was kissing her hair, whispering her name, and loving her as she loved him. She put a hand to the back of his neck, her fingers moving adoringly into those wonderful curls. She could feel his heartbeats, taste him, treasure him again, and even if she had been able to find the words, she could not have uttered them. This passionate but silent reunion was so momentous that everything centred upon it. Upon him. She held him, tears welling from her eyes. He had not been lost forever.

Henry Tudor was pushed into perspective. What a baneful shadow he was, casting his dark presence over her existence. And over England. Jack de la Pole was dazzling light, warm, sweet, rewarding … and so very beloved that she was still afraid this was not happening.

He pressed his cheek adoringly to the top of her head. 'Sweet Jesu, Cicely, I love you so much,' he breathed, his voice thick with emotion.

'As I love you, Jack. As I will always love you. If you fade from my arms now, I will—'

'I am real enough, sweetheart. The pain in my left shoulder is proof enough … to me, at least.' He moved back a moment in order to slide his arm gingerly back into the sling.

She began to pull away in consternation, but he caught her again with his good arm. 'No, sweetheart, I must hold you a little longer. The thought of being with you was the only spur I needed to somehow force my Yorkist hide back here. This is all the balm that is needed to heal me again.'

Tears leapt to her eyes and then wended down her cheeks. 'Richard left me forever, but here you are. I feel so blessed, so very blessed to be granted this boon. But Jack, before anything else, there is something you should know first.'

His smile disappeared when he saw the look in her eyes. 'What is it?'

'Your brother Edmund followed us along Thames Street.'

Jack's eyes hardened. 'That embroidered little fart? Are you sure?'

'Your man, Edgar, recognized him.'

'Yes, and Edmund would know Edgar, too. Tell me what happened.'

She related it all, and he smiled about the cattle. 'I trust Edmund was deposited in horse shit.'

'You dislike him that much?'

'We dislike each *other* that much. It saddens me to say Edmund resents being the second brother. Well, he thinks he is that no more, and could not wait to slip from Oxford to be at court. Tal tells me he brags that he is to be the next Duke of Suffolk, and has been known to wish our harmless father on his way. That same father who wants nothing more than a quiet existence, away from politics and court intrigue, and who has to tolerate his "loving" second son stepping eagerly into my place, without even a moment's show of grief.'

A nerve flickered at Jack's temple as he thought of his father, who could so easily have been a truly powerful and prominent magnate, but chose instead to live quietly on his lands with his Plantagenet princess wife.

'Edmund pretends to be loyal to Henry, but in fact has a grandiose ambition to be the next Yorkist king. Henry will be watching him closely, you may be sure of that. Sweetheart, are you sure you eluded him?'

She nodded. 'Edgar is certain.'

Jack glanced down into the court. 'It seems deserted.'

'Does Edmund know you survived Stoke?'

'I have no idea. I certainly did not inform him.'

'Then he may simply be intrigued to find Edgar here in London,' she said.

'I pray that is the sum of it. Believe me, my "death" at Stoke would have put Edmund in what the Mussulmen call the Seventh Heaven.'

'You must leave London, Jack. You have to soon anyway, because you cannot raise an army here. You will have to go to Burgundy again, as you did before.'

He smiled. 'You are right, of course, but not before you and I have spent time together. But I *will* leave Tal's house before then.'

'I know he is really Sir Humphrey Talbot, *not* Taliesin ap Gruffydd.' She made brief mention of the overheard conversation with Henry.

'Forgive my fib, sweetheart, but Tal did not want to be identified.' He looked at her. 'So, dear Henry still imposes himself on you?' He studied her face. 'My poor darling, how beset you are by your desires.'

'I think you are the only one who has ever understood.'

'Because I am the same as you, sweetheart.'

'What Henry did to you at Knole has made me despise him.'

Jack took a long breath. 'My darling, you have to hide that change of heart He has to be convinced all is the same as ever, because if he should come to suspect you … I need not say more, I think.'

'I cannot bear to think of your agony at his hands.'

'I do not remember any of it, sweetheart. Nothing, from the time Tal and I fled from the hall, until I came around again to find Tal trying to help me. Henry was on the floor, having received a thwack around the head with a candlestick, and a kicking from Tal's enormous boot in his nuts.'

Jack put a finger to Cicely's lips, and drew it sensuously across them, before kissing her again. In a trice her arms went around him and they held each other tightly as the kiss, and the emotions it aroused, swept them both into their desires. But then he drew away a little. 'I … cannot make love to you now, my darling, because I cannot do you justice, and after all this time, I must be able to make love to you with all the skill and passion you deserve.'

'Jack—'

'Please, sweetheart.'

She smiled. 'I was only going to say that I will do whatever you wish, Jack de la Pole. If you want to wait, then I will wait too. It is enough for me that you are alive after all, and I can feast my gaze upon you as a starving creature upon a banquet. But for now, I think it is time for Mary to tend your shoulder.' She went to the door to usher Mary in.

The casket was soon opened, its array of contents fully displayed. For every recognizable ointment, syrup, herb and phial, there were others of a very different order. Dried things, some once living creatures, lay next to others, less distinguishable, steeped in sealed jars. Tightly rolled bandages, deceptively small pads that could soak up infinitely more than their size, and oils in tiny bottles seemed to make up most of the rest, except for the small but precious pestle and mortar that Mary took out first, together with certain special herbs that were fresh because she grew them in pots in a sunny window at Pasmer's Place.

The maid, who had always liked Jack a little too much, blushed as she removed his upper clothes, and then examined the wound.

'You are fortunate, my lord. The blade did not damage your bone, pierce your lung, cut into a vein or across your muscle, but slipped into one of the few places that would do the least lasting damage. When Tal drew it out and put the pad on, he saved you from more harm and from a great deal more loss of blood. You are fortunate.'

Jack smiled at her. 'It does not feel so, Mary.'

She blushed. 'I ... I must clean the wound, my lord, which someone has done very well, but not as expertly as I would like. I must be *sure* there is no rotting flesh that may become poisonous to you.'

'I give you permission to do as you please.'

'Thank you, my lord. It will hurt. A lot.' She glanced around the room, at the ceiling and in the corners, then went to gather all the cobwebs she could find. Returning, she draped them carefully over the edge of the casket, and then nodded. 'My lord, please be so good as to place the hilt of your dagger between your teeth.'

'It will hurt that much?'

'I fear so.'

He did as she said, and then nodded that he was ready. Unable to bear his pain, Cicely looked down into the court again, still fearful that Edmund had managed to trace them, but it remained deserted. She lingered there, her gaze fixed on the entrance from Puddle Dock Hill, but there was nothing to suggest anyone was keeping sly watch.

Mary worked swiftly and efficiently, wiping and dabbing, applying first this and then that. Jack bore it all in silence, but there was perspiration on his forehead, and he closed his eyes for much of the time. At last the maid was satisfied that no more cleaning was needed, and straightened.

'I have finished that, my lord, and just need to apply the salve and some dressings.'

Jack took the dagger away. 'Thank God,' he said with feeling. 'Jesu, lady, you may be a pretty little angel, but you know how to inflict agony.'

'I am so sorry, my lord.' Mary was mortified.

But he caught her hand and pressed it to his lips. 'I tease, sweetheart, for I am truly grateful to you.'

Mary's blush brightened to crimson, and she made much of placing the pad and bandages in readiness, and then mixed the salve a little more.

'It will feel very cold, because there is a secret leaf in it that will dull the pain.'

'And what leaf might that be?' he asked, curious.

'Oh, I dare not tell you, my lord, because it is not in my

aunt's recipe, but is my addition. My aunt would punish me greatly for my impudence if she knew.'

'Really? I find it hard to believe Mistress Kymbe could be such a termagant.'

Mary paused. 'Such a what, my lord?'

He smiled again. 'Shrew.'

'Oh, well, she can, believe me, but I *know* this leaf improves the recipe. You are the first one I have used it upon.'

'Oh, deep joy,' he murmured, catching Cicely's eyes.

Mary took the cobwebs, and with great care laid them over the wound, turning their edges over it until they fitted into it as much as possible. Then she dipped a trembling finger in the green salve and applied it gently over the cobweb and then the entire wound. The coldness was soothing. Next, she dripped three thick liquids—purple, yellow and carnation—onto the pad, and explained that the colours mimicked the wound and the bruising around it. They would draw out all ill humours, she assured Jack.

He winced as she pressed the pad down hard, and worked quickly, bandaging it into place as Tal had done at Knole. Then she slid Jack's arm into the sling again.

'Use this support as much as you can, my lord, for it will ease your wound. Sleep on your other side, or on your stomach. Or in a chair.'

'I do not need telling that, for I learned very quickly.' He smiled again.

'I will leave some of the green salve, my lord. Please have someone examine the dressing every day, and exchange it for a new one every other day. When it is changed, more of the salve must be applied.'

'I will.'

Mary placed her hand upon the pad and whispered something, strange words, melodic and rhyming.

'A spell?' Cicely asked.

115

'For the old gods to hear and be gracious to Lord Lincoln.' She put everything back into the casket and closed it. 'I will have to tend you again soon, my lord, but no one could have done better than me. Except, perhaps, my aunt, although one day *I* will be the very best.'

Jack eyed her in surprise. 'You have such confidence?'

'I must, for it is a great responsibility to be a wise-woman, as is my aunt. Without confidence, I cannot succeed, and the secret powers will not come to me.'

Jack stood, and before Mary knew it, he had kissed her on the lips. 'Thank you, Mary Kymbe,' he said softly, 'I am in your debt.'

Mary gazed at him, her eyes huge. 'A kiss is all the payment I need,' she whispered, seized the casket, and fled from the room.

Cicely had watched. 'You have not lost your touch, Jack de la Pole; poor Mary will now be more foolish over you than ever. How does your shoulder feel now?'

'Sore, but rather numb too, which is a new development. She may be right about her secret leaf. But enough of Mary Kymbe, because I wish to be in comfort with *you*.' He indicated the large raised bed, with its canopy and curtains of dusky blue velvet. 'To simply have you in my arms is all I require, my love, just that sweet delight. And a kiss or two, perhaps, as I tell you what happened after I was parted from Tal. It is a long story.'

Chapter Ten

JACK SAT BACK against one end of the headboard and extended his right arm for Cicely to nestle into the crook.

'What do you know of Knole, sweetheart?' he asked.

She told him what Jon and Tal had said, relating in full the conversation she had with Tal on the duchess's barge.

'So you know all about Roland du Coskäer? In fact, having seen Tal since me, you have told me more than I knew.'

'Is Tal right about him? *Can* he be used to overturn Henry?'

'I believe so, but I will not tell you what we know. Like Tal, it is not because I do not trust you, but because you need to be utterly innocent if and when you *do* learn. And once you know what it is, you certainly will not be able to hide the fact from Henry. It is *that* shocking. Please understand, sweetheart.'

'I do.'

He squeezed her gently. 'So I am once again dead, buried, and providing fodder for fine new willow? How like Henry.'

She frowned. 'But … *someone* was buried at Knole!'

'Or some *thing*.'

'What do you mean?'

'That if Tal saw a body slung over a horse, and Jon saw a burial, the only answer I can provide is the mastiff Tal killed. It would be hard for Tal to know the difference between the body of a man or a great hound at a distance in the dark. I am sure Henry hoped I really was done for, and it suits him to let Yorkists who are in on my survival believe that the tiresome Earl of Lincoln is once again under the sod.'

'What really happened after Tal sent your horse away with you?' she asked.

'I soon knew that I did not have the strength to stay in the saddle for long at the gallop that was necessary. You would not believe the pain from a mere flesh wound could be so insupportable because of the jolting of a horse. Then I found myself in a small glade that was only half-covered with snow, because of overhanging evergreens. I could hear the chase close behind me, and knew I had perhaps a quarter of a minute to act. I halted the horse, jumped down on snowless ground, and then slapped its rump. It was glad to be off again, for it was terrified of the remaining mastiff. I scattered what was left of my orange oil, and scrambled into concealment just as the chase streamed past in pursuit of my horse. The mastiff faltered momentarily, but the trusty orange oil worked like a charm, and the chase continued. I found the stream Tal had used earlier, and waded against the current, away from the house. My feet were soon frozen, but it is amazing the strength and fortitude that can be found under duress.'

'My poor Jack,' she whispered, twisting up to draw his lips to hers.

He smiled. 'Mm, you are nectar to this poor battered bee.'

She snuggled down again. 'Go on.'

'This is not a fairy tale read at bedtime,' he chided.

'Well, I kept pressing upstream, away from the house, until the water passed under a bridge beside a tavern, at the rear of which I found an ox-wagon about to leave.'

'At night? Would that not be to invite robbers?'

'Not when there are armed men in attendance. I do not know who they were, but they had been paid well to see the wagon safely to London. I heard them talking. And when I managed to get into the wagon, I soon discovered that it was laden with bales of costly silk—fit for royalty—as well as lace and skeins of fine gold and silver metal threads for embroidery and the like. I made myself a silken mattress, partly unrolled a bale of exquisite pearl-stitched honey silk, and hid beneath it. A truly fitting bed, I thought as I bled slowly into it. Someone will have been furious when it was found.'

'And you were carried safely all the way to London?'

'Almost all the way. When there was an altercation in Southwark, I took the opportunity to leave the wagon and blend into the crowds, wrapping my cloak around myself to hide the bloodstains. I made for the Black Boar inn, where I had been on a number of occasions. It was once the White Boar, but times have changed, have they not?'

'Yes.'

They were both silent for a moment, remembering Richard, but then Jack continued. 'The innkeeper sent for a friar to clean and redress my shoulder. I was anonymous, the fellow had no idea who he tended. The removal of Tal's original dressing caused a lot of fresh bleeding, which took some time to staunch, so I was weakened again and obliged to rest for a few days if I was to be strong enough to get myself here. I sent word to Edgar, who has become my right hand. He trundled me from the inn, hidden in a wagon of empty tuns, only for me to find I had missed Tal by a matter of hours. I might as well have stayed in Southwark.'

Jack stroked her cheek. 'Forgive me for telling Tal about Leo, but I believed I would die and wished … well … wanted to be certain that Leo's existence was known to those who have remained loyal. I know it is not what you wanted, and that I have seemed to betray my word to you, but it had to be done. Please tell me you understand … and forgive.'

She caught his hand and brought it to her lips. 'I forgive you, Jack. Of course I do. Although I admit to being incensed at first, because I have such trouble keeping faith with Tal.'

'He is a good man, my love. I would—and have— trusted him with my life. Never doubt him. And he is right about Leo. The boy is Richard's son, and if Tal's reasoning concerning a contract between you and Richard is correct, then Leo can be regarded as legitimate. Do you understand? He is Richard's heir, and the true king. I would not stand in his path to the throne.'

She looked away stubbornly.

He was regretful. 'If I have upset you …'

She smiled too brightly. 'I would prefer to be making love with you right now. Or rather, making love *to* you.'

'In Tal's bed?'

She sat up swiftly. 'Oh.'

'I have commandeered it because it is the finest in the house. No lumpy old mattress for me.'

She began to rise from the bed, but he took her hand and pulled it down to his crotch. He was famously well-made— as all the ladies at court had known and sighed over—and at this moment he was far from quiescent. 'When we are in a suitable bed, my lady, I promise you pleasure beyond even *your* wildest imaginings.'

'*That* wild? I will have to contain my desires. But I will hold you to your promise, my lord.' She bent to kiss the exciting mound, and then left the bed.

'You may hold all of me, my lady,' he said quietly.

'I will have to return to Pasmer's Place soon. I left no word to Jon that I was even going from the house. Will you definitely leave here?'

'Yes, tonight, probably. I will let you know where I am, and will soon take you to bed with every ounce of passion I have in me. Which is quite considerable, considering I have not lain with you since the Red Lion.'

'I trust your performance will be as bold as your words, sir.' She smiled, but then remembered Esher. 'Jack, Jon and I have to go to Esher soon. I am not sure exactly when I will go, but please be aware that if I am not at Pasmer's Place, that is where I will be. Henry has something planned, and it involves both Lord *and* Lady Welles. Jon suspects it concerns Roland de Coskäer.' She looked at him. 'Jack, am I to inform Jon of your survival?'

'Does he still think he took my life?'

'No. At least, he will not once I tell him what Tal has told me. And I *will* tell him that much. I can hold my tongue about what you have told me today. I do not need to tell him I have been with you again.'

'You have not quite "been with me".' He smiled.

'I will wait for *you* to rectify that state of affairs.'

He was serious again. 'Do not tell Jon about me. The fewer who are aware, the better.'

'But, Jon would not betray—'

'Humour me, sweetheart. It is better not to put him in the position of having even more tasty titbits to hide from the ravening royal mongrel.'

'Henry is more a replete cat, prepared to wait however long it takes for an unwary mouse to tread his way.' She went back to the bed to kiss his mouth again. 'Just do not be that mouse, Jack de la Pole, for I love you with all my heart,' she whispered.

*

It was after midnight, and the bedchamber at Pasmer's Place was lit only by the muted glow of the banked fire, when Jon returned from his duties at the Tower. The bed curtains were open, and Cicely awakened as he entered.

'Jon?'

'Who else might you have been expecting?' he replied, smiling across at her. His thigh boots and outer clothes had been removed by pages in the great hall, and he was dressed in a scarlet velvet doublet and black hose.

'Jon, there are some things I need to say to you.' She sat up.

He had started to unfasten his doublet, but paused. 'And I am not going to like them, am I?'

'The first one is innocent enough. Do you know of a secret door from Henry's apartments at Westminster?'

'One could not be in your father's household, and *not* know about it.'

'Well, I have told Henry that you mentioned there was another such door at Nottingham.'

He discarded the doublet and the fine shirt beneath it, and came to sit on the bed, his lean face flushed suddenly as the fire shifted. 'May I ask why?'

She explained what had happened. 'As Henry suspected, I *was* reminded of going to Richard, but I managed to explain it away by saying you had told me about my father's women also using the one at Nottingham.'

'I see. Well, I *am* aware of both doors, and will claim responsibility for your knowledge.' He studied her face in the fire glow. 'What else is on your mind?'

'You are acquainted with Sir Humphrey Talbot.' It was a statement, not a question.

'Ah. I have been waiting for this, because I knew as well as damned that you would disobey me. Yes, Cicely, I am acquainted with him. Quite well, as it happens. We met when we were both in your father's household. Yes,

I recognized him at Westminster Stairs. And yes, there is something involving him that I am not going to tell you. I trust that answers everything?'

'Except why you pretended not to know him.'

'Much as I love you, it is none of your business.' There was a pause. 'Did he confirm that he was with Jack at Knole?'

'Yes.'

Jon nodded reluctantly, and got up to remove the rest of his clothes.

She plucked at the bedding. 'The secret that you and he share, is it something that shames you both?'

He slipped into the bed beside her and lay down, pulling her with him. 'Neither of us feels shame, Cicely. We would both do it again under the same circumstances.' His hand sought hers, and enclosed it warmly. 'To turn to a more agreeable topic, I think maybe I can cheer you a little. I had occasion to speak to Mary, and she mentioned how she missed her brother Tom. Now, Henry will never permit you to leave him, but I thought that Mary's desire to see her family could be used to bring the Kymbes, including Leo, to London on a visit. I could secure a house for them somewhere, temporarily … . Would that please you?'

'You know it would. You are so kind and thoughtful to me, Jon.' She moved against him, but guiltily. She was concealing Jack's survival from him, not from choice, but because it was Jack's wish. It was wrong. Jon deserved so much more. Needing to make amends, she leaned over him for a kiss. 'I have been waiting for your return, husband, to show my appreciation of all that you are,' she whispered.

'But what if I am even more than you think?'

'Then you shall have even more appreciation.'

'That is an answer I like, my love, but first, I must exact a promise.'

'What is it?'

'Please, no more interrogation about things you know I will *not* confide.'

She saw the earnestness—and anxiety—in his eyes, and nodded. What else could she do? 'I promise.'

He pushed her gently onto her back, and then propped himself up on an elbow. 'Let your lord show *his* appreciation first,' he said softly.

But as he kissed and caressed her, she thought of Jack. Where was he now? Was he thinking of her? Conscience bit into her. She was with Jon now. *Jon!*

On the cold January day before leaving for Esher, Cicely went to Greenwich to see Bess, who, like most of the court, would not be joining Henry. It was not that he was being secretive, because everyone knew where he was, just that he excluded many, especially his queen.

There had been no word from Jack, and Cicely was anxious. Where was he? But if she knew nothing of him, she certainly knew more about his brother, because as she entered the palace, she saw Edmund strolling towards her. He was flaunting himself, and turning the heads of male and female alike.

He was dressed in red and pale-green parti-colours that alternated between his tightly fitted doublet and even tighter hose, and he walked with a lithe motion that swayed his hips almost to the point of effeminacy, but not quite. His face was perfect, oval and symmetric, with full, sensuous lips and skin as flawless as a maid's. His eyebrows were darker than his wonderful head of pale-chestnut curls, and his eyes were a lighter brown than Jack's, but—like Jack— he knew how to use them to best effect.

In fact, Edmund quite obviously knew how to use *everything* to best effect, Cicely thought, remembering Tal's remark about folly bells. Members of his own sex would never receive what they might desire of Edmund de la Pole, although he might well lead them on. His fleshly gratification would be with women, as was plain in the seducer's smile he bestowed on a young lady in a blue satin gown, who blushed prettily but did not dare to stop. Cicely would be very surprised indeed to discover that he directed such smiles at other youths. Or men. Unless, perhaps, it was for some gain.

He was much closer now, and she saw more detail. Unlike Jack, Edmund's mannerisms were studied, performed before a looking glass until they were honed razor-sharpness, and the cool calculation in his eyes revealed too much experience and immorality for someone of sixteen. Whatever was on Edmund de la Pole's surface, the hidden layers beneath were far darker.

As he passed two gentlemen, who bowed courteously, he responded by placing his slender hands together as if in prayer, and giving a half-bow that flowed like fine wine into a Venetian glass. Those pious hands, and everything else about him, put Cicely in mind of a portrait she had once seen by the artist Rogier van der Weyden.

Edmund drew almost alongside her, and bowed gallantly, hands still together, expression heavenly. She could have halted, made herself known and gauged more, after all, he was her first cousin, but she merely inclined her head and walked on. He did not know her, especially in her finery today, so could not possibly have realized she had been one of the indifferently garbed woman he had surely seen in Thames Street.

The queen's apartments were splendidly furnished, and filled with music. And with card-playing, at which Cicely's elder sister did not excel, and for which Henry had to dig deep into his purse to fund. He also dug deep for her other great penchant of the moment, the keeping of rare and costly greyhounds, very dark brown in colour. She had a whole kennel of them, and indulged their every need, real or imagined. Henry provided well for his queen's whims and pleasures. Perhaps it salved his conscience.

Bess was a month short of her twenty-second birthday, and was everything Cicely was not. Tall, maybe not quite as lissom as she had once been, but very beautiful, with blue eyes and the red-gold hair that was surely the colour that would result if molten gold and copper were blended and then burnished. She also had her forehead shaved high, as fashion demanded, but which Henry did not like. Nor had Richard, which was why Cicely had *never* shaved her own. And never would.

Today the Queen of England wore pale-rose velvet trimmed with black fur, and one of the very new head-dresses that fitted in a shining black band around her face, with a black veil behind and down her back. She was alight with jewels as she hugged her sister and then gestured for them both to be seated close to the flames.

Cicely, dressed in pearl-trimmed peach, held her hands out to the warmth. 'Sometimes the Thames can be as cold as the Arctic.'

'Or as cold as Henry's connubial attentions.' Bess wasted no time about criticizing her husband. 'His weapon of joy is quite joyless to me.'

'And while he puts it to use, I imagine you lie there staring up at the bed tester.'

Bess smiled. 'Of course. If I close my eyes he might think I am enjoying it. Oh, enough of him. I am so glad to see you again, Cissy. We do not often have time together these days.' She became serious. 'I am so sorry about Jack. I did not even know he had survived Stoke.'

'I wanted to tell you, truly.' Cicely's expression did not falter, but she made sure her voice did. She was not going to tell Bess the facts, either.

'Well, I discovered that Henry and Jon had been to

Knole, and Henry took delight in telling me that Jack was finally no more, He grunted it between thrusts. He also said that it was Jon who—'

'Yes.' Cicely told her what Jon had originally told her. That there had been a secret meeting that was eavesdropped upon, and Jack had been killed.

'Would that it had been Henry who had been killed instead.'

Cicely's eyes filled with tears, and she did not know for what deep reason. She hated lying to those close to her, but it began to feel mandatory. Yet these tears were different, and were for three very different men. Jack, Henry … and now Jon too. They all meant so much to her, even—pray God's forgiveness—Henry.

Bess saw the tears. 'Oh, forgive me, Cissy. I know how you felt about Jack,' she whispered, kneeling to hug her.

A lady-in-waiting approached apologetically, and curtsied low. 'Forgive me, Your Grace, but the Lady Ann is here.'

Bess sat back on her heels. 'Our sister Annie, should you wonder which Lady Ann it is.' She nodded at the lady-in-waiting. 'I will receive her now.'

'Your Grace.'

The lady hurried away, and Bess stood. 'Have you seen Annie lately?'

'No, not in some time.' Cicely took out a kerchief to dry her eyes.

'She has changed, and not for the better. All our younger sisters are at Sheen, as you know. Annie is twelve now, and will soon enter my household, but I already receive her from time to time, to acquaint her gradually with Henry's court. Your opinion will interest me.'

Cicely did not reply because at that moment Annie entered. She was very like their mother, tall for her age, with an alabaster complexion, deep-lavender eyes and hair like spun silver. She wore a simple blue woollen gown that suited her youth and virginity, and also went well with her eyes. Her only jewel was a silver pectoral cross studded with green and blue beryl. With her budding breasts and small waist, she was no longer a child, but not quite a woman either, just prettily in between. Soon she would not lack admirers, except that her haughty demeanour and cold expression might deter. Her lineage would not, however.

Her glance flickered at Cicely, and then she curtsied low to Bess. 'Your Grace.'

'Annie. Will you not greet our sister Cicely?'

'Lady Welles.' It was said without a glance.

Taken aback by the obvious discourtesy, Cicely showed disapproval by not responding at all.

Bess frowned. 'That will not do! You are to be civil and respectful while in my household.'

'I was intended to be the future Duchess of Norfolk and therefore wife of the Earl Marshal, which makes me senior to a mere viscountess.'

Cicely wanted to box her ears.

So did Bess. 'Well, perhaps I should remind you that our father intended Cicely to be the Queen of Scotland, which, given your apparent reasoning, makes her very much senior to you.'

Annie flushed. 'I would still be the future duchess if the Howards had not fought on the wrong side at Bosworth.'

It was a grave error to say such a thing in front of Richard's two most loyal nieces. He had elevated his good friend John Howard to the vacant dukedom of Norfolk, which had fallen into abeyance on the death of Elizabeth Talbot's husband, the last Mowbray duke. Now the title was vacant again, because John Howard died supporting Richard. Howard's son, the Earl of Surrey, was attainted and imprisoned in the Tower, and *his* son, fifteen-year-old Thomas Howard, whom Richard had intended as Annie's husband, was one of Henry's esquires. It was Annie's hope that the attainder on Surrey would be reversed and the dukedom restored to him, so that one day Thomas Howard would come into the Norfolk title, *and* be Earl Marshal, making him the premier duke of the realm.

Bess was icily furious. 'If I *ever* hear you say that again, madam, you will be excluded from court. Is that clear? The Howards fought for our blood uncle, Richard, the anointed king. *Never* forget it! Do I need to remind you that the Howards would not have had their lofty titles and positions in the first place were it not for Richard?'

'I am sorry, Bess.' Annie was suitably abashed.

'Your Grace! You have offended me, insulted our beloved uncle *and* been unforgivably rude to Cicely. I am close to banishing you back to Sheen, to *stay* there for good. Do you understand?'

'Yes, Your Grace.' Annie's voice quavered.

Bess resumed her seat, and after a lengthy pause, gestured to Annie to be seated as well. Another lengthy pause followed, intended to impress upon the girl the severity of her transgressions. 'So, you are still determined to have Thomas Howard?'

Annie flushed again. 'Yes, but only if his father has his lands and titles restored.'

'Ambition is not always admirable, Annie. Believe me, I know the truth of this. It is better to settle for love, no matter how lofty or lowly the man.'

Annie glanced at Cicely again. 'As you did, Cissy?' she observed patronizingly.

Cicely was incensed. 'I am *Lady Welles* to you, miss!'

Annie lowered her eyes. 'I did not mean any insult, my lady.'

'Oh, yes, you did. I pity poor Thomas Howard, being hag-ridden by an insufferable, unspeakably arrogant hussy like you. Perhaps he will be better off with the attainders remaining in place.'

'But the attainder *will* be reversed,' Annie replied confidently. 'I will ask the king for it to be so.'

Good luck with *that*, Cicely thought, imagining Henry's reaction.

Bess sniffed. 'You will be fortunate to speak to the king at all, miss, let alone ask him to favour you with such an important boon. And Lady Welles is correct to reprimand you.'

Annie's ears had gone very pink, and there were spots of high colour on her otherwise flawlessly pale cheeks.

'Do you see Thomas very often?' Bess enquired then.

'No, but I will from now on, if I am to be at court a little more.' Annie looked at Bess. 'I ... *am* still to be at court, Your Grace?'

'We will have to see about that. My mind is not yet settled on it. You need to mend your ways, Annie.'

'Yes, Your Grace. I ... I really wish to be at court, to be near ...' Her voice died away and she blushed.

Near whom? Cicely was deeply suspicious. Not Thomas Howard, she was sure. What was this little troublemaker up to?

But Bess imagined it was to have been another reference to Thomas. 'Apologize to Cicely properly, and I may show more tolerance.'

Annie's lips parted, and then she looked at Cicely. 'I *am* sorry, Cissy.'

Cicely permitted the familiarity. 'Annie, my husband may not be an earl or a duke, but he is the king's uncle and Lady Margaret's much-loved brother. He is also noble in spirit and action, a truly honourable lord and I love him very much. I will not forgive you if you *ever* insult him again as you have today. Nor will the king or Lady Margaret, I can promise you that.'

'I really am sorry.'

Was the contrition manufactured? Cicely looked into the lovely lavender eyes, and doubt retained the upper hand.

Bess drew a long breath. 'You may go now, Annie. No, it is not dismissal, rather a little thoughtfulness, for I believe you will find Thomas in the hall with the other esquires. I noticed him earlier. I believe they all go to Esher tomorrow. But do *not* go alone. Who brought you here from Sheen?'

'My nurse, Your Grace.'

'Then see to it that she accompanies you. Do you understand? I will not have you jeopardizing your reputation, or indeed your chastity, *or* bringing shame upon our family. Nor will the king suffer it. Have I made myself abundantly clear?'

'Yes, Your Grace.' But there was a new light in Annie's eyes.

'Well, go then, so that Cissy and I may talk about you.'

Annie only just remembered to curtsey again before scurrying away.

Chapter Eleven

BESS LOOKED AT Cicely. 'What do you think?'

'Pure Mother.'

'Indeed so. Oh, enough of Annie, for I have some news I wish to share with you first. Henry's weapon of joy has managed to get me with child again. I informed him this morning.'

Cicely hesitated. 'Are you pleased?' she asked tentatively.

'Yes, if only because it means Henry will keep his husbandly duties to himself for the coming months.' Bess sighed. 'I *swear* he eats raw garlic deliberately.'

'*Garlic*?' Cicely had never detected such a thing on him, only cloves.

'Oh, yes. Just before he comes to me.'

Cicely did not know what to say. It sounded the sort of thing Henry *would* do. She had to conceal a glimmer of amusement.

Bess tossed her head. 'Just because he does not like the violet water I use. He says it makes him cough.'

'Then use something else.'

'No. Why should I?'

'For the same reason he should stop eating garlic,' Cicely replied sensibly.

'Give in to him? Never. I vow he spends more time in his mother's bed than mine.'

'Bess! You would be very silly indeed to repeat *that*!'

'I would not say it to anyone else.'

Cicely drew a long breath. What a fool Bess was to not court the skilled and considerate attentions of a lover like Henry. He would never be an easy man to contend with, and sometimes he was downright dangerous, but he was certainly not impossible. Or as abhorrent as his queen insisted.

'What does he say of me?' Bess asked then.

'He does not, because he knows I will always defend you.'

Bess gave a smile of sorts. 'You still think me a nitwit, do you not?'

'I know how you struggle, Bess. It is not my place to express an opinion.'

'That is because he loves you and treats you well.'

'And he is not entirely without consideration towards you.'

'I know. You told me that you and he parted acrimoniously at Huntingdon.'

'He thought I was part of a plot to kill him. Oh, do not ask more, for it was so foolish.' She did not intend to mention the violence with which he had treated her on that occasion. 'But the fact remains that I *am* still York, and I let him know it.'

Bess's jaw dropped. 'You continue to say so to his face?'

'If the occasion arises.'

'Jesu, Cissy, how is your head still on your neck?'

'Because he likes what that head can instruct the rest of me to do,' Cicely replied.

Bess stared, and then laughed. 'Well, I am relieved that it is *your* body he is interested in, not mine.'

'Bess, your body is the one that must present him with

heirs. As it seems to be doing right now. I just wish—so much—that you and he could like each other. If you could find some little common ground ...'

'He married me to make his throne safer, not for any other reason, and he could not make it clearer if he pinned a proclamation to the marital bedpost. He only needed to be a little kinder, but he commenced as he meant to go on. Yet with you, he plays the exquisite lover.'

'Please forgive me, Bess.' Cicely felt guilty, even though she had not sought Henry's attention.

Bess smiled. 'Of course I forgive you, Cissy. Heaven alone knows how venomous he might be if he did not have you to turn to. For my part, I no longer think he even needs to visit my bed. A *scowl* would probably suffice to plant his seed in me. Not that I have carried to full term since Arthur. No doubt Henry wonders if I have fallen over purposely, twice, to deprive him of heirs. Would that I had, but—' She broke off, embarrassed. 'Forgive me, Cicely, that was thoughtless of me. I know you want more children.'

'I would give so much to present Jon with an heir.'

'There is still no sign?'

'Nothing.'

'So, since Richard you have lain with Henry, Jack and Jon, and once with John of Gloucester, yet you—'

'Am now barren.'

'At least your poor little boy was by the finest king England has known.'

Cicely thought it was time to tell Bess the truth about Leo. One lie less with which to be burdened. 'Is by,' she said quietly. 'My son *is* by Richard.'

There was silence, during which Bess gazed at her as if she had sprouted horns. 'Do you mean...?'

'I want your vow you will never repeat this. Your *vow*, Bess.'

Bess was still thunderstruck. 'Yes, you have my vow.'

'My baby did not die at Wyberton.' Cicely told her all about Leo.

Bess rose slowly, her gown spilling from the movement. 'I … do not know what to say. You have had so many secrets, and have kept them from me.'

'Not through choice, Bess, but of necessity. And we have not always been friendly these past few years,' Cicely reminded her.

'I know. Well, I have vowed to hold my tongue, and I will.' Bess smiled sadly. 'I would give everything, including *my* king, just to have lain once with Richard. I said once that I would like to see Henry's severed head on a platter, with his equally severed genitals stuffed between its teeth as garnish. I meant it.'

Cicely wondered how Henry would like to see Bess served. Expertly trussed, no doubt, with a very thorny red rose protruding from a very personal place.

Bess inhaled, clearly distracted, but then managed to speak of something else. 'And you do not know what the meeting at Knole was all about?'

'No.' Cicely did not react.

'I gather the house was emptied, even of the great slime himself, Morton, so that Henry, your husband and certain guests from Brittany could have complete privacy. And then there is this strange boy, a Breton, who entered Henry's household a few days ago. Who on earth is he? I have asked various discreet persons, and absolutely no one knows anything.'

'I really do not know anything, Bess.'

'Hmm, I doubt it.' Bess pursed her lips, but then went on more briskly. 'On reflection, perhaps it is best *not* to know what devious, miserable-hearted, fiendishly dishonourable schemes Henry embarks upon. My opinion of him is low enough already, without having to excavate a huge pit in which to accommodate it to the full.'

Cicely laughed. 'What a picture you draw.'

'Why is he being so selective about who goes to Esher?'

'I have no idea,' Cicely replied, truthfully this time.

'Well, if he thinks he can escape *me*, he is wrong.'

'What does that mean?'

'Oh, nothing. Would you care for some wine?'

When Cicely left Bess, she meant to return directly to Pasmer's Place, but was accosted by a page who requested her to accompany him to Lady Margaret. What it was to be sought after, she thought.

Margaret was starched and wimpled so much that she could hardly move her head as she came to greet Cicely, hands outstretched. 'My dear, I *am* glad to see you again.'

Henry's mother knew and disapproved of Viscountess Welles's place in her son's life. She did not like it for many reasons, especially the insult she believed it dealt to her brother Jon ... but her loyalties were divided, because Henry's threats to Jon had driven Cicely into the royal bed in the first place. Blaming Henry for anything at all went against the grain with his doting mother, but in this instance, not even she could deny his guilt.

The rooms were luxurious, although in general the colours were subdued. It was a place of compromise, blending the occupant's religious character with her grand position as the most influential woman in Henry Tudor's England. It bowed its meek, righteous nun's head respectfully, but when it looked up again, it revealed the grandeur and ambition of a cardinal. Her London mansion, Coldharbour, now had the splendour of a cathedral, maybe even of the Vatican itself, and her favourite manor in the country, Collyweston, was being refurbished to the standard of a palace. Henry's beloved mother lacked for nothing.

'Will you drink hippocras with me?' Margaret enquired, indicating a chair by the fireplace and then snapping her fingers at a waiting page.

'I will soon be intoxicated, Lady Margaret, for I have already taken wine with the queen.'

Margaret's smile became thin. She had little time for Bess.

For the second time that day Viscountess Welles sat by someone's fire, this time holding a cup made of chased gold. Margaret waved the servants away, and then made certain all doors were closed before returning to sit close to Cicely.

'Why is the king at Esher?' she asked without preamble.

Cicely was startled, having imagined Margaret would be going there too. '*You* do not know?'

'I would hardly ask if I did.'

'You ask in vain, my lady, for he has not told me. Nor does the queen know.'

Margaret was confounded. 'Not a word? From Henry *or* Jon?'

'The king did say he would send for me when he was there, which he has. I am to leave in the morning. Jon is already with him.'

'Do you know anything of Knole instead?'

'Only what I am sure you already know.' Cicely repeated what she had said to Bess.

Now Margaret was utterly frustrated. 'I was convinced I could wheedle something out of *you*!' she said frankly, but then smiled. 'Clearly there are things my son does *not* whisper in your ear.'

'A great many things, Lady Margaret.' Cicely found herself returning the smile, for there were times—as with Henry—when Margaret could be winning.

The other studied her closely. 'But he tells you of himself, does he not? He tells you things he would never dream of telling me.'

'I am sure he tells me things you would not *wish* to know, Lady Margaret.'

'True. Oh, if only you had been the eldest, he would be so changed.' The thin lips pursed thoughtfully. 'There are two important men in my life, my son and my brother, and they both love you.'

'Is the Earl of Derby not important to you?' *God rot all the Stanleys!*

Margaret glanced at her. 'The only one of my four husbands I have ever loved and really wanted was Edmund Tudor, as I think I have said before. It is as true now as the day I took my vows with him when I was only twelve. No one will ever replace him. I think *you* understand my feelings only too well, my dear. He did not hurt me, and was never unkind. It was wrong to consummate the marriage when I was so small, but he had what he believed to be a pressing reason—involving my inheritance, of course—yet he did it in such a way that … Well, I felt he loved and cherished me.'

Cicely did not quite believe Edmund Tudor to have been the noble-hearted prince that Margaret thought. An under-sized twelve-year-old bride should not, under *any* circumstances, have been bedded. His only redeeming quality had been his kindness and consideration as he did the deed.

'Richard will always be impossible to supplant in your heart,' Margaret observed. 'And now you have lost Jack de la Pole as well. Oh, yes, Henry has told me that much. A terrible quandary for you, I think.' Henry's mother was not entirely without sympathy. 'My dear, if the Earl of Lincoln had remained true to my son, he would still be alive. Instead, he was intent upon usurpation. It was such a waste of an accomplished young nobleman, who was, I admit, an adornment to the House of York, which has never lacked charming leaders.'

There is only one usurper, Cicely thought, and that is Henry.

Margaret touched her sleeve. 'Pray for Lincoln in private, my dear. What you may think of me, I do not know, but I have become fond of you.'

Cicely had to smile. 'I am not a fool, Lady Margaret; you feel this way now because both the king and my husband are content to love me, but if either or both of them should cast me off, you will shun me again.'

'I wish to put old tensions aside and regard each other as friends.' Margaret smiled, and then changed the subject. 'Is your younger sister to be at court now?'

'I think she is being gradually introduced, my lady.' Why was Margaret interested in Annie?

'I saw her an hour or so since. She is a forward minx.'

'Forward minx? What on earth has she done?'

'She flirts unconscionably with young Howard, whom she expects to marry, of course, but she also flirts with that feculent little anus, Edmund de la Pole.'

Cicely's eyes widened to hear such words on such lips, and she was hugely dismayed to hear Annie linked to Edmund.

'And on top of *that*, Mistress Ann—like a she-kitten on heat—now also noses around that odiously disdainful Breton newcomer, who has appeared suddenly at court and is to be whisked away to Esher to be in Henry's entourage. No one knows anything about him, but there is something in his demeanour that I neither like nor want.'

He is probably your grandson, Cicely thought, unsettled by Annie's activities.

'Even worse,' Margaret went on, 'I saw your sister lying in wait for the king when he was walking in the garden, dictating to that *Maître* Fryon fellow.'

Cicely's heart sank finally to the bottom.

'It was just before he departed for Esher. She stepped in front of him, and was bold enough to make her presence known. Most reprehensible. She was all smiles and prettiness as she floated to her knees, like a slowly drifting apple blossom, her skirts billowing softly. What a fascinating little enchantress she was being as she pressed his hand to her forehead, before turning his palm uppermost and kissing that too. *Lingeringly*! It was an appalling display of wanton disregard for propriety.'

Cicely was speechless. Annie had gone that far? *Surely* she did not imagine she could charm Henry as she did a boy like Thomas Howard?

'I hope you and the queen will deal with her privately,' Margaret continued. 'Young girls of that age, no matter how highborn, are *not* to seek the king's attention, for *whatever* reason. Is that clear?'

'Yes, of course. I will attend to it.'

'Waylaying the king indeed. I cannot imagine *what* she was thinking.' Margaret almost bristled with indignation, but then became a little anxious. 'I know what was said of Henry's father, and I do not wish there to be whispers of Henry too. I trust you understand my fear?'

'I do.'

'The young strumpet must reform, or so help me I will have her beaten!'

But there was to be no opportunity to lecture Annie, or for her to be dealt with suitably, because another misdemeanour involving the deliberate ruining of another young lady's blue satin gown had already resulted in her being despatched back to Sheen.

Chapter Twelve

IT WAS ABOUT twenty miles overland from Pasmer's Place to the late Bishop Waynflete's palace at Esher, but the snow made rivers the best means of transport. The Thames was swollen, but not yet in flood, as it would be when the snow melted. Unfortunately, the meandering course doubled the length of the journey, which ended with five miles along the tributary River Mole to the stairs of the now-royal waterside palace.

Sunlight flashed on the wavelets as the small gilded barge conveyed Cicely upstream out of London, the crew pulling rhythmically on the oars. She and Mary were alone on the sheltered seat, which was canopied with rich hangings. Their legs were warmed by several high-quality furs, and as Cicely ran her fingertips over them, she wondered if by any chance they had been supplied by John Pasmer. Why not? He certainly dealt in such superb furs and fells.

Her thoughts turned to Jack again. Why was there no word from him?

Mary sensed her anxiety, and knew its cause. 'Lord Lincoln is well, my lady. I am sure of it.'

'Just as I have him back … he seems to have gone again.'

'You will hear. Soon.' The maid smiled. 'After all, I have

to dress his shoulder, do I not? He will be careful of any infection, and will follow my instructions exactly. Men will either flout all such things, in the mistaken belief that they are strong enough to rise above such petty problems; or they are very careful. Lord Lincoln will be careful.'

'Yes. Oh, yes. I know. I am worrying unnecessarily, but he means so much to me.'

'As you do to him, my lady.'

'Your man will come, Mary. Your "periwinkle".'

'I pray so, my lady, for I grow impatient.'

The short winter afternoon was fading when the red-brick towers of the palace appeared ahead, including those of the impressive four-storey gatehouse built by the late bishop. Because of the River Mole and the confluence with the Thames, there had been a residence on the site for hundreds of years. The water flowed right past a separate kitchen block and a large dovecote, before the barge reached the crowded main steps, where torches burned and servants in royal livery hurried to receive it. There were other barges, as well as numerous small skiffs and similar craft, because Henry's royal business continued as normal.

The gilded vessel bumped gently to the stairs, and a wide gangplank was put in place so that Cicely and her maid could be assisted ashore with ease. Torches fluttered and smoked, and there were courtiers mingling with boatmen and visitors of various stations. She heard trumpets from inside the palace, announcing Henry's arrival at some gathering.

Someone had sent word to Jon the moment her barge came into view, and he descended the steps to greet her. Smiling, she went quickly into his arms, her hood falling back as she raised her lips for a kiss, which he was more than happy to grant.

'I have missed you, my lady,' he said.

She drew back to look at him. 'And I you, my lord.'

'Before you say anything else, I fear we have separate apartments, but I need no directions for finding my way into my wife's bed.' He kept his arm around her shoulder as he ushered the two women towards the tall brick gate-house with its stone-dressed windows and entrance.

When he spoke next, it was for only Cicely to hear. 'Roland is here, as you probably know. The squires and equerries arrived not long after dawn. It seems that from now on Roland is to be addressed in the French fashion, as Roland de Vielleville. The surnames mean the same, I am told. He is seen openly and is Henry's equerry, although prefers to be called an *écuyer*. He is no more pleasant than before. Henry has not paid him any particular attention, but a few discreet enquiries have elicited that no one yet knows why the boy is in the king's household. He is addressed as Master Roland, and is acknowledged as a Breton noble with the right to bear arms. It would seem that Thomas Howard has been singled out to be his companion. What Howard thinks of the situation I do not know, although from what you have written to me of sweet little Annie, he is probably relieved to be away from her. Even the company of a supercilious Breton cuckoo must be preferable.'

'Is … is Edmund de la Pole here too?'

'No.' Jon looked at her. 'Why do you ask?'

'Because Lady Margaret tells me that Annie is not only interested in Thomas, but in Roland *and* Edmund as well.'

'Good God. She has her father's appetites?'

'Or her sister Cicely's.' Cicely smiled.

'But not your natural discretion and common sense.'

'Maybe. I will be interested to see Roland du—I mean, de Vielleville—for myself.' She paused a moment, the reflection of a wall torch in her eyes. '*Is* he Henry's by-blow? For certain?'

'My nephew reveals nothing. He is a mask, as lacking in fatherly display as he is in husbandly warmth.'

'That is not an answer to my question.'

'I realize that.' Jon began to guide his female charges on towards the wide, open courtyard beyond. Directly opposite were many buildings, including the superior apartments and the illuminated great hall, from where light and music issued into the fading day. Henry would be there, Cicely thought.

Then Jon glanced around as the voices of two new arrivals approached from the river behind. He recognized one. 'Greetings, Master Pasmer!'

Cicely turned, surprised. Why would the skinner be here?

The rotund, middle-aged merchant, clad in a mustard-coloured cloak, bowed low. 'Greetings, my lord! How fortuitous.' And to Cicely. 'My lady.'

'Sir.' She wondered how much he knew about her from Tal, and maybe even Jack. Too much, she feared.

The second man brushed past her awkwardly, muttering an apology. He was muffled against the cold, a tall, well-built, older man, she thought. But then she was sure she detected cinnamon. *Tal?* A pang of alarm cut through her. She had told him Henry would be at Esher! Had he come here intent upon something idiotic? For a few moments she could not collect her thoughts.

Jon had not noticed, and addressed the skinner again. 'You look well, sir. Being a member of the Calais Staple appears to suit you.'

'Oh, indeed it does, my lord. I now have so many more contacts than before.'

'I trust you have the furs with you?'

'Certes, my lord. The finest, rarest white sable from the far mountains they call the Urals. I have never seen their like before. *White* sable! When they were offered—enough of them for a fine lining to a royal mantle—I could not help but think of His Majesty.'

'He will be greatly pleased, I am sure.'

Pasmer bowed again. 'I cannot thank you enough for bringing them to his attention.'

'I am more than willing to recommend you, Master Pasmer. Go to your lodgings now and await further word from me.'

'You are truly magnanimous, my lord.' The merchant bowed as low as his almost spherical body permitted, and then hurried on into the courtyard.

Cicely was uneasy to find both Tal *and* John Pasmer, both secret Yorkists, here at Esher, and clearly together. At least, they had been until Jon saw them.

Jon looked at her. 'Is something wrong, sweetheart?'

'I think it was Tal who was with Pasmer just now and then pushed past us.'

'He may well be here legitimately, as Marshal of Calais.'

'Then why did he not greet us?'

'Not even Tal would be foolish enough to come *here* with ill intent. Knole may have been almost devoid of guards, but Esher brims with them. Just look around.' Jon took her arm firmly. 'Forget him, and let us get into the warmth. Come, Mary Kymbe.'

There were narrow timber-built buildings to one side of the courtyard, mostly lodgings, to one of which John Pasmer had taken himself. She saw a brick keep that was much larger than the gatehouse, but of similar design, and behind a projecting wall to keep it separate, an impressive chapel, worthy of the devotions of a bishop. And of King Henry VII.

Jon ushered her on. 'We are to go to the hall as soon as you are ready after the journey. There is entertainment.'

'Why is Henry so insistent that you and I are here, Jon?' she asked curiously.

'Well, it is to do with the boy Roland, of whom I believe I am to be placed in charge, but what you have to do with

145

it I do not know. Ladies are not usually concerned with their husband's squires and pages.' He hesitated. 'Cicely, there is something I have to tell you. I am soon to be sent to attend to my much-neglected duties in Lincolnshire and elsewhere, and I think Roland will accompany me. And no, you cannot come too. Henry will not allow it. And yes, I have tried to persuade him.'

She said nothing. There were times when Henry's control over her life was intolerable.

'Smile again, sweetheart,' Jon whispered, 'Master Pasmer will be asked to find something suitable among his properties, a house with a small garden that will benefit a child, even at this time of the year.' He turned to draw Mary close again, that she too would hear. 'Then I will send word to Tom and inform him that I wish him to bring Leo to that address. With Mistress Kymbe too, of course, provided she is able.'

Mary beamed, and Cicely caught his gloved hand. 'Thank you, Jon.'

As Lord Welles continued ushering his charges towards the lodgings, Cicely had to glance around again. The sky was ruddy to the west as the sun sank behind a bank of charcoal clouds, and numerous shadows thickened across the court. There were deep pools of darkness against the walls and between the many buildings, even though the snow lay thick. Torches did not reach into these places, and although she had not noticed where the man she believed to be Tal had gone, she felt he was there.

Jon showed Cicely his own apartment first. It was very fine, worthy of the king's half-uncle, and then he conducted the two women up an impressive brick newel staircase that spiralled to the equally richly furnished first floor. Before leaving Cicely at her door, he said he would return shortly to take her to Henry in the great hall.

But the moment he had gone and they entered the firelit

apartment, a beloved voice spoke from the doorway of the small room that was to be Mary's. 'Sweetheart?'

Cicely whirled about gladly, her eyes shining. 'Jack!' She ran to him and he held her tightly, obviously finding his shoulder suppler and less painful since Mary's ministering.

They kissed, and for a moment nothing else mattered, but then the stark danger of the situation overwhelmed her, and she seized his hands. 'Are you mad to come here, right into Henry's eyrie?'

'I had to come.'

'How did you even know I would be in these rooms?'

'I heard maidservants discussing which fires they had to tend, and these windows were pointed out as yours. I came up here when you and Jon went to his rooms, and I slipped in behind the back of the maid as she worked on the fire. You can only just have missed her. But that is of no consequence, my darling, because I have come to warn you.'

'Of what?'

'That Tal has come here, intent upon murdering Henry in his bed.'

Mary gasped and covered her mouth with her hands. Cicely was shocked. 'So it *was* him who pushed past me.'

'Yes, but I was watching you and did not see where he went.'

'But what if someone should recognize him? He is supposed to be in Calais!'

'You would not know him. He is clean-shaven, has darkened his hair and combs it differently, and he wears frills and fancy brocades as well.'

She found it hard to take it in. 'Please, Jack, tell me he would not really attempt such an utterly mad thing as this.'

'Sweetheart, when I last saw him he was agitated to the point of rashness. Perhaps if I tell you that today would have been his sister Eleanor's birthday, you might

147

understand more. He has drunk a lot, but not enough to render him incapable, and is intent upon vengeance. Nothing I said or did would stop him, and then he punched me and knocked me out.'

By the firelight she saw there was a red graze on his cheek. '*Tal* did that?'

'He is no weakling, and has always struggled with what happened to Eleanor. He blames himself for not doing anything when your father treated her so badly, and every so often finds it too much to wait patiently for our plan to come to fruition. Today he erupted again.'

She remembered being aboard the barge with Tal, when he had told her of Eleanor. Yes, guilt and self-reproach cut very deep into him.

'There was nothing he could have done against my father. And why is he back here so soon after going to Calais?'

'Because he received word that I was still alive. He made every last-moment arrangement he could for his post to be covered, and returned on the first available vessel. Sweetheart, your husband will soon return to take you to Henry, so there is little time to talk now. Later, perhaps.'

'I do not want to see Henry.'

'You will like him again when you do. He is that sort of man, I fear.' He pulled her close again. 'I have come to you now in the hope that you may recognize Tal after all, and be able to talk him into sanity again. If he can be rescued before he does anything, I would feel a *lot* better. I love the old bastard.'

'I have to tell Jon. He already knows I thought I saw Tal when we arrived. If I express anxiety, and can persuade Jon to help, he will have access to the whole palace without attracting attention.'

'Do not mention me, sweetheart. I would feel safer if Henry's uncle remained in ignorance. Oh, I know Jon would probably not betray me—or you—but nevertheless ...'

She nodded. 'How will I find you?'

'Master Pasmer's lodgings, which is where Tal apparently intends to hide after the deed is done. There is a secret space behind the fireplace. Pasmer found it by complete chance. I doubt anyone else knows of its existence. I have alerted Pasmer to Tal's intentions. He had no idea about Tal's true purpose, and was terrified when I enlightened him. Now he searches as well, but his access to the palace is limited.'

She turned as Jon's voice carried from the top of the staircase at the far end of the passage. He was calling down to someone on the ground floor. She pushed Jack in the direction of Mary's room. 'Hide in there. When Jon and I have left, Mary can dress your wound again.'

He did not argue, but disappeared through the adjoining door, and Mary had already busied herself setting out a suitable gown for attending upon the king.

Jon knew nothing as he waited for his wife to be dressed in formal attire, and minutes later he escorted her towards the great hall. She wore cream, bejewelled brocade, her hair beneath a butterfly headdress. He was not at all pleased to learn of Sir Humphrey Talbot's alcohol-stoked venture. He was even less pleased that Cicely had become involved, and that he too was dragged into it. Finally, he was not in the least satisfied with her tale of an anonymous note—since burned—that had informed on Tal. All these matters would be on the tapis later, and her ladyship would have some pertinent questions to answer.

Jack de la Pole had not been mentioned at all, nor did he cross Jon's mind. To him, Jack was still dead.

Minstrels were playing, and the notes were sweet and accomplished. The hall was of older construction than the gatehouse and private quarters, and the modest court of about fifty, mostly men, was gathered beneath a grand hammerbeam roof. Henry's hospitality was generous tonight. Apart from the minstrels, there were cavorting fools, acrobats, tightrope walkers and some children dancing with garlands. The aroma of good food was pleasing, and the atmosphere convivial.

Numerous torches and candles illuminated the scene, and behind the dais, where Henry sat alone, there was a huge fireplace. Cicely thought how isolated he was, framed against the flames. He was dressed in black, the richest of satin and velvet, with ermine at his neck and cuffs, and a golden circlet around his brow. He was lost in thought, toying with a glass goblet.

She was often struck by how pale he was, but this time he really did look close to white. There were shadows beneath his eyes and even though he tried to appear relaxed, she knew he was not. She wished that—in spite of Knole—she was not so acutely responsive to everything about him.

Her glance moved nervously around the hall. She did not really think that even under the influence of alcohol, Tal would be reckless enough to come where he would be in Henry's sight. But she saw no one who might even remotely fit Sir Humphrey Talbot.

Then she and Jon were announced, and Henry's gaze swung swiftly towards her, warming perceptibly. He smiled and beckoned. There was some whispering, because Winchester was far from forgotten, and the sudden lifting of his mood could not be mistaken. But the undercurrents were muted, and most guests were careful to continue with whatever they had been doing.

Lord and Lady Welles began to make obeisance, but he prevented it, and showed his favour by standing and coming around the table to greet them. His eyes were solely upon Cicely, and she was embarrassed, mostly for Jon, and she allowed Henry to see it. It was not difficult if she thought of the pain he had inflicted on Jack.

He took heed that she was not best pleased with him. 'I have some new wine,' he said briskly. 'Perhaps you would care to try it? It is really very good.' He nodded for a waiting page to bring two more goblets, and then smiled at Jon. 'Uncle, I have a request to make of you.'

'A request?' Jon was wary.

'Will you permit me to dance with your lady?'

Cicely was startled. Henry danced so seldom that it was almost never.

Jon was annoyed, but cleared his throat and indicated consent. 'As Your Majesty wishes.' The strict formality spoke volumes.

Henry moved closer to him and lowered his voice. 'I know what I do to you, Uncle, and I am shamed, believe me. I will not be backward in showing you favour, because I *do* honour and respect you. None more so.'

'Except perhaps when it comes to my wife?'

Henry nodded. 'I fear so.'

Cicely returned her goblet to the page, and Henry's fingers closed warmly around hers. 'My lady,' he said softly.

Touching him again made a maelstrom of her feelings. He was smiling at her, his eyes were steady and warm; he was Harri Tudur. Putting on a face had become second nature to her, and she squeezed his fingers to catch his full attention.

'Henry, you do not look well.'

'A dart? And here I am, putting myself out to be amiable to you.'

'I mean it, Henry. Something is wrong. Tell me, please.'

'I am well enough, *cariad*.'

'You do not appear so,' she insisted.

'You, on the other hand, look exquisite in every way,' he replied, ending the matter as he led her out onto the suddenly deserted floor, from where he gestured to the minstrels. Then he looked at her. 'You are in a miff with me. May I ask why?'

'You humiliated Jon a moment ago.'

'And I apologized to him.'

'It is not always enough, Henry.'

The dance, perhaps already agreed upon, was a measure that every now and then involved a little hop by both dancers. The entire hall fell silent, for the sight of Henry Tudor dancing was diversion enough, let alone seeing him hop as well.

He slipped his arm around her waist as they began to move. 'There, is this not a novelty, my lady?'

'A marvel.' He was determined to make her smile, and she—fool!—was obliging.

'I trust you will not embarrass me with your clumsiness, Lady Welles,' he said then. 'Oh, here we go.'

They both gave a little hop, and were in unison.

'Will that do, Your Majesty?' she enquired.

'Not really, for I fancy that you presumed to hop slightly before me. That is strictly forbidden.'

They twisted around, his other arm moving around her waist.

'I will endeavour to improve next time,' she promised, knowing she was once again enjoying his company far too much. She simply could not help herself.

He nodded. 'Very well. Here we go again.'

She hid her unwilling laughter as they both hopped, this time on the other foot. This man could be so very, very engaging.

He tutted. 'Now you are behind me, madam.'

'I will *not* laugh out loud if that is what you seek,' she said.

'You are *obstinate* to your king?'

They turned again, and executed another hop.

'You were late, Your Majesty.'

'No, Viscountess Welles, *you* were precipitate.'

She eyed him, twisting around to his other arm. 'What is this in aid of?' she asked, raising her face as if to kiss him, but it was only part of the dance.

It was also part of the dance for him to pretend to return the kiss, which he did. Their lips came very close for a second. Too close, perhaps, but it was his doing, not hers.

He spoke softly. 'Now why would you think me guilty of an ulterior motive, my lady? Mm? You imagine that I would have some dastardly reason for behaving as I do towards you?'

'Well, the absence of an ulterior motive would be most unusual.'

'I am dismayed that you have such an opinion of me.'

'You dance very well.'

'And *you* seem insultingly surprised.'

'Well, you can hardly pretend to dance frequently,' she responded.

'Perhaps I have not had a tempting-enough lady with whom to tread out. Quick, hop!'

She almost stumbled, but managed a neat-enough little hop. 'Do not do that, Henry, for it will not look good at all if I fall in a heap at your feet.'

'I would spare you embarrassment by falling with you.'

'*That* would spare me embarrassment? I think not, Your Majesty.'

'It would be interesting, though. Here we go again. Hop, *cariad*, hop.'

They moved together, perfectly, and he gave her a sly look. 'Hopping becomes you.'

'Frogs hop, Your Majesty.'

'True, but I would hardly liken you to a frog, or anything else that resides in a pond, except perhaps, the swan that glides upon it.'

She moved around him again, and he changed arms, but this time held her a little more tightly.

'I do have an ulterior motive, *cariad*. I want to impress upon someone here tonight that you are very close to me and high in my favour.'

'Who? Why?'

'Do not question your king.'

She almost hesitated, but then a hop was required, and she did so, except that she was indeed too early, and they hopped one after the other.

Henry's lips twitched into a smile. 'So, you do not take *everything* in your stride, my lady.'

'That point goes to you, Your Majesty.'

'Does it also place you in my debt?'

She turned for another faked kiss. 'I think I need not ask how I am to pay this debt.'

'Now *there* is a thought. Quick now, for we have to hop again.'

They rose together in perfect harmony, and as the minstrels played the final note, Henry bowed low to her. 'I trust I am incorrigible?'

'Absolutely.' She curtsied.

'Do not be displeased with me, my love, for it grieves me to think I have transgressed.'

She rose from the curtsey, looking deep into his eyes, because she knew he meant what he said.

'Henry, I ...' She faltered, because she really did not know what to say. So she spoke of something else. 'I still think you look unwell. You have to try hard to appear light-hearted tonight.'

'How could I not be light-hearted when I am hopping with you?' He smiled again, a fact that was noted through the hall, and then he led her from the floor, pausing to kiss her hand before returning her to Jon. 'Your lady has a very low opinion of me, I fear, but I will strive to endure.' He snapped his fingers for the evening to continue, because except for the music, the hall had remained silent throughout the measure.

He included Jon in what he said next. 'I have something I wish you *both* to attend to for me, something private and not for transmission to all and sundry. There is a young man here, the son of a late friend, and I wish him to be in the care of those whom I trust. Viscount and Viscountess Welles will be perfect. No, it is not nursemaiding, nor is it insulting.' He exchanged a glance with Jon. 'The father of this young man is—was—very dear to me and I am concerned that I choose his tutors with due care.'

Clearly it was Roland to whom he referred, and Cicely was a little troubled. 'But, *I* am hardly old enough for the role you wish to assign to me, and—'

'You are my choice, Cicely, because not only are you married to my uncle, but I know you to be of singular good sense. And perhaps your youth will be of advantage in this instance, for there can be no more than five years between you. He is to be under my uncle's guidance, but there will be other things that perhaps a woman would be better placed to advise him. My decision will not be appreciated by the young fellow in question, but I deem him to be in dire need of discipline.'

You should be dealing with him in person, Henry Tudor, not absolving yourself of responsibility by making *us* do it all for you, Cicely thought crossly.

Henry looked at Jon again. 'As you know, Uncle, he is not particularly amiable, so I allow you full rein. If he should transgress in any way, you are authorized to punish him. I wish only that you keep me informed of his progress. Do you understand?'

Jon inclined his head. 'Of course.'

Cicely spoke again. 'Who is he?' She had to ask, even though she knew.

'His name, here in England, is Roland de Vielleville. He is Breton, actually named Roland du Coskäer, but I wish him to use the French version. His English is good, but he is unconscionably arrogant. I do not think he is beyond redemption. Not yet, anyway. I have a future in mind for him, but first he must earn it.'

Cicely held his gaze. 'I understand Jon is to go to his duties soon; what will happen then?'

'The boy will accompany him, but you will remain behind.'

There is no need for me to be involved in any way, she thought. Henry was being his usual woodbine self. Perhaps he no longer knew he did it!

He beckoned a servant. 'Bring Master de Vielleville to me.'

Chapter Thirteen

THE MAN BOWED low to Henry and then hurried away around the hall to the furthest corner, where two boys in their teen years were seated, heads together about something.

Cicely recognized one as Annie's Thomas Howard, although she had not seen him in a while. He was a horse-faced, bony-nosed youth, with a lantern jaw, nondescript hair and a rather humourless expression. He was certainly not endowed with good looks and winning charm, so his hoped-for expectations were all that interested Annie.

There was no sign of Edmund de la Pole, but Cicely would have known Roland anywhere from Jon's description. He pouted and adopted the air of a great prince. His long fair hair rolled around his shoulders in the single under-curl that was as perfect as a glued wig, and he was dressed in quilted russet silk that was embroidered with red lions. As he proceeded, nose in the air, towards Henry, he was observed with stifled amusement from all sides.

Henry was not impressed. 'What an arse,' he muttered, and when Roland halted before him, to make deep but supercilious obeisance, Henry was even less amused. 'You may rise, sir, but had better do it with some respect.'

The boy's cheeks went a deep, dull red as he straightened, and Cicely knew he was frightened of Henry but trying not to show it. Even so, he had clearly been brought up with an inflated opinion of himself. Why? Perhaps because he had been treated as a king's son?

Henry presented him to his new tutors, through whom Roland looked as if they were not there. Henry was chill. 'Sir, if you wish your ears to be boxed again—in public, this time—just continue the way you are.'

The boy flinched. 'I apologize, Your Majesty, it will not happen again,' he said politely. His English *was* good, Cicely thought, and with a not unattractive Breton accent.

'Never forget that I am your sovereign lord, boy,' Henry snapped.

'Yes, Your Majesty!' Roland's eyes were bright, and Cicely could feel his almost animal dread of Henry, who was intimidating, it was true, but there was much more to it than that. Something terrible must have happened. But what?

'Very well,' Henry continued smoothly. 'Now I wish you to dance with the Lady Cicely.'

Roland was appalled. 'Alone, Your Majesty?'

'How many partners do you imagine she has in a dance, sir?' Henry was not amused. 'Just do as I say, before I lose patience.'

Roland clearly knew better than to risk such a thing, and hurriedly extended his hand to Cicely. As they descended towards the floor again, she heard Jon distract Henry by broaching the subject of Master Pasmer and the white sables.

No one else danced at the moment because the minstrels were resting, and there were precious few ladies anyway, but the music recommenced immediately.

Cicely felt quite sorry for the boy, in spite of his overweening and rather idiotic self-importance. 'Do you dance, Master Roland?'

'No.'

'No, *my lady*,' she corrected coolly. 'The king is right, you need to do better.'

'You have no authority to—'

'I have the king's authority, and you had best remember it. Now, you are about to dance, and are to acquit yourself well in front of everyone. I think you probably know enough to follow my guidance?'

'Yes, my lady. I have had tuition, but do not like to dance.'

'You must make yourself like it, sir, because you are here to learn to be a courtier as well as a warrior.'

As the music commenced, she took Roland's hand and held it aloft, making him walk forward. Then she turned, held his other hand aloft, and walked back again. He followed her step for step, and by his frown of concentration, was paying full attention.

It was not a difficult dance, lacking such complications as hopping, and the end was reached without Roland appearing clumsy. Clearly pleased with himself, he led her from the floor afterwards, and surrendered her to Jon before making his relieved return to sit beside Thomas Howard.

There had still not been any sign of Tal when Lord Welles escorted his lady to her apartments. Jon was required to return to Henry, and could not stay. Not that he would have done anyway, because he was angry with her for everything; too angry to embark upon a confrontation just yet. He had conducted a careful and very discreet search of the palace, even calling Tal a few times, when it was safe to do so, but there had not been any response. Maybe the fool had sobered, and removed himself from his own madness. But then again, maybe he had not. Jon made his feelings clear to Cicely, and also made it plain he would not spend the night with her. She felt wretched, because he had every right to feel that way. She was sometimes a great trial to him. And a very dangerous one.

She entered her rooms unhappily, for she hated to be at odds with Jon. Mary waited, but there was no sign of Jack, for which she did not know whether to be relieved or not. The very last thing needed now was Jon to change his mind, and come back to find her with the lover who was not only believed to be dead, but was second to Richard in her heart.

Mary explained that Jack had slipped away to Master Pasmer's lodgings, where he intended to sleep in the secret place behind the fire. Cicely knew it was for the best, but being with him again, even for so short a time and under such extenuating circumstances, had left her more in love with him than ever. Plague upon Tal for endangering not only his own hide, but Jack's as well, to say nothing of Master Pasmer, who clearly had no hand in anything, but had been drawn into it, just as she and Jon had.

Jon did not return to her, and she lay alone in the bed, worrying. But it was warm, lying there in the firelit room, and in spite of everything, she fell asleep.

A disturbing dream awoke her later that night. The dream fled as she opened her eyes, but its influence remained. Her heart was beating swiftly, her mouth was dry, and there was perspiration on her forehead. She sat up, pushing her hair back from her face. For a moment she could not think where she was, but then remembered. Esher.

Her mind cleared as she realized there was shouting in the courtyard. What was happening? She slipped from the bed and pulled on her robe to look down from the window. An alarm had been raised, and torches flickered and bobbed as guards ran in all directions. Henry's apartments were bright with lights. The gatehouse entrance was being barred and strongly defended on the inside, and more guards were making for the chapel, as well as the lodgings, which were clearly being thoroughly searched. Tal? Or perhaps Jack! Oh, please God, not Jack!

Her heart began to thunder. 'Mary?'

The maid was already awake and hurried to her. 'My lady? What is it?'

'I do not know, but something serious seems to have happened. I fear what it may be.'

Filled with trepidation, she hurried to the door to the passage, with Mary right at her heels. Her apartment was on its own in this part of the first floor, and there did not seem to be anyone occupying the few others. Men's urgent voices carried up the staircase. Whoever they were, they held torches that sent smoke and monstrous shadows twisting in the stairwell. It was a trick of these moving shadows that allowed Cicely to glimpse someone draw swiftly into a deep window embrasure. A glimpse, maybe, but enough to tell her it could well be either Jack or Tal.

She looked at Mary and put a finger to her lips, before moving towards the embrasure.

'Jack? Tal?' she ventured softly, knowing the risk she took if it was not either of them, but some other, more dangerous fugitive.

'Sweetheart?' Jack emerged, with Tal, clearly in pain, leaning heavily on his arm.

'Dear God, why come here, to me, when there is a danger that Jon—' She broke off, trying to regain her equilibrium. 'Why not go to Master Pasmer's and be in true hiding?' she asked then.

'I would rather answer you in your rooms,' Jack said, glancing back as more voices were heard below, including Jon's.

She went to the top of the staircase. 'Jon?' she called. 'What is happening?'

He came halfway up the steps. His hair was tousled and he had dressed in a hurry. 'Are you all right? I was just about to come up to you. Have you heard anyone up there?'

'All I have heard is the general alarm out in the court-yard. What is going on?'

'Please go back to your bed and bolt your door.' He was able to hold her gaze in the flickering light, and his resentment was very clearly conveyed indeed. It was only too possible that she was hiding someone—Tal alone, he believed—and he knew the imminent danger that might descend upon her. And him.

He descended the steps again, and she heard him reassure his companions. 'It is clear up there. Whoever it is we seek, he is not here.'

Cicely heard them leave, and then the door was locked on the outside and the key taken out. Maybe it was safe inside, but short of breaking and climbing out of a winter-sealed window, they could not leave, either. She stood there for a moment. How was she going to make amends to Jon after this? She had let him down in ways of which he knew ... and in others of which he did not. Yet.

Turning, she went back to Jack and Tal, and tried to sound brave. 'No one will come up here to search now,' she whispered. 'Come, I will try to hide you both.

She put her arm around Tal's waist, to be of what assistance she could to Jack, but Tal was a big man and now almost a dead weight. Between them, they managed to get him to safety, and bolted the door firmly. Candles were lit, and Mary was already setting out her casket in her room. When they removed Tal's cloak, they saw a bloodstained slash across the chest of his rich lavender satin doublet, which he wore with wine-red hose. Such garments were so very different from his usual plain taste that Cicely was quite taken aback.

But, as Jack had said, Tal was different in all ways, from

his dark hair and bristleless chin, to bright clothes that could have been favoured by a much younger man. He could carry off such garments because his body was still firm and muscular. His abdomen was flat and taut, and with his height and good-looking, rather noble features, he was a very attractive man, Cicely thought, imagining he must take after his mother, because everyone knew that his father, the first Earl of Shrewsbury—known as Old Talbot—had been a very dark-haired, dark-eyed man.

Tonight, someone had got close enough to him with a blade to deal him a gash to the chest, as was revealed as Jack undressed him carefully to the waist. Blood oozed as he was made to lie on Mary's bed, so that she could set to work. The maid declined assistance, so Jack and Cicely left her to proceed as she chose.

Jack was contrite. 'Forgive me for bringing him here, my love, but I did not know what else to do. The courtyard is crawling with Henry's men, and we were almost caught. There was no opportunity to get to Pasmer.'

'What has happened? Has he ... killed Henry?'

'No, truth to tell, Henry seems to have come closer to killing *him*. Tal is a damned fool, with his obsessive family conscience. Oh, I do not blame him for wanting revenge, but I do blame him when that desire leads him to take idiotic chances. If he should be caught—if any of us should be caught—Henry's methods will soon extract vital information.'

She looked at him. 'So, you do not think that lying in wait at Knole was an "idiot chance"?' she enquired lightly.

Jack smiled reluctantly. 'Ah, there you have me.'

'I have been so worried about you tonight. And about Tal, but especially you.'

He took her hand and pulled her close to kiss her, and then rested his cheek against her tousled hair.

'I had to seek help to save Tal from himself. I was close

enough to hear Henry screaming for his guards, and then Tal's fleeing footsteps. I grabbed him as he passed, and managed to get him down a back staircase and then outside, where there was already mayhem. How I supported him past the great hall, from buttress to arch to buttress again, without being seen, I do not know.'

'But he actually got close enough to Henry to—'

'Yes, but Henry is that replete cat, always with an ear open and, apparently, a dagger beneath his pillow. Something alerted him and he leapt up, slashed wildly at Tal, and then ran, stark naked, calling for guards. Tal escaped, and I got to him.'

She went to pour some wine, and pressed a cup into his hand. 'When I eavesdropped upon Tal and Henry, Tal's unhappy marriage was mentioned. *Is* it that unhappy?'

'Yes. I did not know a great deal, until he decided to tell me the night before last. I only knew that at one time he and Jane were happy together. She is a Champernoune, an old West Country family. He took the lease of Kingston l'Isle in Berkshire, from his de l'Isle niece and her husband, and all seemed well, but then Jane changed.'

He related what he knew, and Cicely was shocked by the thought of paganism. 'There is such a thing at *Kingston*?'

'I believe there are groups everywhere, Cicely. The one at Kingston follows Woden in particular, and Jane became influenced by its leader, who takes care to be anonymous. Tal has his suspicions about him, but did not divulge a name.'

'Why not?' she asked.

Jack shrugged. 'I have no idea. I asked him direct, but he would not say. Anyway, when he realized what was happening to Jane, he intervened, but it was not until later that he learned she had in her possession a Saxon chalice of great importance that had been kept openly at Kingston church as a *Christian* relic. Christian it is not. She had taken it secretly, together with a white dagger that was also used in diabolical rites up at Wayland Smith. Tal hid them. Now Jane is under the influence of his very Christian sister, the Duchess Elizabeth, at Kenninghall, and is restored to the Church. But she behaves as if Tal is the Devil incarnate.'

'Poor Tal.'

'Well, he no longer loves her. He mentioned a married lady to whom he became utterly devoted. It was entirely one-sided. He was over twenty years her senior, and says he should have known better.'

'He has mentioned her to me. She loved her husband, I think.'

'In a manner of speaking. It was her first husband she really loved, not so much the one she was with when Tal met her. She has passed away now.' Jack avoided her eyes.

Cicely gazed at him, beginning to have an inkling of the lady's identity. The woman had loved her first husband more than her second? The woman who was dead now? How very familiar that sounded. Might it be Richard's queen, Anne Neville?

'You no doubt think the same as me, sweetheart, but Tal did not identify her to me either, and leaping to conclusions would not be helpful. Nothing came of it. The inappropriate emotion was solely his.'

There was a sudden knock at the outer door. Jack returned to Mary's room, and Cicely discovered one of Henry's pages waiting. 'His Majesty requires Viscountess Welles's presence immediately.'

Her fear rose sharply, but she did not let the boy see. 'Please inform His Majesty that she will attend as swiftly as possible.'

He hurried away, and soon Mary had brought a dove-grey gown, and within minutes Cicely's hair had been dressed beneath a headdress and she was ready to face Henry. Well, as ready as she was able, under the circumstances.

Jack smiled to see her looking so lovely. 'I wish you were not taking your beauty to Tudor, sweetheart. I am a much more deserving cause.'

'You are indeed.'

'Henry probably needs you. That is all. He cannot possibly know Tal and I are here, or we would have been arrested long since.'

'I know you are right, but with Henry ... well, you understand, I think.'

He came to embrace her. 'You will be safe enough, my darling, because he has *sent* for you. That is not the act of an angry, betrayed man. If he suspected you, he would have you arrested.'

The door opened without ceremony, and they leapt apart as if stung. It was Jon, and he knew they had been in an embrace, but at first he was too amazed and shaken to see Jack. He closed the door quietly, and shoved the bolt across pointedly.

Cicely closed her eyes. She had forgotten when the page left.

'So, yet again you are in the realm of the living after all, Jack,' Jon said, 'and sniffing around my wife again.' He turned upon Cicely as she protested. 'Do not try to make even more of a fool of me than you already have. Tal is here as well, I suppose? Fortunately, Henry did not recognize him.'

'Yes, he is here,' Jack confirmed, 'but do not blame Cicely, please. I put her in a dangerous position. She helps us. That is all.'

Jon met his eyes. 'Of course. How ridiculous of me to think you and she could be more to each other than cousins. You were not embracing when I came in.'

Cicely closed her eyes in shame.

Jack was angered. 'She wanted to tell you, but *I* forbade her, in the belief it would burden you with more to keep from Henry. You should blame *me*, not her.'

Tal appeared in the doorway to Mary's room, leaning weakly against the jamb. 'Ultimately, it is all *my* fault. I drank myself into rage and came here with the sole purpose of killing Henry.'

'And bungled it abysmally,' Jon said coldly. 'You never learn, do you, Tal? You are sensible and level, and then one day you sink into lunacy. And almost always on this particular day. Oh, yes, I remember the date.'

Tal did not answer.

Cicely was anxious. 'Jon, does Henry think I know something of all this?'

'If he did, he would be right, would he not? But I think he trusts you. As I did. More fool us both.'

'Please do not say such things, Jon. Please.'

'You have gone a little too far, madam. I have always been deemed a fool and a gull to love my wife, and now it seems I really am. Well, no more.'

Jack was appalled. 'For pity's sake, Jon, this is neither the time, nor the place … nor does your lady deserve your censure.'

'No? Can you meet my eyes and say you and she are not in love?'

Cicely spared Jack. 'I do love Jack, Jon, you *know* that, but if you think it diminishes my love for you—'

'Enough! I do not want to hear any more of this false mewling. My eyes have been fully opened, Cicely, and they will stay so. An attempt has been made to murder Henry in his bed, a *Yorkist* plot, in which you, my dear lady, are involved to your slender little neck.' He held up a hand as both Jack and Tal protested. 'Be quiet, both of you. I think you need my help to get out of here intact, so please have the courtesy to let me express my opinion.'

Tal straightened. 'If you imagine you are free of any blame in any way, Jon Welles, you are mistaken. *You* had a hand in what happened in 1483, and if you think I am about to stand by and allow you to—'

Jon's eyes narrowed. 'So, you will hold *that* knife to my throat?'

'If I have to,' Tal replied quietly.

Cicely looked from one to the other. 1483? When Richard became king? She glanced at Jack, but it was plain he did not know what they referred to.

Jon turned to her. 'Your royal lover awaits, my lady. Perhaps Tal has enjoyed your favours as well? Who knows? Or cares?'

She looked at him through tears. 'Please, Jon,' she whispered.

'Get to the king. I need to talk with your Yorkist stallions. And you, Mary Kymbe, can get yourself to the servants' hall, and stay there.' He raised his voice for the maid to hear in her room.

Jack assisted both women into their cloaks, and Jon did not even look at Cicely as she left. From somewhere she found the spirit not to glance back, or allow her tears to fall. She knew the depth of his bitterness, and felt as if a sword had sliced the air between them.

She paused partway along the passage, and put a warning finger to her lips. 'Mary, I want you to hide where the men did earlier. My husband will of a certainty check in a moment to see no one is listening. I will go straight to the king now, but you are to eavesdrop if you possibly can. You may hear something. I need to know what is said.'

'Yes, my lady.'

'I will take the blame should you be caught.'

'Yes, my lady.'

The maid slipped out of sight as Cicely descended the stairs. Sure enough, within moments, the door of the apartment opened again and Jon looked out. Seeing no one, he withdrew again, and as he closed the door, Mary heard him address the others in the room.

'Well, what a fucking pain in the balls you two are.'

The maid slipped from hiding to press her ear to the door, and began to listen to the ensuing conversation.

Chapter Fourteen

WHEN HENRY WAS told Cicely had come, he dismissed the many attendants and guards who clustered around him. His apartments were chaotic, with everyone talking at once and speculation running rife as to who would have had the audacity to try to kill the king when he was so well protected.

The silence when everyone had gone was very welcome, and Henry came to the doorway of the room where she waited.

The fact that the night's events had shaken him was evident. His long hair had not been combed, his movements were swift and nervous, and his crimson robe drained his face, which had been pale enough earlier. The shadows beneath his eyes seemed almost black and he had an air of ... something, she still could not say, except to know that his dishevelled appearance and manner were not solely due to the attempt on his life.

'*Cariad*?'

The word was uttered softly, and with such relief just to see her again, that she could only go to hold him close, although whether to shut out the guilt or hold in the pain, she did not know.

He hid his face in her hair. *'R'wyn dy angen di,'* he breathed, and then in English, 'I need you.' He not only returned her embrace, he drew upon it. For strength. Tonight he made no secret of his utter dependence. His loneliness took physical form, as once had Richard's. Two kings had needed her like this, and she had held them both. And now she had held Jack again, because he too was in need of her comfort and strength. Three strong, powerful men, all of them reliant upon her ... and, maybe, she was reliant upon them.

At last he spoke, but only in a whisper. 'I know that I wrong my uncle, and maybe embarrass you, but if I do not have you close now ...'

'Oh, Henry, forget whatever you think you cannot, because of *course* you can. You are the king.'

He took her face in his hands. 'You really do not understand what you mean to me, do you? It eats my flesh away, *cariad*. My misery when I am without you is a shirt of thorns.' Then he kissed her with everything that was in his heart.

It was distressing to her. He was surrendering so much of himself to her, and yet she was giving refuge to his would-be murderer, as well as his greatest Yorkist foe. Overwhelmed by her own duplicity, she had to pull away.

He allowed her to go from his arms, but she knew he was loath to break the contact.

She looked at him again. 'Have you been injured?'

'My dignity and pride are less than pristine.' He found a rueful smile. 'Fortunately, I had the foresight to put a dagger beneath my pillows and thus have the satisfaction of knowing I cut him before making a nimble, bare-arsed and very unheroic departure. Unfortunately, I was not able to raise the alarm before he managed to get away.'

'Do you think he escaped completely? From the palace, I mean?'

'I have no idea. I pray not, for I would dearly like to have him questioned.'

He looked at her. 'I am sorry to send for you like this, in the middle of the night. Especially when my uncle is here, endeavouring to hunt down my assailant.' He inhaled a little nervously. 'Forgive me, I am more shaken than I realized.' He went to the bed in the adjacent chamber, and sat on the edge of it. His robe was soft, clinging to the outline of his body, and it parted a little, allowing a glimpse of his virility. Not so virile now.

'It would surely be strange if you were not shaken.' She sat next to him.

His hand moved over hers. 'You have been right about my health, *cariad*. I have not felt well for some days now, so it is not only tonight. Oh, it is something I have eaten, I am sure.'

'Are you coughing more?'

He squeezed her fingers reassuringly. 'It is not that. More a general malaise, not helped by tonight's ... episode.' He was silent for a moment. 'A king is supposed to confront everything.'

'Eluding being murdered in your sleep is a little exceptional.'

'Maybe.'

There was such incredible sadness in his strange eyes that he touched something in her heart. 'What is it, Henry? There is something very wrong, is there not? Maybe I can help.' Was it Roland? She felt such a Judas as she smiled sympathetically. A Yorkist Iscariot ...

He smiled ruefully. 'Help? *Cariad*, I fear you will one day do to me what I once did to someone else. The only help you can ever give to me is to be with me. Always.'

'You refer to the lady you will not discuss?' she ventured tentatively.

'I did love her. At first. It was with her that I first entered

172

a fleshly paradise—although not, I vow, as paradisial as the realm I have subsequently known with you.' His tone became momentarily lighter. 'You, lady, know parts of me I had no idea existed.'

She returned the smile. 'You knew they existed, sir, you merely wish to flatter me into your bed again now.'

'Well, I cannot deny *all* of that. But the fact remains that I had a carnal relationship with her, and ... Roland de Vielleville is the result. Ah, I see by your eyes that you had already guessed. Or ... perhaps my uncle told you?' The question was added watchfully.

'I did not need telling, because you gave yourself away at Friskney.'

'So I did. I remember.'

'Be honest, Henry. You cannot be unaware of the speculation about the boy. That he is your son is widely suspected. No doubt it is wagered upon.'

'Well, I have confirmed it now, but only to you. No one else must know.'

'Why?'

He hesitated, and then chose to be amusing. 'Would *you* wish to acknowledge such an objectionable little prick?'

She could hardly probe further. 'Jon already knows, I take it?'

'Yes, I wished him to accompany me to Knole, of which I know you know. I will do my duty as the boy's father, and satisfy my obligations to his mother, but obligation is the sum total of what I now feel for her. Do you understand? I did not love and lose her, I loved and then deliberately and cruelly cast her off. I was ignoble, Cicely.' He met her eyes, his fingers tightening around hers. 'Please tell me you knew nothing of what was to happen tonight.'

She was accustomed to his swift changes of topic, but sometimes he caught her unawares, as now. 'No, Henry, I did not know anything.' *Liar, you did from the moment you arrived and realized Tal was here too.*

'I believe you, *cariad*, I believe you.'

'Who was she?' she asked then.

'Jesu, you are tenacious. It is of no consequence who she was. Do not think I am about to unburden my *entire* soul to you.' He gave her a quick smile, but it was a warning.

She drew away a little. 'Should … should we speak of something else? Something innocuous? Master Pasmer's white sables, perhaps?'

Henry paused. 'How do you know about *that*?'

She explained that she and Jon had met the skinner when she arrived.

'Pasmer is to bring them first thing in the morning,' he replied. 'And I mean first thing, curse it, but there is so much else to attend to that I have to commence with the damned cockerels.'

'I would like to make love with you on such fur,' she teased.

'Then we will. You have my word.'

She searched in her waist purse for the small comb she kept there. Her souvenirs had been left safely at Pasmer's Place. Kneeling up beside him, she rested her cheek against his hair for a moment, for it was hard not to feel for the man he was now. Then she began to employ the comb.

His arms moved around her waist and he kissed the shadow between her breasts.

She continued to comb, talking lightly of this and that, including Jon's forthcoming departure for Lincolnshire. He drew away a little. 'Are you about to ask my permission to go with him?'

'Would there be any point?'

'No. I must have you near, even more so after tonight. There is to be no argument.' He caught her hand suddenly. 'I know that what I did at Huntingdon was wrong in every way. I gave up control to the monster within me, and

174

struck out. There were seconds immediately afterwards when you had it in your power to bring me back to you, but you did not do it. One word, *cariad*, one soft glance, and I would have been rescued. I was trapped within my own miserable self, begging you to take me into your arms, to forgive and understand.'

'It went too far that day. You hit me so hard, and treated me so badly, that I wished you gone. But it is in the past now.' She put the comb aside.

'*Is* it?'

'Yes.' She twisted around, and looped her hair up around her wrist. 'Undress me, Harri Tudur,' she said softly.

He unfastened the rich brocade, and then she rose from the bed to allow the gown to slip to the floor.

The candlelight moved softly over her skin, finding all the curves, shadows and planes, and gleaming on her nipples as she stood before him.

He embraced her, his cheek against the swelling of her breast. 'You are so precious to me,' he breathed. 'Already it seems that what has happened tonight was merely a nightmare. If there is one certain way to drive away all demons, imagined and real, it is to be with you, knowing I am about to make love to you.'

'So, Your Majesty, you have recovered enough for *that*?'

'It would seem so,' he murmured, leaning back a little to reveal just how ready he was.

'My, I believe I am truly flattered.'

'You are about to be more than flattered, *cariad*.' He smiled.

Unable to resist, she pushed his loose robe from his shoulders and down his arms, and then undid the belt. She did not love him, but at this moment, *his* love transcended everything, and she wanted to share the joy he could impart.

175

He lay back on the bed and pulled her down on to him. The pleasure was immediate and intense, and she moved against him, her eyes closed for the sweetness of it. And so she made love with Henry Tudor, and was all he could have wished of her. She wished she was only acting now, but that was not so. Her emotion was real.

The palace was astir but not fully awake when Cicely returned to her own apartment. Snow fell again, thick flakes that wended through the still winter air, filling the thousands of footsteps from the disturbance of the night. Guards were still in evidence, but there was nowhere left to search. Impossibly, the king's assailant had disappeared.

Mary was waiting at the top of the staircase as Cicely ascended. 'My lady?'

'Mary? You ... have something to tell me?'

'Yes, my lady, but it must be said out here.'

Cicely's heart sank, because the maid's face warned of something momentous to be divulged. They drew away from the stairs and spoke in whispers.

'What did you hear?' Cicely asked.

'That his lordship and Tal knew each other when they met in your father's household. Sir Jon was there almost permanently, but Tal was only there for a while, because his post was actually in Calais. They became friendly.' Mary wrung her hands a little. 'My lady ... I do not want to tell you what they said, but know I must.'

'I *asked* you to listen and then tell me, Mary. I will not be angry. So, what did you hear?'

'It ... concerns your father, my lady. Lord Welles and Tal both have their own reasons to hate your father, and took revenge by poisoning him to his death.'

'No!' Cicely recoiled, but knew there had *always* been rumours about her father's sudden death, and Jon *had* been secretive when she asked about it. 'Lord Lincoln did not know, did he?' She knew the answer, having seen Jack's puzzlement over what could have happened in 1483.

'No, my lady. He was greatly shocked.' Mary was agitated. 'I heard them speak of it, my lady. I had to listen very hard, but my hearing is still good. There was a battle called Losecoat Field, and Lord Welles's half-brother and nephew were killed by your father. Tal's grievance was that your father ruined his sister. So they worked together, and both administered draughts to the king when he was ill. One phial contained poison and the other did not, so neither of them knows who actually killed him.'

Cicely leaned weakly against the wall. Jon had already told her he set out for Losecoat in March 1470 to avenge the deaths of his half-brother and nephew, but failed and was almost captured. His life had been saved by the father of the two Talby witches who, each in turn, became his mistress. Losecoat had caused many cruel deaths. Thirty thousand ragged, ill-equipped peasants against the full force and artillery of Edward IV's disciplined army. It had been a bloody massacre, and all these years later the House of York was still loathed in those parts.

'What do you wish of me now, my lady?' the maid asked anxiously.

'Only that you pretend to know nothing of all this. Nothing, is that clear?'

'Yes, my lady.'

'You must *mean* it, Mary Kymbe, because if you speak unwisely to anyone, it will mean the execution of my husband and my friend for regicide. You and I will be in danger too, for concealing Tal and Lord Lincoln. Do you understand?'

The maid's eyes widened. 'Yes, my lady.'

'Is Lord Welles still here?'

'He has gone to see Master Pasmer, and Tal has accompanied him.'

Cicely's eyes widened. 'In *daylight*?'

'Tal wore a hood, but Lord Welles did not. He said that no one would suspect anyone who walked with the king's uncle. And the falling snow would offer some protection as well, he said. I looked from the window and saw them reach the lodgings opposite in safety. Lord Lincoln is still in your rooms. Lord Welles did not wish to risk taking them both. He said that once a plan has been agreed with Master Pasmer, he will come back to escort Lord Lincoln as well.'

Cicely took off her cloak and put it around the maid's shoulders. 'Perhaps the servants' hall would be advisable for an hour or so. It is best I speak to Lord Lincoln alone.'

The maid bobbed another curtsey and then hurried down the stairs, leaving Cicely to continue to her apartment. Not knowing what would await her, she entered anxiously, to see Jack rising hastily from the fireside chair. His shoulder had clearly been newly attended to, and he was not using the sling. He had freshened a little too, and his dark curls shone in the winter daylight.

'Sweetheart?'

She paused, and then closed the door slowly before turning to face him again, feeling that he would somehow see how warm she was from Henry's bed. From Henry's so-beautiful lovemaking. For that was what it had been.

Beautiful.

Jack read her face as if she had voiced her thoughts, and came to hold her. 'Oh, my poor sweetheart ...'

'I deserve your censure, Jack, because I enjoyed him. I feel so unfaithful to everyone, but now, especially to you.'

He put a hand to her chin and raised her lips to give them a fiercely loving kiss. 'I will *never* blame you, because I know you love *me*. Richard alone can challenge me for your heart, and I have inherited more than his claim to the throne: I have inherited *you*.' He smiled, and kissed the tip of her nose.

She managed to return the smile. 'I only hope that I will be able to be as understanding if you find pleasure with someone else. No, do not tell me, for I do not wish to know.'

'Then I will not say a word.'

'Jon said many words.'

'Well, he has always found it difficult, and now, my return is a difficulty too many. I cannot blame him for that, but he *will* come around, sweetheart.'

'I hope so, Jack, because I do want him back. I could not have found a finer man. He stood by me when I needed him. But last night he … was so cold and hard.'

'It was the shock of seeing you with me. A ghost making love to his wife.'

'And now, here I am, reeking of cloves.'

'Take heart from the fact that Tudor does not suspect you. Have you learned anything?'

'Nothing you do not know already.' It was true. 'Jack, what is this about Jon and Tal having poisoned my father?'

He looked at her with a mixture of surprise and dismay. 'I wish you did not know of that, sweetheart. I take it that small maids have large ears?'

'All that matters is that I know.'

'Well, I have only just learned as well. What will you do with your new knowledge?'

She exhaled slowly. 'What *can* I do? It is done, and I feel nothing.'

'It is the reason for the atmosphere between Jon and Tal. They would rather avoid each other now, than be together.'

The door opened and Jon entered. Fresh snowflakes clung to his shoulders and boots. Cicely's heart sank a little as she saw how coolly he glanced from Jack to her, and then back to Jack.

Chapter Fifteen

JON'S FACE MIGHT have been carved of stone as he swung off his cloak and draped it over a chair before going to the window and standing with his back to them.

'Jack, I have settled upon a way to get you and Tal away from here. It is more or less Tal's original plan, which was to be smuggled on board Pasmer's barge, hidden among the furs and fells, and then borne away safely, back to London. Now it will mean smuggling you both.'

'At great danger to you,' Jack said.

Jon turned. 'If it will rid me of the pair of you, then I am almost eager to take the risk.'

Jack met his gaze, but said nothing more.

'Bitter as I am with you, I am not such a cur as to not warn you about your brother.'

'Edmund?'

'Yes. I do not profess to know what he is up to, except that he has something dangerous in mind. All in the name of the House of York, but probably solely to the benefit of Edmund de la Pole. And how do I know? Because Roland de Vielleville did not guard his tongue as he should. He is as thick with Edmund as he is with Thomas Howard. Edmund is malignant, and I have instructed Roland to stay away from him, but you know how alluring the beautiful and dangerous can be.' Jon glanced at Cicely.

'If you should learn more—'

Jon cut into Jack's words. 'I *may* warn you. But do not count upon it, because the way I feel about you at the moment tempts me to let perdition fall about you and your House.'

'Jon, I—'

He was ignored. 'One of my most trusted men resembles Tal's build quite accurately, and now waits in secret aboard Pasmer's barge, as does a second man who, when cloaked and hooded as you will be, could be taken for you. Pasmer has taken the sables to Henry, and is with him at present. When he leaves, the fact that he has been with Henry will be known by the guards. I cannot think that much notice will be taken of him or those with him. Tal will be watching, and will come from the lodgings to join him immediately. The same goes for you and me. No one will question the king's uncle, and as the snow is now very heavy, it will afford considerable concealment anyway.'

He glanced at Cicely again, his face expressionless, and then continued to address Jack. 'We will be loud and friendly, and as natural a group as possible. Then we will all go to the barge, talking about examining Pasmer's furs with a view to purchase. Once you two are safely stowed away, your "doubles" will disembark with me, carrying several furs each. The barge will shove off, and—with God's grace—*you* will be conveyed away from your self-inflicted danger.'

'I cannot thank you enough, Jon,' Jack replied honestly.

'That is very true, Jack de la Pole, but do not ever expect my support again. I accept your reason for coming here, to protect Tal from himself, but I do *not* accept Tal's vengeance for a crime that was actually committed by Edward IV, not Henry VII. Nor do I accept that you are once again with my wife, is that clear? I am no longer prepared to hold my tongue, or turn a blind eye, so if I find you anywhere near Cicely from now on, I will tell Henry everything that I know. I do not care about my wife, and I will publicly abjure her.'

Cicely was stricken. 'No, Jon! Please!'

Jack was appalled too. 'For the love of God, man—'

'Enough! My mind is made up. I will not be made a fool of *ad infinitum*, as you both are pleased to expect of me.'

Tears stung Cicely's eyes. 'Please, Jon, it is not like that,' she whispered. But it *was*. She had not thought twice about going to Jack again. Jon's silent acquiescence had been something she … took for granted. His reaction dismayed her, but she deserved it. 'Forgive me,' she whispered.

'Why should I? Can you tell me that you do not love this man to the exclusion of all others? That he is the new Richard?'

She gazed at him, and then lowered her eyes.

'Then that is the end of it. I always knew you would be a troublesome wife, but all I asked for was your faithfulness. I believed you had to lie with Henry, but why I stooped to overlooking your love for Jack de la Pole as well, I do not know. But my tolerance is at an end.'

'I *am* sorry, Jon, but—'

'But you would do it again!' he interrupted.

'I *do* wish to remain your wife. Please, do not go away from me.'

'I will not share your favours with Henry *and* Jack de la Pole. And … who knows who else?'

Jack intervened. 'Enough, Jon. You *know* there is no one else. This now is my fault. She believed I was dead, and so did you, but I chose to send word to her. I wanted her embrace again, wanted the sweet comfort that she always is. And you know that she is so honest about her feelings. Please, for pity's sake, do not punish her for responding to my message. I wish you could forgive me, but know that I would feel the same in your place.'

'How gracious of you to concede the point.'

'But I do not concede that you have the God-granted right to be so sanctimonious and condemnatory now, Jon Welles, for your record is not exactly free of adultery. Cicely had no choice with Henry, and she did it to save *you* as well as me. Never forget that! But I accept that no one forced her to come to me. I am the *only* other man in her life. Please do not imagine for a moment that she has been deceiving you with all and sundry.'

'How can you be sure you are the only one?' Jon replied scathingly. 'I no longer care if she lies with half the men in London. Do you think I do not *know* she goes willingly enough to Henry? She is *eager* for him, and eager for you! She even pretends to be eager for me. Jesu, man, the woman is insatiable.'

'Damn you, Jon!' Jack cried angrily.

'No, damn *you*, Jack. And damn her.'

'I do not believe you mean any of this in your heart. If you have loved her, you could *never* abjure her!'

'You suggest my love has been inferior?' Jon's vivid eyes were ablaze with resentment.

'Yes, I rather think I have to,' Jack replied simply, not raising his voice at all. 'Please see sense, Jon. Keep Cicely close, because you will be bereft without her. I should know.'

'Well, you will not be bereft any longer, de la Pole, because she has made her choice, and so have I.' Jon addressed her. 'I no longer want you, Cicely, but we will have to talk. In private. When *I* am ready, not when *you* are. And you may be sure I am not ready yet!'

She nodded, unwilling to meet his eyes. She did love him, but perhaps he had never understood her, and perhaps she had always expected too much of him. Now she knew a little of how Henry had felt at Huntingdon. Jon could rescue everything now, with one small word, smile, or extended hand ... but there was nothing.

He turned away again to look from the window. 'There is nothing more to be said for the time being. I prefer to concentrate on the matter in hand.'

Neither of them responded, but Jack moved closer to her and deliberately took her hand. They had been justifiably branded, and he saw little point in pretending it was a misunderstanding. If Jon observed, he gave no intimation.

Master Pasmer's business with Henry did not take long, for the sables were more than acceptable. The skinner emerged into the courtyard, where he was soon joined by Tal. They stood in convivial conversation.

Jon nodded at Jack. 'When you are safe again, and that damned fool Tal has taken his arse back to Calais, if I hear one word that connects you with Cicely, I will see her humiliated at court. And *that* will mean Henry discovering that she has a preferred lover to *him*. Bear that in mind if you think to play at mice behind the Tudor cat's back. You have *both* been warned.'

'I hear you clearly enough,' Jack replied coolly. 'I love your wife, Jon, but if you are prepared to overlook all this, I will withdraw from her life.'

But Cicely's decision was made too. 'No, Jack, for I will not let you go. Jon is right to feel as he does, and I acknowledge it, but *you* are the one I choose.' She looked sadly at Jon. 'You have left me no option but to choose, Jon, and I so wish you had not. My love for you is strong. I have not *pretended* to enjoy your kisses, and if you were honest, you would admit it.'

Jon's face remained stony.

She addressed him again. 'But think on this. If you betray Jack and me to Henry, his wrath will not only descend upon us, but upon you as well, because he will know you have been deceiving him these past two years. He already suspects you of disloyalty, so *please*, think carefully. In your rage to punish Jack and me, you may harm yourself irreparably. Please, Jon, because no matter what you think, or how you hate me, I do love you. Very much.'

He did not respond.

Her spirit rebelled. 'Then know this, sir. I will continue to behave as Viscountess Welles, continue to live at Pasmer's Place and continue as if there is nothing wrong in our marriage. You will have to do all the work where *that* is concerned. And I will always—*always*—be prepared for a reconciliation. We are well matched, and until now have been happy together. Well, generally, because you too have taken lovers.'

'And you regard *my* sins as being equal to yours?'

'I could, should I wish, make your indiscretions seem equal to, or maybe even more than, mine. After all, you installed your witch at Pasmer's Place, and she tried to curse Leo *and* me to our deaths. As her sister had before her. Or do you deny that now? Your well-being has never been in any danger from anything *I* have done. Until now. Here. And for that I still crave your forgiveness.' She turned away.

Jack addressed him. 'After today, Tal and I will owe our lives to you, and to Cicely, and we will consider ourselves to be in debt to you both. If you ever need to call in that debt, you have only to send word.'

But Jon grabbed his cloak, swung it around his shoulders, and left. Jack dropped another kiss on Cicely's lips, seized his own cloak and hood, and then followed, pausing for a second in the doorway. 'You will hear from me, sweetheart.'

'I know. Godspeed, Jack.'

They gazed at each other, and then he had gone.

Cicely felt utterly empty as she watched from the window. The snow was now an almost impenetrable veil, but she could see enough as the two emerged from the entrance to join Master Pasmer and Tal. Then all four stood in casual but friendly conversation, sometimes even laughing. It was quite brazen. No one who saw them could possibly have guessed the truth, that Henry's assailant and the Earl of Lincoln were about to stroll out with Viscount Welles.

Curtains of snow swirled and closed over a scene that, to Cicely, was a nightmare that she knew would not go away, because she was awake already.

Quite when Jon would be ready to speak to Cicely was to remain unknown, because within a day he had sought—and received—Henry's permission to leave for his duties as Constable of Rockingham, Bolingbroke and elsewhere. He departed from Esher, taking Roland de Vielleville with him, and rode away without a word to Lady Welles. She had not even seen him since Jack and Tal escaped.

Yet, in spite of everything, before leaving he still honoured his promise to arrange the renting of one of John Pasmer's properties for the Kymbes. A suitable house was chosen in Hallows Lane, a narrow street close to the Church of St Andrew-by-the-Wardrobe, and therefore close to Flemyng Court as well. She doubted very much that Jon had known of the close proximity of Tal's residence. If he had, she was sure he would not have chosen Hallows Lane.

She was sad, but at least she had Leo to look forward to. And Jack, from whom nothing and no one would keep her. He sent a note, telling that a much-chastened Tal had taken swift passage back to Calais, and he, Jack, had returned to Flemyng Court. He would send Edgar to bring her to him. And this time, Tal's bed or not, she would lie with him again.

Edgar came to escort her to Flemyng Court, and they rode side by side along Thames Street, this time without any sign of Edmund de la Pole. It was late afternoon, and the January day was beginning to fade. There was a raw wind, but she did not feel it any more than she felt the snowflakes touching her cheeks. The light-brown fur of her hood fluttered around her face, and her gloves were tight as she gripped the reins. When she arrived, she would remove the gloves in order to wear one of her precious mementos, Jack's amethyst ring, which tonight she would make him put on again, in order to replace it on her finger, warm from him.

Later, as she lay in Jack's arms, snuggling deep in Tal's astonishingly comfortable bed, Cicely wondered if it was coincidence that when she looked through the crack in the curtains at the great bay window, the clouds had cleared and the moon shone in a starlit sky.

She felt as if those new heavens were mirrored within her. How many times had they made love tonight? Oh, what did it matter? They might have been two lost halves, brought together again.

Now he slept, his lashes dark upon his cheeks, his hair more tousled and wild than ever. He was on his side, facing her, and his good arm was beneath her, keeping her close. Lying there now, if she thought of those moments of utter desolation, when Jon had told her of this man's death, they seemed a lingering memory from another, emptier life. She raised her hand to her lips, and kissed the amethyst, which was not only warm from his finger, but from having been pressed against much more intimate and exciting parts of his body.

His eyes opened. 'How deep in thought you are,' he said softly.

'I was thinking of where this ring has been tonight.'

He drew her closer, and dwelt upon kissing her. A slow, rich kiss that breathed through her, and made her mouth seem it might dissolve. Her fingers twisted adoringly in his hair, and there was no restraint in the way she pressed to him. Oh, how she savoured and enjoyed him. His breath tasted of thyme, and her heart quickened as his caresses became more and more urgent.

'Please … please,' she whispered, 'I want you, Jack.'

He moved on top of her, and their lovemaking was hot and needful, as if it was the first time they had lain together. She felt weightless, adrift in carnal pleasures that brought her original love close again. He was inside her now, long, strong strokes that were also gentle and loving, and when he came, she did too. There was an unworldly beauty in their long climax. They held each other tightly, weak with emotion, their hearts beating swiftly … their bodies warm and sated.

And it was during these precious moments of aftermath that an alien sound was heard.

It came from somewhere downstairs, and was … a single, choked cry? Silence returned in an instant, but Jack almost leapt from the bed to haul his clothes on. He moved like lightning, and she went to help with his thigh boots, which went on with astonishing ease, considering the desperate danger that seemed imminent. Then his dagger was in his palm, and his gaze steady and fixed upon the door as they both listened.

They almost relaxed, until the stairs creaked. Just once. Cicely caught Jack's arm. 'Climb out of the window and *go*!'

'And leave you?'

'I can take care of myself. I am a king's daughter, remember? You must survive, to go to Burgundy and raise an army.' She kissed him fiercely, and then opened the casement. There were horses down in the court, with a single guard. She drew back. 'One man with horses. Make as little sound as you can.'

There was another sound, on the landing this time,

and Jack did not wait a moment more, but climbed lithely from the window, and began the precarious descent to the ground three floors below. In spite of his shoulder, he was still fit and agile enough to lower himself very quietly.

The bells of London suddenly rang out the hour, and he dropped the final yards right onto the unwary guard, who was knocked senseless in a second, and then the Earl of Lincoln had gone, mounting one of the horses and taking the reins of the others to lead them out of the court. The clatter of hooves was lost amid the racket of the bells.

Cicely had already closed the window, and then the shutters as well, before climbing swiftly back into the bed, still naked. She lay under the coverlets as if asleep, praying she would indeed be equal to whatever was about to happen. Henry's name was topmost in her mind. Had he discovered everything after all? Were his spies just on the other side of the door?

The latch made the faintest of clicks as it was raised gently, so as not to warn anyone in the room, but then the door was thrust open with such force that it splintered back on its hinges. Hooded, masked figures rushed into the room, one of them brandishing a lighted torch, the others carrying daggers that they intended to thrust into whoever lay in the bed.

Genuinely terrified, she sat up, hauling the coverlets up to her chin.

'What is the meaning of this?' she cried in her most regal, Plantagenet tone, observing that the men were actually youths of around seventeen.

They gathered around the bed, clearly confused to find a woman alone. Moreover, to find that the woman was clearly *not* a lowborn servant girl. They did not know what to do as they exchanged confused glances.

An authoritative but still-young male voice was heard on the landing, belonging to someone who had followed them up the staircase, and then he pushed into the room. He was as youthful and hooded as the others, but not masked, for she glimpsed the paleness of his face.

'It is done?' he demanded, and when they did not answer, he turned to look at the bed. By the light of the torch she recognized Edmund de la Pole!

He was startled, but then his brown eyes sharpened. He knew he'd seen her somewhere.

'Who are you?' he demanded.

'Why should I answer a mere boy?'

She felt rather than saw his flush of anger. 'Your name, madam!'

'What if I were to say I am Lady Talbot, wife of Sir Humphrey Talbot, Marshal of Calais, whose residence this is? You, sir, have not been invited here, least of all to the bedchamber, so I now demand who *you* are!'

'Where is Sir Humphrey?'

'Calais.'

His glance moved to the amethyst. 'And where is Lord Lincoln?'

Her brows drew together. 'Are you mad? He died last summer at Stoke.'

'You wear his ring, and have not been sleeping alone.' He indicated the crumpled bedding.

'The ring was a gift, and my sleeping arrangements are none of your business.'

He hesitated, and then one of the others leaned close and whispered to him. His face changed. Had he been advised of her true identity? Yes, she thought. She had been recognized.

Edmund came to the bedside, a sly twist on his beautiful lips. 'Have you heard the saying that there is more than one way to skin a cat, my lady? So, you had better forget you have ever seen me. Do you understand?'

'Forget you? Oh, with pleasure,' she replied coldly, but

inside she was hot with fear. He knew who she was, but was still confident and arrogant enough to threaten her! She dared not imagine his character on reaching manhood.

He left, his companions following. Edmund de la Pole would clearly have killed his own brother here tonight. But how did he know Jack was not only still alive, but hiding here? Edmund had recognized the ring, and was capable of seeing to it that Henry knew Lady Welles was wearing it. He might not know she was the king's lover, but he certainly knew she was the queen's sister and married to Henry's uncle. She had not heard the last of Edmund de la Pole, because she was the cat he intended to skin.

She heard Edmund and his friends' fury in the court on discovering their guard unconscious and the horses gone. Their voices awakened the whole household, as well as others nearby, so the youths took to their heels.

Rising from the bed again, and dressing with difficulty, she was glad to have a cloak to hide the untidy lacing at the back of her gown. She went down to find the house in some confusion, although her appearance brought some measure of calm. The cry that had alerted Jack had come from the unfortunate man on duty at the door, but he would recover. She wrote a hasty note to be taken urgently to Tal, to inform him that Jack had escaped safely from an attempted assassination, and making a veiled reference to Edmund as 'he who would be Cain'. Tal would know who was being referred to.

Edgar escorted her safely back to Pasmer's Place, and then rode on to deliver her note to John Pasmer, with instructions that it was to be delivered to Calais with all speed.

The following morning a message arrived from Jack. He was in hiding, but unharmed. He did not say where he was, so she had no way of warning him about Edmund. It was to be the beginning of February before she heard from him again, and by then she would have discovered just how malignant his younger brother really was.

From Jon Welles she would not hear at all.

Chapter Sixteen

THE ATTACK AT Esher appeared to have affected Henry more than seemed at the time. He was a changed man on returning to Westminster at the end of January, and did not celebrate his thirty-first birthday on the twenty-eighth. Nor had he sent for Cicely since Esher.

His temper was foul, and he was best not approached except for something essential. He looked increasingly haggard, Cicely thought, and often coughed. That he occasionally had cramps in his belly was clear in the way he sometimes put his hand to his abdomen. For this he took copious draughts of boiled spikenard root and bilberries steeped in honey, but if either gave any relief, there was no outward sign of it. He was much closeted with Margaret's fourth husband, Thomas Stanley, Earl of Derby, and also with his full-blood uncle, Jasper Tudor. Archbishop Morton appeared to be in full favour again, and his other advisors were always around him like ants.

Strain showed on his face. It might have been due to events at Esher, or anxiety about his health. Or something else entirely. Perhaps Roland de Vielleville? But if he did not send for Lady Welles, she could not help him. Nor did she wish to be sent for. As always, being away from him lessened his fascination.

Then, on the first day of February, when she had decided there would not be any mischief from Edmund after all, word arrived at Pasmer's Place that His Majesty wished to see Lady Welles. The confrontation that ensued was a very sharp reminder of just how flawed Henry was, and how filled with hatred for the House of York.

When she was admitted to the royal apartments, he had been called away unexpectedly. Her grey velvet gown whispered over the floor as she took off her cloak and hood, and draped them over a chair. His half-empty silver-gilt cup of wine stood on the document-strewn table, and by the smell of snuffed candle and melted wax hanging in the air, he had not long departed. His infamous notebook also lay on the table, and she was tempted to peep inside, but it would be just like Henry to have left it deliberately, and in such a way that he would *know* if she had even touched it.

'Eve in the Garden of Eden, my lady?'

He was in the doorway behind her, wearing black trimmed with royal purple. His face was so pale it resembled whey, and his eyes lacked their usual sharpness. She was dismayed. 'Oh, Henry, whatever you take as a remedy, it is not of benefit.'

'I am assured that dried bramble flowers and honey are the next resort.'

He crossed to the table of documents and began to sort through them in a studied way that sent a shudder through her. This was not to be a romantic assignation.

Finding what he sought, he placed a small handwritten note on top of all the papers. But it was of something else that he spoke. 'My mother tells me you are acquainted with Sir Humphrey Talbot?'

Edmund might as well have breathed in her ear, but she was prepared for him. 'Why yes, but only recently. When I

194

left you last time, from here, he was kind enough to make himself known to me. He and Jon are old friends.'

'So I am given to believe.'

'I am sure you remember how very cold it was that day. He offered to convey me to Three Cranes in his sister, the duchess of Norfolk's barge.' Was she being too artless? 'Why do you mention Sir Humphrey?' she asked.

'Oh, come now, I am sure you know.'

'You have heard that I was at Flemyng Court?' She gave him a slightly reproachful look. 'Have you been ordering men to follow me?'

'Why were you there?'

'Certainly not to call upon Sir Humphrey, because he had gone to Calais, and I imagine that is where he is now.'

'Then why … pray?'

Oh, that slight delay, so soft, so ominous. But his own health provided her with a suitable story. 'Because I was in dire need of agrimony and wine, or any other suitable concoction to settle my, er, bowels. Do you wish to know the full details of my indisposition? I can be as graphic and descriptive as you wish.'

'Facetiousness is not becoming.'

Except when *you* employ it, she thought.

The explanation was clearly not what he had expected. 'You were alone,' he said then, and it was an accusation.

'No, I was not.' she answered untruthfully, 'I had Mary with me, and my escort from Pasmer's Place. Henry, what is this about? I was taken very unwell and in urgent need of … well, the necessary facility. Would you have your sister-in-law squat at the side of Thames Street?'

'Why Flemyng Court?'

'Because it was there, close by, and I knew Sir Humphrey. I was admitted immediately, but was too unwell to merely halt a while and then proceed. So I stayed overnight, and yes, I slept in Sir Humphrey's bed. On my own. Would you have had me settle for a meaner mattress when his capacious bedstead was not in use? And I was feeling too unwell to do anything at all, let alone make passionate love to anyone. Even you, Your Majesty, would have gone without that night, I do assure you.'

He said nothing.

'Perhaps I was simply overwrought,' she said then.

'Overwrought?'

'Well, you must know that Jon and I are not on good terms at the moment?'

Again the pause. 'No, I only know that he requested permission to go about his duties as constable.'

'Yes, well, he left without even speaking to me, and I think it will be some time before he does again.'

'What has come between you? Or should I ask, whom?'

She held his gaze. 'A misunderstanding.' She held up her hand to display an amethyst ring. It was not Jack's ring, but another that was very like it, purchased specially for the situation she had been in since Edmund saw the ring at Flemyng Court. For half a heartbeat she knew Henry was taken in, but then he realized it was not fine enough to be the enviable amethyst belonging to Lord Lincoln.

She raised her chin. 'You see? Jon leapt to the same wrong conclusion. It is *not* my cousin's ring. Whoever has informed you to the contrary has been misleading you.' She hesitated. 'But I … I have not told you everything about that night.'

'Oh?'

He knew she had not, and was merely waiting to see if she would give herself away. How she hated him now. 'Armed men broke into the house and came into the bedroom as I slept. They must have known Sir Humphrey was absent, and had come to rob him. Instead, they found me.' She ventured a smile. 'I was truly and alarmingly Plantagenet, and they ran off.'

196

She saw the glimmer of humour in his eyes. 'Is there anything else you wish to tell me?' he asked.

'No. What *is* this, Henry? I would have told you it all before, but you have not sent for me.'

'I have had a lot … on my mind. Including this. Do you know the hand?' He pushed the handwritten note towards her.

She went to look, and knew instinctively that it was Edmund's work. This whole matter had his stamp upon it. 'No. Why?'

'Because the writer appears to know a great deal about your sojourn at Flemyng Court.'

'Indeed?'

'Read.'

She met his eyes for a moment and then picked up the paper, which accused her of sharing a bed with Jack and helping him escape. The amethyst was cited as proof of her licentiousness and treason to the ruling monarch. She placed the note on the table again.

'Well, I trust you know it to be falsehood from first word to last? How *could* I have been in bed with my cousin Jack? He is dead! Unless you know better?' She managed to make her expression change to shock and disbelief. 'You *do* know better? Henry, is Jack alive after all?'

'No, he is not.'

'Then *why* have you given any credence to this poisonous scribble?'

'Because I knew there was a grain of truth in it. Somewhere. Jack de la Pole was almost as close to you as Richard.'

'Neither of them was my lover,' she said quietly.

'Do not lie!' Henry was dangerous again. His eyes were frozen and his whole manner threatening.

'I am not lying!' she said dishonestly, meeting his gaze square on. But her heart seemed to have slowed its beats, and the sun streaming through the window overlooking the Thames was suddenly blinding.

'You will *never* tell me the truth about your royal lovers, will you? First your fucking uncle, then your fucking cousin!'

Something caught inside her, snatching at common sense and fuelling everything with which she despised Henry Tudor.

'How I loathe you!' she breathed. 'Was it not enough to have killed Richard in battle without lying about him ever since? And is it not enough that Jack was killed at Knole, without you accusing me of bedding him *again*? On your own admission you know he is dead, so you *choose* to believe this poison in order to bring about a confrontation. Well? Do I lie?'

He strode over to shake her until her head wobbled. 'Hold your tongue! Do you hear? To whom do you think you speak? A stable boy?'

She did not submit. 'You may be king, Henry Tudor, but you are unworthy of the crown!'

'Unlike your precious uncle, I suppose!' He struck her, grasping her with one hand and hitting her across the face with the flat of the other.

Her breath snatched, but her fury was such that, without hesitation, she gave him a ferocious blow in return. She would have given him another had he not caught her wrist.

'Enough!' he cried. Now he had her by both wrists, holding her away from him with as much strength as he possessed. She tried to kick him where she knew it would cause him most pain, but he evaded her. 'For the love of God, find your senses!' he breathed, his wintry eyes bright, his fingers like vices.

'I will never forgive you for this, Henry. Never,' she cried, tears wet on her cheeks.

'And now you *still* expect me to believe neither of them was your lover?'

Sanity flew out into the winter cold. 'Oh, they were my lovers! And Richard was *the* great love of my life. He took my maidenhead and carried me into Heaven itself. I will yearn for him—for them both—until the day I die. I adored everything about them, but I have never felt anything with you. Nothing! You have *never* meant anything to me, and you never will! Richard and Jack were my soul, and their kisses were ecstasy to me. Do you understand? This is the secret about Richard that you have always feared! I lay with my uncle, and if he were still alive I would do it again. And again, and again—'

The words were silenced as he slapped her again, as hard as he could. 'You bitch!'

Her head was jolted, and his fingers left angry red marks on her cheek. She was silenced at last.

He closed his eyes, released her and turned away. He was as shaken as she, and his breathing was laboured. She heard him whisper of an inauspicious day, but then he spoke quite clearly. 'Go,' he said levelly, but she saw how his hand went to his abdomen, as if in pain.

'You are contemptible, Henry Tudor.'

With an almost strangled cry, he whipped around again and forced her backwards until he had her pinned to the wall. 'And you are the incestuous bitch who took her own uncle as a lover, and who rutted with him like a cheap bawd! Whores are taken against alley walls, madam, but here will have to suffice.'

She tried to wrench herself free again, knocking her headdress askew, but he pressed against her, forcing his lips upon hers and kissing her so cruelly that she could barely breathe. Her head was spinning with fear. She could taste almonds and wine on his lips, but no cloves. Not this time.

He hauled up her skirts, and then his right hand slid between her thighs. She was unspeakably distressed and frightened, and managed to tear her lips from his.

'Behind this monster, do you *still* profess to love me?' she cried.

The words found a target, for his grip relaxed, but only a little. She saw him close his eyes again, as if forcing himself back into control, and then he allowed her skirts to fall. But he immediately took her hands and stretched them down, hard. The act forced their bodies to touch, and she felt the arousal he was now able to suppress, if not entirely banish. He did not speak, he simply stood there, his face against the hair exposed by the unseating of her headdress.

He was breathing heavily, but no longer with anger and lust, only with stress and emotion. It seemed she could now smell cloves again. The scent should have repelled her, but it did not. She knew that if she whispered his name, and moved against him with even the slightest hint of tenderness, he would have been soothed. But, as had happened before at Huntingdon, and as Jon had more recently done to her, she offered only rejection.

Henry remained as he was, his fingers so tightly twined with hers that it was painful. She did not know what he was thinking, or what he might do, and it seemed her frantic heartbeats echoed through them both. She was drained of anger now; drained of everything but fear.

How she wished she had not confessed to a fleshly love for Jack, but above all she wished she had not confessed about Richard. *What a fool you are, Cicely Plantagenet!* Now Henry's mind would almost inevitably turn to the little boy at Friskney, who not only had hair that resembled hers and Richard's, but the latter's clear grey eyes too. And who was surely the right age to have been fathered by Richard at Nottingham. Henry had already remarked that such was her ease and manner with the little boy that she might have been his mother.

He stepped away abruptly, avoiding her eyes and indicating the secret door behind the tapestry. 'Get out.' His voice was choked, he trembled visibly and his face was almost grey with strain.

She could not move.

'*Get out!*' he screamed.

She fled, leaving her cloak and hood over the chair. He slammed the door behind her, and shot the bolt across almost ferociously. As she ran she was sure she heard him cry out again and begin to cough, but she did not dare to go back to him. Nor did she want to.

Chapter Seventeen

CICELY TRIED TO straighten her headdress and smooth her gown before seizing a quiet moment to emerge into the palace's more public area. She also tried to look composed and relaxed, as if nothing whatsoever had happened, but knew she would not succeed. How could she when the mark of Henry's hand was clear upon her face?

She was overwrought, and lacked her cloak and hood to fend off the bitter cold on the return to Pasmer's Place. Then she remembered the safe pass Henry had given her. Perhaps the guards by the steps would find her a cloak *and* escort her home. It was all she could think of. How she wished she were with Jack now. His comfort would be such a loving balm.

Negotiating the main passage was always fraught with difficulties, and this time she came face to face with Archbishop Morton. He was lean and sallow, with a thin face that sagged from his cheekbones and chin, and very bony fingers. His rich vestments were gold and white, and his mitre was studded with jewels. He was followed by a small column of priests, all with hands clasped before them and eyes downcast.

It could not be said Morton walked; rather did he glide,

his crosier tapping occasionally. Cicely almost expected to see a scaly tail protruding from his hem, and horns on either side of his mitre. He had been Richard's remorseless foe, and was still the enemy of all Yorkists. Now he made much of halting and bestowing upon her the sign of the cross.

'Peace be upon you, Lady Welles.' His glance flicked curiously to her red cheek.

She was in no mood to be polite to him. 'Why, if it is not the Archfiend of Canterbury. I trust you are not in good health?' After Henry, it was some small revenge to be rude to this miserable, so-called man of God. She had no fear of Purgatory.

'May God forgive your lack of respect, child. It is clear you are overdue a lengthy confession.'

'Indeed so, but then, when I do confess, I tell the truth. Do you?'

His nostrils flared and bristling with loathing, he glided on without another word. The priests tripped after him like a flock of black geese.

But even as Cicely continued towards the river entrance, she was appalled anew to see Margaret and her ladies coming towards her. Had this day *still* not finished with her? The oncoming ladies were all well-covered from the cold of the Thames, but there was no mistaking Henry's mother.

Nor could Margaret mistake Cicely. Gesturing to the ladies to stay where they were, she came to her. 'My dear, what is the matter? You look as if you have fallen downstairs, or been attacked.'

Cicely could not speak. Her fleeting defiance towards Morton had now evaporated, and she bit her lip in a vain attempt to subdue sobs. Margaret was horrified.

'My dear? Oh, I have to get you somewhere private. The queen's apartments are close by; we will go there.' She looked around and beckoned her ladies. Instructing them to surround Cicely, whose arm she supported comfortingly, Henry's mother managed to escort her to Bess's chambers, where they were admitted quickly.

Sending her ladies away, Margaret ushered Cicely into Bess's presence. Annie was there too, having been permitted another visit. She was cool and pretty in a simple gown of salmon brocade, and her haughty lavender glance took in Cicely's dishevelled appearance. She did not say anything, but her expression was disparaging.

Incongruously, Cicely noticed how straight and gleaming her younger sister's hair was, so perfectly smooth that it looked like fine strands of spun silver. Maybe it *was* spun silver, because the Lady Ann Plantagenet was surely not entirely human.

Annie's ill-concealed sense of superiority did not last long, because she was dismissed by Bess, who was appalled to see Cicely's state. Displeased and resentful, the girl got up, sank into a deep curtsey to Bess and then to Margaret in a way that could—just—have included Cicely, and then she stalked away.

But Margaret was a match for her. 'Come here, girl!'

Annie turned apprehensively. 'My lady?'

'On your knees, this instant!'

There was no hesitation as Annie obeyed. Margaret moved towards her in a way that brought Henry into the room with them. 'If you ever, *ever* insult my brother's wife again, I will make you pay for it. Lady Welles is to be honoured and treated with respect at all times. If you fail to do this, I will see that you are punished until you wish you had never drawn breath.'

'My lady.' Annie's eyes were like saucers.

'And if I *ever* catch you approaching the king again, I will send you back to Sheen so quickly your presumptuous little backside will be in flames! Do you hear me?'

'Y … yes, my lady!'

'Now, get out!' Henry was present again.

The girl's feet flew as she ran from the apartments.

Margaret looked shrewdly after her. 'That one will cause a great deal of trouble. It would be better if she did not come to court at all,' she declared, before returning to assist Cicely into a chair by the fire.

Bess brought a cup of wine and pressed it into her sister's hand. 'Drink a little, Cissy, it will help to restore you.' Her turquoise taffeta gown, beautifully trimmed with bronze cloth-of-gold, rustled as she knelt by the chair, her hand on Cicely's arm. 'Your face! What has happened, Cissy? Has someone dared to strike you?'

Cicely did not answer. How could she to Henry's mother and his queen?

Margaret was not deceived, however. 'Have you been with the king?' she asked quietly, aware that Bess knew of the intimacy between Cicely and Henry.

Cicely closed her eyes and bowed her head.

Bess's lips parted, and she protected the early curve of her abdomen. 'Henry? *Henry* did this to you, Cissy?'

'We had a terrible quarrel that did not stop at words.' Tears wended down Cicely's cheeks. 'And when he hit me, I hit him in return.'

Margaret looked faint. 'Holy Mother, preserve us,' she breathed, and went to pour herself a cup of wine. Belatedly she remembered to pour one for Bess as well.

Bess was shocked. 'You … came to blows?'

'Feelings ran high,' Cicely responded. 'He accused me of … well, of having been Jack de la Pole's leman and wearing his ring.' She held up her hand. 'It is not Jack's ring, and Jack and I were not lovers.' She did not glance at Bess, who knew otherwise. 'Then he accused me of having been Richard's lover, and … well, that was when it became much more than an exchange of words.'

205

Margaret studied her. 'My son is irrationally jealous of Richard Plantagenet,' she said quietly.

Bess sank back on her heels, and Cicely fell eloquently silent.

Margaret drew a long breath. 'My dear, I do still have some influence with him, and maybe—'

'Lady Margaret, what happened today cannot be undone. You see, I told him I *had* been Richard's lover, and Jack de la Pole's.'

Margaret gaped, and so did Bess.

'I wanted to hurt him as he was hurting me, so I lied. I let him think that everything he feared was true after all.'

Margaret's mouth opened and closed several times before she found her voice. 'My dear, if you said *that* to my son—'

'He was justified in hitting me? Is that what you are about to say?' Cicely's tone was challenging.

'No man is ever justified in hitting a woman, my dear, I am simply trying to—yes, I admit it, to find a mitigating circumstance. I do not like to think my son can behave like this.' Margaret put her cup aside. 'I ... think I should go to him. Cicely, do you wish me to mediate for you?'

'No.'

'My dear—'

'No. But I do wish you to make him promise upon St Armel not to take his revenge upon Jon.'

Bess's brow drew together. 'St Armel?'

Margaret nodded. 'His chosen saint. Very well, Cicely, of course I will exact his promise, for I too worry on Jon's account. Although, I do not know what to think about *him* at the moment either. There was clearly more to his abrupt departure than he was prepared to mention.'

'We are ... estranged. And because of the same thing, the amethyst ring that was *not* that of the Earl of Lincoln.' Cicely said it so sincerely that she almost believed it herself.

Bess was startled anew. 'You and Jon are estranged? I had no idea ...'

'He left me after Esher, and I have not heard from him since.'

Margaret sighed unhappily. 'My brother can be mule-headed at times, and sometimes it causes him such pain. As for Henry, well, I wish he was less like me and more like his father. Edmund Tudor was open, forthright and at ease with himself. Henry has been ... made what he is. And I am greatly at fault in this. I will go to him now, and if I can help, you may be sure I will. Bess, I know that you and my son find each other abhorrent, but I also know that he shows a very different side of himself to your sister. I wish it were not so, but it is and there is no point pretending.'

Bess faced her. 'You had best know that *I* do not wish it to be otherwise, my lady. I do not pretend, either.'

The two women looked stonily at each other, and then Margaret swept out. Alone with Cicely, Bess gave vent to her bitterness. 'If there is a devil on earth, it is Henry Tudor. I hope he suffers.'

'Suffers what?'

'Everything awful under the heavens. Nothing is too atrocious for me to wish upon him. I hate him so, and am glad you hit him today. I wish you had been able to hit him many times more.'

'I behaved very badly and very stupidly today, and brought a great deal down upon myself. I am not excusing him, just admitting to sharing the blame. Oh, let us talk of something else. I notice that Annie was her charming self again.'

Bess got up to replenish their cups. 'Ah, well, Annie is in a quandary.'

'Oh? In what way?'

'She is besotted with someone other than Thomas Howard.'

'Who is this new love?'

'Well, there are two of them, actually, one of whom I know nothing at all, save that he exists. The other is the Breton boy, Roland, who looks as disagreeable as Annie herself.' Bess took the other seat before the fire.

'Roland de Vielleville,' Cicely said, her heart sinking. Annie and Henry's illegitimate son? Now *that* would indeed be troublesome! And from Margaret she knew the name of the unidentified love. 'And our dear cousin, Edmund de la Pole, is the third fellow.'

'*Edmund*?' Bess's mouth opened and closed.

'Yes. Lady Margaret noticed and told me.'

'A prospect made in Hell as far as Henry is concerned.'

'That is what I thought,' Cicely replied.

'But Annie would find him alluring, I imagine. He makes me shiver. And this Roland, do you know him?'

'I had to dance with him at Esher. Jon is to watch over him. Anyway, he is now with Jon, so Annie cannot see him for a while, only Thomas Howard and Edmund. Which is enough to be worrisome, without Roland as well, whom, incidentally, I am supposed to help become a courtier. Can you imagine it? But, Henry wishes it and we must hop to his tune.' Hop. The word took her back to dancing with Henry at Esher. *Hop, sweetheart, hop....* New tears stung suddenly.

Bess studied her. 'Who is Roland really, beyond a name? You clearly know something you are not saying.'

'No, Bess, truly. I only know that he is the son of a friend of Henry's, who is now dead.'

'Henry does not have friends,' Bess observed acidly.

'Well, I can only repeat what he said.'

Bess snorted. 'I doubt if my royal spouse will be any more pleased about this than about Edmund.' She was about to expand upon the subject when one of her ladies came scurrying in unannounced.

'Beseeching your favour, Your Grace!' she cried, sinking

into a curtsey that was far too hasty to be elegant.

'Speak.'

'An urgent message for Lady Welles from Lady Margaret.'

Cicely sat forward uneasily. 'What is it?' she asked.

'She requests your presence in the king's apartments, without delay, my lady.'

Cicely remembered hearing him cry out and cough. Maybe it was of more consequence than she realized. She was alarmed, which she knew she would not have been if she hated him.

Bess waved the lady-in-waiting away. 'So, Cissy, yet again you are needed by the king.'

'By the king's mother,' Cicely corrected, distracted. Something was very wrong. 'Forgive me, Bess, but I must go.'

Bess nodded. 'I trust it is something serious, fatal even,' she said, in the tone she would have used if choosing an apple from a bowl. Certainly she did not seem surprised by the urgency with which Cicely had been called away.

Careless of her appearance now, Cicely almost ran through the palace, slipping swiftly out of sight into the secret way to Henry's apartment. She was locked out, of course, for she had heard Henry shoot the bolt earlier, but she knocked loudly until someone came. It was Margaret, whose face was much changed from before. Flustered and very worried, she almost pulled Cicely inside and then locked the door again. 'Thank goodness you are here, for he is very ill. It is the same as before—I believe—but far worse.'

He had not been well since Esher. Cicely felt guilty for not realizing another episode like this was in the offing.

'How bad is he?' she asked.

'Close to unconsciousness, with a fever ... and that cough. But this time he has a violent headache, he vomits, and he soils himself. Oh, he would be so mortified to know. My poor son.' Margaret's eyes brimmed with tears. 'Please, come to him. Comfort him, for he needs you.'

'He may not wish *me* to be anywhere near him. Our quarrel was quite terrible.'

'My dear, he needs you, believe me. He is not a saint, I know, but neither is he all sinner. I have sent for Master Rogers, but the fellow must come from Greenwich. In the meantime we must manage as we did before.'

Master Rogers was the physician and astrologer whom Henry trusted most, which was not saying a great deal. An elderly man, always clad in black, with a long white beard and a black skullcap, he was the only physician summoned when Henry had last suffered a calamity to his health. The planets and stars figured highly in Rogers's diagnoses, and he divined things from urine and stools. Henry believed in astrology and all such arts. Spells and charms were within Rogers's knowledge, to banish bad humours and aid recovery, but he disapproved of wisewomen like Mistress Kymbe, whom he regarded with disdain.

The apartment was as it had been when Cicely left, and her cloak and hood were still over the chair. The day was fading and shadows crowded in. All the light there was came from the fire and a single candle on the cluttered table. There were no servants. Henry would not have sent for anyone, nor would Margaret, because the delicate balance of his health was not to be broadcast, even though to keep it concealed was dangerous to him.

Margaret spoke again. 'When I came into his presence, he was writhing on the bed with cramping pains, and complained of a violent headache that made him spew the contents of his stomach. He had no control, Cicely, and you *know* how that would distress him. A man of his character, grace and elegance, reduced to such humiliation. He hardly knew what was happening. I have managed to undress and clean him a little, and have just pulled the coverlet over him.'

'Pains in the stomach and a headache? Surely that cannot be the result of his chest ailment?'

Margaret looked intently at her. '*Did* you take Richard as your lover?'

Cicely was wiser now. 'No, my lady. I was so unspeakably angry that I would have said anything. Perhaps if you read the note on the table? The one on the very top?'

Margaret went to it, read, and then returned. 'Do you know who sent it?'

'No.'

'I can understand how you felt when faced with such objectionable lies, my dear, but for pity's sake, if Henry should awaken enough to speak to you, *please* reassure him about your dealings with your kinsmen, particularly Richard. The thought of it crucifies him inside, and to hear you say it was true was just too much for him today.'

'You consider this now to be *my* fault?' Cicely prepared to defend herself.

'No, my dear, it is the fault of my son's immeasurable jealousy and preparedness to believe anything with which to feed it. He tries to be strong, but he is not, and you are his greatest weakness of all. Whatever you may think of him, he is my son, my only child, the only tangible living memory I have of his father. You can help him now, and he will recover. One day in the future—may it be many years hence—he will not recover, but I wish to stave off that moment. Please. I implore you, soothe and reassure him. I am *begging* you.'

Cicely was deeply affected, and put a quick hand over Margaret's. 'I will do all you wish, I swear, but do not be surprised if what I said to him today has ended his fondness for me.'

She found Henry on the great four-poster bed as

Margaret described. His hair was spread on the pillow in a way that told of Margaret's attempts to make him as cool as possible. There was an unnatural flush on his cheeks, and Cicely rested a hand to his burning forehead. His breathing was laboured, his eyes closed, and he did not respond to her touch. She could see the blue veins in his eyelids, and the slight flicker of his lashes. As she looked he curled up tightly, clearly in pain.

For a fleeting moment she thought of the poetic justice of it, retribution for anything he may have done to Jack at Knole. But fleeting it was. He was helpless and ill, and his bewitchment enveloped her again.

'Oh, Henry,' she whispered as she hurried to get his half-drunk cup of wine. Then she sat on the edge of the bed to slide an arm beneath his shoulders to try to arouse him a little. 'Henry, drink a little of this,' she urged, raising his head and touching the cup to his lips.

He seemed to come to, but only just. His too-bright eyes opened a little, in a way that made them seem more hooded than usual, and he found it difficult to focus on her. But he knew her.

'I told you to get out,' he breathed, shivering even though he was so hot.

'I am disobeying you, Henry. You will have to get out of this bed and *throw* me out. I did not mean what I said to you earlier. Truly. I was angry, that is all. So please, sweetheart, sip some wine. It will help you.'

She could not tell if her words penetrated. He tried to sip, but only dampened his lips. Then he coughed, that hollow, deadly, consumptive sound she had heard before. What miserable stroke of fate had brought these other afflictions upon him at the same time?

The coughing continued for a while, racking through him, but at last it faded and he lay quietly. He was losing consciousness again, and then his head slipped sideways as he returned to oblivion.

Cicely was about to put the wine aside when something—a hitherto unrealized sense, perhaps—made her sniff it. Maybe the faint drift of almonds had carried to her subconscious. Whatever, she was suddenly back at Wyberton Castle in Lincolnshire, learning of the poisoned damsons with which Jon's vicious mistress, Lucy Talby, intended to kill the new Lady Welles and her unborn child. And she remembered too, tasting almonds on Henry's mouth this very day.

Margaret looked on anxiously. 'What is it?'

'Sniff it, but please do not drink.' Cicely held the cup out.

Margaret breathed the wine tentatively, and then drew back with a horrified gasp. '*Poison*? Someone has poisoned him? Sweet Mother, help him! And he abhors almonds!' She hurled the cup away and sank to her knees to pray desperately.

Chapter Eighteen

As MARGARET WEPT and begged for the Almighty's intervention on her son's behalf, Cicely went back into the other
room to inspect the wine jug. Sure enough, the smell of
almonds was easily detectable. And yet Margaret said he
abhorred them? How could he *not* have smelled them?

But there was no point wondering that now, for the fact
was he *had* drunk it, and had been doing so since Esher,
when he discovered the new wine. A glass or two each
day, sometimes a little more, certainly enough to gradually
reduce him to the wretchedness he suffered now. A cold
finger passed down her spine. Did *poison*, not Tal's attempt
on his life, explain the change in him?

Her hand shook as she replaced the jug. Who could
be responsible? She did not want to think it might have
been Tal, or even Jon, both of whom had committed regicide before. Nor could it be Jack, who wanted Henry *and*
his line excluded from the throne for all time by using
the enigmatic Roland. So who else hated Henry this
much? There was Bess, of course. Her thoughts paused.
Bess ... who had not seemed at all surprised by the almost
frantic way Margaret had sent for Lady Welles, and who
had made such a casually spiteful remark. *'I trust it is*

something serious, fatal even.'

Pushing the dark and shocking thought away, she returned to Margaret, who was still in anguished prayer, kneeling against Henry's bed, hardly able to support herself for the dread that now filled her.

'My lady?' Cicely spoke gently. There was no response, so she touched Margaret's shoulder gently. 'My lady?'

'What is it?' There was anger because truly desperate devotions were interrupted.

'I think this has been happening at least since Esher.' Cicely explained about the change in Henry not only coinciding with the attack upon him, but with the new wine.

Margaret gazed at her. 'Can we be sure?'

'I cannot be *sure* of anything, my lady. Maybe Master Rogers will be able to confirm it is poison, and maybe he can aid Henry's recovery. I may be wrong, but I think the poison might be something called Russian powder, which was administered to me at Wyberton. It too smelled of almonds.'

'One of the Talby witches?'

'Yes.'

Margaret rose, trembling. 'Oh dear, sweet Lord, the poisoner must know that Henry cannot taste or smell almonds. But who? *Who* would do it?'

'When did he lose his sense of smell and taste?'

'He had an ague while on his victorious progress after Stoke. He has regained his taste and ability to smell since then, except with one or two things, including almonds, which he never cared for anyway.'

'Who else will be aware of this?'

'I do not know. Those in the kitchens, I imagine, for they were instructed not to serve almonds to him. But as to who else ...' Margaret shrugged.

'My lady, you may love Henry, but few others do.'

'Including you?' Two words, but they fell chillingly into

the silence.

'So much for your friendship. It is only on the surface; prick you, and your gall soon flows. I have not harmed the king, he is guilty of far more sin against me. I have lain with him many times, but never once have I contemplated murdering him in his sleep. He has been at my mercy, Lady Margaret, and mercy is what has always prevailed.'

Cicely waited for a response, but there was none, so she spoke again. 'My lady, if you *really* believed me to be guilty of trying to murder Henry, you would call for the guards. It would be to Hades with Henry's desire for secrecy, and I would be hauled off to the same room in the Tower where my uncle Clarence was done to death. Or whatever other vile chamber you can think of. But you will not do it because, in your heart, you know I am innocent.'

Henry's mother turned to look at him again, and put the back of her hand gently to his cheek. 'I know I wrong you, Cicely, and crave your pardon. You are the only one who can help now, because you are the only one who is close enough to him. Help me, my dear. He is in no state to issue commands for the discovery of the culprit, or indeed to understand anything but the agony that overtakes him intermittently.'

Margaret took Henry's hand, and bent to kiss it tenderly. The depth of her love almost warmed the air. 'We will not divulge to anyone that poison has been administered to my son. Let the poisoner think himself still undetected.'

Guilt seeped chillingly through Cicely, because she had told Jack of Henry's physical weakness, and Tal knew as well. Henry's enemies were therefore already aware of his unsound health, and she was to blame. Jon knew too. She soaked a napkin in cold water from the hand bowl that was always available and took it to Margaret, who laid it across his forehead.

'Lady Margaret, keeping silent about Henry's health is all very well, but if you had not come here now—and if I had not gone to him when it happened before—how long might it have been before he was found? And this time it is different anyway, because he has to fight his ailment *and* poison.'

'The last thing he would want is for it to be known that he was almost poisoned to death itself. Of course ... this may yet end his life.' Tears ran down Margaret's cheeks.

Cicely hesitated, but then went to put her arms around the older woman. 'I am sure you found him in time, my lady.'

'I so want to believe it.' Margaret returned the embrace for a moment, and then looked at him again. 'He looks so frail.'

Cicely looked too, and wanted him to be as he was when they danced at Esher. *Hop, sweetheart, hop....* She collected herself.

'We must hope Master Rogers will not be too long,' she said, and meant it. Then she thought of Mary. The maid would surely be able to help until the physician came!

But when it was suggested, Margaret was appalled at the mere idea. 'A village wisewoman? Are you mad? I will not hear of it!'

'Mary Kymbe knows old ways, Lady Margaret, and often the old ways are the best. She has learned of a nine-herb charm that protects from poison and will not harm the person to whom it is administered. She may well do him much good. Please, let me send for her.'

'Charms? Protection? You speak of witchcraft!'

'No, I speak of doing everything possible to help Henry.'

Margaret gazed at her, and then at him, so pale and deathly. Love overcame religious objections. She nodded. 'Very well.'

Mary came as quickly as she could, the casket held

tightly, and Margaret scowled at her before retreating to a curtained prie-dieu, thus washing her hands of whatever followed. The maid was fearful of even touching the king, let alone treating him. But then she caught Cicely's anxious gaze, and knew she must do what she could. She bent over him to sniff his breath, and then straightened swiftly.

'It is Russian powder, my lady.'

Cicely nodded. 'Yes, I thought so too.'

Opening the casket at the bedside, Mary began to prepare the mixture of selected herbs, all boiled when the moon was waning. Placing them in a small pestle and mortar, she worked them into a paste, blending in a little apple juice now and then, and whispering rhythmically as she mixed it all into a salve.

'A snake came a-crawling, and bit a man from under,
But Woden took nine glory-twigs and smote the snake
asunder.'

Over and over she repeated the charm, until she deemed the mixture to be perfect, and then scooped the salve into an old, cracked dish, and gave it to Cicely.

'It is not right that I should touch His Majesty's naked-ness, my lady. You must do it. Just smooth it all over him. It will fight away the poison and aid his recovery, and will do far more good than any physician, alchemist or astrologer.'

'Woden's charm?' Tal's wife crossed Cicely's mind.

'It is but a name, my lady. The charm is very old indeed, since before there were Christians. That there is no Woden does not mean the charm will not work.'

Cicely accepted the salve before permitting the maid to leave again. 'Mary, you may return to Pasmer's Place, for I may be here some time and I know Tom and Mistress Kymbe may arrive at Hallows Lane at any time. You would rather be there than waiting around here for me.' She indicated that no mention should be made of Leo within Margaret's hearing.

'They are here already, my lady. I had just received word from Tom when your message arrived as well.'

'Then you must definitely return now. Please convey my greetings to your brother and aunt.'

'Thank you, my lady. I will bring word of them, you may be sure of that.' Mary returned the meaningful look.

'And please, be so good as to embrace Mistress Kymbe for me.' Cicely could almost hear Margaret's nostrils flare with outrage at such familiarity with a low countrywoman.

Mary bobbed a curtsey, collected the casket, and then hurried away.

Margaret emerged immediately, proving she had been listening to every word. 'How very vulgar, speaking of embracing such a person,' she sniffed.

Cicely smiled. 'Mistress Kymbe is a very kind and gentle woman, my lady. I could not have wished for anyone better or more knowledgeable at my lying-in.'

Margaret's lips twitched, and she transferred her disapproval. 'Woden indeed. All this reeks of witchery and wickedness,' she muttered, crossing herself several times.

'It is but herbs and apple juice, Lady Margaret. No harm will come to Henry from its ingredients, but I do believe they will help him.' Cicely put a hand tentatively on the older woman's arm. 'I would never do anything that would hurt his health and well-being. You know that.' *Liar, liar, for you love and help his enemies....*

Margaret looked at her and then nodded. 'Yes, I know.' And she said nothing more as Cicely smoothed the salve into Henry's pale skin, working it gently and continuously, until somehow—impossibly—the green disappeared. And *that* did indeed seem like magic.

It was close to midnight before Master Rogers arrived and

219

immediately expressed outrage that a pagan charm had been applied to His Majesty. But he clearly knew its beneficial properties, because he did not order that Henry should be washed forthwith. It was Cicely's opinion that if—when—Henry recovered, the herbs would not be credited with anything at all, only the matchless skills of the exemplary Master Rogers!

Before the physician's arrival, she and Margaret had been doing what they could to keep Henry comfortable. They managed to persuade him to drink a little wine that had been brought from Margaret's apartments, because it was safe. He was conscious enough to push the cup away as Cicely tried to coax him into drinking more. The quarrel was clearly not forgotten, because resentment darkened his eyes.

'Leave me,' he breathed. 'Get out of my sight. I never wish to see you again.'

She had not moved. 'Make me go,' she replied, as she would have had he been well. She would *always* confront him and speak her mind. 'You may count upon it that when you are nimble enough to get off that bed, Harri Tudur, I will be even nimbler as I leave of my own accord. So put up with me, Your Majesty, because at the moment I rather think I have the upper hand.'

He gazed at her for a long moment, his brows drawing together as if he thought this nightmare was just that, a nightmare. Then his eyes closed. His lips moved again, but she heard no words.

The physician came to the bedside. 'If it were only the same affliction as before, I would by now be certain of his recovery, but there is the poison to consider. I believe it to be a white powder from Russia, produced from the stones of various fruits. It dissolves easily in wine, and is only detectable by its smell and taste. If the victim can no longer respond to those telltale properties—as is the unfortunate case with His Majesty—' He paused, and turned to Cicely. 'I have often wondered if your late father died of this very thing, my lady. My cousin was in attendance and the symptoms were the same as this, including the smell and taste of almonds.'

Margaret eyed him. 'Are you saying that your cousin attended the Yorkist king? I perceive a certain conflict of loyalty in your family, sir.'

'No conflict, Lady Margaret. My cousin would readily and honestly serve King Henry. We serve England's monarch, whatever his House.' He looked at Cicely again. 'I believe that his liberal ingestion of garlic will bring him to recovery.'

Garlic? Cicely almost wanted to laugh.

'There are few more sovereign remedies than garlic. Once he is able, His Majesty must be *made* to consume it.'

'But, he dislikes garlic even more than almonds,' Margaret observed in puzzlement.

Cicely whispered what Bess had told her.

His mother's lips twitched. 'I do not know which of them is worse,' she muttered.

'Nor do I.' Cicely turned to the physician. 'We will see that he eats garlic,' she said.

Margaret and the physician adjourned to the other room, deep in conversation, but Cicely remained with Henry. She gazed down at him. Please let this not be Tal's work, or anyone else she would wish to shield.

A spasm of pain twisted through him, and he doubled up, awakening as the agony overtook him. She managed to push a small bowl to his mouth as he vomited. He clutched her hand as the retching continued.

Master Rogers hastened back, with Margaret at his heels. Cicely would have moved aside, but Henry's fingers were like claws. The empty retching continued to rack his body. Yellow bile was all he brought up, and he lost control

221

of his functions again. He was in such griping pain that he almost wept of it, and Cicely could have wept with him.

She doubted if he realized that he held her hand or even that he gripped a hand at all. It clearly helped him to endure what was happening, and so after several attempts to free herself, she moved a little closer, to let him gain what relief he could, even though she felt her bones would be broken.

Margaret could not bear his misery, and sank to her knees again with his prayer book and rosary.

When the spasms ended Henry's grip on Cicely's hand tightened cruelly. 'Get out,' he whispered. 'Get out, I do not want you here.' Then he released her.

She glanced unhappily at Margaret and the physician. 'I must go, I think. My presence may do more harm than good. I will not return unless I am summoned.'

Margaret was dismayed. 'I am so sorry, my dear.'

Gathering her skirts, Cicely took her outdoor clothes from the chair and left by the back door, which Margaret came to bolt behind her. Once in the passage, Cicely pulled the cloak around herself and eased the hood into place as well. Then she went down through the palace, towards the route to the river. She could have used the safe pass, and in view of what was soon to befall her, it would have been wiser to have done so. Instead she chose to be alone. But there were great dangers awaiting a woman alone in London after dark.

The night air was cold, and torches smoked and danced as a slight breeze wafted upriver from the distant sea. Everything was that odd grey-white hue caused by snow, and tonight it was almost ghostly. No one glanced at her when she hailed a skiff at the stairs and accepted the boatman's hand to step into it. The little craft was poled away from the shore. Cast adrift, she thought wryly.

When the skiff reached Three Cranes wharf, and she

was helped to the lowermost step because the tide had only just turned, the almost deserted quay gave her pause to wish she had used Henry's note after all. Suddenly it seemed a long way to St Sithe's Lane, with shadows and alleys where footpads and other villains might lurk. But the skiff was already sliding away again, downstream towards London Bridge. She had no option but go on.

She hastened across the quay and into the narrow way that led up towards Thames Street. Everything was quiet, except for the few taverns she passed, including the Mermaid in Gough's Alley, a blind way where she had saved Jack and Tal from being overheard by one of Henry's spies—the same whore who had accosted Jack on the Three Cranes steps.

St Sithe's Lane was a long, steady climb, especially in the dark, but just as she came in sight of Pasmer's Place, there was a swift tread behind her. She whirled around and in a blur saw a man, his arm raised to strike. Her brief scream for help was cut short as he chopped the side of his hand against the back of her neck. A truly sickening pain engulfed her, she slumped awkwardly and heavily to her knees and then to the freezing ice-streaked cobbles, striking her forehead in the fall. He caught her ankles and dragged her to the side of the street, where a deep-set, disused doorway offered him the privacy he wanted. The pain was nauseating, but she was too dazed to fend him off as he undid his hose and dragged her skirts up.

He was heavy and malodorous, with a big belly and unshaved chin, and his breath stank of stale ale as he tried to force himself into her, but then someone, another man, began shouting. Frightened, her attacker scrambled to his feet again and fled as the shouts redoubled.

Footsteps ran towards her, and a second man crouched. 'Sweet Jesu, it is Lady Welles!' he cried out in dismay as someone else joined him.

Cicely thought she recognized his voice, but her consciousness was receding, and she knew no more.

A woman spoke right next to her. 'My lady? My lady, can you hear me?'

Confused and a little disturbed, Cicely tried to open her eyes. At first they would not obey, but then she was able to see again. She was in bed at Pasmer's Place, with a pleasant herbal scent enveloping her. The bedchamber was warm and firelit.

Mary was relieved. 'We thought you would never awaken, my lady.'

What was she talking about? Cicely gazed up at her, still halfway between unconsciousness and awareness.

'Do you remember what happened, my lady?' Mary asked, her voice oddly echoing. 'You were attacked in the lane.'

Awful remembrance returned, and Cicely tried to sit up, but blinding pain drove through her head and she fell back. 'Sweet Jesu …'

'Try not to move, my lady. My aunt says you will be well again soon, but in the meantime, you are not to move any more than you absolutely have to. She has been to attend to you, and has left a little phial of her strongest poppy juice to administer when you awaken and feel pain. She says it will help you to relax and rest.' The maid held up a little spouted cup. 'Will you take some, my lady?'

Cicely sipped it several times.

Mary smiled. 'That's good. Oh, Tom waits, in case he should be of use to you.'

'Was it Tom who came to me in the lane?'

'Yes, my lady. He was bringing me back here on his horse when we heard your scream. We saw the man running off. We had stopped him from … well, I think you know.'

'You say Tom is here? Please bring him to me.'

'To your bedside?' Mary was a little disapproving.

'How else may I thank him? I can thank *you* now, Mary, and do so from the bottom of my heart.'

'I will bring him, my lady.'

Mary's brother was in his thirties, tall, sturdily built, clean-shaven and good-looking, with a complexion that was weathered by constant hours in the brisk, open air of Lincolnshire. His long hair was the colour of hazelnuts, but of late had taken a golden tint at the ends. His eyes were hazelnut too. Kind, trustworthy, strong eyes. Like all of him, Cicely thought. He was dressed in black leather, but modestly, without adornment, and his manner was always reassuringly good-natured and calm.

He waited patiently for her to speak, but she was struggling to concentrate, because the poppy juice was beginning to take effect. 'It is good to see you again, Tom-m.' Her lips were unwilling to obey, and he seemed to be fading, as if into a fog.

'The compliment is returned ten times over, my lady.' He bowed over her hand.

She tried to answer, but an incredibly pleasant sense of lethargy was spreading through her. It was delicious, all her aches were melting, and she was drifting away. She was vaguely aware of Mary addressing Tom.

'It is our aunt's most powerful poppy juice, Tom. She will soon be well again.'

'I pray so, Mary, I pray so. When she awakens, will you tell her I have sent word to Lord Welles?'

'I do not know that he will respond.'

Chapter Nineteen

SEVERAL DAYS LATER, Cicely was able to sit by the fire in her bedchamber. She wore leaf-green velvet, there was an ugly bruise and swelling on her forehead and the back of her neck, and her knees were sore because she had slumped on them. But she *was* improving. Her hair was not confined in a headdress, because the weight made her neck feel even worse.

Tom had brought Leo to visit Pasmer's Place several times, ostensibly to see his 'aunt', Mary, but really to see his mother. Cicely was astonished by how much her son had changed in the months since she had last been with him. He was now very close to his second birthday, and less of a baby, more a little boy. To look into his grey eyes was to be with Richard again. So much of him was his father that she wept a little after each visit.

Jon's response to news of her injuries was perfunctory. Writing from Bolingbroke, he said he would await more information before abandoning his duties to return to London. It was a cold, formal letter, and did not merit the dignity of a reply. Let him stay there forever, Cicely thought, hurt. After this, she would *never* let him know she cared.

Henry's illness had not become common fame, and in the absence of any word from Margaret, Cicely had no idea how he was now. She might not have heard anything at all, had not Bess come to Pasmer's Place—in a litter, because of her condition, but still with such royal splendour she almost brought the streets of Cordwainer Ward to a complete halt.

The Queen of England entered Cicely's parlour, a vision in jewels and crimson trimmed with ermine. The delicate veil of her wired headdress billowed as she gestured to Cicely to remain seated, and then bent to embrace her warmly.

'Oh, Cissy, how dreadful a thing to have happened to you. Thank goodness your Master Kymbe was close by!'

'I am recovering well enough, but know I look as if I have been dragged through a hedge.'

Bess inspected her forehead. 'You would not fib to me about recovering?'

'Of course not.'

Bess took a seat. 'Are you not going to ask me how Henry is?'

'How is Henry?'

'Recovering, although, of course, I am not supposed to know he was ill in the first place. But I have my ways of finding out. Poison, I gather, as well as his usual affliction of the lungs.' Bess smiled. 'I suppose I should not be surprised he did not detect anything wrong with his wine, for he cannot smell or taste almonds.'

'So I now understand.' Cicely tried not to see any implication in the remark.

'He told me some months ago, when I offered him some particularly good marzipan. As you can imagine, I have taken great delight in offering marzipan again since then.'

'Oh, Bess.'

'Anyway, at the moment he is being disagreeable again,

so he must be getting better. More is the pity. I had a fancy to wear mourning for him.'

'Do not say that.'

Bess rested her hands across her round belly in a rather odd way, as if something was wrong.

Cicely noticed. 'How are you, Bess? Is everything all right?'

'I … think so.'

'You have doubts?' Cicely sat forward in concern.

'I just feel different.' Bess smiled. 'Perhaps I am carrying a girl this time, which will not please Henry.'

'I am sure Henry will be pleased whichever it is, boy or girl.'

'Speaking of boys, what of your Leo? I know he is in London. Does he flourish?'

'Oh, yes. He is beautiful.'

'Which means he takes after his father, not his mother,' Bess said mischievously.

Cicely smiled. 'He has been coming here to see me, but I do not want to arouse too much interest, so I intend to go to him on his birthday. St Valentine's Day. Anonymously, of course.'

'May I come too?'

Cicely was a little startled. 'Why, yes, of course, but *not* if you display more of today's royal pomp.'

'Oh, I can be discreet when I need to be,' Bess said softly. 'In fact, I can be really devious. Henry would be surprised if he knew. More than merely surprised,' she added with a low laugh that made Cicely want to shiver.

Bess stayed for a while, and left again well before the February afternoon light faded, but several hours later, when it was fully dark, Cicely received the sad news that when Bess alighted from her litter at Westminster, the horses had shifted suddenly and she had been knocked over. She lost her baby. A boy.

Cicely went to her immediately with Tom, Mary and the guards Jon provided for her.

Once at the palace, Mary was sent to prepare the small apartment that Cicely always used, because—Henry's orders or not—she intended to stay for as long as she was needed. Tom provided sturdy assistance for the walk through the candlelit passages to the queen's apartments.

But she could not go inside because Henry, seemingly well again, was visiting his wife. Many of his gentlemen waited outside, and Cicely's arrival on the arm of a man who was clearly a commoner made them talk quietly among themselves. Then the doors opened without warning, and Henry emerged. He wore pine green, and fingered the coiled silver dragon suspended from his collar. His face was grey, there was a firm set to his mouth, and sadness shone in his eyes as he pushed his way through his confused entourage, until coming face to face with Cicely.

He halted abruptly, clearly taken unawares, both by her presence and by the severity of the bruise on her forehead. 'Lady Welles?'

She dropped into a respectful but painful curtsey, from which he raised her, but his quick attention moved to Tom. 'Kymbe, is it not?'

'Yes, Your Majesty.' Tom executed a deep, more than competent bow.

'Why are you not with my uncle?'

'He has given me leave of absence, Your Majesty.'

'Why? What brings you here from Lincolnshire?' The suspicious edge was there. As always.

'I have brought my aunt and my son to London to see my sister, Lady Welles's maid.'

'Ah, yes. Now I recall. I trust your son is in rude health?'

'Indeed so, Your Majesty. I thank you for your kindness.'

Henry waved him away, as well as the guards and his gentlemen, and when they were at a safe distance, he spoke to Cicely. 'I have only just been informed of your encounter with danger, my lady. Why did you not see fit to send word to me?'

'I did not think Your Majesty would wish to be concerned with so minor a matter,' she answered respectfully, because formality was clearly his wish. Of necessity in front of others? Perhaps, although she was not quite sure. There was something in his glance. A great regret? Yes, and it could only be the loss of the baby. She wanted to touch him, to show her sympathy, but everything prevented it.

'I am always concerned about the well-being of my sister-in-law,' he responded at last, his tone oddly level. He was not at ease. His one eye wandered a little, and he smoothed his eyebrow in an attempt to conceal it. Control it, perhaps. 'You ... visit the queen?' he asked then.

'Yes, Your Majesty.' She felt very awkward. Was he angry that she had come here without his permission? 'Your Majesty, if I have offended you, I—'

'I am not offended, my lady. Why would you think that?'

She gazed at him. Because not even with a glance had he shown any fondness.

'The queen will be glad to see you, I am sure,' he said then. 'I trust you can comfort her.'

'I ... am so very sorry for what has happened today.' She was aware of the continuing unkind interest of his gentlemen, watching from further along the passage, and she felt as if her face, already enough of a sight, was now on fire.

'Today? Yes. Quite so.' The tear-brightness was in his eyes again, and she knew he was distressed. But had he let Bess know? Or had he concealed it? This was a time to share emotion with his queen, not crush it as he so often did. As both of them did.

He was a little distracted. 'Be what solace you can to her. If you wish to stay, do so, for however many days you choose, but there is another matter I must discuss with you. Privately. If you would be so good as to attend upon me one hour from now? Without a stray Lincolnshire mongrel sniffing at your heels,' he added pointedly, glancing in Tom's direction.

Cicely blushed and inclined her head as respectfully as she could, given the discomfort in her neck. There was something different about him, and it made her anxious. 'Is something wrong? Please tell me,' she begged quietly, so that only he could possibly hear. 'You have fully recovered from your … ailment?'

'There was no indisposition,' he said coldly, and then walked on, his gentlemen congregating hastily behind him.

The guards resumed their places, flanking the doors, and she struggled to regain her composure, managing to smile at Tom. 'Thank you for escorting me, but I think you should return to wherever you would be were it not for me. I have Mary here, and my guards.'

'Send for me if I am needed, my lady. I will come with all haste.'

'I know. Thank you, Tom.'

Bess was very upset about the loss of another baby. And because it was for the same reason as the first, a fall. She was glad of Cicely, who sat on the bed to hug her tightly. The sisters clung together.

'Oh, Cissy, I *knew* something was wrong. I felt so strange, as if someone was at my shoulder all the time, wishing me ill. And I did not *really* mean what I said about deliberately losing my babies, truly I did not!' More tears flowed.

'I know, sweetheart. I know.' Cicely, stroked the long red-gold hair.

'Two babies, and this one the boy Henry so needs. What if I cannot have another? Everything will rest upon Arthur.'

'You must not think that way, Bess. You are strong and

healthy, and you will recover. What did Henry say to you?' *Please let him have been kind.*

'He was gentle,' Bess conceded unwillingly, for she was loath to say anything good of him.

'You see? He is not as base as you think.'

'Do not defend him. Not today,' Bess whispered, lying back. 'You will stay here for a day or so?'

'Yes, of course. For as long as you need me. Mary is already preparing my old rooms. And the king has desired me to stay as well, to attend you, not for any other reason. I saw him a moment ago, as he was leaving you.' She felt she had to add this, for fear Bess might think she had been alone with Henry.

Bess was remorseful. 'Oh, Cissy, it is selfish to call you when you are unwell.'

'Nonsense. I am your sister and you need me. You are worse now than me.'

'Is Jon to return?'

'No, nor do I wish him to.'

Bess was dismayed. 'You are really so divided?'

'It would appear so.'

Bess squeezed her hand. 'I am sure all will be well again soon.'

'There can be no hope if he does not even return to London. I miss him, Bess, but—'

'But?'

'Oh, nothing. I have upset him greatly, and now … well, he has upset me in return. We need to be together if we are to mend matters.'

'He will return, sweetheart, I know he will.'

'Which will please Annie, I suppose,' Cicely replied, thinking of Roland.

'Oh, she has been busy flirting with Thomas Howard and Cousin Edmund.'

Cicely shuddered. 'I imagine the former's embrace

would be clumsy, and the latter's clammy.'

'Indeed.' Bess managed a giggle. It made her feel better to exchange such silliness with her sister. 'But, I suppose Jon will bring Roland de Vile-Vole back into the fold.'

Someone coughed discreetly behind them, a pretty little cough. Annie, as fresh as a daffodil in yellow. She appeared to have just entered, but might have been there a little longer, Cicely thought, becoming deeply suspicious on receiving an unexpectedly warm smile.

Bess beckoned. 'Come, Annie.'

Cicely rose and moved aside as Annie ran to embrace the queen. 'Oh, Bess —Your Grace—Your Majesty—I am *so* upset for you and the dear king!'

Dear king? Cicely's thoughts returned to sanctuary at Westminster Abbey in 1483, when Bess had spoken of her 'dear Richard'. That was the first time she, Cicely, had begun to realize that Bess felt much more for Richard than she should have. Two years later, Cicely herself had experienced that same intense, incestuous love. But … might Annie regard *Henry* in such a light?

Perhaps this was the time to remind her about Margaret. 'Annie, Lady Margaret has warned you about being forward where His Majesty is concerned. You must not call him your "dear king", but confine yourself to correct conduct.'

Bess nodded as well. 'Indeed so, Annie. It is not wise to refer to him in such a familiar way.'

'But I do not mean anything wrong.'

Bess was stern. 'Maybe not, but that is no excuse. You are still a child, and must behave like one.'

Annie's face was aflame—as much with anger as mortification. Clearly she regarded herself as a woman already. But she murmured politely and dropped into a deep, very respectful, regretful curtsey. Cicely could almost hear her thoughts. *There, my repentance is shown, and that is the end of it, now I will continue to do as I wish ….*

233

Bess managed a smile that was intended to be reassuring. 'Thank you for your kindness in coming here, Annie.'

Her moment of disgrace over, Annie blinked and summoned a convincing wobble to her lips. 'Your poor little baby,' she snuffled, searching in her purse for a kerchief. Then, after blowing her nose very prettily, she suddenly flung herself on her knees before Cicely and hugged her tightly. 'Oh, Cissy! I did so want to be an aunt again!'

The tears seemed genuine, and the girl's whole body shook as she gave in to tears. It was as if she needed to sob away more than just this immediate sorrow. Her fingernails dug through Cicely's gown. 'I *am* sorry, Cissy, I am so sorry for being such a ... a *bitch*!'

Bess was shocked. 'Annie!'

'Forgive me, *please*, but I do so want to be as close to Cissy as I was when I was little.' The girl was imploring. 'Please, Cissy, let me come to stay with you for a while.'

Ah, the grief and repentance was feigned, Cicely thought, the little cat had heard them speak of Roland coming to Pasmer's Place! Cicely did not know what to fix upon with this particular sister, save she was *not* to be trusted.

But Bess was taken in. 'Oh, Annie, how sweet a thing you are. Of course you can stay with Cicely. Is that not so?'

The last was said to Cicely, who could do little more than smile and consent. 'Although I do not know when I will return,' she said lamely, and did not need to *see* Annie's smug smile.

Bess was suddenly weary. Conversation had drained her, and her loss began to overwhelm her again. 'Please, Annie, I mean you no unkindness, but I would like to be alone with Cissy. She knows what it is to ... to lose a baby.'

Annie was all understanding. 'Yes, of course. Cissy, you will not forget to take me to Pasmer's Place with you?'

'Of course not.' Cicely forced a smile. She did *not* want Annie and Roland de Vielleville under the Welles roof. It could only lead to trouble.

She remained with Bess after Annie had gone, and they talked of this and that—mostly silly memories—until Bess felt able to sleep. 'Please come back to me in the morning, Cissy.'

'Yes, of course.'

Bess closed her eyes. 'Everything I do turns to dust,' she whispered. 'Everything fails, no matter how I try. I only want to be happy again.'

Cicely went openly to Henry's apartments, because his summons had been issued in front of his gentlemen.

Candles shimmered, and flames leapt in the fireplace as Henry paced slowly, while dictating a letter to one of his secretaries. He acknowledged her without particular attention, indicated she should be seated, and then continued dictating.

The letter was not important, but he attended to it assiduously. As he did everything. His black velvet hat lay on the table, its brooch shining in the candlelight that shivered in the draught when he sat to read the letter, using the new spectacles he hated so much. The deep shadow beneath his jaw towards his ear was sharply defined, and his hair did not gleam as it should. But then, how could it when he had been both ill *and* subjected to poisoning? It was a miracle he had recovered as much as he had.

She continued to watch him. Sometimes it was almost impossible not to. His elegant, long-fingered hands rested together by the fingertips as he read, and his head was at a slight angle. He was ... spellbinding, she supposed, as he signed the letter, sanded it and applied his signet to the small pool of wax prepared by the secretary.

He was no battle leader, she thought, but a clerk of the highest order, efficient, seldom misled and always achieving the perfect balance. He was no less a king for it, but

Richard had attended to all these things and was an experienced soldier as well.

As the secretary hurried away, closing the door behind him, Henry removed his spectacles. 'You disapprove of my thoroughness?'

'No, but I see what it does to your eyes.'

'The machinations of the French strain me far more. They want me to support them when they endeavour to annex Brittany. I am in debt to both sides, as you know. The situation is thorny.' He met her eyes, with the strange unhappiness of earlier. 'I loathe war.'

'Which will always worry at your heels, and you will always have pretenders to confront.'

'How kind of you to remind me. Your tongue clearly did not suffer when you were attacked.'

'You look so very pale,' she observed.

'Poisoning is apt to have that effect. Fortunately, my habit is often to sip only a little of a cup of wine, and then leave it.' His fingers rapped on the table, and he stood. 'I understand I have you to thank for the poison's discovery.'

'I merely queried the apparent presence of almonds.'

'It was enough. Thank you. Truly. You may have saved my life.'

'You seem surprised. Did you imagine I would say nothing?'

'After what happened between us, I would have expected it.'

'No, you would not, Henry Tudor. We may have quarrelled very badly, but I still would not let you die. Am I to think *you* would let *me* die?'

'You know the answer to that, *cariad*.'

'I am your *cariad* again?'

He gazed at her, something hovering on his lips, but then he spoke of the poison again. 'I have set my spies to trace the origin of the poison, of course, and the whole sequence of events between the wine arriving at Three Cranes and reaching my cup will be thoroughly examined. I will have everyone involved questioned.'

'Questioned?'

He met her eyes. 'Do you think I should be lenient with those suspected of trying to kill me?'

'You are not known for lenience.'

He did not respond, which somehow made her words sound spiteful. She had to say something. 'Have ... have you any idea who might have done it?'

He shook his head. 'Some Yorkist, no doubt,' he said wryly.

'Or just someone who does not like you.'

'The likes of which number in thousands upon thousands?'

Was that the familiar edge in his voice? 'Please, Henry, do not start upon me again.'

'I am calm enough. *Did* you take Richard and Lincoln as your lovers?' he asked, then picked up the little golden figurine of St Armel, weighed it in his palm for a moment, before putting it back.

'None of it was true. I deliberately said those things to hurt you.'

He rubbed his eyebrow, and went to look from the window towards the lights on the Thames. 'You succeeded beyond your wildest hopes. I *want* to believe your denials about Richard, Cicely, for I cannot endure the thought of you lying with him, but I know you did. I would rather believe it was only Lincoln.'

'It was neither of them. I am sorry I said it. *So* sorry.' And she was, because she ought to have been cleverer. Instead, she had lost her temper as much as he had. Now he was almost too calm.

'Why did you not tell me what had happened to you?' he asked suddenly.

'How could I? I thought I had been dismissed forever. You ordered me away when I so wanted to help you. You seemed to hate me.'

'Never strike me again, Cicely.'

'Is that my sin? Shall I make deep obeisance to you, to beg forgiveness? If that is what you wish, I will do it.' She paused. 'Something is very wrong, is it not?'

'I … so wanted to share with you. A private matter. Something so important to me, so vital and yet terrible that—' He did not finish. 'Not that it makes any difference now, and so perhaps it is as well I said nothing. All things being equal.'

A terrible realization began to dawn through her. He was going to end matters between them. The fact was there, touching her across the room, and she could only gaze at him, not wanting to believe it.

He dragged a finger over his eyelid. 'I want you to know that my reason for sending you away was not because I was angry with you, but with myself.'

'Yourself?' She pulled her scattered thoughts together.

'For being in such an abject state, and to be so in front of you.'

She gazed at him. 'It did not matter to me, Henry, my only concern was to help you.'

'It mattered to me. You were the last person I wished to have observing me puking my guts up and shitting myself. Lying there like a baby, needing my arse cleaned, the vomit wiped from my mouth and my cock held to a jar for me to pee. Sweet Jesu, Cicely, I knew enough of what was happening to know how I appeared.'

'It did not matter to *me*,' she said again, because it was true. 'Lady Margaret and I knew how distressed you would be by it, and we felt so much for you. It was not your fault, and if you could have kept control, you would. Revulsion was the very last thing I felt. I wanted to hold you and comfort you, but you would not have permitted any such tenderness, nor do you even now. If you consider my claims about Richard and Jack to have caused you pain, then you must also consider the pain you caused me by dismissing me as you did. And by dismissing me forever, as I know you intend to now.' She wanted him to deny it, to reassure her.

'Still, in the depths of your soul, you support my enemies,' he said softly.

'I am not here now as a Yorkist.'

'What are you here for?'

'You commanded me to come,' she answered. It was the wrong answer and she knew it, but what else could she say?

'You have come to Westminster to see the queen, your sister. Would you have come to see me had I not commanded it?'

'Be fair to me, Henry, you *know* I could not have come to you. You had sent me away.'

'What is Kymbe to you?'

The change of subject should not have shaken her as it did, and she could not hide her shocked dismay. 'Nothing! How can you possibly think it?'

'He looked at you familiarly, I thought.'

'No, Henry. Tom Kymbe and I are acquaintances, we know each other because of Jon and because of my maid. That is all. Please, stop this.'

'You seem inordinately upset.'

'Of *course* I am!' she cried. 'Tom Kymbe is my husband's man, and he escorted me here today because he is good and kind, not because he and I are secret lovers. Oh, Henry, will you *never* stop?'

'No, because I know Kymbe wishes to be your lover! It is written all over him!'

'Stop! Please ...' Her voice broke, and tears leapt to her

eyes. She could not endure this tonight. He made her feel she was about to be arrested. She turned away, biting her lip and trying to hide her unhappiness.

He came to her then, caught her hands, linked his fingers through hers and pulled their bodies together. 'Forgive me, *cariad*, forgive me everything.'

She closed her eyes and breathed the cloves again as he rocked them both gently. What was it that made this man so very different from all the others? Different as a man. It was nothing to do with him being the king. He had such an odd little charm, a way of caressing her senses that she had long since given up trying to resist. They were tied, and even though she was certain it was all now at a physical end, and that she loved Jack a thousand times more, that tie would always be there.

'Say it, Henry. Just say it, and let me go,' she whispered.

He released her and moved away to the table. The cloves went with him. 'Have you sent for my uncle?' he asked, walking his fingertips over the hat brooch.

'Yes. I do not think he intends to return.'

'So, after all the turmoil of making me agree to your match, suddenly it is over anyway?' He walked his fingers over the brooch again. 'I would like to see Kymbe's son.'

'See him?' Cicely was alarmed.

'I wish him to be brought to me. I thought the boy charming and will be interested in his progress. I like children.' He looked away again, and she saw his unhappiness over Bess's loss. *He* had lost as well, but would not say so.

But Cicely's heart thudded like a hammer out of fear for Leo. 'I ... I am sure Tom Kymbe would be honoured.'

He looked at her for a long moment, during which she could not gauge what his thoughts might be, and then he came to her once more. 'I will not keep you longer, for I am sure you have matters to attend to.'

'I mean to stay until Bess is better.' The air seemed suddenly empty, as if something momentous had happened. 'Say it,' she whispered again. 'Cast me off, for that is what you mean to do. I can see the farewell in your eyes.'

'You have been slipping from me, and today, at last, I realize I must let you go. I do not want this to happen, nor have I sought it without realizing, but now that I am confronted ... well, maybe it is for the best.'

'The best?' She could barely collect her common sense. She should be exulting, but was not.

'Yes.'

She was numb. He had become so important in her life that being without him was hard to contemplate. He, who had taken so much away from her, was now taking himself away as well. Was it not what she had always wanted? She could not believe it was happening.

'Henry ... please. I do not understand.'

'It is simple enough, *cariad*. I will no longer send for you or impose upon your life. I release you from your bondage, and I withdraw all my ignoble threats. You are free of me.'

'Without even one small kiss goodbye?' The words were hardly audible.

'I cannot, *cariad*. I cannot. Please do not ask.' She stretched out a hand, but he stayed beyond reach. 'No, *cariad*. For it is all I can do not to break down before you.'

'What did I do? Is it that I am of the House of York?'

'You have not done anything. Parting from you is the hardest thing I have had to do in my life, harder than taking the throne, but I *must* do it. I will not say why, for my reason shames me. I can only ask, again, for your forgiveness. Please, *cariad*.'

'You know you have it, Henry.' Tears wended down her cheeks, and she was so immersed in emotion and regret that she might have drowned of it.

Now he came close again, to put his hand to her cheek

and part her lips softly with his thumb. *'R'wyn dy garu di,'* he murmured.

'What does that mean?' she found herself asking, almost absently, for it sounded the same as something he had said to her before—'I need you'—and yet it was slightly different.

'Nothing of importance. I … will go now. Leave whenever you are ready.'

She nodded, but did not look at him as his soft steps retreated. Then there was silence, broken only by the sound of the fire shifting in the hearth. A great hollow might have been gouged inside her.

The emerald ring he had given her was on her finger, and she removed it slowly to place it on the table next to the hat he had forgotten.

She struggled to appear calm and collected as she made her way slowly back through the palace to her apartment, where Mary realized immediately that something was wrong.

'My lady?' she ventured anxiously as she unpinned Cicely's headdress and loosened her hair.

'I cannot speak of it yet, Mary. Not yet.'

The relief of having her hair loose again made her feel as if she herself had been released, and yet not quite. She turned for Mary to unfasten her gown, but the maid shook her head.

'It … is best I do not, my lady.'

'Do not? Why?'

Jack spoke from behind her. 'Because *I* am here, sweetheart.'

She turned, so glad that she burst into tears. He came to embrace her and run loving fingers into her hair at the nape of her neck. 'Tell me, sweetheart. Is it Henry? Has he—?'

He stopped as he saw the stricken look on her face, and then nodded at Mary to leave them alone. He ushered

Cicely to the bed, where he sat her down on the edge and then sat beside her, his arm lovingly around her shoulder.

'Tell me now, sweetheart. What has the damned Tudor done to upset you so?'

'He ... has cast me off, set me free, liberated me from bondage. Call it what you will.'

Jack was startled. 'I do not believe it. If he has said it, you can be sure he does not mean it.'

'But he does.' She looked at him, and frowned. 'You have cut your beautiful hair. All those curls.' She reached up to touch the shorn locks.

'It identified me too distinctively.'

Her mind leapt to something else. 'Bess lost her baby today, did you know?'

'Yes. The world speaks of it. Some say it is Henry's punishment for usurping the throne. They only whisper it, of course.' He smoothed her hair back from her face. 'Tell me what happened with Henry.'

She described the meeting, and then was silent for a moment. 'He has been part of my life for a long time now, and I have become accustomed to him. Suddenly he has done this, and I do not know what I think or feel. Except emotional.' She bit her lip as the urge to cry came close again. Then she looked him, reproachfully. 'Are you *determined* to put yourself in danger? Why have you come here? Once again into the lion's den. And how did you even *know* I was here?'

'Because word of Bess's loss is spreading, and I knew you would come to her. To these rooms, where you and I have shared the bed before now. How is she?'

'I do not really know. She really does despise Henry, Jack. Deeply.'

'As do many, sweetheart.'

She looked at him again. 'Even without your curls you might easily be recognized.'

243

'Not even Edmund noticed me. I walked past him quite brazenly, but he was too taken up with making ram's eyes at some flibbertigibbet, who would not see trouble if it jumped in her path playing the bagpipes.'

'Jack, it was Edmund who broke into Flemyng Court.'

'I already know. Edgar told me.'

'Well, he cannot have told you Edmund recognized your ring on my finger.'

Jack drew back. 'Are you sure?'

'Oh, yes. And one of his friends identified me to him. I did not show him the respect he considered to be his due, and his revenge was to send an anonymous note to Henry, telling him I was at Flemyng Court, naked, in Tal's bed, wearing your ring.'

Jack drew a heavy breath. 'Edmund is a—'

'Feculent little anus, according to Lady Margaret.'

'Really? I would like to see Henry's face if she said that in front of him.'

'He probably said it first. However, I was prepared for Edmund's revenge, and bought another amethyst ring that on initial glance resembles yours. And I added a story of very loose bowels and indisposition that forced me to seek shelter at Flemyng Court overnight.'

Jack grinned. 'The devil you did. Such initiative. And Henry believed you?'

'I think so. We fell out, but about something else.' She told him.

'He struck you again?' Jack's eyes hardened.

She rose agitatedly. 'Do not do anything, Jack de la Pole. I want your promise.'

He stood as well. 'Cicely, if he beat you—'

'He did not *beat* me. I goaded him, and then gave as good as I got. It was a heated exchange that became physical. I would have hit him twice, had he not caught my wrists.'

Jack's face changed. '*You* hit *him*?'

'Oh, there are other things you cannot know. Someone tried to poison him, and almost succeeded. I must ask … could it have been Tal?'

'No, definitely not. Esher was solely due to Eleanor. He is otherwise a calm and sober man, as dedicated as I am to use Roland as our weapon.'

'Then … Jack, I have a dreadful fear that it might be Bess.'

He stared. 'Bess? A *poisoner*? You jest.'

'Oh, she is capable, believe me. The sweet Bess of the past has gone.'

'Cicely, there never was a sweet Bess. I have never liked her, nor will I ever. And what possible good would it do her to—' He broke off thoughtfully. 'Henry dead, she would be the Queen Mother, and those—such as Margaret—who think she is ineffective, would have a very great surprise to find what she really can be. It will be 1483 again, with a struggle for control of a boy king. If she turns to her Woodville connections, and sets herself up as York against the Tudors and Lancastrians, well, she might easily become the most powerful woman in the realm.'

Cicely found it hard to imagine Bess being so far-sighted, but the ruthlessness was certainly there already.

'We are wasting precious time, my darling,' he said quietly, and kissed her cheek, and then her ear, his soft breath making her shiver with pleasure. She gasped as his tongue explored her ear, tenderly, excitingly.

He pulled her against his loins, and dropped kisses on her shoulders as he unfastened her gown simply by reaching around her. A lover as practised as Jack de la Pole did not need to move behind his lady in order to divest her of her gown.

His lips toyed with hers again. He was the essence of seduction, and the embodiment of masculine temptation as he took her hand and guided it down to his erection, which strained eagerly at the laces of his hose. 'Now then, my sweet lady, I am going to take you to that bed, and lay you down. Then, starting at your pretty toes, my lips will venture slowly up towards the softness of your inner thighs, and after that ... my tongue can pay homage to those hidden places of which I think so very often.'

Chapter Twenty

JON, VISCOUNT WELLES, returned to London on the afternoon of 12 February, with Roland de Vielleville in his retinue. Word of his approach had been sent ahead, and his viscountess waited in the parlour, intending to accord him no more than a courteous welcome.

Annie waited with her, but Cicely wished the girl anywhere but here at Pasmer's Place. Sister or not, she was a vexing, discordant presence. Outwardly fresh and innocent, fair and sweet, when caught in an unguarded moment, she was sleek, sly and serpentine ... and almost unctuous in her fawning capacity for dishonesty. Mary reported that away from Cicely, she persisted in referring to Henry as the 'dear king', claiming that he was particularly gracious, kind and thoughtful where she was concerned. He would have to be warned, and his mother was the one to do it. His discarded lover could hardly approach him on such a delicate matter.

Annie was seated primly at her embroidery, looking as if she did not even know that God had created a masculine gender. She was dainty in a gown the colour of dusty lavender to match her eyes, and had a little silver netted cap that looped prettily behind her ears. Her hair spilled down her back, and the small pendant cross of green and blue beryl rested against her breast. She looked utterly charming, and Cicely was sure it was for Roland's benefit, but no doubt *he* would be too busy being vain to even notice.

In spite of her irritation, Cicely was worried. Annie seemed set on a disastrous course, and might not be so fortunate as to find a Jon Welles to whisk her from the jaws of scandal and ruin. It was this last thought that preoccupied Cicely as she waited. Jon had rescued her when she was unmarried, frightened and with child, and she should *never* forget it. Or that her conduct had given him every reason to feel angry and aggrieved.

It was approaching the early winter dark when Jon's cavalcade finally rode along St Sithe's Lane and into the torch-lit yard, where the snow was piled around and the icy cobbles had been strewn with straw and sand. Cicely went down to meet him, with Annie at her heels. The fading day was bitterly cold as they emerged into the yard, which was now filled with horsemen. Jon's rampant black-lion cognizance fluttered above them on bright-yellow banners.

Jon was travel-stained and tired, wearing a thick cloak over his attire. He saw her, but his face gave nothing away as he began to dismount. 'Madam. I trust you are well again?' he said, his tone expressionless.

'Well enough.' Then she hesitated. Were they to continue as if they had never meant anything to each other? His past kindness and gallantry could *not* be forgotten or pushed aside. Determined to reach him again somehow, she hurried to hug him before he had time to prepare himself for whatever he had originally intended. He felt cold, and smelled of leather and horses, but it was good to hold him again, because he also smelled of rosemary, which *she* had chosen for him. Did he still wear the turquoise ring? She could not see, for he wore gauntlets.

'I am glad you are home again, Jon,' she whispered close to his ear.

'Are you?'

She heard the cool note. 'Please, Jon, do not continue this. We can still be happy together.'

'It can never be the same again, Cicely.' He removed his gauntlets, and as he tossed them to a nearby servant, she saw the turquoise.

'I know that.' She drew back. 'We are not silly children and I remember all that you did for me after Bosworth. There is still time to rescue our marriage, and I really wish to.'

'But not for love.'

'If you loved me, you would have come here immediately when you heard what had happened to me.'

'How is Lincoln?'

'How is *your* latest love?' she countered. 'Oh, do not pretend there is not one. You have often been unfaithful to me when we have been apart. I know it, even if you will not admit it. We have both overlooked our vows, but I do not wish to lose you. Please, Jon, meet me in this. Let us show a united marriage to the world.'

'So that I can look the fool while you bed Lincoln? No, Cicely.'

The wind sucked down into the yard, tearing at the torches and setting wild whirls of smoke spinning.

She drew back sadly. 'As you wish, Jon, but never forget that I made a conciliatory move. You chose to rebuff me.'

'I simply point out what you expect of me.'

Cicely turned to go back inside, but he spoke again. 'You are right. Let us be civilized. My viscountess has come out to welcome me, and I am content to be welcomed.' He took her hand and rested it over his arm.

It was not much, but constituted a beginning, she thought.

He saw Annie in the entrance. 'We have a guest?'

'I fear so,' she answered dryly.

'You *fear* so?'

'That is something to tell you when we are alone. How is Master Roland?'

'Need you ask?' Jon nodded towards the boy, who was alighting from his rather splendid Spanish mount, a bay that was rare enough for Henry himself, let alone his unacknowledged bastard son, whose dark-blue cloak was rich with embroidery. The vivid, pale-green clothes he wore beneath it were even richer, and he carried himself as if he were someone of immense importance. His face still bore its haughty expression, his lips carried a sneering twist, and his hair seemed unaffected by the rigours of riding.

Annie suddenly caught up her gown and hurried towards the boy. As she called his name and he turned, the interest in his eyes was clear.

Jon watched. 'I have already had good cause to have him beaten for being found in … delicate circumstances. His pizzle needs knotting.' He turned to Roland. 'To your duties, *écuyer*!'

Roland glowered as only he—and perhaps his great-uncle, Jasper Tudor—could, but did as he was told. Annie scowled as well, although quickly dissembled to smile sweetly again as she tripped prettily back to the house.

Jon drew a heavy breath. 'The threat of Henry's ire has so far proved to be a very effective deterrent with our brave Breton. If that fails, his pizzle really will be knotted.'

She smiled a little. 'Jon, I am *so* glad we can at least talk again.'

'Talking does not constitute forgiveness, Cicely. Being dragged into your Yorkist affairs was bad enough, but what really hurt me was your deceit. You did not say Jack was still alive. I find it impossible to forgive, do you understand?'

'Yes.' She would not blame Jack, because she had not been forced to obey him. And Jack *had* been thinking of Jon.

'Yes? Is that all?'

'All?' She looked at Jon. 'What more do you wish me to say? I accept your grievance, Jon. Would you rather I did not?'

He held her glance for a long moment, and then gave a disbelieving laugh. 'Oh, Cicely, you are *never* dull.'

'Nor are you.'

'I am your husband, so allow me the last word, if you please.'

She complied.

He sighed. 'Now you have had the last silence instead.'

In the bedchamber later that night, Lord and Lady Welles sat beside the fire that provided the only light. He was still dressed, but she had changed into her nightclothes. He had ordered the main guest chamber to be prepared for him, and she had said nothing to dissuade him. Maybe she was not ready either. Things were so different now, but they could still keep company.

She had told him about Henry, the poison, her suspicion about Bess, and everything else she could think of, because she was determined to never again be accused of keeping truths from him. But she did not speak of Jack, nor did Jon ask. Lord Lincoln was a forbidden subject.

One thing she mentioned was Henry's cryptic remark about not having confided a secret.

'You say that in a rather odd way,' Jon observed. 'Why? Because if you plan to do anything with Yorkist intent, I—'

'I cannot if I am no longer privy to Henry's thoughts.'

Jon rolled his eyes. 'You think he is going to stay away from you? Dear God, lady, he will be playing with himself all night and day.'

'My concern is Leo. He will grow up to know who he is. I can protect him now, but later … he will be such a danger to Henry…. I have to be York, Jon. If—' She broke off, for intentions were forming that she had not seen coming. 'If Henry wants me to return to him, I will. And if he tells me his secret, I—'

'Do not tell me! There can be too much honesty, Cicely. You already stretch my patience. I made threats at Esher that I have not entirely discarded. Do you understand? We may be relatively civil at this moment, but do not think that you have won me over so easily, because you have not.'

She recoiled a little. 'You have made yourself clear, I think. So do you wish to know that the Kymbes have brought Leo here to London? To the house you so thoughtfully secured, for which I am grateful. I am to go there the day after tomorrow. It will be Leo's birthday,' she added.

'I am aware of the date. He was supposed to have been *our* son, was he not? So, it is two years since you first came to Wyberton? Sometimes it seems as if it were only yesterday. How is he progressing?'

She told him, and then added, 'Henry wishes Leo to be taken to him. He remembers him from Friskney. It is a very great honour to the Kymbes, I know that, but … I am afraid, Jon.'

'There is nothing to be done about it. If Henry wishes to see the boy, then he must be obeyed.'

'Come to see Leo with me, Jon.'

'I cannot. Henry expects me to wait upon him tomorrow and the day after. You must still go, of course.'

'Bess is to accompany me. She has told Henry she wishes to show favour to Mary, whom he remembers was once her maid too.'

'Has she been churched already?' He was surprised.

'No, but there has been some arrangement for just this one day, I do not know what. A priest has been persuaded,

Margaret is compliant, and that appears to be that, although Henry insists she is strictly disguised. No one must know she has emerged before her churching.'

'He indulges her because of their lost child?'

'Presumably.' Yes, that was it, she thought, remembering the look on his face when he had emerged from seeing Bess. She sat forward, the flames dancing over her peach robe. 'If he is attempting to mend matters with Bess, he will not find her in the least receptive. She cannot abide him.'

'And has tried to poison him? I still find that hard to credit.'

'I have only told you what I believe, Jon. Not what I know to be true. And Annie really must be warned of the risk she takes with Roland. And maybe Edmund de la Pole. Both thoughts make me shudder, and if Thomas Howard detects her in anything, she will forfeit him.'

Jon paused. 'To be honest, all three make me shudder. Young Howard repels me as much as the others.'

She was surprised. '*Repels* you?'

Jon was silent for a moment. 'Well, it has been reported to me that he likes to beat his whores. He has a liking for buxom laundry girls, it seems, although whether they like his horse face is anyone's guess. I imagine he is aroused by the smell of starch. I also imagine he pays well, too well for them to say anything. But word is getting around. He apparently has no respect for women. If it's true, then he seems to hide it well enough from Annie, because she is, after all, the queen's sister and therefore a great catch for him when he has no actual prospect of becoming a duke.'

'And you believe the rumours?' she asked.

'Short of having witnessed him thrashing a wench until the starch rises in clouds, there is not a lot I can say, except that I first heard it from someone I would regard as reliable. And, on the few occasions I have been in Howard's company, I simply did not like him.'

Cicely did not know what to think. She had never been impressed by Thomas Howard, but had never suspected anything like this.

Jon rose from his chair. 'I will take my leave now.'

'God keep you, Jon.'

Perhaps he had expected she would plead with him to stay, for he hesitated, but then inclined his head and left her.

Chapter Twenty-One

IT WAS MIDDAY on the Feast of St Valentine, a crisp, sunny, still day that was more April than February. Cicely was impatient as she rode slowly along a thronged Thames Street, with Mary and Tom Kymbe. Following them was the tightly curtained but very plain litter that conveyed Bess, and behind it two armed guards for protection. No one in the city's busiest thoroughfare paid any attention.

There was a shadow over Cicely despite her anticipation, because she was to meet Tal a little later. The fact of meeting him was not the reason, rather was it the tone of his message, because it suggested that something was wrong. She had not even realized he was back in London. Perhaps he had never gone away. If so, Jack did not know. Or had not, the last time she heard from him, which had been the previous night.

Tom had brought the note before she even broke her fast that morning. 'My lady, last night I was approached by the knight you call Tal. He gave me this note for you, and said it was urgent. He asked where you be would today and knew you would be visiting Master Leo. I do not know how. He told me to be sure to give this note to you.'

She broke the seal reluctantly, and read. *St Andrew's*

Wardrobe. 2 after noon, tomorrow. T.

'My lady, he will wait at the church in the hope you can be there. If not, then he will contact you again to meet at the Red Lion, as before.'

Cold anxiety lurked in the pit of Cicely's stomach. The noise and colour all around seemed distant as she wondered if something was wrong. But what could it be? Jack was well enough, she knew. And so was Leo, because Tom had brought news of him when he delivered the note. She could only wait, and pray there was nothing to fear.

Hallows Lane was, like Flemyng Court, almost in the shadow of St Andrew-by-the-Wardrobe, although to the east, and the narrow, three-storeyed house lacked window-panes, having wooden slats and shutters instead. Half-timbered and gabled, its upper floors projecting over the cobbled way, it was separated from an adjoining property by a shared alley to a tiny yard strewn with crushed clinker. There was a single stable, and a small walled garden containing two apple trees that in a few short months now would be sweet with blossom.

The alley was too confined and low for riders, so their horses remained in the lane, obliging Cicely and Bess to alight rather publicly, but they both wore unremarkable clothes, and no one could know that the Queen of England was in lowly Hallows Lane.

Tom and Mary followed them into the low, wainscoted hallway, to offer assistance with their cloaks, and no sooner had that been done than Bess waved them away. 'I would like to speak privately with my sister.'

The brother and sister hurried up the stairs to the next floor, and then into a room on the first landing. Bess turned and spoke in a low voice that was muffled by the wainscoting. 'Cissy, there has been a remarkable change in Henry. He has been all kindness and attention since I lost the baby.'

'Indeed?'

'Yes. Not that it changes anything for me. I actually applaud the poisoner's valiant attempt.'

Cicely hoped nothing showed on her face. 'Oh, Bess, you ought to try a little. He clearly is.' She thought again of the moment she had encountered him just after the loss of the baby. He had come face to face with his own guilt. Confronted by it. That was the word he had used. It explained so much of the way he finally parted from her. Such regret, such feeling, such gentleness.

Bess was answering. 'Why should I try? He is a monster, and I am delighted he now suffers from gout as well.'

'Gout?'

'Indeed. He seems inclined to suffer from almost everything. How he remains so outwardly strong I really do not know. By the way, he is going to acquire a monkey.'

'A ... *monkey*? Why?'

'Well, I suspect it is his peculiar notion of humour. You see, he intends to call it Crumplin.'

'Oh.' Yes, it sounded like Henry. Jack had told her of her father's pet name for Richard. Crumplin meant 'small and crooked of body', and Richard's spine curved sideways, which could not be seen when he was dressed, except for one shoulder being slightly raised above the other. Henry would indeed be amused to call a monkey by that name.

'I hope the horrible creature bites him,' Bess said.

'Do you really care so little for the father of your babies? He cared when you lost your last baby, Bess, and you wrong him by thinking otherwise.'

'All he wants of me is living male heirs,' Bess replied. 'Soon I will have to accommodate his person again, and I shudder at the thought. I wonder he does not count the thrusts aloud. One day he will continue dictating to his secretary while he mounts me.'

'Not even Henry would have his secretary in attendance!'

Bess drew a long breath, and changed the subject. 'Jon is beneath the same roof again, I note.'

'But not in the same bed.'

'Oh. Well, no doubt that will change. You were too happy together for his resolve not to weaken. And in the meantime, you could easily have a young, strong, rather attractive Lincolnshire gentleman in his place. Do not look so outraged. A virile man is a virile man, and he is just another one longing for you.'

The furious screams of a very small, very cross Leo ended the calm. 'Me! Me! *Me!*' he screeched.

Bess glanced upstairs. 'Listen to that clamour. You were a screecher too, Cissy.' Her eyes sparkled again. 'Oh, *do* let us go to him.'

They ascended to the next floor, where Leo's loud complaints issued from the door through which Mary and Tom had gone earlier. Sunlight pierced a narrow window, where an elderly, rather cross tabby cat sat. Its ears were turned back and its tail twitched at each yell from behind the door opposite.

'I want! I want!' Leo demanded.

The sisters entered. Elderly Mistress Kymbe—small, bright-eyed and swift-minded—was knitting and ignoring the demands of the angry, red-faced infant who wanted to be picked up.

'No, sir,' she was saying. 'Only when you ask properly, will I cuddle you, but not before.'

Leo inhaled for another bellow, but then saw Cicely and ran to her, arms raised, but he stumbled and would have fallen had she not caught him and swung him up in the air.

He squealed with laughter, his little face lighting up, those memorable eyes dancing with pleasure.

Bess gazed at him. 'Sweet God, Cissy, he is so like

Richard.' Her tears welled and she had to swallow back a sob.

Cicely kissed Leo on the cheek and he squirmed because now that Bess had spoken, and he liked her voice, he wanted to go to her. He held his arms out, as he had once to Henry.

Bess was overwhelmed as Cicely gave him to her and he clasped her around the neck. She held him tenderly, her face filled with emotion.

Tom leaned against the window ledge and vertical wooden slats, his arms folded. His hazelnut eyes were warm as he observed the fond scene, although, perhaps it was not the *entire* scene he watched, just one part of it, or so Bess was to point out later. 'Tom Kymbe had eyes only for you, Cissy. If he is *not* your lover, he certainly longs to be.' Henry's words too.

Aware that Cicely had brought the queen herself, Mistress Kymbe set her knitting aside hastily and tried to sink into a deep curtsey. Cicely swiftly instructed Tom to help her back to her chair, which he and Mary did with great care. Bess was too engrossed in Leo to notice anything.

Cicely knelt beside the chair. 'How are you, Mistress Kymbe?' she asked, making sure her lips could be read.

'Oh, generally well. But how are *you*, my dear? That is more to the point. Did my green salve do its work?'

'Indeed so. I thank you. As the Earl of Lincoln once thanked you too, remember?'

'Ah, that sinfully handsome young fellow. Enticement in human form.' There was a whispered addendum. 'And still not as dead as he is believed to be.'

'How do you know?'

'I see it in your eyes, my dear. There is a colour that is there only for him. I saw it at Friskney, and see it there again.'

Cicely smiled as Leo burst into giggles because Bess tickled him. 'He is so very well. You will never know how grateful I am to you, and to Tom.'

'Tom will always help you, Lady Cicely,' Mistress Kymbe said quietly, holding her eyes meaningfully.

Cicely blushed and glanced at him, to find his eyes upon her. He looked away quickly. Everyone seemed to have noticed, except her, and now she felt awkward.

The old lady spoke of Leo again. 'Apart from that one ailment last year, your boy is a strong, healthy, loving little child. His father would have been proud.'

'Yes, he would. Please do not think badly of me, Mistress Kymbe. I know I should not love as I do.'

'Take care with the present king, my dear, for he is a *very* dangerous man. If he should learn of Lord Lincoln, or of Leo's true parentage, there is no saying what lengths he might go to.'

At that moment the sound of hooves echoed outside, and Tom turned swiftly to look down. 'Jesu, it is the king!'

Cicely was horrified. '*Why*? He wished Leo to be taken to him!'

Bess was guilty. 'He changed his mind and said he would accompany us here today. I did not think he meant it.' She put Leo down, which did not please him, so Tom stepped swiftly to take him up to see the horses and men in the lane below the window.

Cicely steeled herself as Henry's tread sounded on the stairs, but paused on the landing. She heard his voice, low and almost fond, and then he entered with the delighted cat purring in his arms. Clearly the soft-spoken King of England was very much to the haughty creature's liking, for it kneaded its sharp claws on his fur sleeve as he rubbed its ears.

The beguiling scent of cloves entered with him. There was a sapphire brooch in his black velvet hat, and he wore a long sleeveless surcoat, dove grey embroidered with blue and gold. Beneath it was a black fur tunic that would have kept him warm for the ride from Westminster. His cheeks were flushed, and he held his chased leather gauntlets in one hand as he made a fuss of the cat with the other.

He glanced coldly at Bess as everyone made deep obeisance to him. 'I had expressed an intention to accompany you today, madam.'

'I did not for a moment imagine you meant it,' she replied in a rather combative tone. 'Why would *you* wish to see my former maid's nephew?'

'Because I like children. I even have one of my own. With you, if you recall. And I happen to have made the acquaintance of this charming boy, but that too has no doubt slipped your discriminatory memory.' His fingers worked gently into the cat's fur, and the creature was delirious with pleasure. His glance moved slowly over his wife's simple clothes. 'Meekness suits you,' he observed caustically.

Bess's eyes flashed as a savage retort burned on her tongue, but she managed to hold it back.

He looked at Cicely, with a light in his eyes that was gone in a moment because he spoke to Bess again. 'Your absence has been noticed, and the restrictions of churching mentioned, so when you return to Westminster, you will confine yourself to your apartments and follow the usual practice.'

'So, our brief truce is at an end.' Bess spoke as if she were the injured party.

'It was a rather one-sided truce, madam, because you certainly did not observe it.'

Without a word, Bess swept regally from the room, having to step around Henry, because he did not move. The swish of her skirts down the stairs was like the annoyance of a dozen vipers, and there was loathing for Henry in the sound.

Still in Tom's arms, Leo gazed after Bess. 'Lady cwoss,' he observed.

'Lady always cwoss,' Henry remarked dryly, putting the cat down. It immediately jumped up onto a shelf and gazed at him, clearly entranced. He waved away everyone but Cicely and Leo, and instructed Tom to tell the guards and escorts that they were to detain the queen until he, Henry, left.

On the floor yet again, Leo watched them all leave. 'Bye,' he declared clearly.

Cicely went to pick him up, and he beamed at her. 'Cissy,' he said, because he could not pronounce her name. It was also how Bess had come to call her that.

Henry came closer. 'Leo?'

The little boy's expression told of a lingering memory.

Henry thought so too. 'Surely he does not recall me from Friskney?' he said, addressing Cicely, without catching her eye.

'You *are* fairly memorable.'

'The personification of male perfection, mm? Especially without clothes.'

Leo was still listening. 'No close,' he declared.

Henry smiled. 'Not a single stitch, Master Kymbe,' he said.

'Stish,' Leo replied solemnly.

Cicely smiled too, both because of Leo, and because she was inordinately relieved Henry had made light-hearted remarks. It shortened the distance he had placed between them.

'Naked is a state in which my wife has never seen me,' he murmured. 'For which she is no doubt eternally grateful.'

'I have often told her what she is missing.'

He laughed wryly. 'Oh, I think she knows all right.'

'I am told you are to have a monkey.'

He smiled. 'I wondered how long it would take her to tell you. Yes, and yes, I mean to name it Crumplin. And yes, I do so simply to slight your dear uncle. Why? Because it makes me feel better. There, does that answer your unspoken questions?'

'Richard would only laugh. You do know that?'

'The point is, do I care? No, I do not.'

She gazed at him. 'Oh, Henry, you are such a trial to me. And now I also understand you have been suffering from gout?'

'What it is to have a chatterbox for a wife.'

Leo squirmed, wanting to play with some wooden bricks that Tom had sawn and painted for him. Cicely put him down, and it was soon clear he was more interested in the cat, which, no fool, had placed itself beyond reach.

Henry watched him. 'My queen and I are invited to dine—well, a minor feast—at Pasmer's Place after Easter, by which time she will have been properly churched. I wish it to be an agreeable occasion, but have to point out that my wife would rather drink the poison meant for me, than sit at my side through ten courses, or however many there will be. The invitation is courtesy of my uncle, of course. A spur-of-the-moment decision, no doubt regretted within moments of utterance. And I see by your face that you know nothing of it.'

'No, I do not.'

'So, are you and he reunited?'

'In a manner of speaking. It is just that. Speaking.'

'He will not be able to endure *that* for long.' He went to the window. 'Now you have seen my marriage. I trust you are impressed?'

'I am so sorry, Henry. I know how sad you have been to lose the baby, and how you have tried to mend things with her.'

'Well, I do not intend to make an effort in future, you

may be sure of that.'

'Bess is difficult, but then, so are you.'

'Me?' He was all innocence.

'Yes. One word. Garlic.'

'Ah.' He smiled around at her.

'So, garlic *and* perfunctory attention. Please tell me you at least remove your boots for her.'

'*You* have not always wanted me to remove my boots.'

'Thigh boots only. You may certainly toss aside those new round-toed shoes that make your feet look blunt. And I have wanted you in *all* your royal finery as well, to really be sure I am being bedded by the King of England.'

'The usurper,' he said quietly.

'That is another matter, which I do not intend to discuss, Your Majesty. I would rather smile with you than ... well, I think you know.'

'I am sorry about that.'

'You were not well.'

'That is no excuse,' he answered quickly.

'And then you cast me off.'

He turned, regret in his eyes. 'No, I gave you up with more reluctance and misery than I dreamed possible.' He came back to her. 'Who is he? Your new lover?'

'There is no one.'

'Hmm. There is someone else. I can *feel* it.'

Jack de la Pole, if you did but know it. She held his gaze. 'But it is no longer any concern of yours whether or not I have a lover.'

'It is certainly my concern when the king's sister-in-law ventures outside her marriage vows.'

'You hypocrite.'

'Another royal prerogative.' Harri Tudur smiled at her as he reached in his purse and drew out the emerald ring. 'Will you take this back? I fear that when I had it made small enough for you, I certainly made it infinitely too small for me.'

"It … did not seem appropriate to keep it.'

'When I make a gift, Cicely, I do not expect to receive it back. I am hurt you should think to do so.'

'I was the one who was hurt, Henry.'

He caught her hand and pressed the ring into her palm. 'It is St Valentine's Day, and I wish with all my heart that you would be my Valentine again. So, please, wear it once more, as proof that you forgive me for my latest transgressions, and all my other myriad failings. Please, *cariad*.'

She gazed at him. 'Do not be like this with me,' she whispered.

He raised an eyebrow. 'Like this? Like what?'

'Charming and endearing, because …' From absolutely nowhere, and with total incongruousness, she suddenly knew she was going to tell him about Annie. It was nonsensical to choose now, but she had to do it.

'Yes?' he prompted gently.

'I must broach something very delicate, Henry, but I care too much for you not to mention it. Has your lady mother spoken to you of my sister Annie?' She had sent word to Margaret, who may not yet have found an opportunity to speak to him alone.

He was taken aback. '*Annie*? The Lady Ann, you mean? Why in God's own name would my mother speak of *her* to *me*? Unless it is something to do with restoring the Howards to favour! For which they will have to yearn.'

Cicely gazed at him. 'It is not the Howards. Oh, I really do not wish to say this, Henry. You will not like it.'

'Oh, I already realize that. So, what is it?'

'Take more care when you encounter Annie.'

'More care? I hardly know her.' He was genuinely puzzled.

She held his eyes. 'Be careful,' she repeated slowly, deliberately.

Realization began to dawn, just as it once had upon Richard about Bess. 'Sweet God, Cicely, she is a child!'

'Not enough of one to be as sweet and innocent as she looks. She will pursue whatever she desires, and if she thinks *you* can grant it, she is still naïve enough—and therefore dangerous enough—to flatter and fawn upon you to have her way. You *know* how that will look to gossip-mongers. She has been warned, but I do not think she is taking any notice.'

He was nonplussed. 'But, I encountered her *once*, when I was with my secretary.'

'That is all you know, Henry. She lies in wait for you, but has so far been foiled by circumstances. You are her "dear king". She speaks as if she is on intimate terms with you, and—'

'*Intimate* terms?' He was aghast, turning away to snatch off his hat and run his hand through his hair.

'Please avoid her, Henry. Do not give her any encouragement, nor any opportunity, and *never* speak to her alone.'

'I was merely being amiable to my wife's young sister! Who else knows of this?'

'Bess, Jon and your lady mother.'

He was agitated and had to pace. In the process he inadvertently went close to Leo, who knew something was wrong and tugged his hem anxiously. It was a moment when Henry could easily have been impatient, but instead he crouched to quickly bestow a reassuring hand on the top of the boy's head. He said something in Welsh, and his gentle tone banished Leo's anxiety. Nothing could have demonstrated to Cicely more why she was shackled to Henry Tudor, whose charm and consideration could be utterly captivating.

'Promise to be more guarded with Annie, Henry, because I think you understand full well what form the gossip will take if you, your father's son, are believed to be too close to a twelve-year-old girl.'

He straightened, anger flashing into his eyes. 'Oh, now you trespass greatly, *cariad*,' he warned, keeping his voice level for Leo's sake.

'I trespass because I am fearful you will not understand the danger she poses. I want to make you *really* listen to me.'

'Why do you concern yourself? Have I not cast you off, ignored you and—'

'I care for you, Henry. You are my king and have been my lover. I do not wish to see you subjected to unwelcome scandal.'

'As Richard was?' he asked quietly. 'But then, he *was* guilty, with the niece no one suspected.'

'He was linked incorrectly, which you might well be too if you do not listen to me now. Please, Henry, do not attempt to contort my words, because I am truly concerned for you. I always will be, just as I know you will always be for me. It will never quite be over between us, will it?'

'No.'

'Another thing about Annie ...'

'Sweet God, Cicely, are you *determined* to upset my equilibrium?'

'It will be upset far more if I do *not* tell you this. You see, to her you are the means to one of two, possibly three, ends.'

'Which are?'

'Firstly, the Howards *are* of concern to her. She wishes to be Duchess of Norfolk, wife of England's premier duke and Earl Marshal, and will beg you to reverse the attainder on them.'

'And, failing that...?'

'I do not think she would mind becoming Duchess of Suffolk.'

He gazed at her. 'Edmund de la Pole?'

267

'So I understand, from your lady mother.'

'Jesu. And the third?'

'Roland de Vielleville.'

Henry closed his eyes. 'That would be *all* I need.'

'I believe she has read things into his presence in your household.'

'Things?'

'That he is destined for some great favour. No more than that. I do not think she suspects he is your son, for I do not think Roland himself realizes it. I also think she is physically drawn to him, and maybe to Edmund, but certainly not to Thomas Howard. *He* appears to be solely a means to an end.' Then she added vengefully. 'You could send Edmund away, of course, and the others too.' She owed Edmund de la Pole an ill turn.

'If I do that, I believe your sister will only find another object of attention. Better the ones of whom we know. I will keep them here,' Henry replied shrewdly, and then added, 'Howard will not be a good husband.'

'You have heard about him too?'

'Beating his whores? Yes. I have spoken of it with Jon, and am concerned that if it is true, he would not be a suitable choice for my queen's sister. I do not doubt that if Richard had known, he would not have agreed either, but Howard's disagreeable ways had not surfaced then. He was too young.'

'A *good* word for Richard? You must still be a little unwell.'

He smiled.

Cicely looked at him. 'Well, as things are at the moment, with Annie *and* Roland at Pasmer's Place, you may find yourself *having* to arrange a match between them. Which I doubt very much is what you wish for.'

'I have already been apprised of Roland's carnal activities, and have to think I have sired a damned buck rabbit.

But, as I have said to Jon, the boy is *your* responsibility.'

'*Ours*?' She so wanted to remind him that *he* was Roland's father! '*Please* remove him, Henry.'

'Why do you not remove your sister?' he asked reasonably.

'Because Bess wishes her to be with me for a while, so the daughters of Edward IV can be in harmony again.'

'My *wife* understands harmony?' he answered acidly. 'What was the disharmony?'

'Annie insulted me, *and* Jon.'

Henry was cold. 'If she does that again, I will see to it that she is banished from court, once and for all. Make that piercingly clear to her. It should cure her of any further insults or "dear kings". In fact, banishing her anyway seems an excellent notion.'

'Do that and her life will be ruined. She will be unmarriageable, and you know it. She may as well take the veil.' What an unlikely nun Annie would make, Cicely thought, not wishing the fate on her sister.

Henry nodded. 'Yes, I am aware of that, *cariad*. I will only do it as a very last resort. You have my word.' Then he drew a deep breath. 'Cicely, I have complete confidence in your ability—and my uncle's—to keep one young Breton *écuyer* under control.'

'The young Breton *écuyer's* cock is continually out of his hose.'

'Then make sure he has no opportunity to do anything but pee with it.'

'Henry, you are being unreasonable. Bess is set upon Annie being with me, and it would be so easy for you to assist me in this. Why do you force him upon Pasmer's Place?'

'Because I want *you* to influence him, Cicely. *You*, because you are the most exquisitely warm, feminine, *caring* woman I have ever known.'

269

She stared at him. 'Henry—'

'I want that stupid boy to discover what it is to know one such as you, and to respect and appreciate you. No matter what differences you and my uncle have at the moment, I know you will both be civil in front of others. And I am also sure that it will not be long before you are in the same bed again. Do you honestly imagine Roland is going to learn anything good near me? Jesu, I cannot think of anything worse for him than observing *my* marriage. He has been brought up with such notions of self-importance that I think he would look down on Charlemagne. He is to learn how to go on, how to recognize love and respect it. *That* is why he is at Pasmer's Place, Cicely. How more can I say it? To me, you are the perfect woman. Yours is the example he must respect the most, Cicely.'

'But I am an adulteress,' she reminded him quietly.

'Thank God, otherwise I, an adulterer, would never have held you.' He smiled, but then sounds from outside reminded him that Bess awaited. 'I think perhaps it is time to return to Westminster with my sweet consort.'

'But you came here to see Leo, and are to leave already?'

'I did not come to see the Kymbe boy, fascinating as he is. I came to see you. And you know it.'

She held his gaze. 'No, Henry, you came to see me *with Leo*, to feed your suspicions. You knew I would not be present if he were taken to see you, as you originally intended, so you came here, to see for yourself. I know what you are thinking, so before you ask, no, he is not mine. Nor is he Richard's. And certainly not mine by Tom Kymbe, before you think *that* too. My child died not long after birth and I have not been able to give Jon another,' she said firmly, looking him in the eyes and holding her chin up.

'Richard had that hair too. I saw his corpse.'

'No, Henry, you saw him living, when he bore down

on you, unhorsed Sir John Cheney, and then came terrifyingly close to exterminating you. You saw him when he was dragged from his wounded horse, and his helmet and crown were jolted from his head. That is when you saw his hair. *And* his face.'

Henry returned her gaze. 'Yes, I saw him, *cariad.* Exactly as you say. And I almost shat myself with dread. He was a man possessed, and but for chance, he would have killed me. I admit it. If I had half his courage, I would be a different man. My courage is of a different nature, and it will keep me on the throne that I usurped from him. And it will keep me in your heart, because you cannot help yourself. Nor can I. In fact, I am desolate without you. Please tell me you are desolate without me.'

She had to nod. 'Yes, I am.' Was it true? She only knew that he was weaving around her again. And it felt so good.

He smiled and came closer. He did not touch her, except with his lips, which brushed lovingly over hers in a long, tender kiss of such gentle beauty that she could have wept of it.

Then he turned to crouch by Leo again. 'I will see you again, young sir. Be good.'

Leo was pleased and caught his long hair.

Henry extricated himself carefully. 'Goodbye, Master Kymbe.'

''Bye.'

Henry rose to face Cicely. 'You are no longer free of me, *cariad.*'

'And you are not free of me.'

'I know.'

She lowered her eyes, aware of the swing of his rich hem, his soft tread and the fading of the cloves. The cat leapt down and slipped through, just as the door closed.

Leo watched quizzically. 'Gone,' he declared.

Yes, she thought, but he was dominating her again,

and would soon be in her body again. Her feelings were so mixed and troubled that she honestly did not know in which one to have complete faith.

And now she had to go to St Andrew's, to learn what Tal had to say. The apprehension she had lost on entering this house was suddenly found again, with such awful clarity that it was like an icy hand clutching at her stomach. And yet, what could possibly be wrong?

Chapter Twenty-Two

THE CLATTER OF the royal departure had barely faded when Tom escorted Cicely along Hallows Lane towards St Andrew's. She was hooded, cloaked, almost to being shrouded, but beneath it, her composure was in tatters. Being with Henry again had brought back all the uncertainty, unwanted feelings ... and guilt.

They reached the church, to find it locked, with a guard who had instructions to admit only her. Oddly, he put a finger to his lips and opened the door as softly as he could.

Tom was suspicious, and without warning grabbed the man by the throat. 'What is going on?'

'Please, sir! I act for the lady's cousin!'

Cicely's heart leapt. Jack? But then alarm set in. Or ... might it be Edmund again?

Tom was not easily convinced. 'Describe him.'

'Dark-haired, dark-eyed, and—'

When Cicely nodded, Tom released the man, who immediately rubbed his throat. But he managed to speak. 'I am to admit you as quietly as possible, my lady. That is all. He paid me well to disobey my original orders.'

'Original orders?'

'To make a great noise about closing the door behind

you, my lady.'

'Who ordered you to do that?' she asked.

'I do not know his name. In his fifties, very active. He wears a crucifix and a wheel of St Catherine.'

Tal! But why would Jack countermand Tal's order? She looked anxiously at Tom, who nodded reassuringly. 'I will wait here, my lady. You need only call me.' He patted the dagger on his belt.

She turned to the guard again. 'Is my cousin inside?'

'I believe so. I … do not really know. He only told me what to do and paid me to do it. And now, I am not staying around to be punished by either or both!' Without warning he dashed away, disappearing across the cobbles towards Puddle Dock Hill.

Cicely looked at Tom. 'What should I do?'

'Who do you trust most, my lady? The man named Tal, or your cousin?'

'My cousin,' she replied without hesitation.

'Then I will make sure no one hears the door close behind you.'

She stepped in, and Tom pulled the door so softly that she was hardly sure herself if he did it. But the daylight was shut off as well, and she was in the dim, echoing silence. The smell of incense, beeswax candles and old stonework was soothing, but there did not seem to be *anyone* about, let alone Jack or Tal. There was some daylight, finding its cold, pale way through stained-glass windows, and glimmering on the altar, candlesticks and costly vessels.

She was on the point of returning to Tom, when Jack emerged from behind a column close to the newly built sacristy on the north side of the altar. His eyes were bright with warning as he tapped a finger to his lips, and then beckoned. When she reached him, he caught her hand, pulled her into the shadows, and there embraced her tightly.

'Oh, sweetheart, I was afraid you would not come after all,' he whispered.

She whispered too. 'But … I am to meet Tal.'

'I know.' He nodded towards the sacristy. It was unusual for a church to have such a thing, for they were usually the domain of cathedrals and abbeys. The door was closed upon whatever was inside, but she became aware of the low murmur of male voices.

'Who is in there?' she breathed.

'Tal and Pasmer, but they have not begun yet because they still await Henry's French secretary, Étienne Fryon, who will arrive by the sacristy's outer door.'

'Fryon? But—'

'He is our spy. Well, our aunt, Margaret of Burgundy's spy.' Jack glanced at the sacristy door. 'Tal hoped his business with them would be over and done with long before now, so he could meet you. He must be hoping you will be very late indeed. I am glad his timing has been ruined, because it gives me the chance to speak to you first. Now we can *both* listen when Fryon finally condescends to turn up. It is far better that you hear everything yourself, not have it relayed by me.' He searched her face. 'What is wrong? Has something happened?'

'I have not recovered from the shock of Henry coming to Hallows Lane.'

He gazed at her. 'Henry? You did not expect him?'

'Certainly not. He told Bess he wished to come but she saw fit not to mention it. He found out she had already left, and was not best pleased when he arrived. They do hate each other so. However …' She raised her hand to show him the emerald. 'I am to be back in the fold.'

'We will speak of it later. For the moment, I wish you to be strong, and not make a sound when I tell you something.' He put a hand over her mouth. 'Sweetheart, I fear Leo may be in danger of abduction.'

Her eyes widened, and he kissed her forehead to lessen the harshness. Only then, when he knew she would be quiet, did he take his hand away. 'You may have to send Leo away, somewhere Tal is not to learn about. Somewhere Tom Kymbe can see he is safe, but not Friskney. You *do* trust Tom?'

'Yes. Completely.'

'And me?'

'Do you *really* need to ask that?'

He smiled, and bent to kiss her on the lips, but then they heard the muffled sound of a door opening and closing in the sacristy. The voices of Tal and Pasmer became louder, clearly annoyed with the tardy Frenchman, who protested in return.

As they argued, Jack manoeuvred Cicely closer. 'Be ready to get into the shadows again as quickly as possible. Do you understand? If Tal realizes his plan is known—if plan it is—he may take Leo before Tom can get the boy away.'

The voices became clearer, and were not guarded, because it was believed the porch door's closing would be easily heard. John Pasmer was indignant, not with Fryon, but with Tal. Clearly there had been an earlier disagreement.

'And you *refuse* to say who it is?'

Tal answered. 'Because I do not *know*! God above, sir, how can I tell you what is as much a mystery to me? *Someone* tried to poison Tudor, and came close to success.'

'Please, *Maître* Pasmer, Sir 'Umphrey is right, the poisoner—God smile upon 'im—is not from among our ranks.' Fryon's voice was low-pitched and heavily accented.

Pasmer responded. 'What does it matter now? Whoever it is has failed. And Sir Humphrey says he has now received all the irrefutable evidence of the Breton matter. We have to act upon it, unless, of course, you wish to withdraw?'

Fryon was offended. '*Mais non!* I resent the suggestion that I would be'ave in such a way!'

Tal, who had evidently been seated, got up, his chair scraping. 'I am quite prepared to proceed, but I also reserve the right to act on my own if necessary. We must be decisive, and make certain there is no swift attempt to crown Arthur in his father's stead.'

'You *are* certain of these facts from Brittany, Sir Humphrey?' Pasmer asked.

'Oh, yes. History is about to repeat itself, this time at Tudor's expense. I have all the documentation, statements, *everything*. We can now be sure of plucking both him and his spawn.'

Jack whispered, 'I have not seen it, but Tal says it is all we need.'

The Frenchman spoke again. 'You 'ave the notices ready, Sir 'Umphrey?'

'Yes, more than enough. Every church in London will have one fixed to its door, and so will the most important in the rest of the realm.'

'Where do you keep them? Somewhere truly secret, I trust?'

'Here, together with all the documentation. You know the place, and I alone have both the key *and* the secret of how to open it up.'

Pasmer was on edge. 'What of money? You seem to think we have enough, Sir Humphrey, but I am not so sanguine. I am only prepared to donate what I have agreed all along, not a farthing more.'

'Do not fret, merchant, for I have something I intend to sell, a solid gold chalice, Saxon, set with pearls, diamonds and a large, rare sapphire. It is very old and valuable, and will bring goodly funds. So do not fear I intend to impose upon your poor, thin purse.'

Pasmer shuffled. 'And you swear upon all the angels

277

that Lord Lincoln has survived after all?'

'You can count upon it, but he is hardly going to broad-cast his whereabouts. He lies low, and advisedly so.'

Fryon spoke quietly. 'I think maybe it is time I tell you there is a new 'ope in Burgundy. Someone 'oo *may* be senior to Lord Lincoln.'

Stunned silence followed, before Tal answered. 'And the name of this new *'ope*?'

There was a note in his voice, something small but telling to Cicely. She remembered he had spoken to Francis in Calais, and Burgundy had been mentioned. *'There are whispers that do not amount to rumours, if you understand what I mean. An atmosphere.'* He had clearly said the same to Jack, who was not surprised by the course the conversation was taking.

'Well, I already know of the "impression", Master Fryon,' Tal proceeded. 'It is something and nothing, as even my contact, who is constantly at court in Bruges, has told me. With all due respect, I prefer something more tangible.'

Fryon was a little disgruntled. 'Well, to me it was a strong impression, gained when last I was in Bruges.'

'And may I ask why you were there? On Henry's busi-ness, perchance? You being his French secretary *and* spy?'

'I spy *against* 'im, not for 'im. The duchess is my true mistress, as you know well, Sir 'Umphrey. I make no secret of it to you. Do not suggest that I am an enemy in your midst, for I am not.'

Pasmer was anxious to soothe the suddenly troubled waters. 'Please, gentlemen, do not let us fall out.'

Tal spoke deliberately into the ensuing silence. 'Well, I for one do not care what "news" there may be from Burgundy, even if it concerns the sons of King Edward IV, because I regard all of his children to be illegitimate. There is still Warwick, of course, but his cause has been irrepa-rably damaged by calling himself Lambert Simnel, and further by the rout at Stoke Field. He no longer acknowledges his lineage anyway. He prefers to be the sow's ear to the silk purse. To me, Richard III's was the only true claim after Edward's death, and therefore it is *his* line to which I still owe my entire allegiance.'

Cicely felt as cold as ice, and sensed the shock of Pasmer and Fryon. Pasmer became mystified. 'But Richard's direct male line ends with John of Gloucester, who is illegitimate and rendered half-witted by Tudor. Richard wished the Earl of Lincoln to be his heir.'

'Gentlemen, Richard left another *legitimate* son. The only problem is that he is as yet a very small child, little more than a babe.'

Pasmer was confounded. 'Let us be clear here, Sir Humphrey. It is your intention to rid the land of Tudor and his issue, not in support of Jack de la Pole, but to put an as yet unnamed child on the throne instead? And you expect our entire organization to support this anonymous candidate? Give money for him? Raise men for him? Risk *lives*? Sir, many feel they risk enough if it were to be for Lord Lincoln, but for an anonymous infant—?' The skinner's dismay was palpable. 'And you think Lord Lincoln will stand idly by and let this happen?'

'Yes, Pasmer, because he accepts that his own claim is inferior. Inferior. Do you understand?'

Now Fryon expressed annoyance. 'You knew of such a boy, Sir 'Umphrey, and 'ave not said anything until now? How can we be sure 'e is as legitimate as you say?'

Pasmer had been thinking. 'Sir Humphrey, are you saying that King Richard married again in the short time between Queen Anne's death and his own? That is impossible!'

'Just as Edward IV promised marriage to my sister, and then turned it into full marriage by bedding her, Richard promised marriage to this boy's mother. And left flesh-and-blood proof that he had bedded her as well.'

Cicely listened in dismay. Tal was ignoring everything she had begged of him.

Fryon was astonished. 'And Lord Lincoln agrees with this?'

'Yes.'

She looked at Jack, who met her gaze apologetically. 'Yes, sweetheart, I do. Being Lord Protector is what I seek now. Only for Leo will I stand aside.'

'Why will you not identify this boy?' Pasmer asked curiously.

'Because very few know of his existence and that is how it should remain for as long as possible, to protect him from Tudor, and because I wish to convince his mother that putting him on the throne is the only honourable course to take. *Never* underestimate a mother in defence of her child. She fears for his safety, and would shield him, but he is not hers, he is England's. Yet I respect her, and if she can be persuaded to this course, I will feel a lot better.'

'Sir 'Umphrey, why not take the boy from 'er and proceed anyway?' Fryon suggested pragmatically.

'That would be a last resort.'

'Which you 'ave thought of already.'

'Yes.'

Jack closed his eyes. 'So I did not misunderstand,' he breathed.

Cicely was devastated. If she would not give her permission, Tal intended to kidnap Leo!

Jack pulled her closer. 'We can confound him, sweetheart, by removing Leo before Tal knows anything.'

'I *knew* I should not trust him!' she whispered vehemently.

'Do not misjudge him. His loyalty to Richard is a match for mine, mayhap even for yours. He honestly and truly believes your son by Richard should be the next king. He has convinced himself about the boy's legitimacy, and … I am convinced as well.'

'Oh, Jack—'

He put a finger to his lips again, because Pasmer spoke. 'It seems so improbable that Richard took a second wife without anyone knowing. Who might she be, mm? There were rumours at Nottingham, concerning the present queen. But that cannot be. She could not have hidden such a secret while anticipating marriage to Henry, but her sister, Lady Cicely, *was* with child, and present in Nottingham at the relevant time. Jesu, Sir Humphrey, you promote a child born of incest!'

Tal abandoned all pretence. 'Marriage between uncle and niece is not unheard of, dispensation *can* be granted. And this uncle and niece were virtual strangers before 1484. Richard was free, and so was she. Marriage was offered and the boy was born. Can you imagine anyone *more* Yorkist? Richard as his father, Edward as his grandfather and uncle, and Edward's daughter as his mother?'

'But—'

'Enough!' Tal snapped the word. 'You are both to hold your tongues until I have been able to clear certain matters.'

Cicely was so upset that she wept silently, and Jack led her quietly towards the porch, which he opened with great care. The ring handle did not squeak, nor did the hinges groan as they went out to find Tom waiting.

Tom was dismayed to see her tears, and Jack had to catch his attention. 'Tom Kymbe, do you serve any other, apart from Lord and Lady Welles?'

'No, sir. I serve them alone.' Tom was clearly disturbed by Cicely's distress.

'Something has arisen that requires your loyalty and silence.'

'I have ample of both, my lord.'

'I know.' Jack nodded, and then drew Tom a little aside.

'My lady has yet to keep her appointment here, because we have had to listen in upon a very private conversation indeed. Now, as soon as you return my lady to Hallows Lane, I want you to prepare to leave immediately, taking Leo with you.'

'For Friskney?'

'No, not anywhere that is known. Do you have any trusted relatives who live elsewhere in the land?'

'Trusted? My cousin, Roger Kymbe, on the Isle of Wight. I lived with him until my father died and I returned to Friskney.'

Cicely was anxious. 'No! My mother's brother, Sir Edward Woodville, is now Henry's loyal man and has been appointed governor and Lord of Wight.'

Jack was reassuring. 'Woodville will not know anything, sweetheart.' He looked at Tom again. 'You really have faith in this cousin?'

'I would trust him with my life.'

'What are his circumstances?'

'He prospers, and has a small fishing fleet at Fishbourne, on a creek on the north coast of the island. His family is large, but literate, his children having all been educated by a monk from Quarr monastery.'

'That is satisfactory to me. I want you to take Leo to him, and then you must return to your responsibilities at Friskney.'

'You … want Leo to go to my cousin, and be *left* there?' Tom was shaken.

'You will be provided with ample money for Roger's trouble, but Leo *must* be taken from London, because he is in real danger of being kidnapped. Do not tell anyone where you are going.'

'Very well, my lord.' Unasked questions fought on Tom's lips, but he did not voice any of them.

Cicely spoke at last. 'If Mistress Kymbe desires to go

with you, please take her, for I know how attached she is to Leo, but I know she finds travelling difficult. She is welcome to stay at Pasmer's Place with Mary for as long as she cares to, but if she wishes to return to Friskney, I will see that she is taken there in all leisure and comfort. But it is vital that Leo's whereabouts are not known to anyone else. Tom, I realize that he has become your son as well. You have brought him up as yours, you and Mistress Kymbe, and here I am, desiring you to give him up.'

'No, my lady, you order me to keep him safe, and that has *always* been my concern.'

'My child and I have so much to thank you for, Tom.'

'I will always do anything for you, my lady. Please know that.'

Their eyes met, and she saw that his were written with his love. How could she have failed to realize before? He looked away quickly, knowing he had given himself away, not only to her, but to Jack as well.

Jack smiled. 'Kymbe, I do not think there is anything either of us would not do for Lady Cicely.'

It was said with kindness, and he and Tom looked at each other for a long moment. An understanding moment.

Then Jack drew Cicely to one side. 'Sweetheart, about your reunion with Henry. I wish something important of you. I wish you to inveigle Henry's great secret from him.'

'Oh, Jack....' She was reluctant.

'It's important. We have Tal's records and documents, but to hear it all from Henry himself will fill any gaps. Do you understand? He wants to tell you, so make sure your company and your sweet, sympathetic little ears are irresistible. Make sure all of you is irresistible.'

She nodded slowly. 'I will do my best.'

He bent to kiss her, and she knew Tom had turned away.

Jack ushered her to the church door. 'We will go back inside now, Tom, and I want you to slam the door as much as you can behind us, to announce Lady Cicely's apparent arrival. I will hide, but she will have us both within calling distance.'

'Yes, my lord.'

Jack opened the door softly, and ushered her inside again. Tom waited until Jack had slipped away from her into the shadows, and then heaved the door to as loudly as he could. The noise reverberated around the nave, and as the echoes died away, there was the sound of that other door, muffled and distant. Then Tal emerged from the sacristy.

She had to be a supreme deceiver now, and she hurried to him, evincing great pleasure as she held out her hands. He caught them both and drew them to his lips. She felt the topaz ring, which seemed to be the only ring he ever wore.

'Cicely, how good it is to see you looking so much better.' Perhaps he saw the light in her eyes. 'Is something wrong?'

'Nothing at all, unless you count a reunion with Henry. I am glad your hair is its proper shade again.'

'And I am less of a strutting coxcomb in those silks and finery?' He smiled.

'How are you now?'

'Improving. Cicely, I need to thank you again for helping me at Esher. If you had not, well, I would probably have suffered the fate my idiocy deserved.'

'Jack helped you too. And Jon.'

'How are things with him?'

'Strained, but we speak.'

Tal sighed. 'It is all my fault, and I accept the blame without reservation. I have grovelled to Jack, and if I could to Jon, I would, except that I fancy my visage would not be welcome.'

She smiled, for it was easier to seem at ease with him than she had feared.

'Cicely, should you think my gratitude is too easily

expressed, let me say again that I am so much in your debt now that there is nothing I would not do for you. Do you understand? If you *ever* need me, I will come to you, no matter what.'

'You are an honourable man, Tal.' She met his gaze.

For a moment she thought she saw something less than confident in his green eyes, but then it had gone. 'Cicely, do you feel a need to protect Henry?' The question was blunt, and yet not.

'Why?'

'Because I now have everything I need from Brittany concerning Roland de Vielleville.' He explained about the notices and documents hidden somewhere in the church, but said nothing at all about Leo. 'Their content is not for you to know just yet, if only because your astonishment when you learn the truth will be all the more convincing. Please trust me in this.'

'Jack has said the same thing to me. Tal, are these documents the reason you wished to see me today? To tell me you have the proof at last?'

'Yes.' He searched her eyes. 'You have changed towards me today. Why?'

'No, truly, it must be the shock of Henry,' she insisted.

He was amused. 'You cannot have thought he would leave you alone? Not he. Let me recite a poem.

'Oh, cruel fortune, to me most contrary,
Out of her favour to whom had I promised
My service forever, without duplicity.
In thought nor word her never to displease,
Nor from her service ever to depart
Til death had cast on me his mortal dart.'

'A rhyme royal,' she observed.

'How very knowledgeable you are.'

Such rhymes had been introduced by Geoffrey Chaucer, but this was not Chaucer. *'You* wrote it?' she asked then.

'I did, *cariad.* The Welsh poet lurks within this carcass. I wrote it some time ago, but it seems fitting for this moment. I am out of your favour, but have promised my service forever. Whatever has happened to change your view of me, never forget that if I am needed, I *will* come to you.'

'And what of Leo?' She could not help but ask.

'That is something that lies in the future. Please, Cicely, I swear I will not do anything at all concerning him without consulting you first.'

'What if I do not agree?'

'But you will, Cicely. When the time comes, you will. You will understand his importance.'

Two days later, Cicely received a message from Tom Kymbe, sent while he waited to be ferried from the mainland. All was well, and Leo in fine fettle. Mistress Kymbe had come to Pasmer's Place, and was very happy to do so, because she could instruct Mary in all manner of spells, charms, salves and potions. She also extracted from Jon the promise that come the spring, he would allow a small portion of the garden behind the house to be turned over to the growing of medicinal plants.

One night there was a small fire at St Andrew's. It seemed to have been caused by a taper accidentally left alight and knocked over by a cat, which escaped with no more than a singed tail. The altar had been consumed by the flames, and a hiding place discovered beneath it that had perished completely, as had the stacks of papers concealed within. What they had been was a mystery, but Cicely knew Tal's precious, long-awaited proof from Brittany had been destroyed.

Had the fire been deliberate? If so, did it mean that someone present in the sacristy was not as loyal to York as they pretended? Somehow she did not suspect John

Pasmer, and certainly not Tal himself. Nor would Jack have destroyed the long-awaited evidence that would damn Henry. But what of Étienne Fryon, the Duchess of Burgundy's loyal servant?

Chapter Twenty-Three

AFTER EASTER THERE came the occasion of the small feast at Pasmer's Place. Henry had been wrong about his queen, who *was* prepared to sit through ten courses with him. Cicely was less than happy. There would be wine aplenty at the occasion, and maybe Bess perceived a chance of poisoning him again? Cicely prayed not, but could only wait.

The thought of another confrontation between the king and queen, like the one at Hallows Lane on Leo's birthday, was most unappealing. Cicely wished Jon had not issued the invitation, but now the best had to be made of it. She could only pray the feast and entertainment pleased *both* monarchs.

Before then, however, a great problem sprang up involving Annie and Roland. It happened in the small hours on the very eve of the banquet. Cicely and Jon had retired to the main bedchamber to take a cup of warm, honeyed wine together. He came to sit with her every night, and came fully dressed, which told her he intended to retire to the principal guest chamber. She followed her own pattern, and received him in her nightgown and robe. Did she want him to be in her bed again? Sometimes, yes. Other times ... the stiltedness between them was impossible to ignore.

There was a timid but urgent tap at the door, and on Cicely's response, Mary entered nervously. 'My lord, my lady, forgive me, but …' Her tongue passed over her lips. 'The Lady Ann has gone up to Master Roland's room. I … I was returning to my own chamber after sitting with my aunt, when I saw her.'

Cicely was disquieted. 'Oh no! Thank you, Mary. We will attend to it.'

When the maid had gone, Jon got up angrily. 'Damn Henry, damn his libidinous little by-blow, and damn your apprentice jade of a sister.'

They ascended to the uppermost floor of the house. Roland's chamber was at the far end of the passageway, partly within the roof. He was only a squire, and was treated as such, so could consider himself fortunate to be in the house, not wherever his fellows had to make do. It was another frosty night, with little sound, but as they neared the door, beneath which crept the glow of candlelight, they heard Annie's smothered giggles.

Jon kicked the door open furiously. Annie and Roland were sitting together on the bed, he in his nightshirt, she still fully dressed. They scrambled from opposite sides of the narrow mattress. Roland's face was a picture of guilty dismay, and he did not say a word, but Annie burst into tears, caught up her gown and scampered from the room, along the passage and then down the stairs to her own chamber. Roland, on the other hand, became arrogantly haughty, gazing past Cicely at the slope of the roof above the window.

Jon confronted him. 'Well, sir? Have you anything to say for yourself?'

'*Non, monsieur le vicomte.*'

'In English, if you please.'

'No, my lord,' the boy corrected, his chin still fully raised.

'So, you have nothing to say about seducing my lady's young sister?'

'I was not seducing her, my lord, she came to me.'

'And you did *nothing* to ensure she left again without delay.' Jon was icy. 'How old are you?'

'Fourteen, my lord.'

'How old is Lady Ann?'

'Twelve, my lord.'

'You, sir, are old enough to know she should only be in her *own* bedchamber.'

Roland did not respond.

Jon became incensed. 'Your dick, sir, is to be kept only unto you, but I have had far too many reasons to punish you for fucking around! If the itch is so very imperative, I suggest you resort to relieving yourself. You *do* know how to relieve yourself, I take it? Or are you too superior for such vulgar, unholy practices?'

Roland went red.

'Well, profane and forbidden such acts may be, but they are also far less troublesome than the act of tampering with the queen's too-young sister. Do you understand?'

'Yes, my lord.'

'Apologize to my lady for your lamentable conduct.'

Roland's chin seemed to rise even more.

In one stride Jon had shoved him face down on the bed and then placed a booted foot on his exposed buttocks. 'Now then, sir, apologize.'

Roland struggled in silence.

Jon was now very angry indeed, and slammed the heel of his boot down savagely on Roland's backside. 'What have you to say, sir?'

Roland howled in pain. 'I am sorry, Lady Welles! Forgive me, I beg of you!'

Jon released him. 'You are to stay away from the Lady Ann, do you understand? Be caught in another misdemeanour like this, and not only will your hide be thoroughly beaten, but you will be returned to my nephew the king, for *him* to deal with.'

Roland froze. 'Please do not do that, my lord.'

'Give me one sensible reason why I should not.'

'I am afraid of him.'

Cicely wondered again what Henry had done to bring about such dread in his own son, who trembled visibly.

Jon was not impressed. 'Afraid of him? Then you should have thought of that *before*, should you not, *monsieur l'écuyer*? The king *will* hear of this if I become aware of as much as a *whisper* about your conduct from now on. I am tired of your arrogance, surliness, ill manners and laughable airs and graces.'

'*Je vous demande pardon, monsieur le vicomte.*' He hastened to correct himself. 'I am sorry, my lord, and I crave your pardon.'

'You will spend tomorrow here in this room, you will not have food or go about tasks and training with the other young men, and you certainly will not attend the dinner.'

'Yes, my lord.'

Jon stepped away, and then nodded at Cicely. 'See to your sister. I will not venture there with you.'

She turned to go, but Roland suddenly called to her. 'Forgive me, my lady, I know how I have disappointed you. It will not happen again, I swear it.' He scrambled from the bed and knelt facing her. 'I am ashamed, my lady, and I plead with all my heart that you pardon my transgression.'

It was said sincerely, and he did not look up at her or do anything to suggest his usual disdain. He was only fourteen, she thought, remembering herself at that age.

'I will forgive you this time, Master Roland, but my wrath will match my lord's if it should happen again. And my lord and I *do* have the king's ear, so beware of taking chances.'

'*Je suis vraiment reconnaissante, gracieuse dame.*'

He was grateful to her? Yes, she imagined he was, because Jon was ready to deal much more severely with him. She nodded and withdrew.

She found Annie curled up in a ball on her bed, sobbing. 'Sit up, Annie, I have to talk to you.'

Sniffing, trembling and with tears still pouring down her face, Annie did as she was told, but she could not meet her older sister's eyes.

'Well?' Cicely demanded. 'How far did it get?'

'We only k-kissed, Cissy.'

'Is that the truth? Maybe this was not the first time you have sought Master de Vielleville's room? I know he is the only reason you wanted to come here. Certainly you did not come to make up with me. Nor have you mended your ways. So? The details, if you please.'

'This was the first time, and we did not do anything else.' The girl's tears seemed real enough. 'You will not tell anyone, will you, Cissy? If Thomas should learn of it …'

'*Thomas*? You fear him?' Cicely was alert to the rumours.

'I do not *fear* Thomas, I just do not want him to think I am … no longer as pure as I should be. And *please*, Cissy, do not tell Bess, and especially not the king. I could not bear it. Truly I could not.'

'Then behave yourself. And what of Edmund de la Pole?'

Annie glanced up, caught off guard. 'Edmund? He is not interested in me.'

'Are you interested in him?'

'I was, but he was unkind.'

'In what way?'

'He laughed at me.'

Cicely was relieved it was no more than that. 'Stay away from him, Annie, for he is dangerous.'

The girl nodded.

'Who do you really wish to marry? Thomas or Roland?'

'Roland.'

'A mere *écuyer*?'

'He is close to the king.'

Had he guessed who he was? 'And you believe him? He is only here as the king's favour to his father. That will not make him a grand noble, you may count upon it. If you wish to marry well, I suggest you start behaving as if worthy of it.'

Annie hung her head.

'This is your last warning, Annie. Any more ill conduct—*any*!—and the king *will* know of it. His attention has already been drawn to you, and not flatteringly.'

The girl's eyes flew to her in horror.

'He will not be lenient,' Cicely continued. 'You may *beg* to go to Mother at Bermondsey in preference to the low marriage you will be faced with. Do you understand?'

Annie's lips pressed together mutinously.

'*Do—you—understand*?'

'Yes.'

There was a convivial gathering in the brilliantly lit great hall at Pasmer's Place. Minstrels played, there was dancing and singing, and all manner of entertainment, including Henry's favourite fool. The food was magnificent, the wine rare, and the surroundings sumptuous. A surfeit of costly beeswax candles illuminated the scene, and a huge log fire roared in the hearth. Chosen members of the court were present, although Margaret was unwell. Jasper Tudor had refused his invitation in no uncertain terms, displeasing both Henry *and* Margaret, if not Lord and Lady Welles, who had felt constrained to invite him in the first place.

There was sudden excitement and anticipation as trumpets in the courtyard announced the arrival of the royal cavalcade, where Cicely and Jon waited. A hundred flickering torches illuminated everything, and the night was mild and clear. A lovely spring night.

Jon glanced at all the torches. 'Dear God, I hate to think how much this is depleting my coffers.'

'Well, you *would* do it.'

'Thank you for the sympathy and understanding.'

'You are welcome, my lord.'

He smiled. 'And so are our monarchs,' he murmured, as they both made deep obeisance when Henry halted his fine red horse, which danced around nervously, even though two of Jon's grooms strove to soothe it.

Bess was in a gilded litter that bore the royal colours and devices, and when she alighted, assisted by Jon, was very beautiful in a pale-russet brocade gown edged with matching fur. The colour blended exquisitely with her hair, which was swept up loosely beneath a golden headdress and veil.

Henry swung his leg over the pommel and jumped down lightly. He wore black and ermine, the jewels and precious metals of his collar and hat brooch shining as the torches flared in a mild stir of breeze.

Cicely remained in a deep curtsey. 'Your Majesty.'

He bent to raise her. 'Lady Welles.' Their eyes met, and he smiled, his hand remaining beneath her elbow. 'You should wear that gown more often; it becomes you.'

Jon and Bess were already proceeding into the house, and he offered Cicely his arm. 'I was tempted to hope you would wear the plum brocade.'

'In front of the world? I think not.'

More trumpets sounded, and the entire gathering bowed or curtsied. As Henry signified the evening to continue, the music, chattering and entertainment resumed. Tumblers and jugglers preceded the royal couple, who nodded graciously to left and right.

Cicely and Bess left Jon and Henry conversing by the

fire, Bess having expressed an interest in the cold viands displayed on a long side-table. Not only were there viands, but all manner of other cold dishes, as well as wine, mead and all manner of drinks. Jon had acquired some particularly select wine from France, and Bess was interested to sample it. Or so she said.

The attendant servants drew respectfully away as the royal sisters approached. Bess smiled. 'What discreet staff you have, Cissy. Ah, I see Henry has sent his own wine.' She indicated the particular white Rhenish that he had chosen to drink since being poisoned.

'He takes no chances, although I notice his taster has yet to arrive.'

'I believe his taster is … unwell, this evening.' Bess smiled again. Such a pretty smile, just like the Bess of old.

Cicely was uneasy. Unwell? And Bess wished to be where the wine was in readiness? She did not know what to do.

'Henry will not know it has not been tasted,' Bess said airily, and then looked past Cicely. 'Is that not Annie over there? I thought you said she had been forbidden to attend.'

Cicely turned swiftly, but saw no sign of Annie. She scanned the gathering, and then turned back in puzzlement, just in time to see a quick movement of Bess's right hand withdrawing into the folds her gown. A shock jolted through Cicely as a quick glance at the wine revealed a white powder sinking, dissolving and then disappearing. Bess had put something in Henry's wine. Right here, in front of the entire hall!

Bess was confident of being undetected. 'Cissy? Are you afraid I will spoil tonight? I promise I will behave.'

Cicely was in a quandary. She could hardly accuse the Queen of England of trying to poison the king, but that was surely what was happening.

At that moment the signal was given to adjourn to the decorated, white-clothed trestle tables arranged around three sides of the hall. Jon and Henry approached, and escorted their ladies to the dais, where Jon sat at Bess's side, and Cicely next to Henry. She was in turmoil as the wine was brought, and Henry's golden goblet was filled.

'Your Majesty—!' The words blurted, and she did not know what else to say, just that she had his attention.

The formality was unnecessary when they were seated together, and he looked quickly. 'What is it, *cariad*?'

'May I taste your wine, Your Majesty?' she asked in a voice loud enough for Bess to hear. Bess's face changed, and Jon glanced at his wife, aware that something was wrong.

Henry hesitated, but handed her the goblet, which she immediately contrived to drop. She leapt to her feet in apparent confusion. 'Forgive me! Oh, forgive me!'

'It is of no consequence, my lady,' Henry responded guardedly. He indicated the goblet should be replenished, but Bess rose from her seat so abruptly—and clumsily— that she knocked the entire jug out of the servant's hands.

Henry had to move out of the way as the wine splashed everywhere, and in those seconds Cicely leaned close enough to whisper. 'Harri, the food is safe, but please drink only what you see me drink.' She used his Welsh name to be make certain he paid full attention.

He did, and by the curve of his lips and warmth in his eyes, she knew that for those moments she had his complete trust.

The disturbance over, the dinner proceeded magnificently. Henry put himself out to be entertaining and charming, and Jon was genial as well. Bess was quiet, and clearly angry, glancing frequently at Cicely in a way that indicated the sisters' next private meeting promised to be prickly.

It was after dinner, when the entertainment was at its

height, that Cicely noticed Roland in the gathering. Jon had relented at the last moment, and permitted the boy to attend. He was seated at the far end of the hall, between the disagreeable Thomas Howard and a third squire who had appeared in Henry's household. Good-looking, with long, wavy golden hair, Cicely had noticed that he was wont to bestow soft glances upon Mary Kymbe. Enquiries would be made to learn who he was. At first, she wondered if he too figured in Annie's pantheon, but it had soon become clear that he was solely concerned with Mary, who returned the interest.

Annie had not been granted a reprieve. Cicely, more than many, knew the consequences of surrendering to desire. But she had loved Richard completely, without ambition, and his love had been true. Annie acted solely out of ambition, and the likes of Roland de Vielleville, Thomas Howard and Edmund de la Pole would always stand in Richard's shadow. Annie had to be *made* to value herself—and to be wary of the retribution that would be Henry Tudor.

Cicely might not have paid much attention to Roland, had he not looked so uncomfortable. Thomas Howard and the other squire were talking across him, and perhaps that put him out of sorts. Whatever, when he suddenly got up and left the table, his companions hardly noticed. Roland approached Jon's steward, who immediately came to whisper to Jon, who indicated consent, and Roland hurried out by way of the doorway to the stairs hall. He was retiring?

Or was he? Annie's room was also up those stairs. Deciding to be safe rather than sorry, Cicely washed her hands swiftly in the little bowl of water provided. As she wiped them on a towel, clearly intending to excuse herself from the dais, she found Henry's eyes upon her.

'What is it, *cariad*?'

'Young love. Possibly. I am not sure, and mean to be vigilant.'

'*Diawl*,' he muttered. 'I will come with you.'

'There is no need, I—'

'There is every need, Cicely.' He turned to Jon, to whom he spoke over Bess's head. 'Pray attend to the queen, Uncle, for there is something that requires my attention.'

Jon had seen Roland leaving, and nodded.

There was some whispering as Henry and Cicely left the hall, but then the music and merriment resumed. Bess was like a marble statue, looking neither to left nor right.

Cicely took a lighted candle from the table at the foot of the stairs, and then she and Henry ascended. She led him up to the main bedchambers. Annie's door stood open, revealing her room to be empty and lit only by the fire. Cicely's heart sank, and she looked at Henry before nodding upward to indicate the next floor.

His lips pressed together and then he exhaled. 'I take it my delightful offspring is up there?'

'I imagine so. And I fear my sister may be with him. His room offers more privacy.'

'Why in Jesu's name is he not housed with the other squires? Why keep him here, in the same house as your troublesome sister?'

'It was felt he was less likely to misbehave if he was here. Please, Henry, it is difficult enough as it is. Jon and I would rather not see either of them, you may be sure of that. And I did ask you to remove Roland, to which you countered that we should remove Annie. We cannot do either thing, because our monarchs command otherwise.'

He smiled suddenly. 'You are not in the least afraid to be tart with me, are you?'

'If I were *not*, I would say a lot more, and you would like it a lot less.'

'Possibly.'

'Definitely.'

He put his palm to her cheek suddenly. '*Cariad*, you and I have much to talk of, beginning with the wine. Although that is by no means the most important thing on my mind.'

His private matter, she thought. He was going to confide it after all.

'We must have no secrets from each other,' he said softly, and then severed the intimacy by taking the candle to continue to the next floor. As before, candlelight shone beneath the door of Roland's room. A shadow moved as well, and then they heard Roland's dismayed exclamation.

'No! You must not! Please go, you only make trouble for me!'

Henry strode along the passage and thrust the door open with a crash. Roland was in his nightshirt, pressed back against the bedhead, clasping his genitals as if they were in imminent danger of ravishment. His face changed to utter dread as he saw Henry, and he leapt from the bed to his knees, hanging his head so much it seemed he must press his forehead to the floor.

Annie stood at the foot of the bed, and turned. She should have been even more dismayed than Roland, but was not.

Cicely did not know what to think, except that Annie had ignored all the warnings and *this* was the result. 'You really do not learn, do you, Annie? Have you *any* sense?'

'Why should I do what *you* tell me to? You are nothing!' Annie's true colours were fully—and rashly—hoisted.

Henry stepped to snatch her wrist and swing her around until he could give her a hard, stinging clout on the backside through her gown. 'Do not *presume* to speak to Lady Welles like that, do you hear me? Now, on your knees!' His voice shook with fury, and he released her so abruptly that she almost fell.

Annie scrambled to kneel, afraid to do anything but

keep her eyes fixed to his feet.

'Look at me.' He subjected her to his alarmingly uneven stare. 'Why are you here?'

'I … was keeping a tryst.'

'I was keeping a tryst, *Your Majesty*!' he corrected sharply.

She cringed, and repeated it with abject servility.

Roland was stung into protest. 'No! No, that is not true, Your Majesty! I listened to Lord and Lady Welles. I did not ask Lady Ann here. I wanted to stop seeing her at all. She just came into my room! *C'est la vérité vraie! C'est la vérité vraie!*'

'The honest truth?' Henry eyed Annie. 'Well, miss? Do you still insist you are on a tryst?'

Annie knelt there, and did not answer. She did not need to, Roland's sincerity was obvious.

'Answer me!' Henry snapped at her.

She flinched, and her face became red with mortification, anger and rash defensiveness. She forgot to whom she was speaking, and leapt up to point an accusing finger at Roland.

'He is lying!' she cried, and clearly would have blamed the seraphim in that moment. Anyone but herself. Her chin jutted, her body was stiff and her hands were clenched into tight fists, as if she would fly at Roland and pound him with them.

Henry, bemused, did not really know what to do with a twelve-year-old vixen in dire need of discipline. It was one thing to give her a thwack on the backside, but what next? He was suddenly and acutely aware of Cicely's warning.

Cicely came to his rescue. 'Annie, you must crave His Majesty's pardon, for you have shown him no respect. Do it. *Now.*' She spoke quietly but very firmly.

Annie's frightened eyes swung to Henry. 'Please forgive me, Your Majesty. I meant no insult to you.' At that she raised tear-filled eyes to his, and to Cicely's horror, gazed at him mistily, prettily. She meant to appear beseeching, but somehow appeared very different.

Henry stepped back as if scalded, and Cicely snatched her sister's arm to shake her warningly.

'For pity's own sake!' she hissed. 'Have you *any* idea how you are behaving? Does nothing occur to you beyond your own vanity? You are *not* a woman yet, even though you clearly think you are, and you have placed *yourself* in this fix. If Master Roland had been found in your room, then it would have been *his* fault and *his* responsibility. But here you are. Have you no thought of the consequences?'

'Will I now have to marry Master de Vielleville?' Annie asked then.

Roland looked appalled.

Suspicion swept over Cicely. 'Annie, did you come here hoping to be caught?'

Annie's lips clamped shut.

'Did—you—mean—to—be—caught?' Cicely repeated quietly, but she already knew the answer. Annie had decided she wanted Roland, not Thomas Howard, and this was her way of getting him. She had not anticipated Henry's appearance on the scene.

'Answer!' Henry ordered, having no time for Ann Plantagenet.

Annie's bravado deserted her. 'Yes, Your Majesty. I did.' A sob rose—well, seemed to rise—and she hid her face in her hands.

He uttered a ripe, four-lettered Anglo-Saxon expletive and looked askance at Cicely, who strove to stay calm.

'Annie, why do *you*, who intend to be of as high rank as possible, express a wish to marry a humble Breton *écuyer* who has no prospects?' She glanced at Henry, who looked back at her without expression.

'Because he has expectations. He told me so.'

Henry's baleful gaze swung to Roland, to whom he said something threatening in Breton. The boy shook his head violently and was so terrified that he began to cry.

That was when Annie lowered her hands. Desire was suddenly the *last* thing she felt for Roland de Vielleville.

'I see you are at last aware of your foolishness,' Cicely observed. 'Go to your room, and stay there.'

'But—'

'Enough, Annie. Just do it.'

'I hate you, Cissy! I hate you so much! *You* are a slut, not me.'

'*Gwylia dy dafod!*' Henry spat the words and took one furious stride to catch her by the hair and force her to her knees again. 'Apologize!'

Roland seemed more a ghost than a living boy. The only emotion was craven terror. His dread of Henry Tudor would not have been more obvious had it been caught in a shaft of sunlight.

'You are hurting me!' Annie cried, evidently incapable of knowing when she had already gone too far.

He pulled her forward until she was face down on the floor.

'Apologize!' he repeated icily. He was at his most dangerous now, held back by the most delicate of threads, and if Annie continued to defy him, Cicely did not know what he might do. So she said his name quietly.

'Harri?'

He glanced at her, again with that slight puzzlement that followed his outbursts, but then his eyes cleared, and he relaxed his grip a little.

To Cicely's immeasurable relief, Annie whimpered the abject apology he demanded. She would *never* again refer to him as her "dear king".

Henry released her. 'Guard your tongue from now on. I want you gone to your mother at Bermondsey in the morning, and you will stay there until *I* decide otherwise.'

'Not to Mother!' Annie cried in dismay.

'Is it your custom to argue with your king?' Henry asked coldly. 'You are my sister-in-law, and I will *not* have a silly little girl like you bringing *my* family into disrepute. Now, get out, and do exactly as Lady Welles has instructed!'

Annie fled, not even remembering to curtsey.

Henry turned to Roland. 'Stay in this room until I decide what is to be done with you. There will be grave punishment, of that you may be sure.'

'Yes, Your Majesty.'

'Just how many good prospects have you seen fit to mention to the Lady Ann?'

'None, Your Majesty.'

Henry's eyes glittered, and he reverted to Breton again. Whatever he said, Roland protested his innocence vehemently. His father remained stony-faced.

'You had better be telling the truth, because if you are not …' He left unsaid what would follow.

The boy hung his head. He was trembling from head to toe, utterly intimidated.

'And lock yourself in,' Henry continued. 'I am sure you do not wish your fellows to learn you are not man enough to defend your busy little dick from a twelve-year-old temptress.'

With that, he took up the candle again and steered Cicely out into the passage. They both heard Roland shoot the bolt on the inside.

'It is time we talked,' Henry said, shielding the flame with his hand as they approached the staircase.

Chapter Twenty-Four

SERVANTS WERE TENDING the parlour fire, but withdrew hastily as Cicely entered with Henry. When the door closed, he placed the candle in an alcove on the mantel.

'I had not realized you were having quite such trouble with the excesses of young love.'

'Why else would I have pleaded with you? But I confess I did not imagine Annie would be this foolish.'

'What was wrong with the wine, *cariad*?' he asked suddenly.

"I ... feared it was poisoned.'

'Tell me.'

She did not want to, because it would mean accusing Bess.

'Then let me start. I believe my wife has tried to poison me. Am I right?'

She looked away.

'You dropped the wine deliberately, *cariad*, and when I asked for it to be replenished, my queen saw to it that the whole jug was spilled. I am quite capable of interpreting the sequence.'

She nodded unwillingly. 'Yes, I suspected before, but tonight I saw her do it.' She described what had happened.

'So, it was not without significance that my taster did not arrive?'

'Possibly. Probably.'

'Why did you warn me?'

'You have to ask that?' She was hurt.

He drew a long breath. 'Well, yes, I think I do. She is your sister, and Richard was your uncle. Blood is blood.'

She smiled wryly. 'I did not want you dying under Jon's roof.'

'Ah. That explains it.' He came closer, his eyes like a mild winter's day, shafts of sunshine through grey, leafless branches. It was a strange effect, as if he knew all her secrets and yet did not care. Taking her gently by the hands, he drew her to him again. The cloves wrapped luxuriously around her, stirring memories, sensations ... needs. His cheek was against her hair and he swayed sensuously. 'How many times have we done this, mm?' he whispered.

She closed her eyes. 'You break my heart, Harri Tudur.'

'You broke mine a long time since.'

She drew back. 'I could not possibly allow you to take a drink I thought might be laced with poison. I could not do it.'

'I should trust you?'

'You already do, but should *I* trust *you*?' she countered.

'Ah, now *there* is a question, mm? *Cariad*, we both have things we wish to protect above all else, but neither of us knows what we will ultimately prize the most.'

'You would always protect your throne.'

'And what is *your* "throne", *cariad*? What would you protect more than anything else? More than your own life, perhaps?'

Did he know about Leo? She felt as if freezing water poured through her, but she gave nothing away. 'I would protect my husband.'

He smiled. 'What a little fibber you are,' he said softly, and bent to put his lips to the crook of her neck.

'Henry, you toy with me now, and think it amusing.'

He released her.

'And the poison is all because you and Bess hate each other.'

'I do not hate her, *cariad*. I may wish to be free of her, but I would not murder her to achieve it. It would be far too dangerous to my situation. That she hates me, I do not deny. And if she is prepared to kill me, then I imagine, being her mother's daughter, she has a Woodville coup in mind. Everything her mother wanted in 1483.'

Jack's observation too, she thought.

'I would be very interested indeed to know the names of her accomplices,' Henry said then.

'If you nurse hopes of me, I must disappoint. I do not know anything.'

'Short of confronting her now, and forcibly examining the contents of her purse, there is little I can do. It is unlikely the phial is still there, and even if it were, who would believe that beautiful, virtuous Elizabeth of York has been dosing me with Russian powder? She would accuse me of having the phial put there. I am saddled with her, Cicely, because to cast her off will mean losing the support of all the Yorkists who adhere to me because she restores your father's blood to the throne.'

'I do not know what to say, Henry, except that when we return to the hall now, you must not drink anything unless she herself is prepared to drink it.' Cicely paused sadly. 'I have not wanted to say any of this, because I do not want it to be true, Henry. She is my sister and I love her.'

'It has cost you much to save me, has it not?'

'Indecision was fleeting, Henry. You and I have shared too much, pleased each other too much and understood each other too much, although you are not always worthy,' she added a little slyly.

'I will make a note of that last remark in my special book.'

'Which your courtiers begin to dread.'

'Then they should not say things they do not wish me to hear.'

'You employ your imp again?'

He raised his eyebrows. 'Would I do that?'

'Yes.'

'So I would. I am unsound and incurably suspicious.' He waited. 'Madam, you are supposed to protest that I am wisdom personified and a paragon of every virtue.'

'Even though you are not?'

'Even then.' He smiled again.

There was a burst of cheering from the hall, and he glanced irritably towards the sound. 'We should return to the hall. There will already be gossip, and I do not wish to offend my uncle still more. But, *cariad*, there is so much I still need to say to you, and that you, I think, need to say to me. I do not refer only to events tonight, you understand, but to other matters. Secrets that we should share, not keep from each other. And I mean my secrets too. Do not think it is to be an uneven discussion. Trust must be absolute. Absolute. Do you understand?'

He had her attention so completely that all other sounds had died away. There was just the softness of his voice. He *did* know about Leo, she was surer than ever.

Richard's voice came back from the past. *'But between us there must always be trust, complete and inviolate. I cannot settle for anything less.'*

'There is that trust, Uncle.'

Henry came close and took her face in his hands, to caress her lips with his thumbs. 'I go to Sheen in a day or so, for the rest of the month. You and I can meet at the same manor house as before. Are you in agreement?'

'Yes.'

'Do not be afraid, my love, for I do not mean to trick or trap you. I simply need to share everything. With you. Because in my heart, *you* are my only queen. *Beth arall y gallaf ddweud?* That means, "What more can I say?"'

She gazed at him. 'Henry, I—'

But he stopped her words with a kiss, a passionate, loving, needful kiss that threatened to graze her spirit with its sincerity. His arms moved swiftly around her, and she returned it. Being in his arms again was too good.

In spite of his intention to return to the hall, it was several minutes more before they joined the revels again. But only kisses had been exchanged.

The rest of the evening went well enough, although Bess's face had remained thunderous. Henry, on the other hand, was affable and at his best. That night, in the small hours, when the royal guests had gone and Pasmer's Place was quiet again, Lord and Lady Welles sat before the fire in the bedchamber. The warm air was scented by dried lavender flowers in a little rush basket in the hearth, and it was good to just sip warm milk after all the richness of the dinner.

Now, alone with Jon at last, Cicely explained what had happened, and he was bitter about Bess.

'But she did not succeed, Jon, nor did Annie succeed in her mischief. Now I can only hope that we succeed in keeping Leo away from Tal … and from Henry.' She looked at him. 'I am certain Henry knows of him.'

'Until he says so, there is little to be gained by worrying over it.'

'Easy to say.'

He shook his head. 'No, sweetheart, not easy. I am very fond of your boy.' He looked a little sheepish. 'I opened my big mouth at Esher. I would never put Leo at risk. You know that.'

'I did not, but I do now. Such things were said that night, and I must apologize again for imposing it all on you.'

'From all accounts, it was imposed on you first.'

'I cannot bear the thought of keeping Leo from Henry *and* from Tal.' She had told Jon what she and Jack overheard in the church. 'But I think I can dissuade Tal from making any move upon Leo.'

'How?'

'By calling in the great debt he has owed to us since Esher, and which he has stressed to me since.'

'You think it is that simple?'

'I can but try.'

'And now you believe Henry is about to tell you his great dark secret?'

She met his gaze across the firelight. 'I ... pray so.'

Chapter Twenty-Five

BEFORE LEAVING FOR Sheen and her assignation with Henry, Cicely walked with Bess in the garden at Westminster Palace. It was the first time the sisters had met since the dinner, and anyone looking down from the palace windows would have thought the queen and Lady Welles were enjoying a little time together, but the truth was different. There was no enjoyment. Bess had summoned Cicely, and her reason was certainly not sweet and sisterly.

It was a blustery morning, with low, scudding clouds and sharp ripples on the grey Thames. The daffodils bobbed and dipped. They had been in bloom that other day, five long years ago now, in April 1483, when Cicely had overheard her mother and half-brother plotting against Richard.

'So, Cissy, what did you say to him?' Bess's voice was cold.

'The king?'

'You know to whom I refer.' Bess halted, the soft honey fur trimming on her cloak and hood streaming in the wind. Her eyes—the same blue as the gown beneath her cloak—were remote and although she used Cicely's pet name, there was little friendliness in it.

'I do not understand, Bess.' Cicely halted as well. How tired she was of having to convince others of her innocence and sincerity. It made such an accomplished liar of her, when lying was the last thing she wished to do. But a liar was what she had to be; what fate had decreed her to be. 'Truly, Bess, I do not understand.'

'So, when you and Henry disappeared at that cursed dinner, you did not speak of *anything*?'

'We spoke of Annie and the *écuyer* Roland de Vielleville. You *know* it to be so, Bess, for I told you that evening.' Cicely's glance moved to the palace, and there was Margaret, looking down as she had in the past, when other private meetings had taken place.

'It is what *else* you and Henry discussed that concerns me.'

Cicely decided to show irritability. 'We did not discuss anything else, Bess, and if you think that Henry and I were intimate, you are very mistaken.'

'Oh, you may not have done "it", but you both wanted to. I could see it in your eyes. You wind around him like a vine, and he has no wish at all to cut you away. Maybe he had some small vestige of conscience about me, but that has certainly gone now.' Bess snapped her fingers to the air.

'Bess, I was there that night of the banquet, when you told me you hated him. If he has now discarded any thought of reconciliation, you can hardly blame him.'

'Always you defend him. I am your sister, but you *never* take my side.' Bess was all bitter accusation.

Cicely confronted her. 'What did you put in his wine?'

Bess stared at her, caught completely off guard, but then she recovered. 'I did not put anything in his wine. How dare you even *suggest* it!'

'I know what I saw, Bess. Perhaps the phial is still upon your person now.'

311

Bess's hand moved instinctively to the purse, telling Cicely it was indeed still there.

'You did not discard the evidence? Such an oversight.'

Bess's response was to take the phial out and hurl it over the garden wall into the Thames. 'There,' she said triumphantly, '*now* prove anything.'

'So, what was in it? The same as before? Russian powder? Oh, do not protest, for I am your closest sister, we spent our childhood together and were together until you married Henry. You hate him enough to kill him, and you have now attempted to do it twice.'

'Can you prove it?'

'I do not need to prove it. I know it to be so.'

'And now, because of you, Henry believes this lie? How sweet of you to protect your lover. Do you intend to have him to yourself? To ride the royal prick until you—and it— are worn out?'

'If I did, it would be infinitely more than *you* want of him, Bess. Did you really think I could be so close to you by that table and not see what you did? That I did not notice how you urged me to have his wine served, even though the taster had not arrived? The taster who, incidentally, has since been found dead in an alley. And did you then think I would let it all happen, so that Henry was poisoned before my eyes, in *Jon's* house? Did you want Jon's name to be synonymous with an attempt to kill his own nephew?' Cicely looked evenly at her. 'It seems to me that another uncle had such untrue charges levelled against him.'

'Do you know how utterly mad you sound, Cissy?'

'I know *you* know that Henry does not like almonds and cannot smell or taste them, I know how *un*surprised you were when he was taken ill the first time, and how the indignation you show now is not at all convincing. Yes, I told Henry what I thought you had done.'

'Could it be that you love my husband?' Bess enquired coolly.

'I enjoy his kisses, his caresses and his bed, whereas you … *you* throw away every chance to be happy in your marriage. You may be Queen of England, but you are also a fool.'

'You *dare* to speak to me like this!'

'Yes! If telling Henry means you have to stay your hand from now on, then I am glad. He is your king, your husband and the father of your son, as well as the two babies you have lost. You should have comforted each other, but *you* could not bring yourself to do it. You showed much more genuine emotion for Leo than your own lost children.'

'Because Leo is Richard,' Bess said quickly.

'And he is *mine*, Bess. What do you think when you hold Prince Arthur? The truth now. What do you feel?'

'That I hold Henry Tudor's child, not my own.'

'Oh, Bess! Arthur is your own flesh and blood, born of *your* body, of *your* travails. He is yours and he is Henry's. In him the two of you are bound together. Please, Bess, stop doing these dreadful things. My sympathies are with Henry. He does not want you any more than you want him, but he would have tried to make your marriage less of a battlefield. Now it is time for *you* to see sense.'

'I hate you, Cissy. I hate you for the joy you find in the act of love, and the way you steal men's hearts, minds and bodies. And then keep them all. Henry loves you and always will. If he could install you in my place, he would do it gladly. Well, it is *my* joy that he cannot have you.'

'You could have refused to marry him,' Cicely said bluntly. 'If you had refused, there was nothing he could do about it. By placing you in the care of his mother, it could even have been said he abducted you. All you had to do was say no. You could have roused the land to rebellion before Henry even had time to have himself crowned.

Yorkists would have risen again, and Jack would surely have become king. But *you* chose to say yes to Henry Tudor. It was *your* decision.'

'That is monstrous! Of course I had to marry him! To bring peace after all those years of war.'

'You did not *care* about years of war, and decided to make the most of your moment of power. A knife was not held to your throat. And Henry could not have married me because I was already with child, so it was not my fault either. So why did you agree, Bess? Mm? You simply had a fancy to be Queen of England, even with the wrong king. So do not grizzle to me about your dreadful lot, or how much insult it does you when Henry visits your bed. It is all what *you* have made of it. Now, however, I think it is far too late.' Cicely held her sister's gaze. 'So, why poison him now? What is your purpose, Bess? To do in 1488 what our mother could not manage in 1483?'

For a long moment there was only the sound of the breeze in the trees, and the traffic on the Thames, and then Bess smiled coolly. 'Now, *there* is a thought,' she said quietly. 'And in the meantime, Henry has to keep coming to my bed.'

'Unfortunately for him, he has to fuck *you* to get more heirs. And you will be fruitful. You could be enjoying his attentions, as I do. You *are* a fool, Bess. Such a fool.'

'How arrogantly sure of yourself you are, Cissy. My sister, the expert in all things carnal.'

'Practice makes perfect, is that not what they say?' Cicely stepped away quickly as Bess tried to strike her. Her glance moved to the window, and she saw Margaret's astonished face draw back into the room.

'Well, as you say, Henry must practise with me, not you,' Bess said, lowering her hand slowly.

'While *you* continue to practise with poison and other methods? Who helps you in your hatred, Bess?' Cicely asked suddenly, intending to take Bess unawares.

'What do you mean?'

'Well, you were not at Esher, yet the wine there was mixed with poison at your command. Someone helps you. Who is it?'

'So you can trot along to Henry and betray me still more? I think not, Lady Welles.'

'The name Marshal means nothing to you?'

Bess looked blank. 'Marshal? Only the old Earls of Pembroke. Why?'

'It is of no matter.' Cicely was relieved, because it surely meant Tal was *not* involved in the poison. She adjusted her hood. 'I think you and I have probably said all we need to each other. I am sorry I had to tell Henry, but if you had not done it, I would not have had anything to tell. Just know that if ever you need me—really need me—I will come to you. We will always be sisters.'

'And just *you* know that my silence about Leo can no longer be guaranteed.'

Cicely managed a cool smile. 'I fear that Henry already knows.'

Bess gathered her cloak closer as another gust of wind swept in from the Thames. 'I will threaten to expose his sinful relationship with you. He will not take me lightly. After all, I am the queen, the beautiful, trusted, *respected* Bess of York. I would *never* be accused of telling an untruth. I have him where I want, Cicely. Under my pretty thumb.'

'I would not count upon it.'

Walking away alone, Cicely entered the palace to find Margaret waiting for her. It was a surprise, and yet not.

Henry's mother was earnest. 'I must speak with you, Cicely.'

'As you wish, my lady.'

'Come, we can be comfortable and private in my apartment.'

They walked through the palace, and Margaret received deep obeisance from all those they encountered. Cicely smiled. 'How revered you are, my lady,' she said, as they entered Margaret's rich rooms. She turned for a lady-in-waiting to divest her of her hood and cloak, and then went to hold her hands out to the fire.

'Feared, more probably,' Margaret replied frankly, waving all the ladies and pages away and then pouring two small cups of mulled wine.

When they were both comfortable, Margaret spoke again. 'Cicely, Henry has told me what occurred at Pasmer's Place. I must ask, have you sacrificed your sister for him? Is that why you and she quarrelled in the garden?'

'Lady Margaret, I may have told the king about the poison, but Bess is still my sister, and I do not wish to discuss her. Please, I beg that you understand and are not offended.'

'I respect your feelings, Cicely, but I must always do all I can to protect his throne, and above all, his life.'

Cicely nodded resignedly.

'Your sister is an unhappy creature, that much cannot be denied, but she has attempted to *murder* Henry, and in a most cruel, pitiless way. He is not an angel, I have to concede, but for his queen to despise him so much …'

'They should not be husband and wife, my lady, but they have to be. I do not think Bess will do anything more after this. She knows that Henry is aware of what she has done.'

'And she hates you because you saved him?'

Cicely lowered her glance. 'Yes, I believe so.'

'I imagine she seeks to be Queen Mother, and therefore powerful during Arthur's minority?'

The same theory yet again. 'I do not know. Truly. My lady, if you only knew how much *all* of this grieves me.'

Margaret smiled gently. 'But I do, my dear. How

wondrously fortune turns full circle. You, who loved King Richard with all your heart, can now feel the same for his conqueror.'

Cicely's expression did not change. Love *Henry* as she had loved Richard? As she now loved Jack? Never!

'Perhaps it is time for me to tell you that I know your love for Richard was fleshly, and you have a son by him, called Leo Kymbe, whom you have sent into some new place of hiding, as yet unknown to me.'

The words shook Cicely. 'You … are wrong, about everything. Leo Kymbe is *not* my son, by Richard or anyone else.'

'Yes, he is, my dear. I made it my business to see him recently, when he was here in London. I was advised that Tom Kymbe would take him up before him for a ride along Thames Street, so I watched him. He is in Richard's image, and there is much of you in him as well. I am in no doubt whatever that you lay with your uncle and he gave you a child.'

'Then to what terrible corner of Hell will you consign me for such an unnatural sin?'

Margaret chuckled. 'Oh, my dear, you once pointed out that I had met Richard and knew his immense charm. Well, it was true. If even I was drawn to him in such a way, how could you not be? Oh, I loathed him for interesting me, and I blamed him. But the waywardness was in me, not him.'

Cicely was astonished. 'What a revelation you are today, my lady.'

Margaret nodded. 'I am at ease with you, Cicely. You have something within you that has that effect, I think. Besides, you have long since known of my feelings for Edmund Tudor. If nothing else, it proves to you that I am not the sanctimonious, ridiculously holy creature I may choose to appear.' Margaret drew a long breath. 'You may as well know that Henry is now aware that Leo is your

317

child and that Richard was his father. *I* did not tell him, the queen did.'

'Bess?' When Bess had made her threat in the garden, she had *already* betrayed everything?

'She told him after the banquet. I am sorry, Cicely, for I realize what a terrible shock this is, but it is best you know not to confide in her again.'

'If that is when she told him, he already knew. When he and I spoke during the banquet, it was clear to me that he was aware. He did not say so, but I knew.'

'Then I do not know how, unless his spies are as efficient as mine. I would not have told him anything, because of Jon, with whom I am glad to see you reconciled. It is clear my brother has been helping you all along, since Sheriff Hutton.'

Cicely's hands twisted anxiously in her lap. 'What will Henry do?'

'I do not know, my dear. I cherish my half-brother and do not want harm to come to him. You cherish your son, and do not wish harm to come to *him*.'

'He is only a baby. Two years old. I want to shield him from everything.'

'When I first did all I could to bring Henry back to England from Brittany, it was simply to see him restored to his father's earldom. I would have been content to see him at your father's or Richard's court, as the Earl of Richmond. Not that your father could have been trusted not to lop his head the moment he stepped ashore. It was much later that I conspired to see my son on the throne. You too may feel that way one day, my dear. I am sure you still regard the House of York as the rightful ruler of England.'

Cicely did not answer, and Margaret smiled. 'If there is one thing that unites us, my dear, it is our fierce determination to protect our sons. Henry is beyond my protection now, and will behave as he sees fit, but when he was younger, I fought like a cat from Hell itself to shield and guide him. Even if from a distance, with the sea between us. You have hidden Leo, and you are very wise to do so. Do not let him be found, my dear. And as he grows, do all you can to dissuade him from pursuing what his blood dictates. I do not say this to protect Henry, but to protect *you* from heartbreak. Cherish Richard's son, and build a wall around him. That is my advice to you, not as the king's mother, but as your friend.'

'Is Henry searching for Leo?'

'I only know that *my* spies definitely are not. When he was removed from Hallows Lane, I ordered that he was not to be sought. I do not want to know his whereabouts, because then I cannot withhold information from my son. All I know is that Tom Kymbe is now back at Friskney, with a story of the boy's abduction from an inn at Huntingdon. It cannot be disproved, of course.'

Huntingdon. Cicely drew a long breath.

'The route to that town would be most enlightening, I am sure,' Margaret observed thoughtfully, 'because I understand Kymbe and your boy left London for the west. However, Kymbe is now at his home again, without the boy, and the innkeeper at Huntingdon does indeed confirm he had a boy with him on arrival. There was a huge disturbance during the night, after which there was no further sign of the boy.'

Cicely knew it was all a ruse. Tom had taken Leo to Wight, and had now confirmed as much in a very brief note that no one else but she would have understood. Tom was so very good at conveying things to her. He had written that she would hear of a kidnapped child, hired at Huntingdon for the express purpose of disappearing again.

'My dear ...' Margaret hesitated. 'I will do all I can to support you. Loyalty binds me as well, you see, not only to

King Richard, whom they now say was *Good* King Richard.'

'Because he was.'

'Yes. He was, and the struggle to replace him costs Henry's health dear every day. I would *never* have striven so to put him on the throne if I had realized what it would do to him. He needs you, Cicely.'

Cicely felt the mantle of responsibility being placed around her shoulders.

Mary had accompanied Cicely to Westminster, and after the conversation with Margaret, mistress and maid left together, but on the river stairs they encountered Edmund de la Pole. He was with Thomas Howard and the golden-haired squire who liked Mary Kymbe. The maid blushed, the squire blushed, and their interest in each other could not have been clearer had they flung themselves into each other's arms.

His name, Cicely now knew, was Stephen Perrings, and he was dressed in blue. Mary called him Perry, and the moment Cicely had learned his surname, she knew Mistress Kymbe's prediction about the periwinkle flower was correct. And how appropriate that he should even be wearing periwinkle blue.

But it was mostly Edmund who held Cicely's attention now. Jack's brother wore wine red, a very short and tight-waisted doublet and hose that appeared to have been painted upon his person, making the intimate details of his anatomy very clear to see indeed. It proved that said contents of said hose, while substantial, were no match for Jack's. Which was probably another reason for Edmund's dislike of his elder brother.

It could not quite be said that Edmund minced towards her, but he walked in a way that attracted a glance or two, and he tossed his head so that his cloud of auburn curls almost seemed to billow. His cloak, fastened loosely at the throat, caught the breeze and lifted to reveal his perfect, lithe and so youthful body. But would he keep the hearts of those who were drawn to his cause, as Jack did? Cicely doubted it very much. *Would* he have a cause? She wondered. He had originally been regarded as Jack's heir, and therefore Richard's, but the waters had been muddied now, what with something mysterious going on in Burgundy ... and, now, Leo.

He halted before her. 'Cousin Cicely,' he murmured, sweeping an elaborate bow.

'Cousin Edmund.' She merely inclined her head, but before she knew it, he had stepped close enough to embrace her and put his cool lips to her cheek.

'So, my lady, we know each other at last,' he whispered.

She tried not to shudder. 'You have been pointed out to me, sir,' she answered, and moved deliberately back, so that he had to release her. 'Do not presume to be so familiar, sir, for I think we both know we are enemies.'

'Enemies? Am I not the heir to our House?'

'Are you?'

His light-brown eyes rested thoughtfully on her. 'My brother will never return.'

'Hardly, unless the Almighty sends him back with the gift of eternal life.' But she knew this distasteful creature knew Jack still lived.

'Do not think to toy with me, Lady Welles.'

'I am intimate with the king, sir, so do not think to toy with *me*, either.'

'Be sure to always glance over your shoulder, sweetheart.'

'I am not your "sweetheart", my lord, and forbid you to be so familiar. I also forbid you to have any dealings with my sister, the Lady Ann.'

'Who are you to forbid anything?' he asked coldly.

'I am the king's confidante.'

A light hovered in his eyes. 'Ah, yes, I have heard the whispers.'

'Then do not test their veracity. By the way, your handwriting has been identified.'

He laughed. 'My *handwriting?* Do not test the veracity of that, my lady.'

Her mind was quick. 'So, not your handwriting, but dictated by you.'

'Prove it.'

'You, too, should glance frequently over your shoulder, sir.'

'You threaten me?'

'Prove it. Now, step aside, for I do not intend to walk around you.'

His resentment glittered, but he stepped aside, and swept another intricate bow.

She walked on, and Mary tore herself away from exchanging smiles with her Perry. Thomas Howard had remained aloof throughout.

As the two women hailed a skiff and were conveyed away from the steps, Edmund remained where he was, watching until the traffic on the river hid them from sight.

Jon's previously invented duties as constable had turned out to be rather more real than he had expected, and he had to leave again the day after Cicely's encounter with Edmund.

Cicely had not wept over the great schism with Bess, perhaps because Bess now seemed an alien creature. A changeling. Totally different from the sister with whom Cicely had once been so close and loving. But then, it could be said that Bess would think that Cicely was no longer a loving sister, either. Too many secrets and lies had now passed beneath the sibling bridge.

Lord and Lady Welles said their farewells in the parlour

at Pasmer's Place. He was dressed for the long journey to Yorkshire, where unrest was feared to be stirring due to taxes and other grievances. The county was still strong for Richard, and did not take kindly to the usurper who had taken the throne by treachery. Jon's entourage—including Roland—waited in the yard, and a large force of six hundred archers and men-at-arms was camped just outside the city walls, where the great road to the north began.

He and Cicely faced each other a little awkwardly, and his manner was reserved. 'Be wary of Edmund de la Pole, Cicely. He is capable of great mischief.'

'I know.'

'I trust you will remember me to Jack?'

'Do you wish me to?'

He nodded. 'I believe so. I still cannot dislike him, much as I wish to.'

'I will tell him.'

'You do understand why I will not share your bed?'

'Yes.' She smiled a little. 'Perhaps you will remember me as you romp with your doxies?'

'Perhaps.'

Their glances met for a moment, and then he spoke of something else.

'Did Margaret mention Roland?' he enquired.

'Not this time.'

'So, she still does not know about him.' Jon was intent upon her. 'Do not let what is endearing about Henry lead you into folly. Remember Bosworth, John of Gloucester, Huntingdon, and what he did to Jack. You must keep everything in your mind at all times. Never trust Henry Tudor, or indeed Harri Tudur.' He put his hand to her chin. 'Look at me properly, Cicely. As I said before, no matter what Henry *says*, his insistence upon absolute truth between you probably only extends to *you* being truthful to *him*, because believe me, *he* will not be open about everything.

No matter how sweet, seductive and forlorn Harri Tudur appears, there is always the Henry Tudor of whom you are so often—and so rightly—very afraid.'

'I will take every care with Henry. Truly. Jon, I will miss you. May I kiss you farewell?'

He did not reply, but did not move away, so she wrapped her arms around his neck and put her lips tenderly to his. It was a gentle kiss, but did not go further than tenderness. And he did not return it to any great extent. Just a little, perhaps. She released him again.

'You must take care, too,' she said then. 'To Richard's supporters you will always be Henry's uncle.'

'I know.'

'I do love you, Jon.'

He gazed at her. 'As I love you, Cicely. It is just that I can no longer share you.'

'This is where we were at the beginning of our marriage.' Memories returned, brief but brilliant and clear. The moment he rode into Sheriff Hutton, the moment she encountered him when she left John of Gloucester's chamber at dawn, the way he had put his hand over hers when they reached London, the moment he proposed marriage to save her reputation and legitimize her unborn child. The moment he had told her—so gently and kindly— that she must part with Leo in order to save his life. There was no one else like Jon Welles.

'Yes, it is how we started, and perhaps it should have been where we remained.' He gathered his hat and gauntlets from a table and then left without another word.

She looked down into the sunlit yard as he emerged from the house, still tugging on his gauntlets. He mounted, and raised his hand to her, before proceeding into St Sithe's Lane, his mounted men-at-arms following. They made a brave sight, with the Welles banners aloft in the bright spring air.

Mary had come to the door behind her, and Cicely turned. 'Have you put out your cloak and hood?'

'Yes, my lady, and my shoes. But please let me accompany you. You really should not go to the Red Lion alone.'

'I will not come to harm, for Lord Lincoln awaits me.'

'And now his brother hunts him. Perry is anxious for you.'

'Indeed. I am grateful to Master Perrings for his concern.'

Mary said no more.

Chapter Twenty-Six

I⊤ WAS so good to lie in Jack's arms again, even in the shabby bed at the Red Lion. Cicely thought of the last time they had lain here like this, just before he left the country ahead of being summarily arrested—and most likely beheaded—by Henry.

Now, here they were again, but that other occasion intruded upon her thoughts, and she knew it was because since he had come back to her, the talk had been of removing Henry from the throne, but not of how York meant to re-establish itself. She had mentioned it, but he had not really answered. He had to have an ultimate plan, but as yet, she was not in his confidence. Had he even told Tal? Worse, did he even *know* what to do?

She feared he was in limbo, which was not right for a man of action and principle; a natural leader. She was so afraid that his only course would be to flee to Burgundy again, there to join other exiled Yorkists and prepare another invasion. But Henry's private matter had to be exposed first. Whatever it was. Being with Jack like this, she could no longer hold her tongue.

'Jack, what do you plan to do?'

He put a hand to her cheek. 'Never, for a moment, forget

how much I love you, Cicely.'

'You are going to leave England again?' she whispered.

He did not want to answer, but nodded. 'Yes.'

'I knew you would have to, but facing it has been so difficult.'

He looked at her. 'Come with me.'

She stared, and sat up slowly.

He sat up as well, and put a hand over hers. 'We can take Leo with us and be safe with our aunt in Burgundy.'

She closed her eyes, for the thought of being with him, and Leo, was so alluring and unexpected that for a long moment she saw only Paradise, but then she shook her head. 'I cannot, Jack.'

'Why? What possible reason do you have to stay? To be with Henry? With Jon? Because of your sister? The Kymbes? Tal, even? Why? Which of them is worth our happiness, mm?'

'Please, Jack, do not think harshly of me.'

'I could never do that.' He raised her hand to his lips. 'But I would like to know why you think you should stay here.'

'If I go with you, and take Leo, I will be exposing Jon and the Kymbes to the utmost danger. Henry now knows about Leo, and is aware that he was at Friskney, cared for and concealed by Tom Kymbe and Mistress Kymbe. He also knows that Jon has been lying for me. Henry already strongly suspects that Richard was Leo's father, and is not fool enough to overlook the possibility of legitimacy. After all, the example of my father and Tal's sister Eleanor is rather glaring. Tal is already certain of it, and I still fear what *he* may do.'

'Tal will not do anything.'

'How can you be sure?'

'Because his word has been given.'

'But, how—'

'Sweetheart, I do not think you need worry about ever losing Jon Welles. He sent a message to me—through Pasmer—that I was to warn Tal not to make any move at all where Leo is concerned, or he, Jon, would offer a very large reward for the head of the Marshal of Calais on a platter.'

She looked at him. 'Jon said *that*?'

Jack grinned. 'Yes, and he meant it. An urgent message was sent to Tal, and returned by the next tide, with his promise. You need not fear anything from Humphrey Talbot, who *is* a good man, no matter that it may have seemed otherwise for a while. In fact, he sent you this as proof of his good faith.' He reached over for his purse, and took out Tal's topaz ring.

'But … I cannot accept it!'

'Why not? It is not sent as a lover's gift, but as a token of his sincerity. He would be most offended if you refused it. Here, let me place it on your finger, so it is warm from *my* hand. Perhaps that will ease your mind.' He took her hand and slipped the heavy ring onto her middle finger, which was too small, so he placed it on her thumb instead.

'It does not feel right to wear such a gift.'

Jack returned the subject to the reason for her unwillingness to leave with him. 'Sweetheart, I wish you would reconsider, and leave with me.'

'I am to meet Henry at the manor near Sheen. He intends us to share secrets, and I believe he will seek to ensure my silence by revealing his knowledge of Leo. I think he knows that with that held over me, I will hold my tongue about whatever he tells me. Except to you. I will let you know everything, I swear it. Besides, you already know what he will tell me.'

'Not every detail. I did not have the chance to examine all those lost documents in full. But yes, I know what his private matter is. And I still will not tell you. It is best that you are genuinely shocked. Which you will be, believe me. Cicely, I would rather we left together, with Leo. Tal will gain fresh proof, I am sure of it, and—'

'Please, Jack. I have told you why I will not. Oh, my dearest, there is nothing I would like more than to be with you, but my honour will not permit it. I can protect others with my body, because Henry will stay his hand if he has me. I will be *everything* to him, do you understand? I will be *such* a lover, that he will never want another woman. And if I ever *really* believe Leo is in imminent danger, I will send him to you. You already know I will do that, because I want *you* to have charge of him, but only when he is old enough. Until then, I must be able to see him, hold him sometimes, let him know how much his mother loves him. I do not want him to grow up as Henry has, with you in the part of Jasper. I know what I risk, but *must* adhere to what I know is right. Leo can never know his father, but he *will* know his mother, who will one day tell him of Richard.'

Jack rose from the bed, his body pale, and went to the window. There had been snow the last time they were here, not spring sunshine.

'Reassure me, Jack,' she whispered.

'Reassure you? Of what?'

'That you still love me. I know how much you want me to go with you.' She fingered the topaz, which, rather strangely, *did* make her believe in its previous owner's sincerity.

He smiled. 'I love you, Cicely Plantagenet, and I will wait for you, however long it takes you to decide.'

'When will you leave?'

'Soon.'

'When?'

'Tomorrow.'

'Oh.' The knowledge settled wretchedly over her. She

would be without him again, but her mind was set upon what she had to do.

'I understand, sweetheart, and will not hold anything against you.' He smiled and returned to the bedside. 'Except, perhaps, myself.'

She smiled too. 'I do hope so, sir, because if you are to leave tomorrow, I cannot imagine how long it might be before we can be together again.'

'One thing more, Cicely, do not trust Henry! He will promise you the world, and perhaps the moon as well, but you can *never* be sure of him. So now it is my turn to extract a promise. The moment you realize your sacrifice has been in vain, and you can no longer protect anyone by being Tudor's plaything, I want you to promise to join me in Bruges. *With Leo.* So ... promise.'

She nodded. 'I promise.'

He came to pull her from the bed and up into his arms. 'We have spouses, I know, and break more than one Commandment, but we belong together, Cicely Plantagenet.'

She closed her eyes as he held, kissed and caressed her again.

Later, when Cicely and Jack walked back to Pasmer's Place, as unremarkable as any pair of lovers, there was a disturbance in St Sithe's Lane, a rider on a bolting horse.

As it commenced its wild flight towards them, someone behind them shouted a warning. 'Beware! It is no accident!'

Cicely whirled about, and just saw Stephen Perrings draw back out of sight by St Anthony's church at the southern corner of Budge Row. He must have hidden as they passed! She tried to pull Jack to the side of the lane, into the very doorway where she had been attacked, but something about the oncoming rider kept Jack where he was.

There was more than enough room for the horse to

swerve around him, but the rider had no such intention. His face was hidden, but she saw his leg, wearing tight wine-red hose exactly like those worn by Edmund de la Pole ... and there was a dagger in his right hand!

'Jack!' she screamed, hauling upon his arm, but he pushed her back.

'Stay out of danger,' he said quietly, as if all was well in the world, and then he faced his brother again, stepping swiftly from side to side, panicking the horse into slithering to a noisy halt and rearing.

Jack immediately darted forward to grab the bridle. 'So, Ned, you would stoop to this? To fratricide?'

'You do not exist, Jack! And I will *not* give up anything to you!' Edmund cried, trying to reach down to stab him.

Jack caught his wrist and twisted it until Edmund cried out and dropped the dagger. 'And you think to murder me in order to have what is mine?'

'It is now *my* right!' Edmund breathed, his face contorted with loathing.

'I am not dead enough for anything to be yours by right, little brother, and you are not man enough for the task anyway!' Jack grabbed Edmund's boot to haul him from the saddle, but Edmund managed to hold his seat. The terrified horse reared and danced around, finally tearing from Jack's grasp, and set off towards the corner of Budge Row. Within seconds it had gone.

Cicely advanced nervously. 'Jack?'

He pulled her close. 'I am all right, sweetheart,' he said, his voice muffled as his lips were against her head.

'He tried to kill you!'

'I know.'

She clung to him, terrified of what had so nearly happened. 'Mary's new love warned us!' she said then.

'Her new love?'

'Stephen Perrings.'

'Perrings? The name seems familiar ...'

'He is a squire in Henry's household, and I have seen him in Edmund's company.'

'But clearly he is not Edmund's friend.'

'It would seem not.' She was anxious. 'Jack, Edmund *knew* we would come this way.'

'As did Perrings. It had not escaped me.'

'Perry—Mary calls him that—will have known from her, I am sure. But how Edmund knew ...' She gripped Jack's arms suddenly. 'I cannot lose you again, but would rather you were safe and far away from here. Edmund might succeed the next time, so do not wait until tomorrow, go now!'

'Oh, thank you for the comfort.'

She stretched on tiptoe to kiss him, and sink her fingers through his hair for the last time. 'Please, my love, do not delay a moment more. Edmund will not rest until he knows you are dead once and for all.'

'If you only realized how hard it is to leave you ...'

'I do know, Jack, because I feel the same pain, but I cannot bear you to stay and be in as much danger from him as you are from Henry! Go, please.'

He held her tightly, and their hearts pounded together, then, after one last kiss, he went, his boots echoing on the cobbles.

Cicely gazed after him. Her heart felt as if it were splitting in two. When would she see him again? *Would* she see him again? Perhaps he had just walked away from her forever. The salt in her eyes was so hot and stinging that it was several moments before she could continue the final few yards to the gates of Pasmer's Place.

Later, she learned from Mary that the maid had asked Perry to be on guard for anything Edmund de la Pole might do against his brother, so he had followed Edmund to St

Sithe's Lane, and known by his manner that something was planned. Thus he had been able to shout his warning before making himself very scarce indeed. Edmund could not have realized he had even been present.

Chapter Twenty-Seven

THE APRIL WIND was strong as Cicely stood at the bedchamber window at the rear of the small, unimportant
manor house, near Sheen, where she and Henry had met
before. It had been on her seventeenth birthday, 20 March,
1486, St Cuthbert's Day, and his present to her had been
Richard's ruby ring.

Now she watched Henry through the uneven panes.
He leaned thoughtfully against the willow that overhung
the swollen stream in the garden below. There were evergreens, jonquils that shivered in the fierce draughts of air,
and ducks huddled together in the lee of a wall. It was
too cold for April, but Henry did not seem to notice as he
watched the water racing past his feet, the swift current
dragging winter fronds and weeds like drowned banners.
He had been there since arriving over half an hour ago, and
seemed to be preparing himself to face her. She heard him
cough occasionally.

There were two very different men within that lonely
figure, and it was as King Henry VII, the enemy of her
House, that she had to think of him now. She had been
frightened and unsure of him when they first met. Now,
countless acts of love later, she was frightened and unsure

again. Not on her own account, but her child's, and those others who helped her to shield that child.

Even leaning there, deep in thought, Henry was naturally arresting. When his furred cloak lifted and flapped, she saw he wore purple. The jewels in his hat brooch caught the cold light occasionally, and sometimes his hair blew across his face, obliging him to push it aside.

His expression was strained, and she knew that, like her, he was dwelling upon what to say and how to say it. He had told her there had to be complete honesty between them, but what did she dare to tell him? Common sense said one thing, her heart said another. But, looking at him now, she sensed he *had* come here today to be truthful, and because she had decided she must be close to him for a long time yet, she had to risk being truthful with him. Well, as much as she dared without betraying others.

Turning, he looked directly up at the window, and she knew he had been aware of her all along. Their gaze met for several moments, his face gave nothing away, and then he made his way towards the house.

She did not go down to greet him, but waited where she was, with the bed to remind her—and him—of the happiness they had shared here before. Her gown was the plum brocade. If honesty was required, she showed it with this gown, because she knew he liked it best of all. Her hair was loose, and her only jewels were four rings—Jon's wedding band, Richard's ruby, Jack's amethyst and the emerald Henry himself had given to her. Tal's topaz was omitted, for to wear it would concentrate Henry's attention, and not to the good. His Silver Hound was trusted at the moment, and should remain so.

The inclusion of Jack's amethyst was quite deliberate, and an indication that she meant to be sincere in the minutes to come. Although not sincere enough to tell him that Jack was still alive and sheltering in Burgundy to raise an army for another invasion. She smiled a little wryly. Here she was, wondering how honest *Henry* would be, when all the time *she* was not going to be completely forthright either.

At last she heard his steps, always so light. Her pulse raced and her mouth was dry as he opened the door. His outer clothes had been discarded so that he was bareheaded, and as he paused in the doorway, the light from the window shone on his silver collar … and the twisted-dragon pendant.

He smiled to see the plum brocade. 'Do you have seduction in mind, *cariad?*'

'Only if you do.' His smile and use of the Welsh endearment was reassuring, yet the foundations of any pleasure were washed by undercurrents. She sank into a deep, respectful curtsey.

He closed the door softly, and came to raise her. 'There is no need for that, *cariad.*' The brush of his fingers was light upon her bare shoulder, and very cold from the air outside, but the scent of him was more of a comfort than she wished.

She rose slowly, every nerve tingling, the blood flowing through her veins as swiftly as the stream past the willow. She was alive to everything about him. Everything. And it was not simply fear.

He moved away, as if her closeness made him uneasy. 'How are you?' he asked then, clearly for something to say.

'Better than you, I think. I heard you coughing out there.'

'Indeed.' He looked from the other window, which faced over the Sheen road, along which he and his entourage had set off on his royal progress less than a year ago. 'I seem to remember it was here that I promised you the emerald you wear now.'

'Yes, you raised your hand as you rode past at the head of your progress. And you smiled.'

'You also wear Lincoln's amethyst. And this time it *is* his amethyst, as no doubt it was at Flemyng Court.'

He missed nothing, and the first moment of truth was upon her. She met his eyes. 'Yes, for the honesty you wish there to be today. I admit what you have always suspected about Jack. He was my lover, and he gave me the amethyst at Friskney.'

'Warm from his finger?'

'Yes.' *And now from somewhere else as well …*

'Well, his finger will never now be warm again.'

'No.' *Oh, little do you know, Henry …*

'How very small and lonely a word that is. Do you still love him?'

'I will always love him. Death cannot take that away.'

Henry regarded her. 'You believe that I killed him?'

Was it a trick? 'I think so, but that was in self defence.' *Here is a way out, Henry. I offer it to you.*

'No, it was not self-defence. I did not think myself to be in any danger at all.'

It was not the response she had expected. 'What, then?'

'In all honesty? He was still alive when I found him, and there was no sign of his accomplice, who, incidentally, must have been the one who dislocated his left shoulder. Now, I admit that I wanted him dead, and even more wanted to interrogate him first. I would be a liar to state otherwise, but …'

'But?'

'When you and I have made love, and I have slept beside you, how many times could you have murdered me? Mm? But you have never done anything at all. Not once. Well, when I was confronted by your cousin, wounded, in great pain and at my mercy, I could not do anything except try to push the joint back into place. I see you do not believe me, but it is the truth. And that was when I was struck from behind. And kicked. When I eventually regained consciousness, there was no sign of Jack de la Pole.' He smiled almost wistfully. 'I see you still think me a liar.'

Every word he said could be a lie ... or the truth. What he said and what Tal said could both explain what happened. The only person who would have known the truth was Jack, who could not remember.

'*Cariad*, his shoulder was not only stabbed and dislocated, but your husband's dagger had been savagely twisted. Jack was losing a lot of blood and was in agony. If he had received full attention, he would have survived, but as it was ... he did not make it further than the woods just outside Knole.'

'And you saw him dead?' she asked.

He hesitated. 'I believe so. I did not go close enough to examine the body.'

Still possible, she thought. Certainly not an outright untruth. 'Jack has gone, and I accept it,' she said.

'One day it may be my turn. After all, my enemies will never stop trying.' He went to the fire and bent for a fresh log, which he tossed on the flames. Using a poker, he forced it down, setting myriad sparks scattering and swirling. His face was illuminated, and his hair was burnished to bright copper as he straightened. 'Will you now admit to Richard as well?'

She met his gaze. 'Yes. I loved Richard in all the ways of which you have accused me, and I still love him, as I do Jack. It will never change. I cannot help it, nor do I wish to pretend otherwise to you. Richard returned my love.'

'And gave you a child. A boy. Leo Kymbe.'

'Yes.'

'If you are telling me these truths, will you also tell me if my uncle is loyal to me?'

She looked into his eyes. 'Yes, he is. How can you possibly think otherwise?'

'Because I have made a cuckold of him. Perhaps the

338

insult is enough to drive him from my side. As I am sure would have happened at Stoke Field. Jon Welles was prepared to be a traitor to me.'

'No, Henry. Jon is your man, your *blood* relative.'

'If Lincoln had faced me on his *own* account, not that ridiculous Lambert Simnel puppet, more men would have been drawn to his standards, and I would have had a far harder time of it. He was my sworn enemy, Cicely, intent upon my life. I cannot mourn with you, only for you.'

'I do not expect anything more.'

'Where is Leo?'

'I do not intend to tell you.'

Surprise lightened his eyes. 'Indeed? How very defiant.'

'You want truthfulness, Henry, and you have it. I know where my son is, but you will have to torture me to learn anything more.'

'Oh, *cariad*, what a fighting bantam you are. I am sure I could soon find out, if I put my mind to it. And if I put a little pressure on Tom Kymbe.'

'More coercion to make me bow to your will? Do that, Henry, and I will never lie willingly with you again.'

'You love Kymbe?' he asked quickly.

'No, I protect him, as I will protect anyone who has helped me and is in danger from you. Please leave the Kymbes alone. They are loyal to Jon, and have helped me because of him. The only disloyalty Jon has shown to you is in protecting me and keeping my secret. Otherwise, he is your man to the core.' How she hoped she convinced him. 'I am telling the truth. And Leo is no danger to you. He is illegitimate and born of incest. He can never be a true Yorkist claimant to the throne.'

'Oh, what a fool I would be to take *that* at face value!' Henry came close enough to touch a finger to her chin. '*Cariad*, your child's blood descent is irrefutable, and you and I both know how easy it is to forge marriage contracts.'

She lowered her eyes. 'Yes, I know.'

'I have held your boy in my arms, Cicely, and wished that *I* was his father. Oh, yes, I still wish that you could bear my child. I am a fool, I think, because you would never wish for that.'

'I so want another child, Henry, but it is my fate not to have one. By any man.'

'If I had any wisdom now, I would root your Leo out and imprison him somewhere until he is old enough to be considered adult and to have his head lopped.'

'Please do not say that,' she whispered, drawing back.

'Truthfulness is the order of this day, my love, so I tell you what I know I *should* do. I should also punish the Kymbes and my uncle for the treason of hiding a Yorkist child.'

'But … *will* you?'

He turned away, and deflected the subject. 'Did Jack de la Pole know of the boy? Yes, of course he did. Well, that means there will be others who know, because your cousin would convey it to the right places that Richard left a son by you. The choice would not have been left to you. Lincoln would want it realized that one day, in the not too distant future, there will be a boy of the House of York—the son of Richard III and grandson of Edward IV—of an age to challenge me or my heir. *That* will unite Yorkists, because many of them will have discovered to their vexation that I have not advanced their prospects. Lancastrians will have realized the same, because I do not intend the nobility, of whatever persuasion, to have the power it has wielded in the past. I am bringing men of lesser rank to the forefront, and that is how I intend to go on. I am not liked among the populace either, I am well aware of it. They all wish Bosworth had gone the other way. As do you.'

She could not answer.

He changed to yet another matter. 'After all that I have

done to you, how can you bear to be close to me, alone like this?'

'I enjoy being with you. Does that make me a fool? An eager victim? Or a silly woman who thinks she can change you?'

'I pray it means none of those things, *cariad*,' he said softly. 'I am tired of keeping secrets, or fearing to let slip something I do not wish you to know. Tired of starting at every looming shadow. I want there to be complete trust between us, Cicely. I have never, in my entire life, wished to share this utter faith with another. You have become part of me in every way. I have tried to give you up, but I cannot. I cannot do anything without finding you are somehow there with me. You fill my thoughts from the moment I awaken until the moment I sleep again, and then I know you are in my dreams as well, even though I do not always remember them.'

He was silent again, before meeting her eyes. 'I now have your secret in my palm, and with it a power over you that can ensure you remain in that palm forever more. You will do anything to shield your little boy.'

She gazed at him, her heart contracting. Had he fooled her after all? Was this nothing more than one of his cruel tricks?

'Oh, what I see in your eyes now, my love. The fear and uncertainty, the dismay.' He came to her again, and tilted her chin so she could not look away from him. 'I asked for your trust today, *cariad*, and you have given it. It is not misplaced, truly. You see, I think the balance between us should be even, not weighted towards me. You should know things that will place *me* in *your* palm.' His lips touched hers, like a leaf in autumn, and then he drew away again.

What was he about to say? She could hear her heart pounding. Could he hear it too?

'My mind is made up on this, Cicely, and it may be that when you know it all, you will judge me and find me sadly lacking. Perhaps my confession will mean it is soon ended between us forever.'

'Which in turn will mean Leo falls into the utmost peril,' she said. 'So do not tell me anything, Henry. I do not want to know, whatever it is. Please. Leave me in ignorance, because you may wish you had kept it from me. Do not make me a danger to you.' She was suddenly too afraid of the secret; afraid for those she loved.

'I want you to have as much reason to hold your tongue as I will have to hold mine. Besides, you have been a blessed danger to me since I first saw you at Lambeth, and will be a danger to me until the day I die. I realize the risk I will be taking, but still I take it. I have to. You thought you were the one with matters to hide, but I have them too.' His eyes were steady. And warm. 'I need you as I need to breathe, Cicely.'

The words, and the way he uttered them, demolished her guard, and she went to him. To Harri. His lips trapped hers in a kiss that was fresh and sweet, but too vigorous to be honeyed. But she retained the knowledge that she had to bind him to her.

'Make love to me now, Henry, before these things are said. And afterwards I want to rest against you, body to body, your lips close enough to be kissed again and again. *Then* tell me what you must. Please.' The last word was barely audible.

'It may be better that we postpone such a union, *cariad*.' His eyes were closed as her lips continued to move gently over his neck. His arms were around her, one hand enclosing the nape of her neck, his thumb caressing into her hair.

'No. Now.' She turned slowly away from him, holding her hair aside for him to unhook her bodice, and she closed her eyes as he kissed her shoulder. He was swift, for he had unfastened this gown many times. When she was utterly naked, she turned to face him again. His gaze, level and loving, moved over her body.

'We have been apart for some weeks, *cariad*, so I may not be able to take my time.' He removed the belt that rested on his hips.

'I do not need time, Henry, only to be joined to you again.' She eased his doublet away, and lifted his costly but delicate shirt over his head, before putting her hands flat upon the soft hairs of his chest. Then she kissed the place where his heartbeats could be felt.

He removed his footwear and hose and then gathered her closer; she relinquished herself to him, completely, without question. He was her sister's husband and her husband's half-nephew, a threat to all she held dear, but Henry Tudor was good to be with like this, and she, the daughter of Edward IV, niece and lover of Richard III, and beloved of Jack de la Pole, could not stop what was within her.

They lay together beneath the coverlets, and gave themselves up anew to the spell that had always compelled them. As they kissed, and the old longing and need swam deep within her, guilty tears stung her eyes. She knew that these moments would remain with her forever. If he was finally betrayed and destroyed, would she be able to live with herself? Would she? *Would she?*

Their kisses filled with more desire and passion, until at last she was beneath him, and he pushed into her. She heard the almost exquisite satisfaction in his sigh. Once— so long ago now—she had believed she would only be able to make love with Henry if she thought of Richard; she had expected to think of Jack now, but she could not. It was Harri with whom she lay, and with whom she shared every pulse and spasm of his release.

When he could not love her any more, he sank down into her arms, and they lay together, warm, damp and close, still sharing lingering ripples of gratification. He linked her fingers tightly, and hid his face in her hair, but did not stretch her arms above her head. The omission of the fond gesture robbed her of a little confidence, because it took her back to those devastating moments at Westminster, when she realized he was going to end everything between them. She was not only betraying Jack, but Henry himself. Jack—of all men—would understand, because he shared her blood and House, but Henry never would. Nor was there any reason why he should.

He lay over on his back suddenly, breaking all contact. '*Cariad*, it crucifies me not to have told you what I have been at such pains to hide from everyone else. I *must* tell you about—'

'No!' she interrupted urgently, in a last-minute bid to stop the spiral into which she was plunging. She wanted to do as Jack bade her, but she simply did not have enough loathing for Henry. And this, even though he may well have tortured Jack. She could take her pick from the versions of what had happened at Knole. Both were plausible. Now, the lovemaking she had shared with this man was too tender and rewarding for hatred to cling on.

He left the bed and went to pour some wine, but although he picked up the jug, he put it down again without pouring anything at all. 'It does not concern your son, *cariad*, but mine. Roland.'

She drew the bed coverlet around herself and sat up unhappily. 'But you have already told me he is your son.'

'This father has feet of clay. You have probably always thought it, but not even you could guess from what quagmire that clay came.'

'Quagmire?'

'I am two-faced, duplicitous, false, cheating, dishonest, call it what you will. All these words apply to me. If it had all been known when I invaded England, I would *never* have had Yorkist support, and Richard would still be king. You have always called me a usurper, and so I am. Treason drips from my fingers.'

She stared at him. 'What are you saying, Henry?'

'I once asked you to swear on Richard's honour. I must ask the same of you now. Please, my love, swear it.'

Cicely hesitated. 'But you say he would still be alive and still King of England if this terrible secret were known, so how can I possibly swear upon his honour?'

'Please, if the way we make love together means as much to you as it does to me, grant me this indulgence.'

'I am reluctant to make this vow, because I do not think Richard would wish it.' Her throat tightened. 'But ... I swear on Richard's honour.' *Forgive me.*

Henry returned to the bed and slipped in beside her again, to draw her down into his arms and kiss her so sweetly that she could have melted of it.

'*Cariad*, I am not your king now, but your bondman. I belong only to you.'

Sweet God above, what *was* this terrible secret? Her voice shook. 'What can there be about Roland that weighs so heavily? He was born before you married my sister, so what prevents you from accepting him? Most kings acknowledge their bastards, unless they have been born after the royal marriage.'

'What reason do you imagine there could be for my silence about him, *cariad*? Mm? What was the one thing your father had to conceal at all costs? The thing that gave Richard the throne?' His voice was a whisper.

She was stricken with disbelief, and drew her hand away. 'No!'

'But yes,' Henry replied quietly. 'When I married your sister, I already had a wife and son in Brittany. *Now* do you understand the consequence of what I wish to confess to you?'

345

Chapter Twenty-Eight

CICELY WAS UTTERLY appalled. 'You ... you married Bess bigamously? Prince Arthur is illegitimate?' She pulled away from Henry and had to leave the bed as she struggled to absorb what he had said. The room felt suddenly cold, in spite of the fire in the hearth, and she shivered because she was without clothes.

'The answer is yes to both questions,' he said.

The implication was so enormous that she could hardly breathe. How glad she was that Jack and Tal had not told her, because her reaction now was only too genuine!

'Have you nothing more to say, *cariad*?' Henry asked.

'Why did you do it, Henry?' She searched his eyes, which were so dark with guilt and anxiety.

'Because I could get away with it.'

Anger grazed her. 'And *that* is your answer? Glibness, without repentance? Without *conscience*?'

'Sweet Jesu, Cicely, I am nothing *but* conscience!' he cried. 'I am eaten up with it. I wish to God I had stayed in Brittany. No, I lie, for what I really wish is that I had made terms with Richard. If York and Lancaster were to be reunited, I would have been glad to marry whomever he chose. I wanted a peaceful existence, after spending so long being hunted. Instead, I kept my shabby secret, made grand promises to marry Bess, and swept to glory on the back of Yorkist support that would *never* have been mine if the truth were known. Nor would I have had much Lancastrian support either. So I have guarded the sordid truth.'

'Oh, Henry ...'

'*Cariad*, if my marriage had been known, I would have been crushed like the insect I really am, and Richard would still be king. Still your lover. And if my secret is learned now ... I will not long be on the throne, and not long for this world either.' He gazed at her. 'You see before you King Henry VII of England, but if you stretch your hand out to touch me, you will feel no substance. I am a trick of the light.'

'You did not *need* to tell me this, Henry!' she cried. 'You could have kept your secret and taken it to your grave.'

'No, for it is no longer safe anyway.'

'Who else knows?' She already knew of at least two.

'Jack de la Pole knew, I imagine. He had somehow caught wind of it. God alone knows how. His accomplice at Knole will also have known, for one. Who else he may have told I do not know, but it is impossible to believe he acted alone.'

Yes, Jack and Tal are fully aware of the truth, and intend to use it to bring you down. 'If Jack knew, he did not tell me,' she replied. It was the truth.

'Oh, I can tell that you knew nothing until just now.' Henry smiled ruefully. 'My Breton wife knew, of course, but she had urgent reasons of her own to remain silent.'

'She has not wished to take her place beside you, as Queen of England?' Cicely was curious, and noticed that he spoke in the past tense.

He shook his head. 'Definitely not, because she too had married bigamously after me, and wished to remain so.'

She was shocked again. 'Double bigamy?'

'I offer no excuse for what I have done, Cicely. I know it was wrong, and I cannot defend myself. Come back to the bed, *cariad*, for you are too cold.' He extended his hand, but was uncertain and hesitant. A very different Henry Tudor; different even from Harri Tudur.

She went to him, for his appeal was relentless, and he pulled her down into the shelter of the coverlet. Then he lay back with her in his arms.

'Tell me everything, Henry. From the beginning.'

The fire shifted and crackled, and flame shadows played over the room. The wind buffeted outside, but in the bed, together, it was warm. He cleared his throat, to quell the urge to cough, and then rested his cheek to her hair before continuing. 'I was fourteen and a half and, after your father's victory at Tewkesbury, deemed the only remaining Lancastrian heir. I was sent to safety in France in the charge of my uncle Jasper, but we were driven ashore in a storm off Le Conquet in Brittany. Duke Francis wanted bargaining power with your father *and* France, so he offered me protection. I remained in his charge for the next fourteen years.'

He paused thoughtfully. 'In England I was merely Henry Tudor, a hunted, untitled, landless Lancastrian, but in Brittany and France I was the Earl of Richmond, with a claim to the English throne. I was well treated, but separated from Jasper and sent to l'Argöet, where there is a tall octagonal tower known as the Tour d'Elven. I was housed at the very top, the sixth floor, so that escape was impossible. L'Argöet's lord is Jean IV de Rieux, Marshal of Brittany and commander of the Breton army, and therefore not a minor noble. He treated me with honour and consideration.' Henry laughed dryly. 'Not that I was to return the courtesy.'

'What happened?' she asked.

'Well, I lived mostly in the tower, but was often with the family in the *château*, and that was how I met Jean's youngest sister, Tiphaine, who, like me, had been born seven months after the death of her father. I was about seventeen by then, she was fifteen and in Jean's care. She seemed older than merely fifteen, and was very flirtatious, but sweet-natured and kind. She was also very beautiful, blonde, with blue eyes, and a penchant for yellow. It was her favourite colour and she wore it almost all the time.' He paused. 'But that is *not* why I complimented you on your daffodil gown. Please do not think it.'

'I do not.'

'Tiphaine de Rieux would have attracted a good match, which I most definitely was not. On top of which, I was an ugly, gangling youth with divergent eyes and the charm of a grasshopper.' He smiled.

'But you both fell in love?'

'I thought so. I could not believe she favoured me at all, but she was not the innocent she seemed, not that I would have cared even had I known. I was besotted. If I had been all I should have been to Tiphaine, I would never even have *thought* of invading England.'

'You said that you feared my opinion of you would be ruined once I knew the truth. I have not yet heard anything that would do that.'

'Oh, *cariad*, I would have thought your opinion well and truly set already, because you know now that my crime against Richard was far worse than you realized.'

'Does Jolly Jasper know about Tiphaine?'

'Dear God, no! He would have split a gut if he had found out that I had been tampering with the Marshal of Brittany's little sister! You are the only one in whom I ever intend to actually confide everything. Whatever stories may circulate because of those damned Yorkists at Knole, *you* alone will have heard it all from me. You will know, because I will not spare myself.' He kissed her forehead. 'I am painfully honest now, *cariad*. When I had lain with her, believing myself her first lover, honour demanded that I marry her. I regarded it as my duty. And I wanted to anyway. Young passion can be so blind, can it not? We both feared her brother, so we were wed at a clandestine ceremony, by the local priest. It was a true marriage, there is no doubt of that. She became my Countess of Richmond, although only we knew. If de Rieux had found out, I soon would not have had any cock to dibble with. Looking back, Tiphaine and I actually had no idea at all which path to take after that. We were married, but what next? I am amazed we were so hot-headed, particularly me, for it was out of character. Although ...'

'Although?'

'I have since been even more hot-headed over you, *cariad*. Hot-headed, hot-blooded, and hot everything else. When my heart and desire is engaged, I am not in the least the calm and collected man everyone believes me to be.' He smiled apologetically, and then continued about Tiphaine. 'We saw ourselves as Tristan and Yseult, and this Tristan was completely driven by his new-found dick!'

Cicely gave him a look. 'You had not discovered it before?'

'Only in solitude.' He held her closer, and kissed her forehead. 'I am sorry for everything, *cariad*,' he whispered. 'You have no idea how sorry.'

'Tell me more, Henry.'

'Well, Duke Francis decided to have me removed from l'Argöet and returned to live with Jasper, whom I had not seen in some time, and who was not apprised of *anything* I had been up to. Being at a distance from Tiphaine meant that my infatuation—for that was all it was—began to dwindle almost immediately. There were other girls, and women, and I was swiftly in other beds, learning more and more about the fair sex. And the art of making love.'

He fell silent for a moment, remembering, and then continued. 'Barely a month after leaving l'Argöet, Tiphaine wrote that her brother had received an important offer of marriage for her and was forcing her to accept. The prospective bridegroom was Briand du Coskäer, whom I now know to be a ferocious, unpleasant man, all dark passion and no sense. I did not know his true character until it was too late. He is lord of this and that. I have forgotten how many titles he has. Certainly he was not a mediocre match in that respect. He wanted the marriage to take place quickly, because he was in urgent need of an heir. His first wife gave him none and had taken an unconscionable time to die. So selfish. And he such a caring fellow. De Rieux was forcing Tiphaine to accept. She wrote to me in desperation, begging me to claim her.'

'And you did not?'

Henry drew a long, heavy breath. 'I had ceased to be honourable and chivalric, Cicely. There was no hint in her letter that she was with child. Nor did she mention the sort of man Briand du Coskäer was. How honourable I might have been if she *had* said, I do not know, but my only thought at the time was that she could marry the fellow and need never say anything. It is what I hoped.' He paused, and then added, 'I was a shit, and do not attempt to deny it. Is that honest enough for you?'

'You *really* did not know she carried your child?'

'How doubting you sound. I knew nothing, *cariad*, I swear. I convinced myself it was best for both of us if we pretended nothing had happened. So I said and did nothing at all. She managed to send another letter *after* her forced marriage, in which she did tell me of the child she carried, but still did not tell me what a brute du Coskäer had turned out to be. I was implored to forget *our* union, destroy all evidence of it and not to write to her or attempt to see her. I was more than happy to comply. It seems du Coskäer believed he had impregnated her the moment he showed his cock to the fresh air, and eight months after the marriage, Roland was born a du Coskäer, but in truth is Roland Tudor. My heir.' He smiled wryly. 'Do not say it, *cariad*. Both my sons have apparently been incredibly bonny eight-month babies.'

'And neither of them was.'

'Indeed.'

She looked at him. 'And you considered yourself free to marry Bess?'

'Of course not. I knew well enough that in the eyes of God and the Church—and secular law as well—I was still married to Tiphaine. But I *did* think I had heard the last of her, that Roland was safely du Coskäer's heir and would in due course inherit from him and whatever was his mother's. I believed him to be very well provided for. Nor did I know du Coskäer's character. That is the truth, Cicely. I knew nothing of how abominably that bastard treated her, because she gave him no more sons, nor was I aware that he alternately pampered and thrashed Roland.'

'It explains a little of why Roland is as he is.'

'And why he has to be retaught.' Henry leaned his head back. 'I considered it in the past, and then one day last autumn, I received a communication from Tiphaine. She told me she was very ill, would soon die and feared for Roland's safety. She revealed that, in spite of begging me to destroy all evidence of our marriage, *she* had changed her mind and kept everything, even my indiscreet notes in which I referred to her as my beloved wife. Not only that, she had obtained a sworn statement from the priest who married us, in which he identified me as the bridegroom she had wed when she was fifteen. She was afraid du Coskäer had come to suspect Roland was not his child, and she wanted to send the boy to me. It was the last thing

I wanted, and so, to my shame as a father, I did nothing. I was an ignoble knave, *cariad*, and I know it.'

Cicely did not comment, for the self-reproach was appropriate.

'Then, on the day you remarried my uncle, I was handed another sealed note from her to which I finally did respond as she wished. It was impressed upon me that the message was urgent. Someone else had written it for her. Three words. *Please help me.* I knew it was from her because of the yellow wax, although I did not recognize the seal. Some mythological beast or other. Du Coskäer's maybe.'

Cicely looked away. The second note had not been from Tiphaine, but forged by Jack and Tal. Those three words had been chosen because they could mean anything to Henry, and they knew it. Their purpose had been to rattle him, and they succeeded. She recalled how Jon had retrieved the broken seal from the hearth, where Henry had dropped it. They had studied the mythological beast and not known what it was. As forged as the letter itself, no doubt.

'So,' Henry went on, 'I sent for Roland secretly, and first set eyes on him at that meeting at Knole. Guillaume de Boulvriag, his tutor, brought him to me, and also the news that Tiphaine died two days after I received her last message. I am now a widower, living sinfully with your elder sister, whom I have gravely dishonoured, and who is as much my queen as your mother was your father's. Roland is the next rightful King of England. There, is that not a quaint state of affairs? England's first King Roland.'

'And to think of all the things you said of Richard for having accepted the throne. What a hypocrite you are.'

'You never spare me, do you, *cariad*?' he observed softly, tracing a fingertip around her right nipple.

She stopped him. 'Have you finished your story?'

'No, not entirely. You see, my problem *now* is that I do not know what happened to Tiphaine's documents. I have de Boulvriag's vow that he destroyed them, but … '

'You do not believe him?' Surely they *had* to be the papers that had come into Tal's possession and had been destroyed in the fire at St Andrew's.

'Oh, come now, you *know* how sweet and trusting a nature I have, *cariad*,' he said with a hint of a smile. 'Of course I suspect him, and thus I have to fear that proof of my marriage to Tiphaine is still in existence. Somewhere. And the priest may still live, for all I know, and be prepared to swear to the marriage all over again. He was not that old a man at the time, and priests seem to live forever. And might Tiphaine have confided in someone? Given a letter to someone that relates everything? Nor do I even know if Roland is aware of anything. He has convinced your vixen of a sister that he has prospects of some sort.'

'Maybe it is simply bragging. You *have* created an air of mystery around him.'

'*Mea culpa*?'

'In every way. One thing I have noticed is that Roland goes in dread of you. Why?'

He shrugged. 'I do not know. I am strict with him, yes, but that is all. I certainly do not beat him, use thumbscrews, or other instrument of torture.'

She believed him. 'Henry, did you know that Jon and I witnessed your receipt of the letter on our wedding day?'

Henry raised an eyebrow. 'I imagine your curiosity was more than pricked.'

'Yes.'

'Well, now you know how and why Roland de Vielleville has become a cuckoo in the English royal nest. An unpleasant little cuckoo, at that. Between them, Tiphaine and Briand du Coskäer made a sow's ear of him.'

'I feel sorry for him.'

'He needs to earn sympathy, not have it extended to him regardless of his conduct.'

'What will you do now?'

'Sit, wait and hope to God all proof of that foolish marriage has been destroyed after all.'

'What of Bess? And Arthur?'

'I intend to continue as now, pretending that she is my queen and Arthur is my legitimate son. I know I have played her false, but for the life of me, given all she has done, I cannot sympathize. I would love to tell her, just to see her face when she learns that all the fucking she has endured from me has been in sin.'

He caught Cicely's hand tightly. 'I am the culprit in all of this. The moment I chose to invade England without mentioning Tiphaine and Roland, I committed the crime. I threw the dice, and they fell in my favour. Luck. Always luck. I achieved everything, when I had not expected to achieve anything. I promised marriage to your sister in order to gain the Yorkist support that won the battle for me. I am your father all over again. I was already married, but took another woman, named Elizabeth, to my bed. Then I presented my son by her as the heir to the throne.'

'Henry, if I were to pass this information on—'

'But you will not, *cariad*,' he broke in, 'because I give you my Roland for your Leo, do you not see it? Now we both have a secret son to protect and keep secret.'

'Oh, Henry ...'

'You think I am base after all?'

'What would you think if you were me?' she countered. 'You see this as an excellent way to fetter us together, an undeniable reason for us to keep faith with each other. To keep me to you. But sometimes there is too much honesty, Henry.'

'Keeping this from you had become intolerable to me. We belong to each other, Cicely.'

No. I belong to Jack de la Pole!

'The secret I have given to you today is by far more

dangerous to me than anything I know of you. Do you not see it?' He rose from the bed again, and began to dress, not to signify anything, but rather for something to do that would hide his agitation.

She watched him, and then said exactly what Jon had said before her. 'Henry, you expect me to commit treason for you. To join you in it, and allow a bastard boy to ascend the throne after you. I am York! *York!* You have forced this information upon me, and it is not something with which I can blithely comply. That is the one thing Richard would not do, do you see? He would have been a loyal Lord Protector during the minority of my brother, but not after he learned my father had been married before. I am Richard's niece, friend, subject and lover, and I am *proud* to be in his mould and to share his beliefs.'

'But not proud to be my great love?' His hurt was palpable, and he reached for his shirt. 'So, when Leo is old enough to challenge me for the throne, you, his mother, will not support him because he is illegitimate?'

She gazed at him, unable to answer.

'It is a straightforward question, *cariad*. To you, illegitimacy is an insurmountable barrier to the throne. Am I right?'

Be against Leo if he wanted to honour his lineage?

'You see? Nothing is simple.' He came closer, tucking in his shirt. 'Nothing is clear to either of us, my darling. There are areas where mist and fog obscures everything, and finding our way through it can never be easy. I love you, and need you to be close to me. If I had held my tongue about all this, and *then* you found out, what would you have thought of me? Instead, I have chosen to be honest, and now pray you can forgive me and remain my lover.'

'You have had time to dwell upon it all, Henry, to think about what you had to say, but I have only just learned. I must clear my mind and be certain that the answer I give you is one to which I can adhere. Honestly. And with the honesty and consideration for you that you need. Please do not press me for an immediate response that I may not be able to honour. A little time is all I ask. No, not days or even hours upon end. Just a few minutes on my own.'

I need to summon Richard. I must speak with him.... Oh, how long had it been since she had done that? But now, at such a time, when she could not consult Jack, Richard remained her ultimate resort. Her ultimate conscience.

Henry was stricken, but could only nod. 'If that is your wish.'

'It is my *need*, Henry.'

'Please do not spurn me, *cariad*,' he begged, and then almost slung the silver collar around his shoulders, snatched his doublet and boots, and left the room.

Several minutes later she watched him return to the willow tree. His head was bowed, and everything about him suggested dejection.

It should be so easy to despise him, she thought. So easy. 'What would you advise me now, Richard? Mm? Come to me, I implore you, because this is one time when I do *not* know what you would do.'

'It is something only you can decide, sweeting,' his voice said behind her.

She turned gladly, and there he was, her beloved Richard, leaning back against the wall, his arms folded. He had not aged, but was still only thirty-two; still as arresting as ever. His build was slight, and if it were not for the occasionally painful sideways curve of his back, he would have been taller. His long, dark, chestnut hair brushed the shoulders of his grey velvet clothes. Court garments, worn one memorable Christmas. The sovereign's circlet was around his head, but even without it he would have been unmistakably royal. He was more than merely handsome, with a fine-boned face, enthralling grey eyes, and quick lips that played in a tender smile. Richard III, King of England and France, Lord of Ireland. Master of her soul, and, in her eyes, the perfect man and perfect monarch.

'I swore upon your honour, Richard, and crave your forgiveness,' she whispered.

'My poor Cicely, how life tests you,' he said gently.

She moved towards him, and he opened his arms to her. Then she was in his embrace again. It was imagination, she knew, but oh, how real the costmary, and the warmth of his body beneath his rich clothes. The moment she touched him, she was again in the heaven taken from her at Bosworth. She had been so strong for months, not giving in to this need to be with him again, but now, with so much to decide upon, she *had* to speak to him.

His lips were loving on her cheek. 'You do not need me, sweeting,' he said softly.

'I do. This time, I do.' She linked her arms around his neck and hid her face against his hair. 'Hold me as tightly as you can, Richard, please. I need you so much now, because I do *not* know what to do. And my guilt weighs so heavily I feel it will stop my breath.'

'Guilt? Because of that mangy mongrel Tudor?'

'Yes, and because he has told me such things now that I could weep from the bewilderment. Forgive me. Please.'

'There is nothing to forgive, because none of it is your fault. It is his, and he accepts it. He gives the impression of being strong, except in health, but he is not. He really does need you as he says.'

'You defend him?'

'I am not real, merely your conscience. You are prey to the wonderful passions awakened by our love, and now I am gone, you have turned to Jack, who well deserves to have you. But Henry casts a spell on you that is born of his incredible love for you. Do you understand? No one else will ever see the loving man that you do. So, with Jack gone to Burgundy, you call me back again.'

She leaned back to drink in every detail of his face. 'You still plunder all that I am, Richard. No one else, not even Jack, will ever mean as much to me.'

'When I saw you in sanctuary at Westminster Abbey, in 1484, so frightened of me and yet so full of spirit … I knew you were my reflection—an echo of my own heart. Oh, I did not desire you, not then, for you were so young and my niece; it was much later, when I knew you more, that what I felt changed to something it should not have been. But from the beginning, we understood each other. We were in harmony.'

'You were the perfect uncle to me, Richard. Never fear otherwise. And when I was of age, you were still the perfect uncle and king. You broke no rule, nor did anything for which you could be censured. I am blessed, because I have known a love so true, pure and without blemish, that it will sustain me until the day I die. No, do not remind me that we were all we should not have been as well, because it does not matter to me.'

He put the backs of his fingers to her cheek. 'If we could have been together, we would have changed the world itself, mm?'

'*You* could.'

'I had some merits, but not as many as all that. I was York, however, which perhaps brings us to the reason you have called me,' he said quietly.

'What do you mean? I do not understand.…'

'Yes, you do, sweetheart. What if *I* were to ask of you the thing Henry asks? Would you doubt me? Would you consider it to be treason? Would you ask for time? Answer me, Cicely.'

'I would never doubt you, Richard, but would do anything you asked.'

'Why?'

'Because I love and trust you above all others.'

'Being loved and trusted would not make me right, or infallible. You are trapped by the emotions Henry Tudor stirs in you, so much so that even knowing what he has done—most recently to Jack, because you *do* believe Tal—you are still able to woo him and tie invisible, silken ropes around him. And find immense pleasure in his lovemaking, as he finds in yours. You are well matched between the coverlets, sweetheart. Now, he has told you everything that has been concealed, and he trusts you. But you, sweeting, are tied to him too. To protect those you love and cherish, you have already decided to stay at his side and in his bed for as long as you possibly can. If you are to do that, you *have* to support him now. You have no choice. York is still a very long way from overthrowing him. A very long way, no matter what Jack and Tal may think. They still have no proof.'

She looked away. What he said was so obvious that she felt almost foolish.

'And, Cicely, in one other thing, Henry is right. You would ultimately have *no* qualms about Leo taking the throne, illegitimate or not. It is what your father was prepared to do as well.'

'For which *you* condemned him,' she said quickly.

He smiled. 'So I did, but you would not be opposed to Leo becoming king, so how can you blame Henry for being willing to let *his* illegitimate son, Arthur, succeed him?'

'You did not let my brother ascend the throne, nor John of Gloucester. Instead, you chose Jack because he was legitimate.'

Richard met her eyes. 'There is not a lot I can say to that, for it is true. But if I had not had Jack, I might indeed have thought of John.'

'No, you would not.'

He smiled a little. 'On another matter, Tal is right, I *did* say I wanted you as my queen, I *did* lie with you and give you my child. I was almost as guilty of that as your father with Tal's sister, although I did not say or do anything to trick you, nor did I discard you afterwards. It is therefore arguable that Leo is legitimate. Henry has no option but to fight to keep the throne, and he will. And his luck will stay with him. At least, that is what you believe. The stars like Henry Tudor. But if Leo challenges him one day, it will take all his—Henry's—resolve and tenacity to take up arms against your son. The fact that Leo is also mine will not be his real issue. It is you, sweeting. He loves you so very much, as I think he has proved today.'

She searched his face. 'Leo may not choose to—'

'He will *have* to, sweetheart, as I had to. Events of 1483 *forced* the crown upon me. I did my duty. So, in due course, will Leo. And just consider that if the truth comes out, Henry Tudor's legitimate heir is Roland de Vielleville, who has no Yorkist blood whatever. But through Bess, Arthur is at least half York.'

'So, I must go along with Henry's deception?'

He smiled. 'You know you must, for it is the only way that you can do what your conscience—and love for Jon and Leo—insists upon. Jack and Tal know of his marriage, but someone as yet unknown destroyed their evidence. Now they seek it again. You have to decide if there is any point in relaying to them what Henry has told you today. Look at me, sweetheart. Henry did not tell you anything that you could prove in a court of law, unless he stood up in the dock and confessed it all. Which will *not* happen. So it remains word of mouth alone, without a single page of proof. The House of York has to produce solid evidence if it is to rob Henry of all his support and see an end to him and his line. Even Henry does not know if such evidence still exists, so unless Tal's agent somehow manages to find something, somewhere, there will *never* be a way to unseat him because of this other marriage and the siring of Roland de Vielleville. Do you understand?'

'But the priest who performed the marriage may—'

'Priests can be paid to say anything. The *original* evidence is needed, not anything concocted since. We are talking of removing a King of England from the throne, Cicely, and although I was plucked in battle, you will never catch Henry in battle again.' He gave a half-laugh. '*Now* do you accept what I am saying?'

'Yes.' Her mind was clearing, as always it did when she used him in this way.

He smoothed her hair from her face. 'Proof is everything, sweetheart. I am you, and can only say things you know but are not acknowledging. Do you feel better now?' He put his fingers beneath her chin and made her look at him.

'It is impossible *not* to feel better when I am with you.'

He smiled. 'And in your heart you will always pray Leo will never answer the call of his lineage, and will thus remain out of danger from Henry, who *will* leave him alone until he senses him to be a very real Yorkist danger. You are right to think of sending the boy to Jack, who is the very best man in the world to care for him. I approve of your choice. But not until Leo is old enough to know *why* you send him away.'

'Oh, Richard, all of it has made *such* a liar of me.'

He laughed. 'And it all started with me. Because I made you so close to me, you started to lie to Bess and to your mother.'

'So it's all your fault.' She laughed too. 'But seriously, I seem to have been born to keep secrets.'

'Yes, and others *will* insist upon confiding more, mm?'

She smiled a little ruefully. 'Yes.'

'It is good that you and Jack love so much, sweetheart. But I know that I will always be first in your heart, and that you accept I have gone now. I died knowing that we were the greatest of loves.'

'Hold me tight, Richard,' she whispered, and he did.

'Cicely, your only course is the one you have already set out upon. Tell Henry you will support him, and thus purchase all the time that is needed for Leo to decide for *himself* what he wishes to do. When he is of age, there is nothing you, his mother, can say or do to prevent him. Protect him now, but accept that his future is his own.'

His lips found hers in a loving kiss that stirred every dear memory, every sensation and every desire. The taste of mint was so poignant and beloved. Oh, to really make love with this beguiling man again. But it was all chaff before the wind, fleeting, imagined and already fading beyond her reach.

She tried to cling to him, but he was slipping away. 'Richard!'

He did not answer, and she was alone in the room. But her mind was now as clear as the finest crystal, and she knew what to tell Henry.

Taking up her cloak, which lay over a chair close to the fire, she wrapped it around her naked body and went down through the house, where there was not a servant to be seen, because they had been charged to show the utmost discretion. As she went out into the cold, the wind snatched at her loose hair, but she felt warm and confident as she made her way towards the willow.

Henry did not hear her coming, and started as she appeared beside him. His glance was anxious. '*Cariad*?'

She moved in front of him and pressed close, so that his arms moved around her instinctively. 'Henry, I will keep your secret and stay close to you,' she said gently, her voice almost lost in the hurry and splash of the stream.

'Oh, *cariad*...' His voice was choked and she could feel how he shook with stifled tears. '*Cariad*, do ... do you understand now why I had to tell you? Why I needed you to know everything?'

'I think so.'

'Neither of us wishes to face the inevitable future, sweetheart, but perhaps, until then, we can enjoy the present? And each other?'

He flung his cloak back, unfastened the dragon from his collar and pressed it into her hand. 'There, now you *know* this Tudor dragon is your captive,' he said, closing her fingers over it.

'No, I do not, Henry Tudor, you only want me to *think* I have you thus.'

He smiled and bent his head to kiss her. No mint now, or thyme or even rosemary. Just cloves. And Henry Tudor.

Who knew what the future would bring, because she had not been as open and forthcoming with him as she promised. And how could she know if he had been completely truthful? One day, Leo would have to learn the devastating truth about his royal birth. What would happen then?

She could not help glancing up at the bedroom window, willing Richard to be there. He was. And it was so easy to imagine Jack there too....

Her fingers closed tightly around the silver dragon, until it pressed against Henry's emerald, and those precious Yorkist jewels, Richard's ruby and Jack's amethyst. In that hand she held a microcosm of England's fate—plus her own and her son's.

Author's Note

HISTORY IS FACT. Historical fiction is fact with the addition of make-believe. My version of Cicely Plantagenet's story is the latter, and should *not* be taken any other way. I am a storyteller, not a historian. So I must repeat that the love between Cicely and Richard III, John (Jack) de la Pole and Henry VII are my invention. As, of course, is Leo Kymbe. I have invented Mistress Kymbe and Mary, whose (equally fictitious) new love, Stephen Perrings, is also a fictional character. Edmund de la Pole is fact, although I doubt if he was the awful figure I have depicted. But ... who knows? The same applies to Ann Plantagenet, who might have been the perfect sister.

Throughout his reign, Henry VII went in fear of his life. His hounded early years had caused him to be secretive, suspicious, trusting of no one, and the years after his usurpation were spent endeavouring to keep a desperate hold on his stolen crown. The attempts to poison him described in this story, and his queen's guilt, are not true. Nor, to my knowledge, is/was there any such thing as Russian powder. It is meant to suggest a blend of arsenic and something cyanidic that *could* have existed in the fifteenth century.

Henry's marriage to Elizabeth of York may have been harmonious, but he was described at the time as 'unuxorious'. I have chosen to take this latter view.

Jack de la Pole died at the Battle of Stoke Field in 1487. His last resting place is not known, but the story of the willow stave through the heart is a strong tradition in the area. This may, of course, have been a friendly act by his supporters, because the willow would grow, and the tree would 'always' mark the place of his burial. That tree has long gone, of course. But he is still there, I'm sure. His demise in battle being fact, it is obvious that he cannot have survived to be included in this book.

The connection between the factual merchant John Pasmer and the equally factual Welles London residence, Pasmer's Place, is (I think) a reasonable supposition, but his involvement with the Yorkist rebels is my storytelling, as is the fire at St Andrew-by-the-Wardrobe.

Jon (John) Welles and Sir Humphrey Talbot are wronged by being saddled with the crimes of regicide and attempted regicide. Jon was loyal to Henry, his half-nephew, throughout his life, or so it appears. Nor can I justifiably make Humphrey a Yorkist supporter who made an attempt on Henry's life. The poem (from *Anciennes chroniques de Flandres*) has been associated with Humphrey, although whether he actually wrote it, or to whom it may have been dedicated, is not known to me. He was of a religious disposition and went on pilgrimages, dying at St Catherine's Monastery on Mount Sinai. His residence in Flemyng Court is fictitious.

I cannot imagine he enjoyed seeing his sister Eleanor thrown to the wolves by Edward IV, who almost certainly *did* marry and desert her. Richard III believed she was his brother's wife, and thus she became the reason for Edward's children being illegitimate. And was why Richard became king. But then Henry VII threw her to the wolves again, because he needed Bess to be legitimate. Unfortunately for him, legitimizing her legitimized her siblings too, thus giving her brothers a much stronger right to the throne than Henry himself. Catch-22. Henry's constant dread of their return seems to me to prove that he did *not* believe they had been murdered by Richard III.

Now to the matter of Henry's 'bigamy' and fathering of Roland de Vielleville (de Velville, de Cosquer, du Coskäer and various other spellings). It is often said that there is no smoke without fire, which may indeed be the case where Roland is concerned. The rumours were strong, and there seemed no particular reason for Henry to show interest in him. Henry did *not* acknowledge Roland, which leads me to deduce that either the boy was not his son, or that there was some very good reason for keeping the fact a secret. Henry VII's dynastic marriage was vital to his retention of the crown.

Henry had spent half his life in Brittany. That he would have had lovers is obvious, and that he had at least one illegitimate child is not beyond belief. That he actually married while there is my fiction and so, therefore, is Tiphaine de Rieux and her husband Briand du Coskäer. But Jean IV de Rieux was a real person, and Marshal of Brittany. If Roland was Henry's son, someone like Tiphaine must have existed. We just do not know the facts. Yet.

My assessment of Anne (Ann/Annie) Plantagenet's disagreeable and calculating character is another of my flights of fancy. She may in fact have been a sweet young thing who would never say boo to a goose, but that would not be very interesting, would it?

There *was* a close friendship between Cicely and Henry's mother, Margaret Beaufort, which might have arisen because Cicely was married to Jon Welles, the halfbrother of whom Margaret was very fond.

I have tweaked names and their spelling in order to

differentiate between characters of the same name, e.g. John of Gloucester, Jack de la Pole and Jon Welles. Having three Johns would be tiresome for the reader.

Throughout this book I have continued to show my support for Richard III, and make no apology for so doing. I still believe him to have been innocent of the crimes assigned to him by history. Edward IV relied heavily upon Richard, who was known for his fairness and good rule. He was an enlightened man, determined to advance justice for the people, and concerned that women should be treated well by their husbands. These are not the qualities of a monster. But he cannot have been an angel either, being a successful and courageous medieval prince who knew how to command armies and hack his way around battlefields. He was *very* well loved in the north, where he ruled with all the power relinquished to him by his brother the king. If he had then been left to get on with ruling, I believe he would have been very good for England.

Sandra Heath Wilson
Gloucester
September 2015